Praise for Jamie Brenner's

The Forever Summer

"A captivating tale of family secrets and strong women."
—Kim Hubbard, *People*

"Soap-opera twists and turns are tempered with the believable goodness of the characters, the messiness of their journeys, and just a hint of unpredictability as events unfold... Engaging...An excellent choice for summer vacation reading."
—*Kirkus Reviews*

"A gem of a novel about strong women, the meaning of family, and the secrets we keep. It's the perfect read to get you into a Summer state of mind." —Brenda Janowitz, *PopSugar*

"*The Forever Summer* sweeps you away with a page-turning story that will stay with you long after the sun sets on the beach. Brenner is a glorious storyteller. She has created a world, richly described and inhabited by a modern, intergenerational family of women who are strong yet flawed. Secrets revealed, love lost and found, and the abiding strength of family fill these pages with a particular wisdom and humor. Put your feet up, sip a cocktail, and let Jamie Brenner surprise and delight you with the first great read of summer."
—Adriana Trigiani, author of *All the Stars in the Heavens*

"A satisfying, quick read about family, relationships, forgiveness, and discovering strength after loss. Brenner's rich narrative descriptions of Provincetown and its cast of characters have added the Massachusetts town to my list of travel destinations." —Sarah Huffstetler, *Fort Worth Star-Telegram*

"*The Forever Summer* paints a poignant portrait of a family in turmoil, striving to make peace with the past and forge a path into the future. Brenner is a natural storyteller with a gift for creating true-to-life characters. You'll definitely want to curl up with this one!"

—Emily Liebert, author of *Some Women*

"With *The Forever Summer,* Brenner has established herself as a must-read summer author. I fell in love with the untraditional families coming together in charming Provincetown and the secrets that ultimately made them stronger. A vacation read that's as essential as sunblock!"

—Karin Tanabe, author of *The Gilded Years*

"Two women on very different paths come together in the most unlikely of circumstances, both tentatively exploring the boundaries of their newfound bond in Jamie Brenner's *The Forever Summer.* Love and relationships are tested in this charming tale of sisterhood and resilience set against the beautiful backdrop of a Cape Cod summer."

—Zoe Fishman, author of *Inheriting Edith*

"This celebration of family in all its traditional and modern varieties is such a pleasure to read that you'll want to make a reservation at the Beach Rose Inn, where happiness and redemption are discovered among the twists and thorns of life."

—Nancy Thayer, author of *Secrets in Summer*

ALSO BY JAMIE BRENNER

The
Forever
Summer

A Novel

Jamie
Brenner

Little, Brown and Company
New York Boston London

Copyright © 2017 by Jamie Brenner
Excerpt from *Drawing Home* copyright © 2019 by Jamie Brenner

Little, Brown and Company
Hachette Book Group
1290 Avenue of the Americas, New York, NY 10104
littlebrown.com

The publisher is not responsible for websites (or their content) that are not owned by the publisher.

Printed in the United States of America

Originally published in hardcover by Little, Brown and Company, April 2017
First Back Bay trade paperback edition, April 2018
First Little, Brown and Company mass market edition, June 2019

10 9 8 7 6 5 4 3 2 1

For my grandmother
Frances Rubin Carver.
I miss you.

The

Forever
Summer

Provincetown, Massachusetts

Spring

The annual opening of the Beach Rose Inn marked the unofficial start of summer. It was part of the rhythm of life in Provincetown, like the ferry service from Boston, the whale-watching tour schedule, and the route of the Fourth of July parade. Amelia understood this, and it was something she had weighed carefully in making her decision to close it.

The old house had been in her family for five generations, and every spring required pre–beach season maintenance that she had long managed like clockwork. There was reshingling, repainting, flower-bed upkeep, cable and Internet upgrades, and of course a multitude of unpredictable repairs depending on how harsh the New England winter they'd just endured had been. And then, once the summer got into full swing, the work really began. For fifteen straight weeks, from May until early September, her home was filled with guests. Some were new, some were old (more like friends than guests, really), but all of them kept Amelia and her partner, Kelly, on their toes all season long.

And she loved it. At age seventy-five, she had been running the inn for so long, she couldn't imagine a summer without it. But things changed, and it was time to slow down.

But then, the phone call. Out of nowhere.

Amelia was in the kitchen, standing at the sink, when the call came in. She had been looking out the window at the long wooden table that stretched the length of the backyard to the tip of the sand that framed Cape Cod Bay. Her guests always took their breakfast at the table, dining communally, making new friends, relationships that she had heard often lasted well beyond their vacation week.

"May I speak to Amelia Cabral?" The young woman's voice shook.

"Speaking," said Amelia, prepared to tell her the inn would be closed that summer—perhaps closed indefinitely. After months of such conversations, they had not gotten any easier.

"Hi, um—I'm sorry to bother you." A long pause.

"Yes, dear. How can I help you?" Amelia prompted gently.

"Mrs. Cabral, my name is Rachel. I live in LA. And I'm pretty sure you're my . . . grandmother."

The word hung in the ether between them, heavy and weightless at the same time.

Amelia had thought that at her age, the days of surprises—good and bad—were long behind her. She had been standing in that very spot when a call had come in nearly three decades earlier, news so devastating all she could do was grip the countertop as if it were the only thing tethering her to the earth. And as the young woman told her story, that's exactly what Amelia did once again.

When she finally hung up the phone, she had to hug herself to stop the shaking.

Funny, Amelia thought, *how we greet both extremely bad news and extremely good news in the same way: disbelief.*

In a daze, Amelia walked out the back door of the house into the early-spring sunshine. Her first thought was that she had to tell Kelly, stalwart Kelly, who had helped her keep the inn afloat all these years and had only reluctantly supported her decision to close it for the season. What would Kelly make of this?

What did *she* make of it? All Amelia knew was that she'd spent the last thirty years filling the house with strangers. But in a few weeks, she would have family under her roof.

After all this time, her family.

Chapter One

New York City

The restaurant was opulent, trendy, and loud. Her fiancé had chosen it for her birthday dinner. Her fiancé, who was not at the table.

Marin stood and waved when she spotted her parents walking into the room. They had driven up from Philadelphia for the night to celebrate with her. Her mother pulled her into a hug as soon as she reached the table.

"Happy birthday, sweetheart! Thirty. I can't believe it," she said. She was dressed in a classically cut pale blue suit. Very Main Line. Very Mom. Marin felt a pang of sadness. Her mother didn't know it, but she was about to become very upset.

"Marin, you're looking well," her father said. "All the long hours at the firm must agree with you."

Marin beamed. She lived for her father's pride in her career. At least one of her parents would be happy with her tonight.

Her mother looked around. "Where's Greg? Is he running late?"

"No," Marin said slowly. "He's not running late."

The three of them sat down and the waiter handed them menus. The restaurant was prix fixe, offering very few options. Marin had no appetite.

"What's going on?" her mother asked. "Is he sick?"

"He's fine, Mom. But we broke up."

"What?" Her mother looked like Marin had slapped her across the face. "Why on earth? Did you have an argument?"

Her father summoned the waiter and ordered a martini. Marin asked for a glass of chardonnay.

"No. Not an argument. I just wasn't happy," Marin said. It was the partial truth.

"You're spending too much time at work. Relationships need to be nurtured, Marin. You can't just go on autopilot because you have a ring on your finger," said her mother, her voice going up an octave.

"Blythe, please. She's entitled to a career. Don't blame it on that," said Kip. "And Greg's Wall Street hours are no doubt longer than hers."

"Mom, it's all right. It's for the best. I'm sorry to disappoint you but—"

Blythe shook her head. "You're not disappointing me. I just want you to be happy. Why didn't you talk to me? When did all of this happen?"

Marin did feel guilty for not confiding in her—the first time that she had frozen her mother out of her personal life. But it was temporary, and necessary, and one day her mother would understand. At least, she hoped she would. It was hard to explain something messy like this to a woman who had been happily married for thirty-two years.

"Last night. I just realized it wasn't the right thing for me. I'm not ready to get married. Or maybe I don't want to marry him. I don't know. Either way, I had to be honest—with him and with myself..."

The waiter brought their drinks, and her father raised his glass. "It's not easy to admit what you want when it means making an unpopular decision. I'm proud of you."

Her mother glared at him.

"Thanks, Dad."

"Did you give back the ring?" Kip asked.

"That's what you have to say about this?" said Blythe.

"In New York State it's considered a conditional gift. There's a contractual obligation to return the ring."

"Who cares about the damn ring!" said Blythe.

"Yes, Dad—I returned the ring. And Mom, breakups happen. It's going to be fine."

Her mother nodded glumly, unconvinced.

"Of course it's fine," her father said, drumming his fingers on the table.

"Come on—isn't there something else we can talk about? This is supposed to be a happy occasion," Marin said, smiling, hoping to lighten the mood.

Her parents exchanged an odd glance. If she wasn't mistaken, her mother shook her head at Marin's father, ever so slightly.

"What's going on?" Marin said.

"Absolutely nothing," said her mom. Too quickly.

A silence settled over the table, mercifully broken when the waiter came to take their dinner orders. The atmosphere at the table finally turned positive when her father asked her about her law firm's newest client, a high-profile personal-genetics company.

Marin beamed. "I can't really say that much about the merger in the works but it's a big step for me to be put on the case. I mean, I'm pretty low on the totem pole, but still..."

Kip nodded, gently shaking his glass so the ice clinked together. "You have to walk before you can run. Just keep your head down, work hard, play the game, and you'll get there."

They both knew what he meant by *there*. Partner at the most prestigious law firm in New York City. Or maybe the head of her own firm, like the one her father had founded in 1982 in Philadelphia, where Kipton Bishop was arguably the most powerful attorney in the city. And at the age of sixty, he showed no signs of slowing down. It was actually surprising that he'd made it to her birthday dinner. After a lifetime of seeing him work eighteen-hour days and travel the globe, she was used to it being just her mother and herself more often than not. Honestly, she didn't know how her mother had done it all of those years, staying at home, tending to the house and her vegetable garden. Waiting for her father's rare appearances. Marin shuddered. For as long as she could remember, she'd always been very aware of the fact that she never wanted to be the one left behind.

Throughout dinner, under the table, Marin checked her phone. She appreciated her parents driving up to Manhattan to celebrate with her, she really did. But the evening was dragging.

Finally, the text she'd been waiting for arrived.

Sure, come on over.

The waiter approached with a large cake covered with extravagant shavings of white chocolate. It was lit with a single candle.

Please don't sing. But no, it wasn't that type of place. The waiter placed the cake in front of her, and her mother reached across the table and squeezed her hand. "Happy birthday, sweetheart." She sounded so forlorn, it was as if her own engagement had been broken off.

Marin closed her eyes, blew out the candle, and thought of the person waiting for her on the other side of the city.

"To many more," chimed in her father, finishing his drink.

The waiter sliced the cake and served them each a piece. "So what does Greg think of all this? He's just accepted it?" her mother blurted out. Marin had to give her credit—she'd held out until dessert.

"Blythe, don't push," her father said, ignoring the plate in front of him while Marin ate half her slice in two big bites. With her mouth full, she couldn't be expected to talk.

"It's a natural question, Kip. I mean, two years, planning a life together...that doesn't just evaporate." Her mother patted her ash-blond hair as if the mere thought of such chaos had set it askew. "Are you sure about this? I just don't want you to do something you'll regret."

Marin nodded. Yes, she was sure. You didn't break up with a man like Greg Harper on a whim.

"Thanks so much for dinner. Really. I miss you guys," Marin said, reflexively checking her phone again.

"You're not running off, are you?" her mother said.

"Let her be, Blythe. Knowing Marin, she's probably going home to burn the midnight oil." He gave her a conspiratorial wink.

"Well, she needs to learn how to relax. Honestly, Marin. Your priorities—"

"Are exactly where they should be," said her father.

"It's just been a long week," Marin said. "And I'll see you in the morning for breakfast."

Again, her parents exchanged that strange look.

Marin kissed them both good night.

Outside, she took in the warm spring air before hailing a cab. It felt like the first time she'd breathed all night.

Blythe Bishop shuddered in the freezing lobby of the Plaza Hotel.

Breakups happen. That's all her daughter had to say on the topic? Oh, what was she thinking? Blythe wrapped her arms around herself, trying to take comfort in her elegant surroundings.

Yes, breakups did happen. But yesterday, Marin had had a three-carat diamond on her left ring finger, a deposit on a wedding venue, and plans to go dress shopping with her mother next week. Now what? All that was just... gone?

Marin was too career-obsessed. That was the problem.

Thirty and single. Oh, Blythe knew it was old-fashioned to see that as a bad thing. But most of Marin's friends on the Main Line were already married, living in big, beautiful homes in Penn Valley, having their first babies, with the days of office hours and career stress long behind them. Was it so wrong to want that for her own daughter?

"You need to give Marin more credit," said Kip. "She's the captain of her own ship."

"I just wish she'd open up more about what happened with Greg. Even though she's the one who ended it, it still can't be easy. They ordered the invitations."

"It's not really our business," Kip said, walking briskly to the elevator. She followed him inside, and each pressed a button.

"Well, as we're her parents, it actually is our business." After thirty-two years, she still didn't understand half the things that came out of that man's mouth.

"Marin had the balls to end it because she knew it wasn't right for her. She's a tough cookie," *Like me,* she knew he was thinking. Also, *And unlike you.*

"I'm afraid she's going to end up alone," said Blythe.

"Well, maybe that's what she wants. It's her life."

The door slid open on eight, Kip's floor.

"This is so strange," she said, following him uninvited out of the elevator. "Kip, this doesn't feel right."

Standing in the quiet hallway, she blinked back tears.

Kip scratched his jaw with his room key card. He looked uncharacteristically tired.

"No more stalling, Blythe. We have to tell her."

"This just isn't the best time to—"

Kip held up his hand as if halting traffic. "Stop. I don't want to hear it. This breakup with Greg doesn't change anything. Tomorrow at breakfast, we're telling her."

With that, Kip summoned the elevator for her. Case closed.

Chapter Two

Marin walked quickly in the shadows of the tree-lined side street at Sixty-Eighth and Lexington. It was May, and after a long winter, the trees were full of leaves and in bloom. It was a perfect spring night, and she had made it past the first hurdle.

The thought of seeing him had been the only thing that got her through dinner. She knew her parents meant well, but God—what was she supposed to say? *I broke off my engagement because I experienced the most intense physical attraction I've ever felt in my life to a different man?* She didn't know what was worse: being the object of their worry or dealing with their disappointment if she told them the truth.

Marin reached the brownstone on Sixty-Eighth and Lexington and rang the doorbell. Her gaze lingered on her empty ring finger. It was still a shock not to see the Tiffany diamond ring Greg Harper had placed on her hand three days before Thanksgiving at the charmingly impossible-to-get-into restaurant One if by Land, Two if by Sea (made famous when Obama took his wife there on their New York City date night). Marin had worn the ring for nearly six months; when she said yes to him, she really had intended to wear it for the rest of her life.

What would Julian say when she told him she'd broken off her engagement?

He answered the door still dressed in the suit he'd worn to the office but without the tie. His reading glasses were a tip-off that she'd interrupted him working. Marin felt a pang of guilt. She should be working too. Burning the midnight oil, as her dad said. Instead, she was distracting Julian. And being distracted by him.

At age thirty-two, Julian Rowe was the youngest partner at the law firm she'd dreamed of working at since undergrad: the fabled Cole, Harding, and Worth. He'd built his career in M and A—as a young associate, he'd ridden shotgun on some of the most groundbreaking cases the courts had heard in recent years. And then, a few months ago and two years into her own tenure at the firm, she'd been assigned to his team to work on a merger between a pharmaceutical giant and a small but extremely profitable company providing DNA home testing.

There was almost enough work and a steep enough learning curve to keep her mind off the fact that Julian Rowe was beautiful.

Almost.

When she first saw him—tall, with near-black hair and deep, dark eyes—the first word that came to mind was *striking*. He had the perfectly chiseled nose of a young Clint Eastwood, and he spoke at a slight remove, as if his brilliant mind barely had time to stop and convey the information—it was already on to the next item of business. He had the remnants of a British accent from his first twelve years growing up in North London. Everything about him was achingly serious.

Marin wanted him—instantly. She'd never felt such a pure physical attraction in her life. She walked around the office charged up, adrenalized, all of her senses heightened. She felt like one big raw nerve. When he spoke to her, it took all of her effort to absorb what he said and not just stare at his lips. Over the conference table, she found herself leaning too close. She could barely sleep at night, she was so eager to get back into the office.

And all the while, she was planning her wedding.

"How's the birthday girl?" he asked with a kiss after letting her in. He took her light cashmere wrap and hung it in the coat closet.

"Better now," she breathed, his arms around her.

"I was surprised to hear from you. How did you get away? Didn't you have dinner with your parents and—"

"Long story," she said.

"Come on in," he said. Julian occupied the entire four-story brownstone, which he had been renting for years from a widowed socialite who had moved to Palm Beach. The first night Marin saw it, she told him she'd always dreamed of having a place just like it.

"When the time is right I'm going to make an offer on it," he'd said.

"What makes you think she'll sell?"

"I'm a lawyer. I know how to feel these things out."

"Well, I'm a lawyer, and I don't."

He'd regarded her with his usual heart-stopping intensity and said, "I find that hard to believe. You seem like a woman who goes after what she wants."

That night, she had believed she would never see

the town house again. Yes, they'd slept together. But it was just a onetime thing—just to get it out of their systems.

Of course, that first night had been the point of no return. How naive to think it would turn out any other way.

She thought of her mother's expression when she'd told her the wedding was off, and winced.

"Cover your eyes," Julian said, leading her into the house by the hand.

"Why? What are you doing?" This playfulness was a side of him she had seen only recently, maybe in the past few weeks of their two-month relationship. Every time he revealed a new facet of himself, some detail of his growing up, some endearing quirk of his personality, it was like a precious gift. All she wanted was to know him completely, and the sense that he was beginning to trust her more, to open up, thrilled her.

He told her to keep her eyes covered, and she allowed him to steer her from one room to the other.

"Okay—you can look now."

They were in his living room. A flickering light caught her eye—a candle atop a chocolate cupcake on one of the antique side tables.

"Oh, Julian," she said, kissing him.

"You didn't give me much notice that I'd get to celebrate with you tonight. I planned on sometime later this week."

"You didn't have to do anything. Really. I just wanted to see you."

The candle needed attention, and she knew Julian would not prompt her with something as clichéd as *Make a wish,* so she bent over the table and gently blew it out. He poured her a glass of wine and she curled up on his plush leather couch. Across the room, a glass table was covered with files and two laptops.

"You working on Genie?"

He nodded. "What else. But I'm about ready to wrap up."

The DNA-testing company Genie was taking up all of his time and most of hers. It had also spurred on their relationship, sending it out of the sexual-tension zone into the sex zone.

It happened during one of a seemingly endless string of very late nights at the office working on the Genie merger. Her fiancé, usually tolerant of her long hours, was starting to complain. Marin knew his impatience with her work schedule was understandable, but it still irked her. And it made her second-guess her decision to accept his proposal. This was why she had never been keen on the idea of marriage—and why she was certainly not open to the idea of children. Greg did not want children either, so that was one less thing to worry about. No one could do it all, have it all. And she had known from a young age that she wanted to be successful. Like her father.

As much as Greg said he supported her work ethic, she knew she was testing his patience. And so, on a Wednesday night at nine thirty, she decided to tear herself away from the computer and call it quits. But before she left, she stopped by Julian's office to drop off a box of files—a box she could very well have left for the interoffice delivery in the morning. He was like the pull of gravity.

I'll see him for a minute, and then I'll leave. Home to my fiancé, she told herself. Looking at her ring.

Maybe she wouldn't even talk to him. She'd just drop the box off with a wave and be on her way. But when she reached his office on the ninth floor, with its view of the

Empire State Building lit in purple, she saw him in the midst of something that compelled her to ask:

"Sampling the wares?" She smiled in a way she would be the first to admit was too flirtatious.

Open in front of him on his desk was one of the Genie testing kits. The red-and-green DNA-strand logo on the packaging was unmistakable. And there were dozens of them stacked around the office. It was typical for clients to gift the firm samples of their products. But for her, the DNA-testing kit was one of the less appealing offerings.

Apparently, though, not for Julian. He held the plastic test tube with a detachable lid in one hand and the instructions in the other. When he looked up to find Marin in the doorway, he raised the test tube like he was making a toast.

"Yes. They keep asking me if I've done a test. I guess you could say I feel a professional obligation. And a little curiosity, I'll admit."

Marin drew closer to his desk. She reached over and picked up the empty cardboard Genie box, grateful for the prop. She knew she was crossing some sort of line, but she couldn't stop herself. It was like she was watching someone else's actions from afar.

With a smile, he handed her the small instruction sheet printed on shiny paper. She didn't need to read it; she knew how it worked from their first meeting with Genie: All you had to do was mail in a saliva sample, and a few weeks later Genie e-mailed you the results. It was so user-friendly, it was no wonder the company was blowing up and attracting a multibillion-dollar buyer.

She took the paper from him, and his fingertips grazed hers. Swallowing hard, she pretended to read the instructions but the words swam in front of her eyes. *Just go home*.

"You should try it too," he said.

"Really?"

"You're on the team," he said, smiling, his midnight eyes meeting hers in a challenge that was, dare she think it, flirtatious in its own right.

And in the state she was in, thrilled by the barely professional interaction, Marin happily agreed.

Things felt different after that. Nothing happened that night, but somehow it felt like they had a secret. And she realized that they did: they were attracted to each other. And it would have to stay a secret; even if she hadn't been engaged to another man, it was strictly taboo for a partner to date an associate. The firm had a strict no-dating, no-fraternizing, don't-even-look-twice-at-your-subordinate policy.

It was a fairly standard attitude for law firms, but everyone at Cole, Harding was especially sensitive since the Incident: Two years ago, at a summer-associate drinks event, a senior partner had told one of the young women that he wanted to fuck her seven different ways. The woman talked. For the first time in the firm's proud five-decade history, it found itself written about in the *New York Post*'s Page Six instead of the *Wall Street Journal*.

That partner had gone from making seven figures to teaching at CUNY, and the rest of them had suffered through a week of sensitivity training and a sexual-harassment seminar. The zero-tolerance policy had been enacted.

And yet she and Julian couldn't stay away from each other. As much as they tried, it was less than a week after the Genie incident before he invited her to his town house. They both admitted their sexual attraction and agreed they needed to "defuse" the situation.

At his town house that first night, they didn't speak. They didn't make it past the entrance hall. Handsome, reserved, professional Julian Rowe fucked with reckless abandon. Afterward, her entire body throbbed. They lay tangled together on his floor, making small talk about the fabulous house he rented and wanted to buy. And then she forced herself to get dressed and go back to the apartment she shared with her fiancé.

It was terribly wrong, but she couldn't bring herself to stop. When she weighed everything in her mind, leaving Greg was easier to imagine than staying away from Julian was. And once she admitted that to herself, she knew what she had to do.

"Marin," Julian said now.

She looked up, startled. "Sorry. I was just thinking…"

"Where does Greg think you are? I don't want you to get yourself into trouble."

She toyed with the wrapper of her cupcake and licked chocolate frosting off her thumb. Her heart pounded.

"I ended it with Greg." She was afraid to look at him, unsure how he would take the news. When he didn't say anything, she was forced to face him to gauge his reaction.

It didn't seem positive.

"Are you upset?"

"I'm not upset." He stood and began pacing. "But Marin, this wasn't supposed to ruin your relationship. This was supposed to be a temporary thing, two adults letting off steam, dealing with their attraction to each other. I mean, we work together. We can't be a couple."

Her stomach plunged with disappointment. "That's fine," she snapped. "But I still can't marry a man I'm not in love with. So it has nothing to do with you, if that makes you feel any better."

"Don't be angry with me. I think you're taking this wrong." He sat next to her and reached for her hand. "Look, I'm crazy about you. I am—you have to know that." He kissed her. "This just took me by surprise. And we have to be careful."

"I know that! I'm not trying to escalate anything. I just can't live a lie."

"I respect you for that, Marin. I really do." He hugged her. "I know it couldn't have been easy."

It hadn't been. Greg took it badly. He was angry and called her all the names she deserved to be called, even though he didn't know the worst of it: that she was having an affair. Greg Harper had never lost anything—had never had something fail to go his way—in his entire life. He hadn't even bothered to ask her why or see if there was something they could do to salvage things. She was taking something away from him. She was doing something to him that was out of his control. He was clearly more upset about losing face than about losing her. Whoever said hell hath no fury like a woman scorned had clearly never burned an alpha male.

It had been ugly, but the way it all went down just validated her decision.

Now it was done. Julian could choose to let it put a damper on their relationship, or he could see it as a positive. Either way, she felt as if a weight had been lifted off her.

Marin stood up. "I should get going. Thanks for the birthday cupcake."

He reached for her hand. "Don't go. Stay."

She was shocked to feel tears prick her eyes. She hadn't realized how desperately she needed to hear that word.

Chapter Three

Blythe woke up just before six in the morning, two hours before her alarm. This was not surprising. One month into her separation from Kip, she still wasn't used to sleeping alone. Add a strange hotel room to the mix, and it made for an exhausting night of tossing and turning.

Blinking in the darkness, she stretched out in the enormous bed of her suite. With the blackout curtains closed, there wasn't even a hint of light. Even though the sun was just beginning to rise, she knew that midtown was bright and awake around the clock, and if she stepped out onto Fifth Avenue, she could start her day.

But she didn't want to start her day—not when it meant telling her daughter that after three decades of marriage, Kip had asked her for a divorce.

When Kip moved out four weeks ago (leaving his clothes and golf equipment and scotch collection in their home on Wynnewood Lane—the house they'd bought as newlyweds), she'd felt certain he'd be back. He was subletting a town house at Oak Hill, but that would get old fast. She knew Kip, and of this she felt certain. Yes, there were problems in their marriage, but that had long been the case. So why divorce? Why now?

Was it a coincidence that he'd first expressed his desire to separate on the heels of Marin's engagement? Had he been suppressing this impulse, thinking that their grown daughter needed them together still? And that her impending marriage, the first step toward creating a family of her own, somehow released him from this obligation?

If that had been his reasoning, then wasn't the broken engagement the perfect time to pause and think it over?

We're telling her at breakfast. No more stalling.

She couldn't do it. She wasn't ready to admit defeat.

A glance at the bedside clock told her that it was a little after six. Kip hadn't slept past six a day in his life.

Blythe didn't bother putting on makeup, though she was tempted to at least dab a little concealer over the dark hollows under her eyes. But now that she had the idea to talk to Kip, she couldn't risk missing the opportunity. What if he was already getting ready to go to the hotel gym? She pulled on her own sadly underused yoga pants, the Yale zipper hoodie she'd had since Marin's freshman year, and her Uggs.

Pressing the button for Kip's floor, Blythe ran through her pitch. *There's no reason to rush into telling Marin. We haven't even worked out the details ourselves.* Of course, she already knew what he'd say: *There's nothing to work out. You keep the house. Whatever you need…*

I need you, she thought to herself. But she had not yet said this—not aloud. Not to him. But this morning, she would.

And it was true—had been true for as long as she could remember. Even during the times when she didn't want him. *Want* and *need* were two different things. What was it some philosopher had said? Substitute the word *need* for *love* and I'll show you love in its true dimensions. Something like that. She hadn't studied philosophy. She had not attended college. She'd married Kip instead.

Blythe padded down the eighth-floor hallway, passing two men dressed in business suits as she rounded the corner to Kip's room.

She paused a minute, then ignored the Do Not Disturb placard and knocked.

No response.

Blythe knocked again, more self-consciously this time. A housekeeper passed by, pushing a cart of linens and towels. She waited until she was halfway down the hall to knock again. Maybe he was already at the hotel fitness center. Did she dare track him down there? And then she heard the brush of metal on metal as the front door unlocked. Surprisingly, Blythe felt her heart race. The way it hadn't for Kip in a very long time.

Her husband answered the door, but barely; he cracked it two inches. She could see that he was still in his powder-blue Peter Elliot nightshirt, the one she'd given him last Christmas. His eyes were half closed with sleep.

"Are you okay?" she said, because illness was the only possible explanation for his not being up and about.

"Blythe, what the hell are you doing here at this hour?" he whispered.

At this hour? Had she made a mistake? She felt her face flood with color as she glanced at her watch, half expecting it to read 4:15 instead of 6:15.

"It's after six," she said.

"Kip? Who is it?" A female voice. From inside her husband's hotel room.

Blythe froze. Kip responded to the query, though in the white-hot shock of the moment, Blythe couldn't for the life of her make sense of what he said. He stepped out into the hall and closed the door behind him.

"I'm sorry," he said, rubbing his brow. "I should have told you sooner. But you've been having so much difficulty with even the concept of divorce. I wanted to take it one thing at a time."

When he looked at her, his eyes had softened from his initial flash of irritation.

"Do you...love her?" she asked.

"Yes."

Marin walked into the lobby of the Plaza, buzzing with energy despite getting only a few hours of sleep.

Julian was happy she was free. *She* was happy she was free. Now she could enjoy her parents' company in a way she hadn't been able to last night.

She spotted her father, dressed in a pair of gray slacks and a lightweight argyle sweater. At six foot two, with a thick head of salt-and-pepper hair and bright blue eyes, her father was a dashing man. She'd always wished she looked a little more like him, but she took after her mother's side, the Madigans. Not that her mother was a slouch in the looks department; she was a very pretty woman, with high cheekbones and deep-set hazel eyes and full lips. But Marin had always coveted the more refined, classic features of the Bishops.

"Where's Mom?" she asked when she reached her father, looking around. The lobby was bustling with well-heeled guests arriving and departing and bellhops pushing brass carts full of luggage.

"She has a terrible headache," he said.

"Oh no! Should I go up to your room and see her?"

"No, no—she's resting," he said, looking away.

"Are you sure?" Marin felt a stab of guilt. Her broken engagement was making her mother literally sick. She would have to make a trip to Philly. Schedule a mother-daughter lunch. Confide in her about Julian.

"Yes. She sends her love and feels terrible but said to just call her later."

"Okay, well, do you want to eat here or go somewhere else for breakfast? There's a place I like just a few blocks—"

"Marin, there's something I want to discuss with you." His expression was serious. Stern.

Marin's first thought was *How did he find out that I'm seeing someone at my firm?* The law world was a small one, especially in the New York, Philadelphia, Boston triad. Oh, he must be disappointed in her. So unprofessional!

She was afraid to meet his eyes. "Is everything okay?"

He nodded, arms crossed in front of his chest. "Your mother and I are divorcing."

Chapter Four

Traffic heading east on LA's Freeway 10 was bumper-to-bumper.

After five minutes of not moving an inch, Rachel Moscowitz leaned on her horn. Not very Zen of her, but even mindful breathing wasn't helping today. She was out of a job. Again! And this time, it wasn't even her fault.

Her phone rang, and she put it on speaker.

"Rach, it's Fran," her mother said.

"This isn't the best time. I'm in crazy traffic."

"This will just take a sec; can you swing by my house after work and pick up Hugo? I'm in Joshua Tree and I forgot to board him."

"What? Now?"

"It's been a few days and he's probably out of food."

Un-fucking-believable. Her mother shouldn't even have a houseplant, let alone a cat.

"Fran, I am having a really bad day. Isn't there anyone else you can call? Where's Tad?" Tad, her mother's boyfriend du jour. Just a few years older than Rachel.

"We broke up weeks ago. Didn't I tell you?"

No, she had not told her. Because she called Rachel only when she needed something. The thing was, her mother's house in Brentwood gave Rachel a place to stop on her way home and wait out the worst of the traffic.

"Fine," she said. "I'll feed Hugo. When are you coming back?"

"I'll text you."

The call ended before Rachel could tell her that she'd lost the job she'd been sure was finally the start of a career.

Oh, she'd been so excited to land it. One of her mother's Reiki clients (yes, her mother was a certified Reiki master; she was also an ordained nondenominational minister and a licensed real estate agent) was a producer on the reality show *Celebrity Family Tree*. Post–Reiki session, the woman mentioned she needed a research assistant. And Fran, in a rare display of helpfulness, got Rachel an interview. The producer didn't seem to mind that Rachel's résumé featured only two years of credits from UC Berkeley, a brief stint waiting tables at an organic café, a few months as a salesgirl at a vintage shop on Melrose, and sporadic turns as a dog walker.

"I like your energy," the producer had said. And Rachel did have good energy! She worked at it. If there was any useful lesson her mother had imparted to her, it was the power of positive thinking.

But then, the emergency staff meeting. Her boss, Judy, gathered them in the conference room and delivered the news: Production was halted indefinitely.

She would try not to let her new unemployed status get her too down. Or the traffic. Or the fact that the extra key to her mother's house was missing from underneath the potted plant next to the front door.

Rachel sat on the front steps, the midday sun beating down on her.

Where was the damn key? She had one at her apartment, but it was all the way across town in Silver Lake, and that wasn't going to do her much good at the moment. She dialed her mother, and it went straight to voice mail.

Unbelievable!

Her mother had a way of disappearing, going completely off the grid for months at a time. Fortunately, she also had a way of leaving her windows unlocked. And since the last thing Rachel wanted to do was get back into her car, she walked through unkempt grass to the supply shed in the backyard. She dragged a metal ladder to the house, propped it against the area closest to her mother's bedroom window, and climbed up, cursing. *Positive thinking, positive thinking,* she told herself.

Her phone buzzed in her back pocket. She ignored it, trying not to look down as she climbed to the second floor. She reached the window and pushed the sash up and open. Success! After heaving it higher, she leaned inside and eased her body to a safe landing on top of her mother's desk. It was covered with piles of papers and books and loose change, much of which went flying, displaced by Rachel's body.

A sharp cry made her look up, lose her balance, and roll off the desk onto the floor.

"Hugo, you startled me."

Hugo, her mother's two-year-old tabby, meowed again, rubbing his body against Rachel's. The cat, usually more circumspect, must have been attention-starved. Or just starved.

Rachel took the stairs down to the kitchen, and sure

enough, the cat-food bowl was empty. The water bowl was also empty. And it had to be ninety degrees in there.

"Oh, Hugo. I'm sorry." Rachel found a bag of Iams under the sink, poured a generous heap into the metal bowl, filled the water dish, and sat at the kitchen table. Now that she was there, she was in no rush to get back to her own apartment. She would have to tell her roommate that she had lost yet another job. She'd have to move out. Maybe even move back in with Fran.

Her phone rang, startling her. She looked at the incoming number: Judy Ross, head of research. Her boss. Or, as of this morning, former boss.

"Hi, Rachel—I know you're probably not even home yet but I'm already getting some calls from the press. I doubt anyone would call you but if they get stonewalled by the higher-ups, you never know..."

"I won't say anything. But between you and me, I just can't believe he ruined our show." And yes, even though she was just a research assistant, she felt invested enough in the production to think of it as her show too.

After all, she'd been there when the research team made the discovery. They were working on the episode featuring Scott Anders, beloved rom-com hero, sometime action star, and poster boy for Hollywood political activism. He was so outspoken about human rights, he made Angelina Jolie look apathetic. So what a surprise for the *Celebrity Family Tree* team to discover that an ancestor of his had been one of the most notorious slave traders in the South.

Rachel wasn't completely sure what happened next, but when the episode was edited, somehow that fun little factoid didn't make the final cut. And someone on staff must have been pissed, because it was leaked to the press.

That Scott Anders was descended from slave traders didn't get a lot of play, because you can't help the family you're born into. But you *can* help what you do in the here and now, and Scott Anders had leaned on the producers hard to make them bury the discovery. The whole selling point of the show was that the viewer was "with" the celebrities when they learned about their heritage. The veracity of the entire program came into question; Scott Anders denied accusations that he'd asked executives to suppress the truth about his ancestors, throwing *Celebrity Family Tree* under the proverbial bus. And the network pulled the plug.

"But Judy," Rachel said, "if you can still try to find me any leads on my father, it would mean the world to me."

For as long as she could remember, Rachel had ached to learn the identity of her father. All her mother knew was that he was a white male in his twenties. She chose him as her sperm donor because he'd written that he liked to travel.

Rachel used the show's resources to do a little digging. She didn't have his name, but she'd had her DNA tested and found out that she was half Southern European and half Eastern European. Since her mother was an Ashkenazi Jew, that left her father as the Southern European. Even better, Genie, the DNA-testing company, reported that another user in its database was a 50 percent genetic match to her. A half sibling! And through the company, she was able to e-mail her.

For the first time, she had more family than just her self-absorbed mother.

But a week after sending the e-mail through Genie, she still had not heard back from Marin Bishop of New York, New York.

Maybe the e-mail got dumped in her half sister's spam folder. Her half *sister*. She could scarcely get her mind around it. Yes, that had to be it—foiled by the spam folder.

Rachel would try her again. She'd find a way to e-mail her directly. If there was anything she'd learned from her two months in research, it was how to be persistent in reaching out to a source. And this woman, this half sister, was a source of the most valuable information she could imagine. Rachel had to believe that she belonged somewhere, and she'd certainly never felt it with her mother. But maybe when she found her father and her sister, all the puzzle pieces would fit together and she'd feel whole for the first time in her life.

"That's another reason I'm calling you," Judy said. "I didn't have time to talk to you about this at the office with everything that's going on. But I found it. I have your father's name."

Chapter Five

Divorce! Marin hadn't seen it coming.

Sitting at her desk where she was usually the picture of organization and control, she was unglued by her father's words—*long overdue* and *a new phase of life*. New phase of life? Her father didn't speak like that. And so she asked him, "Is there someone else?" His response: "Yes." The second blow.

She stared blankly at her computer screen.

How could this be happening? She'd gone home to Philly two months ago for her mother's birthday. Her parents had appeared the same as always. There wasn't a single sign anything was wrong, and now they were divorcing and her father was in a new relationship? Then again, she'd brought Greg with her that weekend. So much for appearances.

She was going to lose it if she didn't talk to someone, and the someone she most wanted to talk to was just one floor above her.

It was wrong, and she hated herself for her weakness, but she needed him.

She abandoned her desk and headed for the elevators.

Julian's secretary was not at her desk and his door was closed. Marin knocked once and opened it. All she wanted was to see his face.

When she saw it, he had a deer-in-the-headlights look. Senior partner Hilton Wallace was sitting across from him.

Hilton Wallace had probably once been an attractive man. But in his midfifties, he had the generic appearance of bloated affluence. Golf and tennis on the weekends couldn't combat the decades of long hours behind a desk. He had steely blue eyes and the deepest crow's-feet Marin had ever seen, lines that appeared to have been carved into his face rather than slowly worn in over time. And at the moment, they gave his face a particularly stern look.

"Hello, Marin. Surprised to see you in this neck of the woods," Hilton said, leaning back in his chair, looking at her pointedly.

"Sorry to interrupt! I just…there are a few Genie documents that aren't in that file box you sent down. Dina isn't at her desk or I would have asked her—"

"I'll have her check the document list when she returns," Julian said curtly.

Fuck, fuck, fuck. She backed out of the office and retreated to her own.

Closing her own door and leaning against it, she decided to do what she should have done in the first place: call her mother. She got her voice mail and left a message saying she was going to come home on Saturday.

Until then, Marin had to put it out of her mind. Yes, her parents were splitting up. *Deal with it—you're a grown woman.*

Marin opened her e-mail.

She scrolled through her messages, one in particular catching her eye. It was from a name she didn't recognize, the subject line: *Please Read.*

Hi, Marin:

I tried reaching you through Genie, but when I didn't hear back I figured I might have gotten dumped in your spam folder so I thought I'd e-mail you directly. I hope you don't mind.

I recently did a DNA test through Genie and I got a notice from them that I have a very close relative in their database. You! So close that you're either my grandparent or my half sibling. I'm guessing from your profile you're not my grandmother (LOL). I know this probably comes as a shock to you—it was for me, even though I always knew it was a possibility since I have a single mom and my father was a sperm donor. Maybe you're in a similar situation? Either way, I'd love to hear from you. Number's below. Call any time.

Rachel Moscowitz

Marin blinked at the screen.

What. The. Fuck.

She hadn't heard a thing from Genie since mailing in her test kit. She'd practically forgotten about it.

Holding her breath, she opened a browser and logged in to her personal e-mail account. Sure enough, more than half a dozen e-mails from Genie hovered near the top, sandwiched between the entreaties from Equinox to rejoin and sales alerts from Barneys and Bergdorf's.

Your Kit Has Been Registered.

Your Sample Has Been Received.

Your Complete Genie Ancestry Reports Are Ready to View.

With shaking hands, she clicked on the third message. *Sign in to your account using the user name and password created during the kit-registration process.*

User name and password? She struggled to remember them. It took three tries before she got into the site. *Stop being emotional.* It was important to approach this as she would any new information that required analysis: Methodically. Professionally. Detached.

After a few minutes of clicking around, she felt more relaxed and in control. She focused on the Ancestry Composition section, which had a global map on one side of the page and a list of percentages and regions on the other. At the top, it told her she was 99.2 percent European. She would have guessed 100 percent, considering both of her parents' families were from the UK, but probably in this day and age, no one was purely 100 percent anything. The 99.2 percent was probably remarkable in itself.

The map was colored in the regions where Marin's ancestry was located. Not surprisingly, the UK was lit up—her father's great-great-grandparents came over from England and Scotland, and her mother was Welsh. But oddly, the region of Southern Europe near Spain and Portugal was also highlighted.

She checked the percentages on the right and frowned. According to the site's breakdown, she was 50 percent

Southern European. That didn't make sense. Even if one of her parents had an ancestor from Spain or somewhere in the region, she wouldn't be 50 percent Southern European.

Well, that explained the strange e-mail. There had been an error.

She was tempted to ignore the e-mail, but if she just left it out there, the woman might try to contact her again. Better to just terminate the inquiry.

Dear Ms. Moscowitz:

Thank you for getting in touch. Unfortunately, there seems to be some mistake. I wish you the best in your family research.

Marin hit Send and logged off.

She didn't need the distraction of abstract information about her alleged family tree. Her real family, her here-and-now family, was coming apart at the seams.

And she had no idea what to do about it.

Chapter Six

When in doubt, garden.

It had been Blythe's personal motto for years. Her love of gardening came from her mother-in-law—the most valuable gift the woman ever gave her. It was prompted by Blythe's confessed frustration with Kip's seemingly endless workdays and his weekend devotion to the golf course.

"No need to feel like a golf widow, my dear," said Nina Bishop. "It's not that your husband is too busy. It is that you are not busy enough."

Blythe had looked across the room at toddler Marin. Not busy enough?

But later, when she thought about it, she realized there was *busy* that made you feel like you were treading water every day and *busy* that gave you a sense of accomplishment. It wasn't that motherhood didn't give her satisfaction, but it was a different kind than what she'd felt when she danced.

"Start simple," Nina had said. "Lettuces. Pole beans."

And she did. She learned about ground pH and working the soil. Buying and sowing seeds. Transplanting. When to harvest. Weeds. Pest control. By the time Marin was in second grade, Blythe had a robust, rotating crop of lettuce, French beans, tomatoes, beets, kale, rhubarb, and—to Marin's delight—pumpkins. Kip, not a huge fan of vegetables, had requested only one item in all of Blythe's years of gardening: corn for popping. And she grew it.

This morning, Blythe knelt in the soil in front of her Brandywine tomatoes checking for invaders. Yesterday, she'd spotted a tiny green fruitworm inching its way up the side of the stake. Blythe had swiftly vanquished it.

She only wished she could do the same to Kip's new girlfriend.

Candace Cavanaugh, the divorced daughter of one of Kip's golfing buddies at the club. She was twenty-five years his junior. Who'd have thought Kip would turn into such a cliché?

"It's a delicate situation," Kip had said to her. "If it was anyone else, I wouldn't worry so much about appearances. But we need to do the right thing here…"

In other words, sometimes people had flings and there was a lot of looking the other way, because marriage was marriage. But this time, there was no looking away. Other eyes were on the ball; specifically, eyes from the Philadelphia Racquet and Hunt Country Club. Kip would not be party to a scandalous situation. The divorce papers were being filed.

For the first time since she was nineteen years old, Blythe would have to plan for a life without Kipton Bishop. Perhaps she was just lucky it had lasted as long as it did. After all, he'd arrived in her life when she needed a safety net.

Blythe had moved from Michigan to Philadelphia to join the corps of her third-choice ballet company, the Pennsylvania Ballet. Both the ABT and Joffrey had rejected her.

With each passing day, all she heard in the back of her mind was her parents' plea—logical, maddening, and ultimately ignored—to go to college and keep one foot in ballet (so to speak) and then pursue a professional dancing career later *if* that was what she still wanted. But why should she put off what she knew she wanted? There was no *if*.

The *if* became a *what if*.

What if she failed? What if she wasn't asked to return the following year?

By the spring of that first year, her confidence was at an all-time low. The night she met Kip had been the Pennsylvania Ballet's annual gala. The theme was Diamonds on Broad Street, an homage to the third act of Balanchine's *Jewels*.

Blythe remembered the dress she wore that night—a white silk sheath, size 0. She still had it in storage.

Select dancers had been chosen to perform that evening, and Blythe was not among them. Instead, she stood among the crowd of wealthy dance benefactors— some of whom had paid ten thousand dollars a plate to be there—listening to the company's artistic director introduce the evening's theme.

" 'Diamonds,' brought to life by the music of Tchaikovsky, conjures the spirit of the Mariinsky Theater, where Balanchine trained. Mary Clarke and Clement Crisp have written: 'If the entire imperial Russian inheritance of ballet were lost, "Diamonds" would still tell us of its essence.' "

Blythe clapped politely, wanting to be anywhere else. She was an ornament, like the white calla lily centerpieces, the hundreds of shining silver candlesticks on loan from a Philadelphia socialite, and the ice sculpture in the center of the room evoking imperial Russia. The guests came for the food, the photo ops, the performances, but above all, they came to mingle with the dancers themselves.

An older couple approached her, a man in a tux and a woman with silver-threaded blond hair wearing an elegant white-beaded gown. Even among the hundreds of other well-heeled dance patrons, they made an impression. Out of everyone she'd met that night, these two seemed the most excited to be there.

The woman asked Blythe if she was one of the performers.

"I'm a member of the company, but I'm not performing tonight," she said. Then she added, "It's my first year." A lame excuse. But this couple didn't know any better.

"How lovely. Congratulations," the woman said. She introduced herself as Nina Bishop. Her husband, Preston Bishop, told Blythe his wife had been attending the Pennsylvania Ballet since "before you were born."

"My grandmother brought me to *The Nutcracker* when I was four," Nina said. "I don't remember it, of course, but it somehow inspired a lifelong passion."

Something else was mentioned, something about the importance of supporting the arts, but Blythe barely heard. A man walked toward them, a young Robert Redford. It was clear he intended to join them, that he would be interrupting this talkative couple.

"Kip! There you are. I thought you snuck out on us." Nina pulled him into their little circle. The man, who Blythe guessed was five or six years older than her, said something about leaving soon, an early day at the office. When Blythe retold the story, she would remember that Kip had started to say he was leaving but then noticed Blythe and reconsidered. In reality, Nina had introduced her to him—"She's a dancer!"—and insisted he stay and that Blythe join them at their table. And then, and this part was true, Kip had said to her, "No offense, but I don't share my parents' passion for the ballet. Maybe you can help me understand what I seem to be missing?"

Her heart fluttered, the way it did when she was in the midst of a particularly difficult lift. Love at first sight? Not exactly. But there was something, a spark. Enough to help her imagine an alternative life to one lived on stage. Maybe a fulfilling life, one in which she might set herself up for success rather than failure.

A year later, when she walked down the church aisle on her father's arm, preparing to take her vows in front of two hundred people, she said one silently to herself first. *I will be a good wife to Kipton Bishop. I will make him happy.*

And now, her husband was with another woman.

Blythe heard a car crunch the gravel of the driveway. She stood up, brushed off her sweatpants, and walked around the side of the house. Marin's Saab was an extravagance to keep in Manhattan, but it made visiting home a blessedly simple two-hour drive.

"Hi, sweetheart! I'm in the garden. What do you have there?"

Marin pulled a large plastic shopping bag out of the passenger seat.

"I brought you bagels." She looked like a walking Michael Kors ad, with her perfectly tailored navy pants, a pin-striped blouse, and half a dozen gold bangles clinking musically as she headed toward the yard. Her glossy dark hair was up in a high ponytail, her brown eyes hidden behind reflective aviator sunglasses. Blythe swelled with pride. Her baby.

"Honey, you didn't have to do that. Thank you." Marin knew her parents couldn't find decent bagels in suburban Philadelphia—at least, not like in New York. Oh, New York. Though Blythe had gone through a phase of resenting the city that had lured her daughter away, she had to admit it wasn't all bad.

They convened in the breakfast room, an addition to the house made ten years ago during renovations to the kitchen. It was an airy, open space with wide Spanish tiles and a skylight. It had a table for eight and a love seat in the corner that was Blythe's favorite spot in the house for reading. French doors led to the garden.

Blythe brought out a pitcher of fresh-brewed iced tea. Marin set her phone on the table and scrolled through her e-mails.

"Sorry—I just need to check this quickly."

Blythe sat across from her and waited patiently for Marin to finish tapping away on her phone. When Marin finally looked up, the first thing she said was "So why did you leave New York before I had a chance to talk to you?"

Well, that didn't take long.

"I guess I didn't know what to tell you," Blythe admitted. "I had hoped we wouldn't have to have the conversation, that your father would come to his senses. But that was before I knew the whole story."

"Candace Cavanaugh." Marin's lips pursed like she'd just bitten into a lemon.

Blythe nodded glumly, then shook her head. "But it's not just about that. At least, I can't imagine it is. Marriages are complicated. I just thought we were past a lot of the more—" She waved her hand as if swatting a fly. "Still—it doesn't change the important things. Your father and I are still your parents, and we are here for you. We'll always be a family." She tried to smile.

Marin reached across the table and took her hand. "Thanks, Mom. I'm okay. Really. I'm just concerned about you. And look, I know we've always been able to be honest with each other. I'm sorry I've been . . . secretive about my breakup with Greg. I wanted to talk to you. I did. I mean, I do."

"You do?" Blythe perked up.

"Of course. Mom—you're my best friend. But I'm trying to be discreet and I need you to be as well. The truth is, I met someone else."

Blythe gasped. This was the last thing she'd expected. "Who is it?"

"You won't tell Dad about this, you swear?"

"Believe me, at this point, that is not an issue."

"Oh, Mom. Are you two not speaking?"

"We are." Barely. "Enough about that. Who *is* he?"

"It's someone at work."

Blythe tensed with alarm. "Oh, Marin. Please tell me he's not married."

"No! No, it's nothing like that. But he's in a senior position, so it's kind of an issue. We're keeping it secret. I feel weird even telling you this much."

Blythe didn't know what to say. There she was, assuming Marin had let her work obsession get in the way of her relationship when in actuality she'd started a new relationship—at work! Oh, she hoped Marin knew what she was doing.

"Please don't get mad at me for asking this, but are you

sure you needed to break up with Greg? I hate to say it, but people do have flings and it's not necessarily something to end an engagement over." Or a marriage, for that matter.

Marin shook her head quickly. "It was the only thing to do. Being with this new man ... it made me realize what a mistake I was making by committing my life to Greg. I don't love him, Mom. At least, not enough." The unspoken words were loud and clear: *Not the way I love this new guy.*

"And this man at the office—he feels the same about you?"

Marin beamed. "I think so."

Blythe had never seen her look so happy about a man. Not ever. She was positively glowing. Marin's reticence fell by the wayside, and she went on and on about this new man's good looks, his long-lashed dark eyes, his faint British accent. The way his sharply analytical mind worked. His brilliance.

"Okay, okay." Blythe laughed. "I get it. I'm happy for you. Just be careful, please."

"I am. Don't worry," Marin said, checking her phone again. "Hey, Mom, can I ask you a kind of crazy question?"

"Sure," Blythe practically sang, so thrilled to be her daughter's confidante once again. "Ask me anything."

"Is there any chance Dad is part Spanish or Italian or something?"

Blythe felt the color drain from her face. She looked down at her shorts, suddenly focused on a smudge of dirt. "Not that I know of," she said, trying to sound casual.

"Portuguese? Anything like that? I know he likes to say his family is more British than the Crown, but I mean, what's the real story there?"

"Where is this coming from?" Blythe felt her body go cold with alarm.

"It's silly, really. But you know that new client I told you about at dinner last week? Their product is a home DNA-testing kit and since I'm part of the team, I sampled one. It came back that I'm fifty percent Southern European—Spain, Portugal, that region."

"Oh. Well, there must be some mistake. Or maybe I'm half Spanish." Her forced laugh came out like a yelp.

"You'd have to be a hundred percent Spanish."

"Well, then it's a mistake." The guilt—oh, the guilt. Like an anvil on her chest.

Marin nodded. "I figured."

Blythe, hands shaking, stood up from the table. "Well, anyway. Come out back. I want to show you my Swiss chard."

Any excuse to get closer to the ground, on her hands and knees. Before she fainted.

Marin had plenty of time to think while stuck in GW Bridge traffic heading back into the city. She never would have planned to drive into Manhattan on a Saturday night—she'd intended to stay over in Philly. But her mother practically shoved her out the door.

"I have a lot going on here and I know you're busy with work. We'll have a longer visit next time," she'd said.

Strange. Usually her mother found any excuse to get her to stay longer. On the plus side, Marin would have more time with Julian. She drove straight to his town house.

"This is a surprise," he said, hugging her. "I thought you were staying in Philly the entire weekend."

Files were everywhere, and his laptop was on the glass coffee table. She had asked him once why he didn't just use the house's second-floor office, and he said he never meant to spend all night working in the living room— he'd start out opening his laptop to do just one little thing and the next thing he knew, three hours had passed. She was the same way.

"Yeah. So did I. But my mother seemed to want some space." *Oddly.*

"How's she taking the split?"

Marin shrugged. "It's hard to say. I think she's putting up a brave front. But I know she's not used to living alone. And this just seems out of nowhere."

"It might seem like that, but it never is. There's always something."

"I just can't imagine what."

"Of course not. There's no marriage more mysterious than one's own parents'."

She knew he was thinking of his parents' divorce. It was the source of a lot of pain for him growing up. His father had left when Julian was nine, and Julian had never seen him again after his mother moved them back to New York. Growing up with a lonely, underemployed mother in the picturesque Rye suburbs, he always felt like an outsider. He made up for it by being the captain of every sports team and getting straight As and flawless test scores. He attended Harvard on a full scholarship.

He told Marin that only recently had he and his father been back in contact. Julian suspected he just wanted money.

She felt stupid complaining to him about her parents.

He stood from the couch and reached for something in the drawer of one of the antique side tables. When he turned back to her, he was holding a small orange box wrapped in a brown bow.

"We never got a chance to properly celebrate your birthday," he said, smiling.

"You didn't have to get me anything," she said nervously.

Something about Julian spending money on her made her uncomfortable. Greg Harper had thrown money around like it meant nothing, and to him, it hadn't. He'd been born with tons of it, and as a banker he earned even more. Julian had a huge salary at the firm, but because he had struggled growing up, he approached any purchases with great seriousness and care. He wasn't cheap; he just thought about everything because every dollar meant something to him. It was almost as if how it was earned and how it was spent was a moral issue and not just a financial one.

The box was from Hermès.

"Open it," he said, moving closer to her and rubbing her back.

Hesitantly, she slipped off the bow and lifted the lid to find a delicate platinum key chain, her initials engraved in ornate cursive on the oblong oval base.

She gently removed it from the box and looked at him.

"Julian, it's beautiful! Thank you. But you really didn't have to…"

He kissed her, holding her face, and she wrapped her arms around him. Her chest to his, she felt the rise and fall of his breathing. She wished she could stay like that forever.

I love him, she thought. *I'm completely in love with him.*

He pulled back, took her hand, and pressed something into her palm.

A key.

The Hermès chain suddenly took on much more meaning.

"Julian…"

"We have to be careful at the office, but I want to see you more. As often as you can come over here."

Her heart soared. This was happening. They were going to be together.

"Oh, Julian. I'm sorry about the other day, barging into your office like that."

He kissed the bridge of her nose. "It's okay. No harm done. I get it—you were upset. But you really can't do it again. I don't want to raise any red flags."

"I know," she said. "But I *am* working on Genie. It's not totally outrageous that I would have an issue to discuss."

"You just wouldn't necessarily burst into my office with it."

"True." She tried to push the next thought away, but she couldn't. "Julian, did you ever get your results from Genie?"

"Sure. Didn't you?"

"Um, yeah. Why didn't you mention it?"

"I didn't really think about it, to tell you the truth. No big revelations. Why?"

"I was just wondering." She glanced away. "What's the probability of Genie results being wrong?"

"Very low. There's always a slight margin for human error, but to the knowledge of the executives at the company, that has not happened."

Her heart began to pound but she kept her tone casual. "I mean, this is serious stuff. People get emotionally invested."

"Like I said, the probability of an individual's results being wrong is extremely low."

"But it's possible."

"Anything is possible. Why—did you get something surprising in your results?"

Now was the time to tell him about the e-mail. But no, things were going so well. It was a magical day. Why spoil it?

"No," she lied. "Nothing at all. I was just thinking, you know—from a legal perspective. There could be lawsuits."

"Of course. But there haven't been. I think even when people get surprising or questionable results, they can just retake the test and confirm, and that's pretty much what's happened in any cases of doubt. And the test comes back exactly the same."

She rested her head against his shoulder. She would forget about the e-mail.

It was just a mistake.

Chapter Seven

Where are you off to?" Rachel's mother asked, having finally arrived to reclaim her cat. She was trying, with limited success, to lure Hugo back into his carrying case.

Rachel, halfway through packing her oversize duffel bag, debated whether or not to tell her mother the truth. She decided it would take more effort to be evasive. And why bother? Her mother wouldn't care. She'd always been direct with her about her paternity. Very casual about it. Maddeningly so.

"I used the research department at the show to track down my father."

"Get out! Did you find him?"

"Not him, exactly. But I found his mother. She lives in Provincetown, Massachusetts. I'm going to spend a few days there."

"Intense," said Fran, pulling a joint out of her handbag.

"Please don't smoke in here," Rachel said.

"It's medicinal. I'm way hung over. Sean took me to a

new place in Venice last night that supposedly served only organic wine, but I suspect it wasn't."

Rachel zipped up her duffel bag with an irritated flourish. She hated to admit it but she'd hoped her mother, upon learning about the trip, would have something insightful to say. But Fran seemed to exist only on the surface of life. Anything too heavy, and she tuned out. Their entire relationship had been less like a mother and daughter's and more like sisters'. It would be too much to ask of Fran to actually mother her. This odd dynamic had been the envy of all of Rachel's friends growing up. "Your mom is so cool," they would tell her again and again when Fran scoffed at the notion of a curfew and didn't bother checking Rachel's report cards. Her idea of motherly advice was sharing the details of her one-night stand with Anthony Kiedis of the Red Hot Chili Peppers.

"Rach, is this whole trip about losing your job?"

"What? No. I told you, I've been researching my paternity for a while."

"I don't want you freaking out. Just try to find a new gig."

"Are you seriously lecturing me about the job? You've never stuck with a career in your life."

"You should do as I say, not as I do. When's the last time you did yoga?"

"Okay, Fran. When I get back from the trip, I will find a new job. Don't worry."

Her mother, satisfied she had done her parental duty for the day, turned her attention back to the cat. Rachel was tempted to confide in her mother about the first leg of her trip—a quick stop in New York City to try to meet her half sister. Then she decided against mentioning it. She had her own doubts about it, and she didn't want Fran to discourage her.

She knew she should maybe let it go for now and just be satisfied with the person she'd reached out to who *did* want to see her: her grandmother. Grandmother! Amelia Cabral of Provincetown, Massachusetts. But she couldn't resist one last attempt to get through to Marin Bishop. This time she would do it face-to-face.

Fran lit her joint, and Rachel sighed.

She simply could not accept that her crazy mother was the only answer to the question *Who am I?*

"I have to get going, Fran. I'll give you a call when I'm back."

"Hugo seems to want to stay here," she said.

"No one is staying here. We're all leaving."

After a final glance around the apartment, Rachel walked out with her stuffed duffel bag heavy on her shoulder.

It was against Marin's nature to leave something unfinished. Friends had long teased her about her obsessive attention to detail, her determination to wrangle life into order. And so Monday morning, after a sleepless Sunday night, she knew she had to hear more from this Rachel Moscowitz person. Not that she thought there was any validity to what she was saying—she'd felt absurd even bringing it up to her mother. But until she was able to get new results from a second DNA test, the strange woman's e-mail was just hanging out there, a big question begging to be answered. She couldn't ignore it any more than she could leave work with a pile of paperwork on her desk.

At eight in the morning on a Monday, the office was

still relatively quiet. Quiet enough for her to make the call without the risk of interruption.

She closed her door, pulled up the e-mail on her phone, and then dialed. Her heart beat fast, and in a weak moment, she prayed for voice mail. And she got it.

"Hi—this is Rachel. My voice mail, actually. Leave a message!"

"Rachel, this is Marin Bishop. Um, as I said in my e-mail, there's clearly been some sort of error. But I did want to just ask you a few questions, if you don't mind." She left her number and hung up like her phone was on fire. It was only after she turned back to her computer that she realized that the 310 area code was in California, so it was only five in the morning where Rachel Moscowitz lived. Okay, she would have a few hours before she had to deal with a possible call back. She could relax.

A knock on her door.

"Come in," she said, hoping it was Julian, knowing it wouldn't be. She wouldn't see or speak to him all day, and if they happened to pass each other in the halls, there was a good chance they wouldn't even make eye contact.

The door opened. "Hilton would like to see you in his office." It was Carol Rand, executive assistant to Hilton Wallace. Carol had been at the firm since before Marin was born. Marin wondered what that would be like—doing the same job for thirty years, never advancing, never being in a position of power. How did Carol get up in the morning?

Marin smiled. "Before the ten o'clock meeting or—"

"Now, if you can step away."

Marin slipped out from behind her desk, smoothed her gray pencil skirt, and followed Carol to the elevator bank.

"Did you have a nice weekend?" Carol asked.

"Yes, thanks. You?"

The woman nodded. "Time with the grandchildren. Nothing beats that."

The elevator, smelling faintly of coffee, whisked them up to the twentieth floor. The partner section of the firm was silent as a tomb, everyone working behind closed frosted-glass doors. Hilton's office, which she rarely saw, was at the farthest end of the hall, a corner space with a view of the Freedom Tower. Carol opened the door for her.

"Marin's here," she announced. Marin stepped inside and had to bite her lip not to audibly gasp at the sight of Julian sitting in the chair opposite Hilton Wallace. Julian barely glanced at her, which stung, even though she knew he was doing the right thing.

"Close the door, would you, Carol? Thanks."

Marin's stomach tightened like a fist.

"Marin. Julian," he said, nodding at them. What was this about? It took all of her willpower not to glance at Julian to see if he was anxious or if this was just business as usual. "I won't insult the considerable intelligence of either one of you by pretending you don't know why you're here."

Marin's stomach dropped. With all her considerable intelligence, she suddenly *did* know why they were there. But where had they gone wrong? How had a senior partner found out about their relationship?

Julian and Marin, both trained negotiators, said nothing. Hilton, understanding this, nodded and steepled his fingers under his chin.

"I'm sure you are both aware of our firm's policy on fraternization."

Marin felt her morning coffee rise to the back of her throat. Should she speak up and deny it? She wished she could talk to her father, as if this were a game show and she was allowed one lifeline call. But this was no game, and there was no way out of what Hilton Wallace said next. "I'm asking you both to tender your resignations, effective immediately."

Chapter Eight

The sound of a ringing phone roused Marin from a deep daytime sleep that felt like she'd been drugged. Her first thought, squinting against the sunlight streaming into the living room, was that she was certain she'd turned off the damn phone—had turned it off days ago. The last call she'd taken had been from her father, who'd told her to "get back on the horse" and come home to Philadelphia, where he would have to pull strings to get her a job. And there it was—her ultimate punishment. It wasn't losing her job or even potentially losing Julian. It was her father's disappointment.

The ringing, shrill and persistent. She realized it was the house phone; it must be the doorman calling up from the lobby.

Julian. Why had it taken him so long?

They hadn't seen each other since the excruciating dismissal from Hilton Wallace's office.

At first, walking out of Cole, Harding, and Worth with the security escort by her side, her laptop repossessed by the firm, a single box of her belongings in her arms, she told herself they would rally. They would both find new jobs. The firm would not be punitive; the partners simply didn't want to risk a sexual-harassment lawsuit. They were being thorough—that was the nature of the business.

But Julian didn't see it that way. He had actually said that his life was ruined. She didn't have the nerve to ask if he meant by her, Hilton Wallace, or himself.

That first night, he told her he needed a little time alone.

"I have to process this."

"You blame me," she said.

"I don't. I don't blame you, Marin. If anything, I blame myself for being so reckless. And I just need some space to deal with that right now. Alone."

She told herself this was a natural, understandable reaction. After all, she had things to figure out herself. They spoke on the phone a few times, but the distance between them was painfully obvious. This will pass, she told herself. It has to.

And then, two days later, the Page Six blind-gossip item: "Legal Lovebirds." *Which two rising stars at a top-notch law firm had a hard fall from grace when they fell for each other? Hint: The affair derailed more than their professional reputations. The lady lawyer was formerly engaged to UBS banker Greg Harper. But all's well that ends well: Harper has happily landed in the arms of NY News1 anchor Sarah Stall.*

It was officially public; it was officially ugly. She had cheated on her fiancé, she had slept with her boss. She had lost her job. (The one bright spot? Her guilt over breaking up with Greg was at least partially alleviated, seeing as he had already moved on. The news anchor was young and pretty and, well, what did she expect?)

She cringed to think of Greg reading the Page Six piece. She hadn't told him there was someone else—had wanted to spare his feelings. And yes, she'd also been a little afraid that he would be vindictive. Greg was a Wall Street guy—he was type A. You didn't make seven figures by age thirty by sitting back and letting things happen to you.

How had they gotten busted? She lay awake at night, replaying their relationship moment by moment, a film on a constant loop, looking for the slipup. Had it been the day she'd walked into his office when Hilton was there? Marin would probably never know. And, really, what difference did it make? The damage was done. And Julian blamed her. He said he didn't, but she knew better.

She kept looking at the key he'd given her, a tangible reminder that he did care for her—this wouldn't all just disappear. She was tormented by the constant temptation to go over there and see him. At least he hadn't asked for the key back, she told herself.

Not yet.

She checked her phone obsessively, hoping for something from Julian. It was painful, not only because there was never a voice mail or text, but because every time she opened her e-mail, it was a minefield of well-meaning friends who had heard from so-and-so on Facebook blah-blah-blah.

And then, a voice-mail message she *didn't* want: Rachel Moscowitz was coming to New York. On her way to see her biological father's family. "They're Portuguese," she said. "And I guess, so are we!"

What a mistake to have called her. A moment of weakness. Oh, if only she could forget everything that had happened that last day in the office!

She reached for the phone, but it had stopped ringing. She dialed the front desk.

"You called?" she asked the doorman. It came out like a croak and she had to clear her throat. How long had it been since she'd spoken to someone?

"Yes, Ms. Bishop. Your mother is on her way up."

Marin closed her eyes. Not Julian, but her mother. Of course. How long had she thought she could put off her mother? She looked around at her comforter and pillows on the couch where she'd fallen asleep in front of the TV every night this week and where she spent most of the day.

No more hiding. She dragged herself across the living room to open the door.

"Hi, Mom."

Blythe strode in without a word, her blond hair perfectly coiffed, dressed in gray slacks and a lightweight baby-blue cashmere wrap. She dropped her car keys on the small wooden entrance table and pulled Marin into a hug.

"You've had me so worried. Are you okay?"

Marin knew Blythe could answer her own question just by looking at her daughter's unwashed hair, her ratty T-shirt, the yoga pants she'd both slept in and worn during the day for the past week. She knew her cheekbones stood out. She'd had no interest in food and had barely eaten anything; her face had been carved into sharp edges.

Marin folded herself back onto the couch. Her mother sat next to her, moving aside a crumpled ball of tissues and the TV remote.

"Marin, it's going to be fine. These things happen."

"No, they don't! Do you have any idea how bad this is? No top firm in Manhattan will hire me. I'm radioactive. I'm in Page Six, for God's sake!"

"It will blow over," she said. "Yesterday's news."

Her mother didn't understand. How could she? She'd never made such colossally bad decisions. She'd never sent her own life into a tailspin.

"I'm going to use the bathroom," Marin said. "Do you want coffee or anything? I can call for delivery."

"Goodness, Marin. You don't even make your own coffee in the morning?"

"I get it on the way to the office." With that, she dissolved into tears.

"Marin, sweetheart, please don't despair. Go shower and get dressed—you'll feel better when you do."

Marin sniffed into a tissue. "I really screwed up."

"At the risk of sounding trite, things do happen for a reason. That could be the case now. Time will tell. For the moment, you can't punish yourself like this. So get dressed, and I'm going to run to the grocery store, and we'll have a nice dinner here tonight. And we'll talk it through. Just as we always have everything else."

Marin leaned into her mother's hug. "Okay. Take my keys in case I'm in the shower when you get back."

Blythe kissed her on the forehead on her way out the door.

Sorrow overcame her, and she choked back more sobs. God, she felt like a child. Her mother was right; she had to pull it together. She had to start facing things like she always had, like her father did: head-on, with resolve. She would fix this.

Her phone rang, and she wiped tears from her eyes so she could find the phone on the couch. The incoming number made her breath catch in her throat, and her instinct was to ignore the call, to send it to voice-mail purgatory and then erase it.

Instead, in the spirit of facing things head-on, she touched the screen.

"This is Marin."

"Marin? It's Rachel. Rachel Moscowitz."

Marin stayed silent, and Rachel pressed on, her words coming in a rush. "I got your message and I'm literally in New York for just a few hours before I head to Cape Cod and I couldn't pass through here and not try to see you. If you could just give me a few minutes, just for my own sense of . . . I don't know. I don't know what I'm looking for, honestly."

Marin, already at rock bottom, wasn't afraid to fall.

"Where are you right now?"

* * *

The Times Square Starbucks was jammed with tourists and the squatting homeless. Marin looked around and recognized Rachel Moscowitz from her quick Google search on the cab ride over. Marin was surprised by how pretty she was, with a long tumble of honey-blond hair and skin burnished by the California sun. She was dressed with the casual, inexpensive boho chic Marin could never pull off without looking like she'd just rolled out of bed.

Rachel stood leaning against the wall next to the mugs, CDs, and eco-friendly bottled water for sale. An oversize duffel bag rested at her feet.

Marin took a deep breath and approached her.

"Rachel?"

The woman turned, widened her big brown eyes. "Marin!" She pulled her into a hug. "Oh my God, I'm so happy to meet you!"

Marin nodded, unable to speak. Taken aback by those

eyes, their almond shape mirrors of her own. Finally, she choked out, "We should find somewhere better to talk."

"What? Oh, sure. I didn't really know where to go. This is only my second time in New York. The last time I was here I was ten and we were visiting my mom's friends. They took us to see *Wicked*."

"Let's get a cab," Marin said.

They filled the five-minute ride with small talk about LA and New York. Really, they could have walked the short distance to the restaurant, but Marin wanted to sit. She needed a contained environment. She wanted the illusion of control.

Le Pain Quotidien at Fifty-Third and Fifth was Marin's go-to place when she wanted to get out of the office for a few minutes. It was familiar and comfortable to her and she needed this to steady herself.

Marin chose a table on the second level, making a sharp right at the top of the stairs to get a spot on the balcony. She ordered coffee, and Rachel ordered green tea and a blueberry muffin.

"So," Marin said.

"Thanks for meeting me," said Rachel, toying with a packet of sugar. "I know this is pretty crazy."

Marin nodded, looking into the eyes that were disconcertingly familiar. "I just can't take these test results at face value. It's nothing against you. But my parents have been together for over thirty years. I don't see how this could be true."

Rachel nodded, tapping her mug with her index finger. "I get it. It's simpler for me because I always knew my father was a sperm donor. Maybe your mom had fertility issues and just never told your dad. Crazier things have happened."

What?

"Or maybe Genie made a mistake with my results," Marin said quickly. Though she had to glance away from Rachel as she said it.

"Sure," Rachel said. "Look, I'm not here to, like, mess up your life. I just wanted to meet you. In case it's true. I never had a sister, or a father. I've never had anyone but my mom and she's...well, she's not very motherly. So I guess I got a little overexcited when I learned about you. And about our—I mean, my—father."

Rachel told her about her job in the research department of a television show and how her boss had cut through the red tape of the sperm bank to learn her father's name.

Marin swallowed hard. "Did you contact him?"

"I wanted to contact him. More than anything. But it's too late."

Marin felt her emotional detachment peel away like a shedding skin. Her mouth was suddenly dry. "What do you mean, too late?"

"He died. A long time ago."

Marin, in all of her jumbled and conflicted thoughts on this issue, had not considered that possibility. She nervously ripped at her packet of sugar.

"I'm...sorry to hear that."

"Yeah. That's the bad news. But good news is that his mother, my grandmother, is alive and well and living in Provincetown."

"Did you reach out to her? Your grandmother?"

"Sure. I wasn't discouraged by your rejection." She smiled to show Marin she was just teasing. Ugh, why did she have to be cool? It made it harder than Marin had anticipated to blow her off. "And she actually sounded kind of psyched to hear from me. Invited me to stay for as long as I want. She runs a bed-and-breakfast. So that's where I'm headed."

Rachel pulled up a photograph on her phone of a three-story beach house with dusky gray shingles and wraparound terraces.

"Here's a view from one of the bedrooms." A backyard leading to a stretch of sand and a wide expanse of water. Marin could smell the salt air.

"You should come with me," Rachel said. "There's plenty of room."

"What? Oh—no. I told you, this isn't even connected to me."

Marin didn't miss the slightly wounded look on Rachel's face. She wished she'd responded a little less sharply. "I have a lot going on here," Marin said. "Work—that sort of thing."

"Totally. I get it. I don't know—I thought maybe you'd want to get away."

Marin's phone buzzed. Her mother texting to ask if she wanted red or white wine with dinner. She ignored it, turned off her phone, and shoved it into her bag. "I'm sorry—what were you saying?"

"Oh, just that I thought maybe you'd want to get away."

"Why would you think that?"

"Look, I'm not a stalker or anything, but I really didn't think you'd actually meet with me, and on my way to New York I Googled you again and, um, your…situation came up."

Marin pressed her face into the palm of her hand. "The Page Six piece."

The overwhelming reality of the mess of her life felt crushing. Suddenly, it was hard to breathe.

"Are you all right?"

"No."

"I'm sorry. I didn't mean to freak you out—unloading all this on you. I guess it was selfish of me. I should hit the road."

"How are you getting to Provincetown?"

"I'm renting a car. A six-hour straight shot to Amelia's."

"Amelia?"

"My grandmother." She grinned.

Marin envisioned hours on the road, heading away from the city. Quiet. Anonymity. A cottage by the sea.

That's when Marin noticed the packet of sugar in Rachel's fingers, the way she'd made a row of tiny rips along the base, turning it into fringe. Marin looked at her own yellow wrapper, torn in the exact same pattern. She slid it across the table to Rachel, and their eyes met.

"Okay," Marin said, practically a whisper. "I'll go with you."

Chapter Nine

Blythe juggled the heavy shopping bags from Whole Foods, marveling at the outrageous cost of the produce and kicking herself for not thinking ahead and bringing her own from the garden. She was so scattered lately. But with everything going on, who could blame her?

When she walked into Marin's lobby, a doorman scurried out from behind the front desk to help her.

"Thanks—I've got it," Blythe said. "If you could please just press the elevator button for me."

Marin's building on Eighty-Seventh between Park and Madison was a starkly modern space, opulent in its minimalism. Lots of chrome and white. Blythe would never feel at home walking through the wide revolving door into the cold and impersonal lobby. When Blythe was Marin's age, she and Kip already had their two-story Colonial that Blythe fell in love with at first sight.

But there were other aspects of being the young Mrs. Kipton Bishop that she had not embraced with such enthusiasm. For instance, the family country club.

Blythe had been dating Kip for a month when he first

brought her to Philadelphia Racquet and Hunt, where the Bishop family had belonged since the club's founding in 1897. Kip was unabashed in his reverence for the place; Blythe, walking into the front hall, all dark wood filled with portraits of illustrious past members (all white men), was struck by an inexplicable but immediate sense of alienation. She should have taken to it; like ballet, it was a closed society with its own set of rigid rules and expectations. Except here, it was name and lineage and money that counted, not blood, sweat, and talent.

She hated golf. And she was young; she had no interest in passing the time playing cards upstairs in the ladies' lounge. What else was there to do at the club? She wasn't used to being idle, and how many hours could she lie sunbathing by the Olympic-size swimming pool? And so Kip spent his weekends at the club, and Blythe spent them at home—alone. His long hours at work during the week, she understood. The club, she resented. She felt trapped.

What a different life her daughter was living. She had her freedom, her independence, but where had that gotten her? In a span of one month she'd lost her fiancé and her job. And from what she was hearing, it didn't sound like the new man in her life was being very stand-up about the debacle. After all, it was partly his fault.

Blythe had fought the urge to drive straight up to New York the day Marin called her with the news about her job. Kip had been the one to ultimately talk her out of it, reminding her that Marin was an adult and that whatever was happening was a result of her own choices. But after days of no response to her calls and texts, Blythe couldn't take it any longer.

And from the moment she'd walked into the apartment, Blythe knew she'd waited too long. She could tell Marin had lost weight since she'd last seen her, just a week earlier. She looked tired and pale. And when Blythe hugged her, though Marin had never been much of a hugger, not even as a small child, she felt her daughter fold into her arms.

Blythe had to admit it felt good to be needed. She hated to see her daughter hurting, but at least she could do something about this. At least here she didn't feel completely out of control—unlike everything with the divorce.

Kip had her served with papers. He was so businesslike! Her friends told her that enough was enough—she needed to get her own attorney, no matter how generous Kip claimed he would be. Reluctantly, she'd made an appointment for the following week to meet with Patricia Graf, Esquire. "The best," she'd been told. A "shark in Chanel."

Blythe shook the thought away. She would deal with that crisis next week. For now, Marin was the only thing that mattered. She would help her get some perspective on all this and rally. She would start by cooking her a nice meal.

"Marin?" she called after she'd let herself into the apartment. She dropped two bags on the floor and closed the door behind her.

No response. Blythe checked the bedroom. Nothing.

She must have gone out, finally back to the land of the living. Blythe just hoped she'd gotten her text about the wine and hadn't run off to buy more.

Blythe smiled, satisfied. She knew coming here was the right thing to do!

She unpacked the groceries: boneless chicken breasts,

Italian bread, olive oil, eggs, butter, lemons, a bunch of kale, kosher salt, anchovy fillets, Worcestershire sauce, garlic. Everything she'd need for Marin's favorite chicken piccata and a new recipe she was trying out for a kale Caesar salad. She hoped Marin hadn't returned the food processor she'd given her last Christmas; she'd need it for the dressing.

She heard the apartment door open.

"Hi, sweetheart," Blythe called, closing yet another near-empty cabinet. "I'm just looking for your food processor."

The door slammed shut, and Blythe looked up to find Marin was not alone. She had a friend with her, a beautiful young woman with tawny, sun-burnished skin and long wheat-colored hair. The young woman carried a large duffel bag.

"Oh! I didn't know you were having company…"

Marin didn't say a word to her, instead telling the new arrival that she could just drop her bag in the living room.

The woman smiled—apologetically?—at Blythe and gave her a small wave. Marin, uncharacteristically rude, made no move to introduce them. Blythe scurried out from behind the kitchen counter. What was going on?

"I'm Blythe Bishop, Marin's mother," she said, holding out her hand. The girl smiled brightly, seeming genuinely happy to meet her.

"Rachel Moscowitz," she said.

"You two know each other from…"

"Mother, can I speak to you a minute? In my room," Marin said.

"So you're sure I should cancel the rental car?" Rachel said.

"Yes. We'll take mine."

Blythe refrained from asking the obvious: Where were they going?

Marin led her mother into her bedroom, closed the door, and scoured the room with her eyes as if she were mentally packing.

"Where are you going?" Blythe asked, because how could she not?

"Cape Cod. Provincetown."

Blythe swayed on her feet, a deep, primal alarm sweeping through her.

"Oh?" she managed.

"Yes. Rachel is going there to meet her father's family, and I'm going with her."

"Going with her? Why?"

"Well, Mother, because my life is falling apart and I need to get away and this opportunity to do so just fell in my lap and I'm taking it."

"Marin, you're upset—with good reason. But this isn't the time to run away from things. You should be with family."

"Funny you should say that. Rachel is under the impression that we are family—close family. Half sisters, in fact."

Blythe's heart began to pound. Had she really thought Marin's question from last week would go away? That she could give Marin a cursory denial and no one would ever speak of it again?

"Is there anything you want to tell me, Mother?"

She hated the way she was calling her Mother, as if it were a title like colonel or president. Not a term of endearment, not what you called the closest person in the world to you.

She swallowed hard. "Where is all of this coming from?"

"I tried talking to you about this at the house. The DNA-testing company. Rachel found me through them. We were matched up by the closeness of our genes."

"And she...never knew her father?"

"Her father was a sperm donor."

"A sperm donor?" Blythe said, confused.

"Yes. Mom, just tell me the truth—did you have a difficult time getting pregnant? Did you have to use a sperm donor?"

Blythe didn't know what to say.

"Mom, you might as well tell me. I'm going to find out. Is Dad my biological father?"

There were no words, and so Blythe said nothing. Seconds ticked by. She watched Marin's face flood with color.

"Answer me. You owe me the truth. Is he my father?"

Blythe pressed her hand to her chest as if forcing out the word. "No."

Marin sank to the floor and sat at Blythe's feet like she was a toddler again.

"But does that matter? Marin, this is all a technicality. You're more like your father than like me!"

Marin put her head in her hands. "Does Dad know?"

"No."

"What?" Marin looked up at her. "How could you lie about something like this? What were you *thinking?*"

"Please, please just let this go. I don't want this to disrupt your life."

"My life? Or *your* life?"

Blythe couldn't bear the way Marin was looking at her, like she was the enemy.

"Either of our lives. Or your father's."

Marin nodded slowly, wiping away tears and reaching

for her bed to pull herself up again. "Well, maybe you should have thought about that when you went behind his back thirty years ago."

With a sob, Marin stormed out of the room, slamming the door behind her. Blythe stood unmoving except for the tremble in her legs. As much as she wanted to hide in there forever, she knew she couldn't—the sooner she went into the living room to salvage the situation, the better.

She found Marin and Rachel in the kitchen with shot glasses and a bottle of Tito's vodka. They turned to look at her with identical brown eyes. How had she not noticed before?

"Marin, please don't drink. Let's finish talking."

"Just go, Mother. I'm leaving first thing in the morning."

"Don't run away. I'm sorry—I'm sorry that I didn't tell you sooner. But don't punish me. Don't shut me out and deal with this by turning to people you barely know." She glanced at Rachel, who bit her lower lip in a way that mirrored Marin's habitual nervous gesture. "Rachel, maybe you can go without Marin? Give us some time to—"

"No!" Marin said angrily. "Rachel is my... sister. And the woman in Provincetown might be a stranger, but she's also my grandmother. And she wants to meet us."

Blythe felt herself start to sway. "What woman?"

"I found my father's mother," Rachel said. "She runs a bed-and-breakfast. She invited me to stay for the week and I told her I was trying to convince Marin and she said the more the merrier. She sounds very cool. So nice."

"So you're not trying to find your... father?"

"I tried," Rachel said. "But he's dead."

Blythe reached for the wall, pressed her palm against

it. *Breathe,* she told herself. How could he be dead? How could she not know? But then, how would she?

"I'm sorry to hear that," she managed. "Do you know what happened to him?"

Rachel shook her head. "I'm hoping my grandmother can tell me more. Tell me a lot of things."

Blythe felt a terror like she'd never known. She would lose Marin over this—she knew it. She couldn't let it happen. The past had caught up with her, and she couldn't hide anymore. And she certainly couldn't leave her daughter to meet it alone.

"I want to go with you," Blythe said.

Marin angrily slammed down her shot glass. "Absolutely not."

At the same time, Rachel smiled and said, "Awesome."

Chapter Ten

Provincetown

Amelia watched Kelly fix the final piece of sea glass along the outermost edge of the heavy panel. It was a large piece, commissioned by a client who wanted something "authentic" and "beachy" to display as a centerpiece of her newly acquired, multimillion-dollar home on the East End.

Amelia Cabral had been creating mosaics for as long as she could remember, but it was Kelly who had turned it into a business. For Amelia, it was a family tradition that evoked fond memories of her childhood summers on the beaches of Provincetown, when her mother had taken her for long morning walks and they collected shells. Her father would give them discarded bits of wood from whatever furniture piece he was working on, and her mother would sand them and then glue them together to make picture frames. Amelia's job was to artfully arrange the shells and create unique mosaic patterns for the frames. Her mother sold them to tourists for five dollars apiece.

Like many families four or five generations deep into life in Provincetown, the Cabrals had had to adapt to the decline in the seaport, and they'd made money however and whenever they could. Her mother spoke of picking and selling blueberries when she was a child and, as a young woman, cleaning rooms at the Provincetown's one small hotel. It was the influx of artists—many of whom would go on to be the greats of their eras (Jack Kerouac, Jackson Pollock, and Norman Mailer had all, at one point, called Provincetown home)—who showed her there were other ways to earn a living. For survival, there had to be. That's when her mother, inspired by photos of the elaborate artwork in the walkways of Lisbon, began creating her own mosaics.

Years later, after Amelia had established—and destroyed—a life for herself in Boston, she would remember the other means by which her mother, widowed at a young age, learned to support herself: she began renting out the rooms of their home to the artists flocking to Provincetown. Oh, there had been nothing official about it. It wasn't a bed-and-breakfast, as they called them nowadays. Word simply spread among the creative community that if you needed a place to sleep and work you could try Renata at 157 Front Street. That had been back in the days when the sea, and not tourism, had been the backbone of the town. Now the same strip was called Commercial Street, and Renata's informal lodging house was now the Beach Rose Inn, reestablished in 1989.

Amelia had thought the old house had seen the last of its stories, the last of its transformations. But now, her granddaughters were on their way. Who would have ever imagined?

"It's a beauty," Amelia said, appraising the mosaic from the doorway of the studio. "I'm tempted to buy it out from under that woman."

"You can't afford it, darling," Kelly said. "But I'm working on something for you next. A surprise."

Amelia smiled. "Give me a hint."

Kelly shook her head, a sly smile on her face. Amelia felt a pang of guilt. She had a surprise for Kelly as well. And probably not a pleasant one.

Amelia hesitated, then pulled a chair out from the worktable. She might as well tell her now. No sense waiting until they had guests in the house.

"I sent a letter to Nadine," she said.

Kelly set down her glue and placed both hands on the table, her shoulders dipping forward.

"I had to tell her," Amelia said. "It's her brother's children. She has a right to know."

Kelly sighed. "Of course. I get it. I've never been happy about this situation, Amelia. You don't have to be apologetic on my account."

"Well, she's been so hurtful."

"She's your daughter. And like you said, she has a right to know. It has little to do with me at this point."

"I asked her to come here."

Kelly looked startled. "Did you hear back from her?"

Amelia shook her head.

"Okay, well—I just don't want you to set yourself up to be hurt. That's all I care about."

"The only thing that can hurt me right now is the continued silence."

Kelly put her arm around her. "You have two granddaughters coming. Granddaughters! Let's focus on the positive."

"I will. I mean, I am. But I also feel like this is my last chance with Nadine."

She could see Kelly wrestling with the idea of Nadine

showing up, of seeing her again after three decades. After all of the hurt and anger and terrible things said. Yes, Kelly was concerned for her. But she knew that, selfishly, Kelly didn't want to revisit the past. But Amelia, twenty years Kelly's senior, didn't have the luxury of waiting any longer.

By a miracle of fate, the past was arriving on her doorstep tomorrow. And she would welcome it with open arms.

* * *

Two hundred and ninety miles from New York City. One hundred and seventeen miles from Boston.

Provincetown might as well have been on the moon.

Four hours into the drive, Marin was steeped in regret. With her mother and Rachel chattering happily the entire time, you'd never have guessed that (a) they'd just met the night before, and (b) her mother had just been revealed to be the world's biggest liar.

But what did Rachel care? She had what she wanted: an instant new family. Oh, why had Marin agreed to go? She'd been caught up in the moment. Or maybe it would have been a decent idea, if her mother hadn't hijacked it.

"Get off here," her mother chirped from the backseat. The sign in front of them read DOWNTOWN NEWPORT.

"Okay, Blythe!" Rachel sang happily.

"Recalibrating," monotoned the GPS.

"Wait, why are we getting off here? We decided to do this in a straight shot," Marin said, sitting up in the passenger seat. She knew she should have stayed behind the wheel.

"Oh—I thought we agreed to have lunch in Newport. The beach is supposed to be really cute," Rachel said.

"I never agreed."

"Majority rules, Marin," said her mother.

It was something her father used to say to quell dissent on family road trips. In the context of this trip, the comment infuriated her. She turned around to the backseat, glaring. "Mother, you invited yourself along on this trip and, frankly, I still don't understand why. But the least you can do is stay out of things."

"You need to get over your anger."

"Get over my anger? You've been lying to me my entire life!"

"That's why I want to be with you... to help you understand—"

The GPS interrupted in its mechanical voice, "I'm not sure I understand."

"Goddamn it," said Marin.

"I'm not sure I understand," repeated the GPS. Rachel turned it off.

"We really do have to eat," Rachel said, casting a sideways glance at Marin. With the open windows, the breeze fanning her long hair out like a kite, the gold in her hair glimmering in the sun, she looked like an actress in a happy-road-trip movie directed by Nancy Meyers.

"Fine," Marin muttered.

She had to admit, the harbor was pretty, with red-shingled restaurants like the Barking Crab and stores like Egg and Dart on Bowen's Wharf, and it made Manhattan seem very far away. She exhaled, thinking that maybe, just maybe, things would be okay. But the moment of optimism, a fragile balloon, was punctured by thoughts of Julian.

Still not a word from him.

They circled around until Easton's Beach appeared on

their right. The ocean shimmered, turquoise and calm. Marin had had no idea the Atlantic could look like that. The ocean of her childhood, the Jersey Shore, was dark blue or gray, rolling with steady waves. The squawk of a seagull cemented her sense memory of those days, and she felt like crying for the loss of everything she had believed to be true about her life.

Rachel parked in a wide-open lot, the noonday sun beating down on them.

"Where are we going?" Marin asked, following her mother and Rachel, who was consulting Yelp.

"There's a snack bar on the beach," Rachel said.

"A snack bar?"

"It has four and a half stars. Famous for its lobster roll," Rachel said, holding up a photo on her phone.

"Fine," Marin said, hating how miserable she sounded but unable to switch gears. The sun, the sand, the beautiful day—none of it could cut through the cloud over her heart.

The snack bar was a long wooden counter in front of an open kitchen. It had a soda-fountain machine, a display of soft pretzels, and popcorn like at a movie theater. A hamburger was $5.25. Marin couldn't remember the last time she'd paid less than ten or eleven dollars for a burger. Fish sandwiches, clam cakes, crab cakes, hot dogs…even cotton candy. The entire place screamed *Fun! Enjoy!*

Marin and Blythe ordered the same thing: the twin lobster rolls with French fries. Rachel ordered only dessert—churros.

When their order was ready, lobster rolls placed in paper plates, sodas balanced alongside salty piles of fries, they carried it on trays to a table on the deck.

"This is the first day it really feels like summer," Blythe

said, smiling and looking around at the panoramic view of the beach.

"This food *tastes* like summer," Rachel said, biting into her lobster roll.

Marin slumped back in her seat, reached into her handbag and searched for her phone. She had made a deal with herself that she wouldn't check her e-mail until they had arrived in Provincetown. But this stop in Rhode Island counted—didn't it?

She cupped her hand around the screen, shielding it from the sun beating overhead. *Updated just now.*

Nothing.

"Oh my God, Marin!" her mother shrieked.

A bird was on her tray—a slender seagull. And then the seagull was flying away with her lobster roll.

"What the fuck…" Marin said.

In that instant, a second bird swooped in and snagged Marin's other one.

Rachel, mouth full, stifling laughter, simply pointed to something behind Marin's back. She turned. There, propped up against a Coca-Cola vending machine, was a large handwritten sign: *Please be careful with your food. We cannot be responsible for it once it has left the counter. Caution: Seagulls will take your food!*

Marin, inexplicably, felt her eyes fill with tears. "I'm not even hungry," she said.

"Oh, hon—here. Take one of mine."

"I'm fine," she snapped. "I knew we shouldn't have stopped."

"Marin wouldn't eat lobster until she was in college," Blythe said to Rachel. "When she was little, we used to go to a fancy seafood restaurant in Center City and she would stand by the lobster tank and sob."

"Aww!" said Rachel.

Marin rolled her eyes.

By the time her mother and Rachel were finished eating, Marin realized she was, in fact, hungry. But for some reason, she couldn't admit it.

They piled back into the car.

Chapter Eleven

To Blythe, the enormous white wind turbines in the distance were like churning arms, beckoning her. For the past hour, the surrounding scenery of sailboat-dotted waters, narrow bridges, and tree-lined highways had made her feel she was enveloped in a fantasy world. With the sunroof open, the classic-rock station playing songs she remembered from her teen years in the early 1980s (Rachel and Marin refused to believe Bono had once been godlike to girls everywhere), she felt the type of nearly pure joy she'd thought was behind her forever. And the only thing preventing it from being absolute happiness was the palpable misery of her daughter.

Yes, of course it was all a shock. Was Blythe in the wrong? Completely. But she had to believe that Marin would forgive her eventually. To believe otherwise was unthinkable. Marin said she didn't understand why Blythe had invited herself along. One of the reasons was that she didn't want her simmering in her confusion and anger while on a trip with a bunch of strangers.

The other reason she had insisted on joining the girls on their trip? Frankly, she was curious. This woman, Amelia, was her daughter's grandmother. It seemed almost impossible that some stranger had such a close connection to her daughter. Of course, logically, she always knew it was so. But it felt no more real than other facts about the universe that she didn't think about on a day-to-day basis. Now that this person, this grandmother, had been unearthed—well, Blythe had to meet her. What facets of Marin might be evident in this other woman's face, in her personality?

And yes, it would also bring her back to the man who was Marin's biological father. But she would not think of that now.

She stared at the back of Marin's head, her glossy dark hair pulled into a careless knot at the nape of her graceful neck. She was checking her phone. Again.

"Have you heard from Julian?" Blythe asked, knowing she shouldn't. But this silence from Marin was new and unbearable to her. Shutting her out of the breakup with Greg, the disaster at her office. And now whatever was going on with this new man.

"Leave it alone, Mother," she said.

"What's his deal?" asked Rachel. Blythe nodded. *Yes, you go, Rachel! Ask away. Marin won't ignore you. She's too polite.*

Marin sighed, shifting in her seat.

"We met at work. The firm had a strict no-dating policy—I was his subordinate—and someone found out and we were both asked to resign."

"Yeah, I mean—I gathered some of that from the article online. Totally sucks. Does he mind that you're skipping town in the middle of it?"

Marin shook her head. "He doesn't want to talk to me right now."

"He doesn't?" Rachel and Blythe said in unison.

Marin shot Blythe a look. "No. He needs time to...process it."

"That's a bit selfish, if you ask me," said Blythe.

"No one did."

"Do you think he blames you?" asked Rachel.

"I don't know," Marin admitted.

"That's ridiculous!" Blythe said. Her vehemence startled even herself. But really, to hear Marin speak like that—it was so defeatist. So unlike her. "Your father said the firm overreacted."

"Oh, my *father* said?" Marin replied sharply. "Tell me more about what my *father* thinks."

The comment hung in the air, and a silence followed for what seemed like an endless stretch of driving.

At nearly three o'clock, seven hours after they'd left New York City, Rachel turned the car onto Commercial Street in Provincetown.

She smiled. Could this quaint, narrow street brimming with colorful storefronts, buildings no more than three stories high, be as much a part of her as the brassy beauty of Los Angeles? Yes. Yes, it was. She felt it.

People were walking everywhere, spilling off the sidewalks, flanking her slowly moving car in couples and groups, a few bikes rolling by, announcing their presence with tinkling bells. Up ahead, a pedicab. Inching along, she drove half a block. To her left, Cabot's Candy. Her right, a small art gallery. Inch by inch. They passed the large, red-brick post office. The white clapboard library. A café called Heaven.

"Oh, it's so lovely!" Blythe said.

It was—it really was.

She felt bad that Marin wasn't enjoying the trip. Yes, her mother had lied to her, and it had to be upsetting. But Blythe seemed like a pretty amazing mom. Rachel couldn't imagine having grown up with a mother like that. With Fran, everything was "me, me, me." With Blythe, it was all about Marin. Just the way she looked at her, so adoringly. She cared about what was going on with Marin and her boyfriend. She came along for their trip! Fran was probably off in Ojai or Joshua Tree again, and who knew when Rachel would hear from her.

She glanced beside her at Marin, who was staring out the window.

"What do you think?" Rachel said. "Cool, right?"

"I can't believe that car in front of us is just stopped in the middle of the road like that."

Yes, the car in front of her, a red Jeep, was practically parked while the driver chitchatted with a guy on a bike and his friend, who was leaning into the car's window. This would be unthinkable in LA, the cause of much honking and yelling. But something told Rachel this was just business as usual in Provincetown.

When the Jeep resumed moving, Rachel made it another block. There, on the left, loomed the three-story gray-shingled Georgian house with a wraparound veranda, red-brick steps, and terraces framed in white fencing. A hanging distressed-wood sign read BEACH ROSE INN.

Rachel's heart began to beat fast.

Amelia had instructed her via e-mail to just find street parking. But being so close to meeting her grandmother, enveloped in the charm of the strange and wondrous town, such practicalities were too much for her. She could barely think straight, let alone deal with parallel parking.

"I'll do it," Marin said, unbuckling her seat belt after Rachel fumbled the first two spots she tried to squeeze into. She pulled the car across the street from the inn, directly in front of a place called Joe Coffee.

"I actually could use a cup," Marin said.

Was she kidding? How could they delay for even a minute? Their grandmother was right there, waiting for them.

Rachel noticed a chocolate Lab resting on the front porch. She was about to say, *No, let's just go inside*. But Marin was so unhappy. If a little caffeine would cheer her up...

They made their way up the path to the café, passing round tables topped with turquoise umbrellas. The table closest to the door was occupied by a group of half a dozen men, all with trim salt-and-pepper beards, trendy eyewear, and colorful T-shirts. Their raucous laughter gave Rachel the urge to pull up a chair and join the conversation.

"Do you want anything?" Marin asked her, taking her place in line.

"I've got it, sweetheart. Tell me what you want," said Blythe.

"No, I've got it, Mom."

"Nothing for me, thanks," Rachel said, biting her lip to keep from saying, *Just hurry up!*

Luckily, the barista worked quickly. She had blond dreadlocks and eye shadow fit for a midnight rave. Her pink T-shirt read VAGINA IS FOR LOVERS.

Marin and Blythe, coffees in hand, followed her back outside. Rachel had to force herself not to walk double-time. *Hurry, hurry.*

"Let's sit at a table for a minute," Marin said.

Okay, now she was pushing it.

"Marin! We just drove seven hours. Not to mention the twenty-two years it's taken me to get here. I can't wait another minute!"

Marin looked stricken, and that's when Rachel realized she was stalling.

"Fine. You go on ahead," Marin said.

"Oh no—we're doing this together."

"You know what?" Blythe said. "Why don't *you* two go on ahead, and I'll wait here. You should meet your grandmother on your own. I'm going to get a newspaper and have my coffee. I'll join you in a bit."

Marin looked torn. She clearly didn't want to sit and wait with her mother, but she wasn't ready for Amelia's house either. And so Rachel did what any sister would do.

She took her by the hand.

Chapter Twelve

Panic. That was the only word to describe Marin's feeling as she followed Rachel up the red-brick steps. Overhead, red geraniums dangled from a wicker basket.

Marin hung back as Rachel approached the front door, and a large chocolate Lab bounded up to her and licked the hand she put out in protest.

"The door's open," Rachel said, reaching for the doorknob.

"Wait! Shouldn't you knock or something?"

"It's a B and B—I think we can just walk in."

Before this could be quietly settled between them, the dog rushed headlong through the open door, announcing them with a bark.

Inside, the only hint that the place was an inn and not just a picture-perfect private beach cottage was the white wooden wraparound desk to the right of the front door. The space was light and airy, all white and gray and sea green. White walls and woodwork, a white wicker table between two pale gray couches facing each other. Small, weathered-looking wood-topped tables covered in knickknacks—antique copper candlesticks, glass bowls filled with gray and moss-green stones. To her left, a framed antique map of Provincetown above a wooden shelf lined with mismatched green and blue glass bottles.

One entire wall was covered with mosaics, some tiled in vivid blues and greens, others monochromatic and made from pale stones and shells. The piece that really caught her eye was an enormous stained-glass starfish.

"Molly, enough barking! What's all the fuss about?" A redheaded woman emerged from a doorway in the far corner of the room. She wore a V-necked white T-shirt and army-green cargo pants, her hair pulled into two messy low pigtails. She had high cheekbones and creamy skin brushed with freckles. The crow's-feet around her green eyes and grooves around her delicate mouth were the only indicators of her age. "Oh—hello, girls. You must be the granddaughters!"

"Uh, yeah," said Rachel. Marin simply nodded.

"I'm Kelly." The woman held up one finger—*Just a sec*—and pulled a walkie-talkie-type device from her back pocket. "The girls are here," she said, before turning back to them with a smile. "Amelia will be right down. Excuse this rambunctious beast. She's our friends' dog from down the street and for some reason she makes herself just a little too at home here. I'm going for a grocery run. See you at dinner—oh, any food allergies?"

Marin and Rachel both shook their heads.

"I'm, um, a vegetarian," Rachel said.

"I used to be, until Amelia turned me to the dark side," she said with a wink, and then she disappeared back from whence she'd come.

Marin turned to Rachel.

"Who is that?"

"Kelly."

"Yeah, I get that. Does she run this place or something?"

Rachel shrugged. "Amelia said the inn was closed for the season. That's why she has room for all of us. So I'm not sure if that woman works here or what."

And then: footsteps on the staircase. An older woman in a blue batik-print dress made her way down, greeting them with a little wave. She was medium height and slender and had chin-length white hair, a broad nose, and a warm smile.

"Rachel," she said, immediately hugging her. "You're much more lovely than even your photos!" She turned her dark eyes on Marin, and they suddenly welled with tears.

"You look just like my Nicolau," she said, grasping her firmly by the hands. "I wasn't prepared for that."

Marin glanced helplessly at Rachel, who shrugged.

The woman gazed around the room. "Are we missing someone?"

"Oh—yes. My mother. She's at the coffee place. Getting coffee," Marin said awkwardly.

"We have coffee here," Amelia said, as if that were absurdly obvious.

"She'll be here soon," Marin said.

Amelia seemed to contemplate this. "Why wait? Let me show you to your rooms so you can get comfortable. Mom can catch up."

Blythe had a direct view of the Beach Rose Inn from her table outside of Joe Coffee. She wondered how long she should wait before going inside.

It was extraordinary, how things happened in life. That

she should be sitting there, on the verge of divorce, despite the decision she'd made all those years ago in order to save her marriage.

And this glorious day: a cloudless sky, the sun bright but not too hot. The type of weather that made it seem like it would never rain again. A mirror image of that early-summer afternoon when she'd first met Nick Cabral.

She knew when they said good-bye that she wouldn't see him again. But she never imagined she would someday meet his mother—the mother who had done something so egregious, Nick never wanted to talk about her and said he didn't care if he ever saw her again.

"This is my new start," he'd said of Philadelphia, where he was earning a degree in studio arts. Where he was spending lazy summer afternoons making love to Blythe, a married woman.

By that point, she had felt like her life was already a tired story. There would be no new starts for her. She, the wife of an ambitious corporate lawyer, living in a big house in the suburbs. Her marriage was lonely. She couldn't remember the last time Kip had touched her.

Her infatuation with the dreamy, dark-eyed art student was a distraction, a temporary indulgence. It was wrong, but she couldn't stop herself.

What did your mother do that was so bad? I mean, she's still your mother.

She's dead to me, he replied.

Blythe could envision his face exactly as he'd said those words. So much hurt in his eyes, the set of his strong jaw. She'd leaned forward and kissed him.

She grabbed her coffee and stood up. It was time to meet the woman who was dead to Nick—Nick, who was truly dead to them both now. *Nick.*

It hurt so much, more than she would have imagined. But how could she have imagined any of this? And then she remembered one of the last things Nick had said to her, something about the universe having its own plans.

He had been right.

Chapter Thirteen

They were mid-tour of the second floor, standing in the doorway of the bedroom Marin would call her own for the next six nights. Sunlight streamed in through the windows and glass-paned door that opened onto a terrace. The queen-size bed had a white bookcase headboard, sea-green sheets covered with a white down comforter topped with a colorful crocheted afghan throw that had to be handmade. The wooden side table had delicate white china knobs painted with cornflowers. A piece of driftwood rested against one wall.

Marin spotted the place where she could curl up and lick her wounds all week: a plank bench covered in mismatched cushions in front of a window, the ledge decorated with eclectic treasures, including old-fashioned wooden clothespins bleached from the sun, a smattering of round, smooth stones, and a mason jar filled with blue sea glass.

Downstairs, Molly barked loudly.

"Your mother must be here," Amelia said. "Just leave your bag, hon, and you can unpack later."

"Actually, I'm going to unpack now. If you don't mind."

"You're not coming downstairs?" Amelia looked surprised. She probably thought it was strange, maybe even rude, for Marin not to greet her mother.

Amelia seemed about to say something, but then thought better of it. "Okay, dear. Whenever you're ready. I'll get your mother settled." Marin thanked her, feeling impolite, feeling terrible, but wanting so desperately to be alone.

Marin turned to look at herself in the seashell-mosaic-framed mirror hanging above the white dresser. For the first time in her life, the puzzle about her looks was complete. The features she had that she had never been able to match to either her mother or her father (her brown eyes, the slope of her nose, her attached earlobes), she identified on Amelia.

Marin flopped on the bed, on her back, staring up at the ceiling. A fan whirred gently. She watched it churn and thought about her dad. What was she supposed to do about all of this? Living with the secret was unthinkable, but telling him the truth would only hurt him. It was, as he would say, lose-lose. Another thing he would say: When you don't know what to do, don't do anything.

Watching the fan made her feel dizzy. Her stomach churned. She was overcome with homesickness, not for a place, but for the life she'd had just two weeks ago. Now she was completely unmoored, dislocated—literally and in every figurative way. Even Julian seemed like a dream. He felt so unreal, it scared her.

She scrolled through her phone until she found a selfie she'd snapped of the two of them in his bed one lazy Sunday morning. Julian had a rare unguarded look, his shiny dark hair mussed, a smile on his face.

She moaned, her arm bracing her midsection, the pain

almost physical. Beyond her window, the ocean stretched. An offering of peace, of happiness.

Marin dialed his number, prepared for his voice mail yet again. But for the first time since the day after they left the firm, he answered.

"Hey," she said nervously. She was completely unprepared for an actual conversation. She was barely prepared to leave a voice mail. "How are you?"

"Doing okay. How about you?" The question was perfunctory, she could tell. She'd breached his request for space. But how much space and time did he need? She was three states away.

"I'm okay. I wanted to let you know that I left the city for a few days. I'm spending some time in Provincetown. A cute little place called the Beach Rose Inn, but it's closed for the season. It's a long story..." Her babbling was met by Julian's reproachful silence.

She wished she'd told him about Rachel before now. It was an impossible conversation to have in their current fragile, disjoined state. It would seem emotionally manipulative.

"I'm in Chicago," he said matter-of-factly. Chicago? In all the time she'd known him, she'd never heard him mention it.

"Visiting?"

"Job interview," he said.

Her stomach dropped.

"Wow. That's...exciting," she managed. If he moved to Chicago, that was the end of whatever hope she had for continuing the relationship. Long hours and long distance were an impossible combination.

"I'll see if it works out," he said. She could imagine the determined set of his jaw.

More silence. She wished she hadn't called. This conversation was worse than the silence.

"Okay. Well, keep me posted. I'll be back in the city on Saturday."

"Marin," he said. There was an unsettling sympathetic tone to the way he said her name. "I just need to focus on work right now."

Oh.

"By 'right now,' you mean..."

"Take care of yourself, Marin."

Dinner was called for six o'clock. Rachel was the first one out back, seated at the long table with a view of Cape Cod Bay. It was all so charming—the house, the yard. The way a foghorn sounded in the distance. The seagulls assembled on the wooden dividers, and thick twine roped off the yard from the shrub-filled sand stretching to the water.

The tabletop was four wide planks of faded wood, scarred from use. Eagerly waiting for everyone, Rachel dug her fingernail into one of the deep grooves.

"Hey, Rachel," Kelly said, sliding onto the bench beside her. "You are getting the star treatment. Amelia actually made a vegetarian dish tonight. Never thought I'd see the day." She winked at her.

"I heard that," Amelia said, setting down a bowl of white bean salad and a breadbasket.

Blythe trailed behind her. She had changed into a pair of linen pants and a sweater. Marin's mother was so great. She even looked like the perfect mom: still beautiful without seeming to try too hard; elegant. Unlike Fran, with her obsessively ropy yoga body wrapped in clothes that Rachel would deem too young even for herself, her perpetual tan, her tattoos. She shook the thought away.

"Oh, Amelia, this is just lovely," Blythe said.

"Yeah, this table is really cool."

"Our friend Paul made it for us. Years ago, we had several small tables out here. But then we thought it would be nice to have more of a communal dining experience for our guests—so people could get to know one another instead of just sitting in separate groups. And it was one of the best decisions we made here because over the years, many guests became friends, have gone to one another's weddings and such." She and Kelly shared a smile. "It worked out quite beautifully."

"So you cook dinner for your guests?"

"No, just breakfast."

"As I said, star treatment," Kelly said, grinning.

"Well, hon, they're family, not guests." Amelia looked around the table. "Is your daughter not joining us?" she asked Blythe.

Blythe looked uneasily at Rachel.

"Let me go check. I'll let her know we're out here," Rachel said.

"You can get to the second floor from the kitchen. There's a back staircase," Amelia told her.

Rachel walked quickly into the house, hoping Marin had simply lost track of time and was not pulling a full-on boycott.

The kitchen was so charming it made her want to cook. It felt both modern and retro, with pale wood floors, bone-colored cabinets, marble countertops, whisks and ladles hanging from copper piping running along one wall. Chunky wooden shelves supported by iron brackets were filled with an eclectic collection of plates and bowls. On the counter, a toaster oven, a wooden bowl holding a mortar and pestle. A pale blue tin that read BREAD on the front. A sugar bowl that looked like handmade pottery. A yellow teapot, a china creamer. On the windowsill, pieces of green sea glass. Rachel reached out to touch one, resisted the urge to slip it into the pocket of her jean shorts, and headed upstairs.

On the second floor, she hesitated a few seconds outside of Marin's room, then knocked.

"Who is it?" Marin called out.

"It's me—Rachel. We're all out back for dinner. Everyone's waiting for you."

"I don't want dinner."

Rachel felt her first flash of annoyance toward her sister. Marin wasn't the only one dealing with heavy shit. Rachel felt out of sorts too. She didn't know what she'd expected—that she'd meet Amelia and all the pieces would magically fall into place? That she would have an innate sense of homecoming, that the shadow of loneliness that she'd carried her whole life would disappear? Well, it didn't feel that way.

Yes, Amelia and Kelly were cool. And she was excited to be spending time with them. But she realized now she had been kidding herself that it didn't matter that her father was gone, that meeting her grandmother would be enough. She felt an urgency to connect to him somehow. She just didn't know what she could ask or what she could find in that house that would satisfy her.

"Come on, Marin," she said. "The food looks great and...I mean, you don't want to be rude, do you?"

"Go away, Rachel."

The tone of her voice did not leave much room for negotiation. Reluctantly, Rachel retreated down the stairs.

Chapter Fourteen

Blythe knew as soon as she saw Rachel's face that Marin would not be joining them. She tried not to feel despair. They were, after all, in Provincetown for a week, and she couldn't expect things to be perfect the very first night.

"I feel bad about your daughter," Amelia said to Blythe. "This was all an unwelcome surprise to her?"

"It's complicated," said Blythe. "She'll come around." *God, please let her come around!*

The food was delicious—grilled shrimp with garlic and cilantro, rice, stewed green beans. And the small talk over the meal was pleasant enough. It seemed no one wanted to get too serious, to burst the idyllic getting-to-know-you bubble. But when Amelia and Kelly retreated into the kitchen to get the dessert and coffee, Blythe couldn't help but ask Rachel: "How does your mother feel about all of this? You contacting Amelia, coming out here?"

"Oh, my mother? She doesn't care."

"Doesn't *care?*"

Rachel shrugged. "She's always been very casual about the sperm-donor thing. She wanted to have a kid on her own and there was never any secret. I don't mean to get too personal, but were you ever going to tell Marin the truth? I mean, didn't you worry she'd find out someday?"

Blythe gulped her wine and looked away, toward the water. "As I said earlier—it's complicated."

"Are you upset with me for getting in touch with her?"

Blythe traced the rim of her glass with her fingertip. Was she upset with Rachel for opening this can of worms?

"No. No, of course not."

"And her father? I mean, you know—the father who raised her?"

"Do you mind if we don't talk about this?" Blythe glanced back at the house, regretting starting the conversation.

"I'm sorry! I just...you know, I'm so full of nervous energy."

"Have you always lived in Los Angeles?"

Rachel took a swig of her beer. "We moved from Philly to LA when I was two."

"You're from Philadelphia?"

"Yeah. My mother grew up on the Main Line. She didn't like it and beat it out of there as soon as she was eighteen."

Rachel's mother "beat it out of there" at the same age Blythe had been when she'd arrived, never expecting to spend her entire life in Philadelphia.

"So tell me about yourself, Rachel. Aside from all this family drama. Do you have a boyfriend back in LA?"

Rachel shook her head. "No. I don't have a boyfriend. I've never, you know, been in love or anything."

Blythe nodded. "None of you girls seem to be in a rush these days."

She supposed, in that sense, they were a lot smarter than she had been.

* * *

It had started in the summer of 1988. The Tracy Chapman song "Fast Car" was on constant radio rotation. Blythe went to see the movie *Cocktail* three times. It was terrible, and still she could not stop watching it.

That was the first time Blythe realized there was something about the summer that simply made her feel unmoored. The warm air, the flowers in bloom, the backyard pools unmasked from their winter tarps, the long days and the glow of fireflies at night. All of it heightened her loneliness, made it that much more unbearable.

Last summer, the first of her marriage, had been no different; the humid air, thick with pollen, evoked a painful yearning. It was the strangest thing. By August, she was in such a state of longing she could barely sleep. Night after night, she reached for Kip, hoping to sate herself with his body. He often turned away. He had to be up early; he was stressed. He was uninterested.

When September rolled around, she was thankful for the first fallen leaves, the silence of the cicadas. The season of early darkness and bare trees would hopefully silence that thing inside of her. And it had. By Christmastime, she was thinking, *I can do this*.

But summer returned, and with it, the restlessness.

She sat on the steps of the Philadelphia Museum of Art, watching the cars round the traffic circle heading toward Kelly Drive. The roadway was named after rower John B. Kelly Jr., who happened to be the older brother of Grace Kelly—Philadelphia trivia courtesy of Kip's mother.

But she didn't want to think about the Bishops. She'd had an argument with Kip that morning, and just for a few hours she wanted to try to forget about him. It was a perfect Saturday afternoon, hot but not humid, a breeze off the river. She'd begged him to spend a few hours with her. They didn't have to do anything crazy (though she would have loved to drive to the shore and walk on the beach and get cheesesteaks, sandy feet stuffed into their untied sneakers)—even just a walk around Suburban Square would have been nice. But he was working, as he was every weekend lately, and when she expressed frustration, he told her to "grow up."

She climbed the seventy or so steps to the museum entrance, pausing to look behind her at the handsome vista of her adopted city. It was a great town, she couldn't complain. But four years after moving there, what did she have to show for it? Her dancing career had fizzled out. She was a lonely housewife.

Maybe, she'd thought, the answer was a baby.

"A baby?" Kip had said, as if she'd suggested a trip to the moon. "You have zero body fat."

Was that an issue? The thought upset her. She gained ten pounds. The doctor told her she was fine. Still, no baby. She made the mistake of expressing her frustration to Kip.

"The time isn't right—for either of us. I have to really buckle down, Blythe. We'll start a family when I'm more established."

But she was afraid he'd never be "established" enough to slow down, to be a husband, let alone a father.

The doctor had told her to check with him in six

months if she didn't conceive. But at the half-year mark, she didn't have the nerve to make the follow-up appointment. Of course she hadn't conceived; her husband never touched her anymore.

Again, she complained to Kip. "Maybe we should see a marriage counselor?"

"Blythe, you have to relax. I have enough on my plate right now. Stop trying to control everything."

Control everything? She had control over nothing. Her life was shapeless and empty. When she had first learned ballet hands, her instructor had told her to hold her middle finger and thumb as if a fluffy cotton ball were suspended between them. That was where she existed right now—in that tiny, amorphous space.

The Philadelphia Museum of Art was hosting a new exhibition of the Cubist masters: Picasso, Braque, Léger, Gris. Blythe was interested in the Cubist movement mostly because it coincided with the height of the Ballets Russes; Picasso had even collaborated with Sergei Diaghilev.

Her first stop inside the museum was the gift shop, where she lingered among the Impressionist posters, miniature Liberty Bells, and big expensive coffee-table books. She spotted a writing journal with Degas's *Dancers in Blue* as the cover art, picked it up, and flipped through the blank pages. She imagined holding it in her bed at night, filling it with her frustrations and her dreams and her longing.

She bought it.

The entrance hall was surprisingly crowded. It was such a beautiful day outside, she'd expected the museum to be virtually empty. In her mind, everyone was enjoying the first blush of summer the proper way—outdoors—

except for her. But no, the line for tickets stretched the entire length of the museum's first floor. Inexplicably, Blythe felt like crying. The universe was conspiring against her.

After an hour, a uniformed museum docent walked the length of the line, asking people to come back in half an hour, one hour, two, depending on where they were in the queue. They needed to open up space in the lobby. The crowd was a fire hazard.

As everyone herded toward the door, a man behind quipped, "I can't believe this many people are interested enough in Cubism to stand in line for an hour."

She turned to him, her frustration needing an outlet. "You stood on line for it, so I don't know why you can't believe it."

He wore jeans and a black Cocteau Twins T-shirt. His eyes were nearly black.

"I have to be here—it's a school assignment. Believe me, I can think of a lot better ways to spend a summer Saturday."

She wanted to say, *Oh yeah, like what?* But her second glance at him shut that right down. He was too good-looking. It would sound flirtatious, an invitation. She noticed he was carrying a sketch pad. She couldn't resist asking.

"Where are you in school?"

"University of the Arts," he said, adding, "School is the only reason to be in a town like Philly."

Something about his overt negativity, his impatience, the way his dark eyes claimed her face and her body in that merciless way only artists possessed, gave her the feeling of emerging from underwater.

She wanted to tell him she'd come to the city for artistic ambition too. She wished, in that moment, that it was *still* the reason she was in the city.

Outside, the sun was hidden behind fresh clouds.

"So what are you going to do for an hour before we are allowed back in?" he said. His black eyes were an invitation. Her heart leaped.

Looking down, the dozens and dozens of steps between her and the street seemed an impossible hurdle. She was rooted in place. There was nowhere to go because she didn't want to exist beyond that very moment. She didn't want to lose the feeling of the world suddenly expanding. "I have no idea," she said.

"I do. I'm going to make love to you," he said.

"Excuse me?" Was he for real? Who *talked* like that?

"I need inspiration." He glanced behind them. "And I'm not going to find what I'm looking for in there."

"I don't even know your name," she said, stalling.

"My name is Nick."

Chapter Fifteen

Amelia was a creature of routine: Every summer morning she served breakfast to her guests from seven to nine. Then she biked to Herring Cove Beach to take a long walk and scour the sand for shells and sea glass and other small treasures.

Now it was after nine and the table was still empty except for a brazen seagull that perched on the end of the bench. Amelia set out the hand-painted cake tray with her signature egg tarts, then returned to the kitchen to make fresh coffee. Looking out at the table through the window, she wondered if the entire breakfast would go to waste.

Were they all late sleepers? Just when she was about to give up and head to the beach, she spotted the glossy dark ponytail of one of the girls.

It was Marin. The quiet one. The one who looked so much like Nick.

She must have gone out the front entrance and walked the long way around to the yard.

Amelia would talk to her. It was strange to have

these young women in her home, knowing they were her granddaughters. She knew it, she could see it, but she could not yet feel it. What she felt the most was the sting of no response from her daughter to the letter. Kelly had been right; she shouldn't have opened herself up to hope. But she would open herself up to these girls. Her expectations were not unrealistic. Truthfully, she had none. They could not change the past, but they were an undeniable link to it.

Nick, a sperm donor. Of all things! She'd have given him the money for school. It had been tight then, with the inn just getting off the ground, but she could have figured it out. Otto would have helped. In the first few years after their divorce, he'd written her off, but certainly not the kids. But then, it was a good thing Nick hadn't come to them for money. If he had, then he would be really and truly gone now. Instead, she had this beautiful young woman sitting in her backyard.

Marin sat on the edge of the bench near the farthest end of the table, staring out at the water. Sunglasses covered half her face and she was dressed in white jean shorts and a black tank top.

Amelia took a deep breath and pushed through the swinging screen door to the rear of the house, carrying the chipped yellow porcelain coffeepot her own mother had used. Marin didn't turn away from the water until Amelia set the coffee on the table, next to the orange juice, *broa* (Portuguese corn bread), and a bowl of fresh berries.

"Good morning, dear." She poured coffee into one of the cups, a lovely pale blue patterned china she'd found at an estate sale with Kelly a few summers back. "Do you take milk in your coffee?"

Marin looked at her almost blankly. "What? No, thanks. Black is fine."

The pain in the young woman's eyes was unmistakable. Amelia understood—it all must be quite a shock. Rachel had explained that she'd always known about the sperm donor but told her in the last phone conversation before her arrival that Marin hadn't had any idea.

"I know this has to be a big adjustment," Amelia said.

Marin turned back to the water. When it became clear that she was not going to respond, Amelia felt uncharacteristically compelled to fill the silence.

"If it's any consolation, I simply could not be more thrilled to meet you girls. And your mother seems lovely. Maybe later this afternoon I can show you around?"

The back screen door slapped shut with its familiar thwap. Amelia turned to find Rachel bounding toward them.

"Good morning!" Rachel said.

"Did you sleep well, dear?" said Amelia.

"Totally! Like, better than I have in so long. Wow, this all looks so amazing. Thanks." She reached for the coffee.

"I was just telling Marin that I'd love to show you around later today."

"Yes! I want to see everything. I feel like a week is barely going to be enough time."

Amelia laughed. "It's a small peninsula, but in some ways you're right. I've been here most of my life, and I'm still discovering things."

"I love that! How many generations of your family have lived here?"

"Your great-great-grandmother settled here when it was just a remote fishing village. No one could have imagined it would become—"

"Excuse me," Marin said, standing abruptly. She headed for the house, taking her coffee with her.

Amelia and Rachel shared a glance of mutual concern, and the unexpected, easy intimacy was startling.

While she felt bad that Marin was unhappy, she couldn't help but feel a swell of happiness that she was connecting with at least one of her granddaughters.

"She's a stress case," Rachel said, reaching for a piece of corn bread. "This looks awesome."

"I feel bad that she's having a hard time with this. That it's a source of pain and not joy."

"She'll get over it."

"What makes you so sure?"

"She pushed me away at first too. And now she's here. So I'm not worried about it."

Amelia smiled. What a bright and optimistic soul.

"You know what I really want to do? Like, ASAP, if it's not too much trouble? I want to see photos of my father."

Amelia felt her smile falter. When was the last time she'd been able to look at a photo of Nick? Aside from the anniversary of his death every year, she kept the memories of what had been lost tucked away—literally and figuratively. The photo albums from her life in Boston, the years of raising Nick and Nadine, were boxed up in the attic, along with their baby books and the baby clothes she'd saved in case she was ever blessed with a grandchild.

She bit her lip. Here was the grandchild, all grown up.

"Oh, dear. Of course I have photos. I just need some time to get them down from storage."

"I'm so excited. I've been dreaming about this forever."

She put her hand on Amelia's and squeezed.

* * *

Coming here was a mistake, Marin said to herself, pulling open the drawers and throwing clothes back into her suitcase. Really, what had she been thinking? Her father always advised clients not to make big decisions when they were dealing with death or divorce, and what had her past weeks been if not a sort of death and a sort of divorce? She was in mourning—mourning the loss of her job, her relationship, and, yes, her father.

She wanted so much to talk to her dad and tell him what was going on. But her mother was right in saying that it would only hurt him.

She turned her focus to the logistics. If she drove back to New York now, she would be leaving her mother and Rachel stranded. But they could rent a car. Or take the ferry to Boston and fly back. They would figure it out. All she knew was that she needed to get out of there as quickly as possible.

Suitcase packed, she rolled it into the hallway, hoping for a clean getaway.

No such luck. Down the hall, Kelly's red hair waved like a flag as she hoisted a huge rectangular mosaic and inched her way toward the stairs. Her T-shirt read NO ONE LIKES A SHADY BEACH.

Marin backed into her room.

"Marin?"

Too late.

"Um, yeah?"

Kelly slowly set down the obviously heavy object, balancing it against her knees. Her green-eyed gaze settled on Marin's suitcase.

"If you have a sec, can you help me get this out to the truck? I overestimated my stamina here. Or maybe I underestimated the weight of this beast."

Cornered.

"Um, sure." What else could she say?

She looked at the piece, a giant mermaid of tiles and shells and all sorts of things that should have created a hot mess but instead came together in a glorious riot of color and texture.

"Where's it going?" Marin asked.

"A client commissioned it so I'm driving it to her house on the other end of town." She eyed the suitcase again. "I can drop you off somewhere if you need a lift."

"Oh, I...no, that's fine. Thanks." She kicked her suitcase back into her room.

Marin grabbed one end of the mosaic while Kelly handled the other, and they hobbled down the stairs in awkward, synchronized steps.

"Whew. Thanks. You're a lifesaver."

They continued their step-and-stop movements out to the front of the house, where they lifted it into the back of Kelly's Dodge pickup.

"So you work here full-time even though the inn isn't open this summer?" Marin said.

Kelly smiled. "I don't work here, darlin'. Amelia's my wife."

Oh! Marin felt herself blush for her naïveté. Should she somehow have guessed that? Some New Yorker she was; how could she have made such an unsophisticated assumption?

"I'm sorry. I feel like an idiot."

Kelly laughed. "Don't. It's the age difference, right? It throws everyone." She opened the driver's side, climbed in, and then stepped out and peered back over the truck at Marin. "Why don't you come for a ride?"

"What? Now?"

"I could use the company. Amelia would usually come with me, but frankly she's so excited to have you all here, I doubt I can tear her away from the kitchen."

Marin thought of the packed suitcase in her room. If she left now, she could be back in the city by late afternoon. And yet, she found herself saying, "Sure."

Chapter Sixteen

Toward the east, the town became markedly more residential. The houses had a stately beauty. They were homey and grand at the same time.

"This would be a great walk if we weren't lugging the mosaic," Kelly said.

"How far is the drive?"

"Not long. A few minutes."

"Oh. I thought you said these people were all the way on the other end of town."

"They are. The whole town is only three miles long."

Marin couldn't imagine living on a small peninsula. As far as she could tell, the place was two blocks wide. "How many people live here?"

"Year-round? Maybe three thousand. But in the summer—I'd say another twenty thousand."

What? "That sounds kind of crazy."

"Of course it is. Provincetown is most definitely crazy. And so are the people who love it." She looked over at Marin with a smile.

Marin turned to her window. She wished they could

just keep driving and driving. She wouldn't have to think beyond the sand dunes in the distance, Kelly, her amiable guide. There was something steadying about Kelly. She couldn't imagine her ever fucking up. Something about her suggested she never had a moment's self-doubt.

"So who commissioned the mosaic?"

"A woman named Sandra Crowe. She came here from Boston last summer for an art auction and ended up buying a house. Now she fancies herself a painter. Not that there's anything wrong with being a hobbyist— in the summers, this town is filled with people who want to indulge their artistic sides. But Sandra drove our friends crazy pushing for shows in their galleries. Finally, our friend Bart let her show in his gallery for a few weeks. In the end he lost money, but at least he shut her up."

"Took one for the team," Marin said.

"Exactly. The East End is technically the fancy part of town," Kelly said, steering the truck around a bend. "Back in the day, you would not be hanging out on this side of the wharf."

"I wouldn't?"

Kelly shook her head. "Nope. You're from the working class, doll. Portuguese fishing family."

Great. Not only was she a disgraced attorney, she was from a lineage deemed undesirable by her grandmother's own native town.

To the left, in the shade behind hills and dunes, a Colonial Revival mansion. The sprawling front lawn was a patchwork of purple and red flowers. The house, all white, had a starkness to it that reminded her of Greg Harper's summerhouse in East Hampton. She shook the thought away.

Kelly pulled the truck into the circular driveway and parked.

"Mind helping me get the piece to the front door? Then your service is fulfilled—promise." Her smile was heartbreakingly lovely.

"Sure."

They resumed their positions around the canvas and stepped in tandem up the stone walkway until they reached the front portico.

"I used to have a dolly to transport these things, but I have no idea where it went. I think some guests used it to get stuff into their car and took off with it in the trunk."

A young woman with a blond ponytail wearing khaki pants and a white polo shirt answered the doorbell.

Kelly, clearly surprised, said, "Tanya—what are you doing here?"

"I'm working for Mrs. Crowe this summer."

"Really?" Kelly's inflection conveyed the unspoken words *That's the best you could do?*

"Well, I would rather have worked at the inn again, but..."

Kelly turned to Marin, made the introductions. "Tanya goes to the Rhode Island School of Design. This is, what, your third summer in town?"

"Fourth," Tanya said. "Kelly, this mosaic is one of my favorites of yours. Really awesome. And it's being given the place of honor around here, apparently," she said.

"Oh yeah? Where's it going?" Wiping her brow, then putting her hands on her hips, Kelly surveyed the two-story entrance hall.

"In the dining room."

"Sounds good. All right, kiddo. See you around."

"Wait! Don't go. She's out back and she's expecting you."

"Another time. We have to run."

"Kelly, don't leave me hanging. She'll kill me if you don't say hi."

Kelly groaned. "Fine. Lead the way."

The house had dramatic high ceilings and was air-conditioned to an arctic temperature. It was all white walls and monochromatic pale furniture. The only splashes of color came from the oil paintings and sculptures.

"This will just take a minute. Hopefully," Kelly said to Marin.

Sliding glass doors opened onto a deck and a comma-shaped swimming pool. A woman in a white one-piece bathing suit and an oversize white hat stretched out on a chaise longue. She waved them over.

"Hi, Sandra," Kelly said.

"Hi, darling. Is my new baby here?"

"Yep. Tanya has it in the foyer."

The woman clapped in delight, like a child presented with an ice cream sundae topped with a sparkler.

"You have company today," the woman observed. Closer now, Marin guessed she was in her late forties, maybe early fifties. It was tough to say for sure; half her face was hidden behind Jackie O. sunglasses. Her lipstick was a glossy neutral shade, not too brown, not too pink—a color only a makeup artist could successfully pick out for you. She wore a rope of gold around her neck.

"This is Marin Bishop. Marin, Mrs. Sandra Crowe."

They exchanged greetings, and then Sandra pushed her glasses up and looked at Kelly. She had the sort of well-preserved beauty Marin was used to seeing in Manhattan.

Sandra tied a black sarong around her waist, slipped into her gold Tory Burch flip-flops, and said, "Let's go take a look!"

They followed her into the entrance foyer, where the mosaic was propped up against the wall. Sandra gasped and again clapped her hands in delight.

"It's beyond! *Beyond.* Oh, Kelly. You are a genius."

"Glad you like it."

"Like it? I'm obsessed. Do you think you could do another mermaid? I would love to do a stained-glass piece on the window in the master bath."

"Sure. We can talk about it."

"Fabulous. Why don't you two stay for breakfast?"

"Thanks, Sandra, but we have to get back. I have a friend's birthday party this afternoon."

"Well, another time. But before you run off, tell me, is it true that the inn isn't opening this season?"

"That's right," Kelly said.

"Amelia isn't unwell, I hope."

"No, she's just fine, thanks for asking."

"It's a lot of work, the inn," said Sandra.

"Work we've loved."

"But how long can you do it? You remind Amelia that I'm ready to take that load of a house off her shoulders any time she is ready. You two should enjoy yourselves a little! Travel light."

"I'll let her know, Sandra. But she's not selling anytime soon."

The sunglasses went back on. "Just be a doll and relay the message. Oh, and I'm having a Fourth of July party. You and Amelia *must* come. You too," she said as an afterthought to Marin, clearly having already forgotten her name.

"We'll check our calendars," said Kelly noncommittally.

"It's cocktails and dinner before everyone heads over to the fireworks. And I'm going to officially unveil your mosaic. I'm sure my friends will be lining up to commission pieces of their own."

Kelly nodded. "Well, how can I say no? Thanks, Sandra. We'll see you in a few weeks."

Back in the car, Marin asked, "Is Amelia really thinking of selling her house?" For some reason, the idea of Sandra Crowe owning the house made her sad.

"Not anytime soon. The house has been in Amelia's family for five generations. But the truth is, there isn't any family left to care for it." She looked pointedly at Marin. "You should stay the week. It's just a few days. You *were* on your way to leave this morning, weren't you?" Kelly said.

"Yeah," Marin admitted. "Okay. I'll stick around for a few days. But as far as Sandra's Fourth of July cocktails, you're on your own."

Kelly laughed.

Rachel hoped she wasn't being selfish, pushing so hard to see photos of her father. But why did Amelia keep the only photos of her lost son stashed away in the attic?

She stretched out on the plush queen-size bed in her glorious room. The sun streamed in through the gauzy white curtains as the ceiling fan churned the fresh breeze blowing through the window off the bay.

A knock on her door.

"Come in," she called out.

Blythe poked her head in. "Sorry to bother you, but have you seen Marin?"

"Not since breakfast."

"I want to go to the beach and thought it might be a nice thing for the two of us to do together. But she's not in her room."

Rachel sat up. "Maybe she went for a walk. Where's the beach?"

Blythe came in, pulled a map from her handbag, unfolded it, and pointed out Herring Cove.

"We should rent bikes," Rachel said.

"I haven't been on a bike in thirty years."

"Well, you know what they say—it's just like riding a bike!"

Blythe laughed.

"Knock, knock," Amelia said outside the open door. "May I come in?"

"Sure! We were just thinking about renting bikes. Is there a place nearby?" And then Rachel noticed the photo albums in her arms.

"Yes. Although Kelly and I have bikes if it's just the two of you."

"Is that . . . you have the photos of my father?"

Amelia nodded. "I'll just leave them here for you to look through at your leisure."

"Oh, don't go!" Rachel said. "I want to look at them with you so you can tell me things. Like, where they were taken and stuff."

Amelia hesitated.

Blythe folded up her map and headed for the door.

"You don't have to leave," Rachel said.

"I'll find you later," Blythe called out without so much as a glance behind her.

Hmm. Wasn't she curious to see a photo? After all, Nick Cabral was Marin's biological father too. Rachel could imagine her own mother being indifferent, but Blythe was so *involved*.

Amelia sat on the edge of the bed with a sigh. "Rachel, you know I'm delighted with this turn of events. Meeting you and your sister is the best thing that has happened to me in a very long time. But I can't say it isn't complicated. Nick and I parted on bad terms. He was angry with me. At the time of his death, we hadn't spoken in a few years. And the fact that we never had a chance to resolve our issues is very, very painful."

Oh, what had she done? She was a bull in an emotional china shop.

"I'm sorry! I can go through these myself. I didn't realize...I'm really sorry."

Amelia smiled sadly, her eyes tearing. "You have absolutely nothing to apologize for, dear girl." She hesitated, then opened the top album. "I brought two. One is from his childhood, when he was about ten or so. This one is from the last summer he spent in this house, between his junior and senior years of college."

"So he was almost my age."

"Yes."

Rachel hugged herself. Now that the moment was here, the moment she had longed for her entire life, she was afraid. Gingerly, she reached out and touched the page. It was covered in plastic, so the surface was shiny, catching the glare of the sun. Rachel tilted her head, leaning close to get a clear view of the photos.

She sat back against the wicker headboard and took the album gingerly from Amelia. Her eyes fell on the photo on the upper right corner of the page. A young man in weedy grass pulling at a tennis ball clenched between the teeth of a large golden Lab. He was tall and lanky, with dark hair falling into his eyes and a smile on his face.

"That's him?" she breathed, a question, even though she knew it was.

"Yes. That's Nick behind this house. Before we had the communal table."

Wow. No way around it—her dad was a hottie. He reminded her of that Mexican actor, Gael García Bernal.

The photo below was a shot from the beach on an overcast day. Nick, in long bathing trunks and a Boston University T-shirt, was bending over a cooler. A dark-haired young woman, tan and slender, stood beside him, her facial expression suggesting they were midconversation.

"Who's that?"

"My daughter. Nadine."

"You have a daughter?"

Amelia nodded, tight-lipped.

"Does she live around here too?"

"No. She lives in Italy."

"Did you... does she know about Marin and me?"

"I sent her a letter."

A letter? Did she mean an e-mail? And wouldn't the existence of two previously unknown family members merit a phone call? Maybe this was some sort of old-fashioned thing Rachel just didn't understand.

She turned back to the photos. Mentally, she said the word *Dad* over and over, but it was hard to reconcile that hot guy with a paternal role. What would he look like today?

Amelia's phone rang, and she answered it while Rachel continued to slowly page through the album. A few pictures were of Nick and an older man, tan with silver hair, not terribly tall but broad-shouldered and handsome. Her grandfather?

"What do you mean, she canceled? The party is this afternoon!" Amelia made a tsking sound and stood up to pace around the room. "She is so unprofessional. I don't know how she is still in business. Only in this town." Silence, then: "I'll do what I can, but you know I can't just whip something up for dozens of people in two hours."

Amelia set her phone on the bed.

"Is everything okay?" Rachel said, closing the album with her hand still inside, holding her spot.

"It's our friend Thomas's fifty-fifth birthday, and the party is this afternoon," Amelia said. "And the caterer just canceled. Just now! I'm going to head over there and help figure out what to do about the food."

"I'll go with you," Rachel said.

"Oh, hon, you don't have to do that. I'll be fine. You're here for only a few days. You should go to the beach."

"No. I want to help. I didn't come here for the beach, I came for family, and that's what family's for, right?"

"Well, when you put it that way." Amelia smiled.

Chapter Seventeen

Where had everyone gone? Blythe couldn't find Marin or Amelia or anyone, for that matter. She passed by Rachel's empty room and looked inside.

The photo albums were just sitting there. On the bed. *Just sitting there.*

She never would have sought them out. Every instinct told her to ignore them.

Blythe glanced down the hallway in either direction and then went in and closed Rachel's bedroom door.

This was madness.

She sat on Rachel's bed. The album was navy blue with gold piping along the edges. The spine was worn. When she opened it, the book crackled. It smelled musty and like old glue. Blythe's pulse raced.

There he was, the face that had existed only in her mind for thirty years. Achingly beautiful and alive. She gingerly touched his image: Nick on the beach, at the water's edge. She had not known this Nick—carefree. Sun-kissed. Happy.

"Oh, Nick," she whispered.

By the time she'd met him, he'd abandoned this town built on sand. He'd sworn off Boston, the place where he'd been born and raised. He would barely speak of his mother, the woman whose roof Blythe was now sleeping under.

Nick Cabral had been, ultimately, not knowable.

That first day, leaving the art museum, Blythe had lied to herself—unconvincingly—that they were just going to talk. And yet, walking the few blocks to his apartment on Green Street, they barely exchanged a word. Had it been a longer trip, one involving a bus or a cab, she might have changed her mind. But the sun, the heat, the fluttering pulse of the city in the first rush of summer, ushered her along like a hand on her back.

His studio apartment was cluttered. A guitar rested against the wall next to a bike with chipped blue paint. Half-unpacked boxes of clothes served as the only bedroom furniture. Near the small kitchenette, a round wood table was covered with sketch pads, pencils, and boxes of art charcoal.

Blythe couldn't help but mentally compare it to the first time she'd stepped into Kip's pristine, sprawling apartment on Rittenhouse Square.

Stop. Just one hour of not being Mrs. Kipton Bishop. That was all she wanted.

Nick opened his small refrigerator. "I have beer and white wine. It's been open a week or maybe more but it might still be okay."

It was eleven in the morning.

"Oh, no. I'm fine. Thanks."

He popped open two beers and handed her one. Okay, she'd have a beer. Why not? They sat at the table. She touched one of the sketchbooks. "Can I look?"

"You can look. There's nothing in it."

She flipped through the pages. All blank.

He told her he hadn't been able to draw since leaving Provincetown, where he used to spend his summers.

"Why not?" she said.

He didn't answer.

She sipped her beer. Blythe was not a beer drinker. *Liquid bread.* But that didn't matter anymore. If this man saw her naked, he would not know that he was bearing witness to a new, rounder, fuller version of her body, the one she had since she'd stopped dancing. A body her husband had not touched in months. She wondered if, no longer a wispy pixie girl, she was somehow less attractive to Kip. Or was it really just work? Or was marriage itself to blame?

Nick stared at her, his artist's eyes dark pools of desire. He saw before him something he wanted. He took her by the hand and she followed him to the queen-size mattress on the floor. The bed was made, and this small evidence of some sense of order and discipline in his life was comforting.

When he touched her, she gasped. Pressed body to body, she lost all reason. Good God, had she ever felt such ridiculous desire? She'd slept with three men: a dancer at the company, a journalist she'd met at a party and dated for a few months, and then Kip.

But this? Never this.

Afterward, naked and breathless, side by side in the bed, she waited to feel guilt, regret, even surprise at what had just happened. But all she felt was an overwhelming sense of relief. If he'd pressed her for words, if he had been the type of man who wanted to talk to her after fucking her senseless, she would have told him that it felt like he had given her back *herself*.

Nick reached for a lighter next to the bed and sparked up a joint. He offered it to her but she shook her head. Blythe did not smoke, did not drink, did not do drugs. But she supposed, since she'd followed a perfect stranger into his house in the middle of the day and had had sex with him, it was not a stretch for him to assume she would indulge in any number of vices.

The pot was probably her cue to leave, but she didn't want to go. She was in no hurry to get back to her life.

"I came here to dance ballet," she blurted out. "Came to Philly, I mean."

He glanced at her. "So you're a dancer?"

She shook her head. "Not anymore."

He inhaled, held it, blew the smoke away from her. "So now what?"

"Well, I got married."

Nick nodded. "I noticed the ring. How's that going?"

"Not well. Obviously." She pulled the sheet up higher.

He turned on his side, propped himself up on one elbow, and looked at her.

"What do you know? Two artists who aren't doing shit. A fine pair we are." His gaze was gentle and kind and this touched her more than his passion. She waited for him to say something else, but he didn't. After a long silence, he put out the joint and pulled the sheet down, baring her breasts. And then he moved on top of her, inside of her again, and she realized there was no "going back" to her life.

Could she last the week? Marin thought maybe—if she could just avoid her mother.

The more she thought about the magnitude of Blythe's deception, the less she could believe it. She felt like her mother, the person who had always been the closest in the world to her, was a stranger.

She followed Kelly into the inn, the back entrance, through the kitchen.

Marin saw the note first. It was written on Beach Rose Inn notepaper and stuck to the refrigerator with a magnetized strip of photo-booth pictures of Amelia and Kelly dressed up for some formal event.

> *Catering fiasco at Thomas's: they canceled! I'm trying*
> *to pull something together. Come over when you can.*
> *Love, A*

"It's always something," Kelly said. "Come along—meet our friends."

Marin hesitated. With Amelia and Kelly both out of the house, it was the perfect time to make her getaway. But looking at Kelly's flushed, smiling face, she just couldn't do it. Still, she wasn't exactly in a party mood.

"I think I'm just going to hang out here," she said.

"It's up to you, but I really wouldn't pass this up. You haven't experienced Provincetown until you've attended an 'I made it to fifty-five' party."

"I've been to birthday parties for people older than fifty-five."

"With AIDS?"

Oh. "Okay. Give me five minutes to change clothes."

The number of restaurants and shops dwindled as they headed west on Commercial. They walked until they reached a lovely shingled cottage with turquoise shutters and matching rocking chairs on the front porch. Kelly bounded up the stone steps waving at two men dressed casually in shorts and T-shirts. One was African American with salt-and-pepper hair and glasses; the other was tall and angular with the strong jaw and cleft chin of an old-time movie star.

"How's the birthday boy?" Kelly asked, hugging the silver fox.

"Thomas is having a good day today," he said, then he smiled at Marin. "I'm Bart. Welcome to our home."

"Marin," she said, shaking his hand.

"Oh, the granddaughter," the second guy said.

Under other circumstances, this would have annoyed her. Why should these strangers know her personal business? But she was the one crashing their party.

"Yes," she said.

"I'm Paul. Come on in. Amelia's in the kitchen," he said, tugging her along. Marin followed him, leaving Kelly deep in conversation with Bart.

"So how long are you in town for?" Paul said.

"Just until Saturday morning," she said. *It's only a few more days,* she told herself.

The house, like Amelia and Kelly's, was a perfect beachy-shabby chic. The living room had a skylight and wall-to-wall bookshelves filled with hardcovers. Marin would have loved to check out the titles but Paul ushered her toward the kitchen.

Thomas and Bart's kitchen was spacious and full of light, with a farmhouse sink, pale hardwood floors, and a white marble island. It was bright with green accents—lime-green Shaker cabinets, a bowl of Granny Smith apples, a row of large Perrier bottles on the countertop.

"Look what the cat dragged in," Paul said to Amelia. She looked up from the counter.

"Hi, dear—I'm elbows-deep in dough or I'd give you

a welcome hug. Make yourself at home. It's going to get very crowded here in about an hour, so if I were you I'd stake out a spot and relax."

Three men bounded into the kitchen and started picking from a tray of artfully arranged crudités. Amelia swatted them away while ticking off introductions.

Marin knew she would never remember all the names. The men were unabashedly fascinated and delighted by her sudden appearance in Amelia's life.

"So you're Rachel's sister?" one man asked.

"Half sister," Marin said, the words still unbelievable to her own ears. But somehow, in this place, it wasn't quite as strange as it might have been somewhere else. "Is Rachel here?" she asked Amelia.

"Out by the pool," Amelia said.

Marin grabbed a carrot stick and headed out through the French doors to the back of the house. A porch overlooked a flower garden, an old-fashioned gazebo, and a small swimming pool. That's where she spotted Rachel, perched on the edge of a chair, talking to a remarkably good-looking guy. He looked like one of the Hemsworth brothers, Chris or Liam or whatever their names were. Either way, definitely swoon-worthy.

And she couldn't help but notice that her sister seemed to be swooning.

Rachel had been surprised, when she arrived at the house, at how quickly Amelia was enveloped by her friends and how extraneous Rachel instantly felt. Oh, she was welcome. And she was certainly a curiosity.

"Nick's daughter. After all this time. Remarkable!"

She learned she was in the home of Thomas Frost Duncan, an award-winning poet and longtime Provincetown resident who was celebrating not just his fifty-fifth birthday but twenty years of surviving with AIDS.

Thomas had short-cropped white hair and piercing blue eyes. He sat folded in an Eames chair and looked much older than fifty-five. As if reading Rachel's thoughts, he said, "I never thought I'd reach forty."

Unsure what to say to that, she asked about his poetry.

"I didn't think your generation was interested in poetry. Just your hundred-and-forty-character Twitter haiku."

"Such a cranky old man. How do I put up with you?" Bart said, his warm brown eyes crinkled with affection. "Don't mind him. In fact, you should go back to the pool with the other young people."

"Sure," said Rachel. "I'll go check it out."

She wandered over to the back patio. It was quiet out there except for a lone guy sitting poolside in a lounge chair. She didn't want to disturb him. She stood indecisively between the house and the pool until the man sensed her awkward presence and turned around.

"Hey there." He gave a half smile, then turned back to the water.

Whoa. He had cheekbones you could ski jump off and blue-green eyes the color of the bay. When she was young she had been obsessed with a made-for-TV movie about a girl who turned into a mermaid. The mermaid (and Rachel!) fell in love with a hunky lifeguard, played by a gorgeous Australian actor. This guy looked just like him. All he was missing was the accent.

But this wasn't a movie, and she shouldn't be crushing on some dude. That was not why she was there. This was a family trip, and shame on her for even noticing that he was great-looking. Besides, this was a crowd of gay men. She was an idiot.

She sat on a chair near him but not too near.

"Hey. I'm Rachel," she said.

"Luke," he said. "How do you know Thomas?"

"Oh—I don't. I came with my grandmother. She's good friends with him."

He nodded with a polite smile. Dimples! What was wrong with her?

"So how do *you* know Thomas?" she asked.

"He's my father."

"Really?" she said, not bothering to hide her surprise.

"Yes," said Luke. "You know, most people here are on their second lives."

She shook her head. "I don't know that much about this place. I just got here yesterday."

"Oh, well—you'll see. P-Town is the land of reinvention. Everybody's got a story."

I just want your story, she thought. "Do you live here?" she asked.

"Just visiting," he said. "I teach at the University of Rhode Island."

Cute *and* smart. "What do you teach?"

"Urban planning."

And socially aware. *Stop it.*

How old was he? Early thirties, she guessed. She started to say something but noticed he was distracted, fixed on something or someone over her shoulder. She turned to see Marin. Marin, looking like a radiant, dark-haired angel in a diaphanous white sundress.

Rachel felt an unfamiliar pang of territorial angst.

For the first time since learning about Marin, Rachel wanted a few more minutes of being an only child.

Chapter Eighteen

Marin stood in front of the row of lounge chairs while Rachel stumbled through introductions to the hot guy, followed by an awkward explanation of their half-sister-hood.

"Interesting," he said. "And I thought I had a complicated situation with my dad."

Kelly and Paul appeared.

"We're going to duck out and get a drink," said Kelly.

"Correction," said Paul. "We're going out to get drunk."

"You're leaving?" Marin asked.

"Bart's friends are in recovery, so this party is dry; Paul and I want to have a celebratory round," Kelly said. "In case you'd like to join us."

Marin had two choices: Continue to talk with the hottie—and suffer the dagger eyes of Rachel—or get good and drunk.

"Sounds like a plan," she said. "Lead the way."

Rachel's sigh of relief was shockingly blatant—or maybe Marin had imagined it. Suddenly, she was really annoyed with Rachel. Annoyed with her innocent doe eyes. Annoyed with her for her pathetic, obvious crush on this guy. Annoyed with her for the endless pit of need that had dragged Marin into her life and turned Marin's own life upside down.

"Care to join us?" Marin said to Luke. He seemed to consider it, then said, "It's a little early for me. Thanks, though."

"Suit yourself," Marin said.

The bar was, as everything here seemed to be, within easy walking distance. A-House was nestled on a side street off Commercial. It was a white clapboard building with an American flag waving atop the porch roof. A hanging wooden sign out front read ATLANTIC HOUSE BAR. It was old-fashioned and non-remarkable-looking, but when Marin glanced up she noticed beautiful stained-glass windows on an upper floor. They didn't really fit with the rest of the exterior. But this was what Province-town seemed to be so far: at first glance, you saw one thing; after a closer look, you saw something you wouldn't necessarily expect.

Inside, it was dark and smelled like decades' worth of faded cigarette smoke. Behind the bar, Christmas-tree lights. And in the farthest corner of the room, another small, stained-glass window. Mariah Carey played over the sound system: "Vision of Love."

The bartender looked up wearily, as if it were the end of a late Saturday night instead of eleven in the morning in the middle of the week. He had a sun-weathered face, a buzz cut, and a full sleeve of tattoos. Marin couldn't tell if he was forty or sixty.

Marin, Kelly, and Paul sat at the bar, front and center.

Directly behind the bartender was a carved wooden bust of a merman.

"Hey, Chris. Three kamikaze shots," said Paul.

A kamikaze? Marin was a wine drinker—that was it. To her left, a giant screen played the Mariah Carey video that went with the song.

"To Thomas's birthday," the bartender said, sliding the shots in front of them and downing one himself.

"To Thomas," Marin said along with Kelly and Paul. She swallowed her shot. Vodka with lime juice? She wasn't sure. All she knew was that it was strong.

"Fifty-five," Kelly said. "And I can't believe I'm past fifty."

"Yes, you are, sweetheart. But you don't look a day over thirty-five. You and Julianne Moore. The hottest old redheads in the world."

"Thanks?" Kelly said, laughing.

"I hate that you didn't have a big party last year. I say we have a ridiculous, all-night soiree right here for your next birthday. It should have a theme."

"I'll drink to that." Kelly waved the bartender over for another round. "But you better check in with my better half. You know she always has something planned."

"Don't I know it, you lucky bitch. You and Amelia, Thomas and Bart—you all make me almost believe in marriage. Though it is a little sickening to be around all that love and devotion." Paul turned to Marin. "What about you, gorgeous? Do you have a boyfriend? Some hot suit waiting for you back in New York?"

Marin burst into tears.

"Oh, honey! Was it something I said?"

"No," Marin sobbed. She missed Julian so much, the emotional pain was nearly physical. Her entire body ached.

She couldn't let it end with that last terse phone call. She should have told him the real reason she was in Provincetown. Given him a chance to be her friend again. They didn't have to figure out the other stuff yet.

"Oh, look what you've done, gossip queen!" Kelly admonished Paul, throwing her arm around Marin. "Just ignore him."

"It's okay. It's fine. It's just..." And the whole story came rushing out: her job, falling for Julian, getting busted at work and fired.

"No fraternization at work? This whole town would shut down," said Paul.

"Marin, this will sound trite, but trust me—I had a very bumpy start in my relationship with Amelia—"

"Understatement!" chirped Paul.

"Can I finish, please? Hon, you have to just say to yourself that if it's meant to be, it will be. It sounds like a cliché but clichés are just recycled truths."

They downed their drinks, and then Kelly ordered another round and headed off to the bathroom.

"I hate to be a lightweight but I really can't keep up with you two," Marin said.

"We're just getting started. Kelly needs to get blitzed, I can tell."

"Really?"

"Birthdays can do that to you at our age. And she had her own health scare last year. So I think this just dredges up that old ugly beast, fear of mortality."

She glanced behind her. Kelly was still in the dark, nether regions of the bar.

"Is she okay now?"

"She's fine. But these things make you think. *Carpe diem* and all that."

Marin wanted to say something, but the thought floated away. She was well and truly buzzed. Chris slid the next round across the bar.

"Carpe diem," Marin said, and they clinked their shot glasses together.

Kelly reappeared and scolded them for not waiting for her.

"You know what we never did?" said Paul. "We never got our tattoos!"

"We never got our tattoos," Kelly repeated.

"You promised."

"What tattoos?" said Marin.

"Long story," said Kelly.

"We should go *right now,*" said Paul.

"Amelia will kill me. She hates tattoos."

"Honey, you're a breast cancer survivor. You've earned the right to mark that in some way."

"That's true!" said Kelly. "Maybe I'll get her name. That way she can't be too angry, don't you think?"

Marin nodded. At that point, it all sounded perfectly reasonable to her.

Had Marin been flirting with Luke? Rachel couldn't tell if she was just being jealous and ridiculous or if there was actually a vibe between the two of them. Then again, why would Marin be interested in Luke? Wasn't she supposedly still hung up on her ex-boyfriend back in New York?

So much for sisterly loyalty.

The poolside was, by that time, populated with guests who had spilled out of the crowded house. Lunch organized itself in a sort of free-form potluck.

"I see my dad in the summers mostly," Luke told

Rachel over paper plates filled with tuna salad and chips. "I alternate Christmases between him and my mom."

He had grown up in New Jersey. Thomas had been a high-school English teacher, his mother a school administrator. "When I was twelve, my dad basically announced, 'This isn't right for me, I need to live my authentic life.' And that was it."

"Your poor mother. She must have freaked."

"You know, not really. She was upset, but not upset with him, because she knew he couldn't change the way he felt. If he could have made it work with her, he would have. I guess the split was as amicable as it could be under the circumstances."

Rachel told him about her single-mother upbringing, her father a father only in his genetic contribution. And that she had learned of his death only last week. "Now it's too late," she said.

"I'm sorry," Luke said. She immediately regretted complaining. Such a downer!

"No—I mean, it's fine," she said. "I'm here, Amelia is amazing. I'm really thankful to meet my grandmother."

"And your sister."

Are you thinking about my sister?

More people trickled out to the pool. Everyone wanted to say hi to Luke, all of them full of recollections of the last time they had seen him and anecdotes about what had happened since his visit the previous summer. Rachel started to feel silly just planted by his side, so she reluctantly excused herself.

Inside the house she found Blythe perusing the living-room bookshelves. She stood out, overdressed in a pair of well-tailored gray slacks and a cream-colored summer-weight cashmere cardigan with a scarf knotted around her neck.

"Amelia texted me that you were all here but I don't see Marin anywhere," Blythe said.

"Oh, she and Kelly and Paul went to a bar."

"Really?" Blythe said, incredulous. Not happy.

Rachel nodded. "Apparently the party is dry, and they all went out for a drink."

"Marin isn't a big drinker. And certainly not a day drinker."

Rachel shrugged. "We're on vacation."

Over Blythe's shoulder, she spotted Luke heading toward the front door. Alone. He noticed her and gave a little wave.

"You're leaving?" she called out, realizing she sounded like a girl upset that the boy she liked was ditching the middle-school dance.

"I need a little breather. I'm going to stop by Herring Cove for a while."

"Herring Cove?"

"The beach," he said. Then, after hesitating for a second: "Do you want to come along?"

That would be a definite yes. No use pretending otherwise.

"I'll see you later, Blythe," she said, leaving Marin's mother looking confused, possibly about to protest.

Maybe having an overly involved mother wasn't all it was cracked up to be.

Luke opened the passenger door of his Jeep and she climbed in. The sky had grown overcast, and the breeze had turned into wind.

"There's a sweatshirt or two in that duffel in the backseat if you're cold," he said. "It will be even windier at the beach."

She turned around and unzipped the duffel. It felt

strangely intimate to be going through his stuff, but it had been his idea. She pulled out a navy blue University of Rhode Island hoodie and pulled it over her T-shirt.

"Thanks."

She stole a glance at him in profile and bit her lip. He was ridiculously handsome, clearly intelligent, nice as hell.

She tried not to think of the way he'd looked at Marin. Rachel was not adept at the politics of love and relationships. She'd never had a serious boyfriend—*serious* meaning lasting more than a few weeks. Which was especially ironic, given that her mother was never *without* a boyfriend, usually someone inappropriately young and almost always underemployed.

"Why didn't you ever get married?" Rachel had asked her once.

"Because men are for fun, and marriage is work," her mother said.

And so, on some basic level, Rachel didn't get the point of relationships. She'd never seen one work out. She'd also never yet experienced that all-consuming rush of infatuation that seemed to drive everyone else in the human population.

Luke turned on the radio, and an old Kings of Leon song filled the car. Rachel felt a surge of energy, a high-powered adrenaline rush that took her breath away. He drove northwest onto Bradford and she closed her eyes, the wind whipping through the open-topped Jeep. Minutes later, he pulled around a bend and into a nearly empty parking lot. Luke jumped out and came over to open her door.

"This is the beach?" she said.

"Yeah. Past these dunes."

The hills of sand were threaded with plants and a smattering of deep pink flowers. Rachel took off her sneakers.

"We don't have flowers growing on the beaches in California," she said.

"They call them beach roses," he said.

Rachel followed him down a path to a wide patch of wet sand. The ocean was gray and foamy, and not many people were around.

"This isn't how I imagined the beach. Where is everyone?"

"It's late in the day and cloudy...the tide is high. If you were here midday in July, you'd barely have room to walk."

He picked up a stone and, with a twist of his wrist, threw it into the water, where it skipped three times before disappearing.

"Impressive," she said, half joking, half serious.

"I'm rusty. I used to get at least two more skips out of it."

Rachel picked up a smooth white rock. With a twist of her wrist, she tossed it into the sea, but it promptly sank.

Luke scooped another few rocks out of the sand and handed one to her. "You have to hold it kind of loosely, like this." He positioned her fingers around the rock. His nearness was dizzying. "And then move your wrist like a hinge—just launch it." He held her hand in his to give her a sense of the motion. The stone sailed from her fingers but still disappeared without skimming the surface of the water.

"I suck at this," she said.

"It just takes practice. How long are you in town?"

"Until Saturday."

"That's plenty of time. You'll master it."

"I accept the challenge." She was shocked at her own flirtatiousness.

They stood facing each other, total eye-lock. Somewhere in the distance, a foghorn sounded. It felt like the roar of her heart.

"We should get back to the party," he said.

No, no, no—she felt a door closing. A door to what, she didn't quite know.

But she had to find out.

Chapter Nineteen

Just minutes after the three of them stumbled drunk into Coastline Tattoo, a small shop nestled in an alleyway, a text message lured Paul away.

"You suck!" Kelly protested when he said he was going. Marin smiled. She hoped she was like that when she was in her fifties. She was so relaxed, so comfortable in her own skin. There were no other words for it: she was cool.

"Not all of us have the loves of our lives waiting for us at home. Some of us have to take it when it comes. Or when it's ready to come."

"Ugh! Go."

Marin laughed—for the first time in how long?

They flipped through the artists' books to find designs.

"Are you really getting Amelia's name?"

"Maybe. I need to find a good font. I'm thinking this kind of cursive." She pointed out an ornate, swirling treatment of the words *Marine Life*.

"I might get a flower," Marin said. "Maybe a little daisy inside my wrist."

"Is that your birth-month flower?"

"What? No."

"You should find a design that has personal meaning."

Marin shrugged. "I'm too drunk. This is a bad idea. I'll just keep you company."

"Yeah. If it doesn't have meaning, don't do it. That's the problem today—we've lost all sense of the rites of passage. It's important to mark things, you know?"

"I'm not sure I'd be marking anything today except my life at rock bottom."

"Well, that's not a bad place to be."

"How do you figure?"

"Nowhere to go but up," said Kelly. And then Marin remembered thinking she was at rock bottom the day that Rachel had called from the Times Square Starbucks. She'd thought, *Why not meet her? Things can't get any worse.* And then the truth came out.

But what could possibly get worse now?

Kelly flipped a few pages and then stopped, pointing to an image. "This is the one. If you get it, I'll get it."

"Matching tattoos? No offense, but we just met yesterday."

"And in a week you'll leave, and maybe our paths will never cross again. Something to remember me by."

Marin leaned closer to look at the drawing.

"What is it?"

"A beach rose," said Kelly.

By late afternoon, Thomas Duncan's house was filled to capacity, and there were more people outside than inside. Amelia held court in the living room; someone was asking her, "How could Kelly sell one of her mosaics to that awful Sandra Crowe?" when she spotted Luke Duncan slipping out the front door with Rachel.

She smiled. He was a handsome young man, and Amelia could remember the first time he'd visited Provincetown, a lanky preteen with big eyes and floppy, boy-band hair. She felt a pang of envy; Thomas had his life with Bart, but he also had his son. She ached for Nadine in that moment. Having Marin and Rachel somehow made Nadine's absence all the more acute.

Nadine still hadn't responded to the letter, and now Amelia had to admit that she likely would not be doing so. If Nadine had nothing to say to a letter with such dramatic news, chances were that her daughter would never return. Not for her nieces—probably not even to bury her mother, when that day came. It was time for Amelia to accept that Nadine did not want to be part of a family.

As a teenager and even in college, Nadine always had to have a friend around during times that should have been just for family. Once, Amelia overheard her on the phone calling a friend her buffer. Amelia felt wounded by this but it wasn't something she could bring up lest she be accused of eavesdropping. Nadine was constantly accusing her of something, ranging from the innocuous and typical "You don't understand" to the more damning "You're ruining my life." During Nadine's high-school years, Amelia had accepted this as normal. Her more seasoned mom friends told her that all young women needed to reject their mothers in order to establish their own womanhood. Although as much as Amelia wanted to embrace that modern, intellectual explanation for what was happening, she couldn't remember rejecting her own mother. She had always revered and cherished the woman.

So, no, she didn't understand Nadine's attitude toward

her. She accepted that she couldn't necessarily change it, but it never sat well with her.

It had been different with Nick, her firstborn; from the very moment he locked his cloudy dark eyes on her, she'd felt a bolt of electrifying connectedness. That feeling never ebbed, never waned. Not until that last summer.

Every year the Cabrals spent June through August at Amelia's mother's house on Commercial Street. When Renata died, in the mid-1970s, she left the house to Amelia, and the Provincetown summers continued. By the time Nick and Nadine were teenagers, the house was filled with an endless rotation of their visiting friends. This continued during the summers after they started Boston University. Nadine, more often than Nick, had a constant stream of friends—the aforementioned buffers. At that point, Amelia welcomed the buffers as well; her three-decade marriage to Otto Cabral was stale. She accepted this as the natural course of things. She doubted her own parents had had a rewarding, passion-filled marriage until the end. (She was certain there was a year or two in which they'd barely spoken to each other.) Yes, when she'd married Otto, she'd been mirroring her parents' marriage. It's what she thought she wanted in life. It had made her mother happy, and surely she was just like her mother. But as she got older, Amelia realized she wasn't so very much like her mother after all, no matter how much she adored her. She was not able to find satisfaction in a marriage that ranged from lukewarm companionship to downright apathy. Yes, she had her children and her cooking, her house and her friends. But it wasn't enough.

And so the summers were a welcome distraction. Morning walks on the beach, the elaborate meal preparations, late dinners by the bay that started at sunset and didn't end until the last person crawled off to bed.

That final summer, Nadine's roommate and new best friend had come along with her, a bright, artistic, high-spirited young woman who brought out a giddiness in Nadine that Amelia had rarely seen. Even Nick, usually annoyed with the cloying adoration of his younger sister's friends, seemed to go out of his way to spend time with the two of them.

Sometimes Amelia sensed the kids were crowding their guest, who seemed more interested in spending time with Amelia in the kitchen than in going to the beach or chugging margaritas at the Canteen. When Amelia (who enjoyed the company more than she cared to admit) asked the girl about this, she locked her wide green eyes on Amelia and said, "I guess I'm an old soul." Amelia's heart lurched, an undeniable free fall that terrified her. Three weeks into the summer, and Amelia was in love with Kelly Hanauer.

It was impossible. It was madness. She would not indulge in such thoughts, in such feelings. But one afternoon, when Otto went off fishing and Nick and Nadine went whale watching, an hour in the kitchen teaching Kelly to bake *rosquilhas secas* turned into a bottle of wine at the edge of the bay. And the irrepressible redhead kissed her.

"This cannot happen," said Amelia.

"It already has," said Kelly.

Chapter Twenty

How did Amelia find the time? First thing in the morning, Blythe saw her setting out a full spread of fresh-baked bread, berries, coffee, and organic granola. As if she hadn't just whipped a party together the day before.

"I hope you're not doing all of this just on account of us," Blythe said.

"Please. It's my pleasure. Ask Kelly—I don't know what to do with myself if I'm not taking care of guests. Did you sleep well?"

"I did. Perfectly."

Well, not perfectly. She'd fallen asleep before Marin got home, and she woke up at two in the morning worried about her. Blythe crept out of bed and down the hall and peeked into the other guest room to make sure Marin was there. At the sight of her, safely curled up, only her dark ponytail visible against the pale sheets in the moonlight, Blythe was finally able to go back to sleep.

Amelia set out a plate of golden-brown zucchini bread. Blythe thought of the Black Beauty zucchini she'd grown two years ago and looked around the yard in appraisal.

"Did you ever think of having a vegetable garden? You have the perfect space for it."

Amelia shook her head. "It's a lovely idea but the soil here takes a lot of work. This town was literally built on sand and silt. People with gardens sometimes have the soil shipped in. It's just more trouble than it's worth for us."

"That's such a shame," Blythe said. She made a mental note to call her neighbor and ask her to check on her tomatoes.

"Good morning!" Rachel bounded out of the house, her long hair loose. She wore a flowing Indian-print sundress. "I'm starving."

Rachel sat on the bench across from Blythe. The sun reflected a narrow ring of gold in her eyes. They were lighter than Marin's but the same wide, almond shape. She couldn't get used to seeing similarities between the two of them. But it was small, tangible things like that that made the absurdity of their situation feel real.

She wished she knew what Marin was thinking. Nearly a week since Marin had confronted her with the truth, and she was no closer to getting her daughter to talk to her, let alone forgive her, than she had been on day one.

"Maybe the three of us can go to the beach this afternoon," Blythe said to Rachel. "I just have to find a bathing-suit shop first."

When she had left Philadelphia, she had packed for only a few days in New York, not a trip to the beach. Had that really been less than a week ago?

The back door swung open, and Blythe looked up hopefully. Sure enough, Marin appeared. She wore her usual sunglasses and her new uniform of black yoga pants and a rumpled T-shirt. She made her way to the table without a word, sat down, and slumped over, her head resting on her arm. She reeked of alcohol.

"Hi, sweetheart. Coffee?" Blythe said, trying to sound chipper and not alarmed.

Marin nodded.

"Did you go out last night?" Rachel asked.

"Yeah," Marin said, sitting up and sipping the coffee. Even though half her face was behind sunglasses, Blythe could see the sickly pallor of her complexion.

"Are you okay?" said Blythe.

"Fine."

That's when Blythe noticed it: something shiny and red on the inside of her daughter's right wrist, the size of a quarter.

"Marin, what in God's name is that?"

"What?" Marin said.

"This?" Blythe said, grabbing her wrist.

Rachel and Amelia peered over her shoulder.

"You got a *tattoo?*" Blythe said loudly. Marin had never even pierced her ears. The most outrageous aesthetic choice she'd ever made was ill-advisedly highlighting her hair the summer between sophomore and junior years of high school.

"Can you please not yell? My head is splitting." Marin took her coffee and walked back into the house.

"Oh my God," Blythe said.

Rachel put an arm around her. "She's fine."

"You don't even know her! She is not fine. She is not herself. My daughter is having a meltdown."

With that, she stormed into the house.

* * *

Marin flopped down on her bed, facing the ceiling. She was so hung over, the whir of the ceiling fan made her stomach lurch.

Did she really have *that* much to drink? Enough to get a good buzz on, sure. But to throw up three times?

Still, she had to admit it was worth it. Kelly was fucking awesome. She looked at the red flower etched inside her wrist, and smiled. Even if she hadn't loved the tattoo—which she did—the look on her mother's face would have been well worth it.

Marin closed her eyes and draped her arm over her face to block out the sunlight. She imagined her office in New York. The conference room. The lobby. Life at Cole, Harding, and Worth was going on without her. And the truth was, it didn't feel that strange. She didn't miss it. What did that mean?

A knock on the door. Marin ignored it.

"Marin," called her mother. "We're going to the beach. Want to come?"

"No," she said.

"It's going to be a beautiful day."

Marin forced herself out of bed and opened her door a crack. Her mother smiled at her hopefully.

"I can't get sun on my tattoo," Marin said. "I'm going back to sleep."

She closed the door again.

She was just dozing off when another knock disturbed her. She wanted to yell at whoever it was to leave her alone, but she forced herself to call out—with just a modicum of civility—"Who is it?"

No answer. Another light rap. Groaning, she sat up and dragged herself to the door. She opened it to find Kelly.

"Amelia will kill me if you're too hung over to leave your room today," she said.

Marin sighed. "I am pretty hung over. But I also just can't deal with my mother. Or anyone."

"So you're hiding in here?"

"That's the plan."

"For how long?"

"You can wake me up when it's time to drive back to New York."

Kelly put her hands on her hips, cocked her head to one side. "I have a better idea. Come hang out in my studio. I could use an extra set of hands for a project."

Marin rolled her eyes. "Kelly, you don't have to do this."

"Do what?"

"Babysit me. I'm fine, okay? There's just a lot going on, and I want to be alone."

"I hate to break it to you, but I'm not asking *for you*. I actually do need help with something, and if you wanted to be alone, you've come to the wrong house. You've come to the wrong town, actually. In case you haven't noticed, we're all up in everyone else's business. I think that's printed somewhere on the brochure."

Marin couldn't help but smile. "I'm not very artistic."

"I don't need talent. I need manual labor. Come on."

Marin followed Kelly up one flight of stairs to her third-floor studio.

The first thing that struck Marin about the room was color; it was everywhere. It wasn't just the mosaics on the wall. Small end tables were tiled in cobalt and sky blue; a full-length mirror was covered in pieces of china, pale pink and moss green and red. A vivid green mermaid statue shone with opaque glass. The room was enormous, probably intended as a master suite. In the center, a wide rectangular table stretching nearly the length of the room. It was covered with plates of colorful tiles and glass, bowls of pebbles, a teacup brimming with shattered china. The table was also littered with tools: a metal ruler, a T-square, an odd device that looked like gardening shears with two round wheels at the top, giant rolls of tape, tubes of glue.

"Oh. Wow," Marin said, walking around. The walls were lined with floor-to-ceiling shelves and cubbies that were filled with plastic bins labeled by color and material: sea glass, tiles, china, and crockery. Some shelves were piled with dishes; others had towers of teacups. One long shelf was filled with sheets of stained glass organized by color: vivid greens and blues and purple in every shade from deep, dark violet to the palest lavender to cotton-candy pink.

"I have to say, it's my favorite place in the world. This used to be Amelia's bedroom—back in the day. But when I got serious about mosaics, we converted it into a studio."

"It smells good in here. Like spicy vanilla."

"Oh, that's perfume. It's from a fancy store, Calypso. Amelia gave it to me as a stocking stuffer one Christmas. I don't wear it, but I do spray it around. Very expensive air freshener." She smiled.

Marin kind of loved her. "How did you get into this whole mosaic thing?"

"Amelia taught me. Her family—*your* family—has been making them for generations. She just showed me because she thought it was a hobby we could do together, but then I got kind of obsessed. And since I moved here in my twenties, I had no idea how I was going to earn a living. I just got a hundred percent focused on it, and luckily it worked out."

"You made all of these?" she said, touching a tabletop lighthouse design constructed from mirrors and glass.

"Yep."

"You're seriously talented."

A panel on the floor was one of the few monochrome pieces, all pale stones and white stained glass. A sheet of paper was taped to it: *Glass and stone on panel, twelve inches by thirty-six inches, $1,600.* The lawyer inside of her, the one who calculated her worth by time sheets and hourly rates, wondered how long it took to make one of these pieces. She asked Kelly.

"It always varies, depending on the size, the material, the design. My energy level. And I'm really busy right now—that's where you come in. I'm making a surprise piece for Amelia."

She unrolled a large sketch and set it on the table.

"It's a Beach Rose Inn sign she can hang out front to replace the old one. My not-so-subtle hint that I want her to reopen next summer."

"Is this a color legend?"

"Exactly. I'm going to fill in this entire sketch with colored pencil but I'm working off this for now. This shows the areas that will be tiles and smalti. The lettering is going to be all shells that Amelia has collected over the years, and then here will be a beach rose. These notes are my materials: sea glass, Venetian tiles, smalti, shells."

She gestured for Marin to follow her to one of the shelves.

"All of these bins are filled with stuff Amelia found."

The containers were labeled: ANGEL WINGS, MOON

SNAIL, BLUE MUSSEL, SLIPPER SHELL. On the bottom shelf were mason jars filled with sea glass.

"She collected all of this stuff?"

Kelly nodded. "Every morning for years, she's walked the beach looking for pieces to bring back to me."

Marin decided she wanted to walk the beach looking for its treasures at least once before she left.

"That sounds like a great morning routine."

"Personally, I like to work first thing in the morning—or very late at night. It's when my mind is most open and creative."

"I want to collect a few things to bring back to New York. To remind me of this trip."

"Go along with Amelia tomorrow. I'm sure she'd love it. Okay, are you ready to get to work?"

"Yes," Marin said, surprised by how excited she felt to do something productive.

"Okay, so you see these mosaics are constructed of hundreds of little pieces. Some are tiles, some are glass, some are smalti...all need to be cut. That takes time, and if you can do some of the cutting, that frees me up for working on the actual sign."

"Don't you have a lot of this stuff already cut? I mean, all these shelves..."

"I ordered specific materials for Amelia's piece. Like this metallic smalti that's too expensive to buy for no reason."

"Smalti?"

"It's special material produced in Venice just for mosaics. It gives us more options than tile because it has various opacities and the colors are extremely vivid. It arrives in sheets and has to be cut by hand." She picked up the odd tool that looked like gardening shears with wheels at the top. "A wheel cutter. Amelia calls it a nipper." She handed it to Marin. "Are you ready?"

"It's worth a try."

Blythe stood outside on her bedroom balcony hoping for decent reception and dialed Kip's phone. Straight to voice mail. Undeterred, she called his office. His secretary started giving some song and dance about a meeting, but Blythe—uncharacteristically—cut her off and said, "Just get him on the line."

"Blythe, this isn't a good time," Kip said when he picked up.

"Have you spoken to Marin?"

Kip sighed. "Not since the middle of last week. I've left messages on her phone. You said you were heading up to the city. Are you still with her?"

"Yes. Actually, I thought she should get away for a few days, so we're in Cape Cod."

"A change of scenery is probably good for her."

"It hasn't been good for her. She's getting worse." Of course, she was omitting a large piece of the Marin puzzle. It was impossible to convey Marin's mental state without telling him the truth about what was going on. But she didn't want to have that conversation over the phone.

"She's had a rough few weeks. She'll rally," Kip said. "Do you want me to talk to her? Put her on the phone."

"She's locked in her room. She's depressed. I'm really worried."

Blythe realized that the only way Marin would accept the situation was if Blythe and Kip showed a united front. She would have to tell him the truth. What was the worst that could happen? He was filing for divorce. Their marriage was over. She didn't want to hurt him, but if it meant saving Marin's sanity, she'd do it.

Kip sighed. "When are you getting back? I'll drive up and spend some time with her."

"I think you should come out here."

"To the Cape? Blythe, I'm bogged down here. I can't just pick up and fly out there right now. Get her back to New York and I'll talk some sense into her."

"Kip, I realize we are getting divorced. I am not asking you for me, I'm asking you for our daughter. For once in your life, put family first."

Chapter Twenty-One

Amelia waited until the house was settled. After years of running the inn, she had a sense of when the inhabitants were in their rooms and it was time to unwind.

Next to her in bed, Kelly brushed out her hair with one hand while holding her e-reader with the other. Amelia couldn't understand how she could choose that device over actual books, but Kelly insisted it was easier on her eyes.

Amelia was irritated with Kelly. It was rare for her to feel that way, and the emotion took her by surprise, so much so that she was almost paralyzed by it. All day, she'd been waiting for the feeling to pass, but it hadn't. And so now it was time to say something.

"Can you put that down for a minute?" she asked, taking off her glasses. She pressed her fingers to the creases of her eyes. She was exhausted; it was one of those days when she felt her age.

"Is something wrong?" Kelly asked, sensitive enough to know the answer to that question.

"I'm a little disappointed by the way you're handling Marin's fragile emotional state."

Kelly sat straight up and placed the e-reader and the brush in her lap.

"What do you mean?"

"Getting her drunk in the middle of the afternoon? Getting *tattoos*? Her mother is very upset and I can't say I blame her. Marin should be spending this week getting fresh air, taking long walks, talking. Discovering the town. We should be helping her deal with all of this in a healthy, constructive way."

Kelly had always been impetuous; she did what she wanted, when she wanted. She was a rule breaker. It was a trait Amelia loved, and it was that fearless exuberance that had helped shake Amelia out of the rut of her marriage, out of her life of resignation, of duty. It was what had made it possible for Kelly to drop everything and move to Provincetown all those years ago. But it was also the thing about Kelly that frustrated Amelia the most.

Kelly sighed. "Okay, when you put it like that, it sounds bad."

"And Paul is a terrible influence on you."

"This has nothing to do with Paul. Listen, Marin was leaving, okay? She was not going to spend another night here. If I hadn't found a way to connect with her, she'd be back in New York at this very moment, probably never to be heard from again. Instead, she's asking me if you will take her on your morning walk tomorrow. She wants to go with you."

Amelia raised an eyebrow. "Is that so?"

"Yes. I told her you'd wake her in the morning."

Silence settled between them. "So what you're saying to me is the ends justify the means?"

Kelly nodded. "Something like that."

"Kelly."

She sighed. "Okay, fine. Maybe I went too far. I'm sorry. My heart was in the right place."

Amelia squeezed her hand. "I know. It always is."

"So much for a calm, uneventful summer," Kelly said, turning off the light on her side of the bed.

Amelia propped herself up on one elbow, gazing at her wife. Kelly's long hair was loose, and her bare face looked not a day older than the girls'. It was that Irish skin, shielded from the sun out of necessity year after year. She leaned over and kissed her.

"It's just one week. Things will get back to normal," Amelia said.

"I'm not complaining! I love having a full house. And I know you do too." Kelly smiled, a hopeful, almost childlike expression taking over her face. "I was think-ing we should ask them to stay another few weeks. They really should experience a proper Provincetown Fourth of July."

"Do you think they'd want to?"

Kelly shrugged. "It's worth a shot."

"Can you believe this whole thing?"

"It's amazing. Beyond amazing. And you know, it's making me think we were too quick to shut down the inn. I know you thought I needed to take it easy because of my health scare. But having the house full of people is a good thing. I think it's good for you, especially."

"It was hard to cancel on people and to turn away guests," Amelia admitted. "I felt particularly bad about the Millers." The Miller family had had standing reser-vations for the first week in August since the summer of 1996. Amelia and Kelly had watched their children grow up. "They must be so disappointed. They didn't even respond to my e-mail. I can't blame them, I guess."

"I'll call them. I'm sure they're over it by now," Kelly said. "So next summer we'll reopen. Maybe Marin and Rachel will come for a while. And we'll make it up to the Millers—give them a free weekend or something."

Amelia smiled. "Okay, then. We'll call this our one-season vacation." She turned off her light and spooned Kelly. "By the way, have you noticed that love might be in bloom?"

"Who?"

"Rachel and Luke Duncan."

"What happened with his girlfriend? That pretty Asian woman he brought last summer?"

Amelia shook her head. "Thomas said Luke ended it just before he came out here. I certainly hope that's the case if he's flirting with Rachel."

"What is it about this place and love at first sight?" Kelly said with a sly smile.

Amelia started to say something, then stopped. Kelly was being romantic; she knew that. But it hit the wrong note with her. Love at first sight was not always harmless and romantic.

Oh, the agony when their affair had first begun! Amelia played all the mental games with herself that people do when they cross a line. She told herself it was just this one time. Then she told herself, *Okay, it's the summer and then it's over.* She assured herself it was harmless as long as no one found out.

But of course, someone always finds out.

Unfortunately, in their case, that person was Nick. Nick, who was supposed to be with his father at a fundraiser at the theater one night but who came home early and went straight to Kelly's room. Nick could no longer wait, could no longer be subtle; he was ready to profess his adoration for Kelly, his need to be with her.

Instead, he walked in on her making love to his mother.

Chapter Twenty-Two

Marin dug her toes into the wet sand.

"Some days I just pick up whatever strikes my fancy," Amelia said. "An oyster shell. A channeled whelk. A sand-dollar skeleton if I'm lucky. Other days, I'm on a mission. Maybe it's green sea glass, or white pebbles."

Marin nodded, bending down to roll up her cargo pants, then tying the drawstring tight to keep them high on her hips. The edges were soaked. The pants had enough pockets to hold whatever she collected that morning. She checked that the bandanna tied around her wrist to shield her tattoo from the sun was still in place, then tilted her face to the sky.

"I have this idea of getting a mason jar and filling it with sea glass from this week and then keeping it next to my bed at home," she said.

"Well, it's a lovely thought, but you won't find that much sea glass in the time you have here."

"I guess I could start with what I find and then just buy the rest to fill in."

Amelia looked at her like she had two heads.

"Buy it? Doesn't that defeat the purpose? When you find it yourself, it has meaning. It marks this day, this walk—this moment in time. Your hands pluck it from the place that produced it and make it your own."

Well, when she put it that way. "I guess I'll just see what I can find."

Amelia nodded her approval.

They walked in silence, both scouring the sand. It crossed Marin's mind that maybe she should ask about Amelia's son. It wasn't that she particularly cared to know—he was nothing more to her than twenty-three chromosomes. An anonymous sperm donor that would have remained anonymous if it weren't for damned technology. But was it rude not to at least acknowledge him? Surely he had walked that very stretch of beach. She shook the thought away; she would not let the donor take root in her mind, in her heart. To ask about him made him too real. It was a betrayal of her father.

Marin spotted something round and pale green. She scooped it up, wet sand getting underneath her fingernails, and showed it to Amelia, who held it up to the sky and pronounced, "It's a pebble, not sea glass."

"How can you tell?"

"No light is coming through it."

Marin stuck it in her back pocket anyway.

Amelia stopped walking. "So Kelly and I were talking last night, and we'd really love it if you would consider staying another week or two. Maybe until the Fourth? It's a fun day here in town and would be the perfect way to end your trip."

Marin's first impulse was to say no, to give her a litany of reasons why she had to get back to New York. But she couldn't come up with a single one.

"That's really generous of you, Amelia. Thanks. I'll talk to Rachel and my mother about it."

"It might not be my business, but I would be remiss if I didn't tell you that I think you need to forgive her."

"What? Who?"

"Your mother."

Marin looked at her sharply. "No offense, but you really don't know the first thing about it."

"Maybe not," Amelia said, using her hand to shield her eyes from the sun so she could look at Marin. "But I know that life is complicated, that people make mistakes, and that it never pays to judge those who love you."

"She lied to me—and my father—my entire life. That's not a mistake, it's a choice."

"Perhaps," she said. "You know, my son, Nicolau, was not speaking to me at the time of his death. We hadn't spoken for several years."

"I didn't know that. What happened?"

"I fell in love with Kelly. While I was married to his father."

Okay, not ideal. But still, it paled in comparison to Blythe's deception.

"Well, I can see how that would be…upsetting. But I still think what my mother did was worse. Way worse. I mean, you can't help who you fall in love with."

"I think Nick believed *he* was in love with Kelly."

"What?"

"They were contemporaries. Kelly was my daughter's best friend. We were all spending the summer here."

"At the inn?"

"Well, it wasn't an inn back then. It was our family home. And yes, at the house."

Marin couldn't believe it. The drama that had taken

place under that very roof! Her biological father, now cast in the light of a tragic romantic figure.

"That sounds...difficult."

"After more than a quarter of a century with Kelly, it's hard to look at our relationship as a transgression, though I suppose it was that. Regardless, I never meant to hurt my children. But I did, and I've had to live with that for thirty years. That's why I don't want to see history repeat itself with you and your mother."

"It's not the same thing," Marin said. "Not at all."

And truly, thirty years of anger didn't seem out of the question to her.

The front porch of the Beach Rose Inn was people-watching central.

Rachel had found a book about Provincetown on the shelf in her room, *Land's End*, by Michael Cunningham, and brought it to the porch rocking chair along with a mug of coffee to settle in for an hour of reading. But how could she focus on *reading* about Provincetown when it was unfolding in front of her in all its dramatic glory? The thing that amazed her the most was the way everyone seemed to know one another. It was so unlike LA, that sprawling metropolis where you kept seeing people you thought you knew and then realized they were just actors from TV shows you once watched.

And now, someone she *did* know appeared on the steps. Luke Duncan.

He carried two serving trays.

"Oh, hi!" She jumped up to help him and took one of the trays, a heavy ceramic hand-painted dish she recognized from the day of the party.

"Thanks. My dad sent me to return these to Amelia."

"Great," she said. *Great?* Her heart thumped. And it wasn't the strong coffee.

He looked around the porch. "What are you guys up to today?"

"I'm just... reading." She pulled her book off the chair and waved it at him.

"That's a good one."

He started to say something else but was distracted by voices just beyond the stairs, and then Marin appeared, trailed by Amelia.

Rachel realized that Marin was truly beautiful. She wore drawstring pants slung low on her hips and a white tank top; her cheeks were flushed from either exercise or the sun, the bright color serving to highlight the deep brown of her eyes. Her shiny dark hair was in a messy knot on top of her head, a few tendrils escaping so artfully it was as if she had been styled for a beach photo shoot.

And Rachel was not the only one who noticed.

"Hey." Luke smiled at Marin, literally *turning his back to her*.

"Hey," Marin said, focused on unwrapping the red bandanna around her wrist.

"Let me get those from you, dear," Amelia said, taking the trays from Luke and Rachel and leaving the three of them to shuffle awkwardly on the porch.

Marin continued to attend to her wrist, unveiling her tattoo, while Luke watched in rapt attention. Rachel struggled to think of a way to dismiss her.

"Did you just get that?" he asked her.

Marin nodded. "Yesterday. After we left the party."

He reached for her hand and held her wrist at an angle so he could see better. Rachel's stomach lurched with jealousy.

"A beach rose?"

"Yeah."

"Awesome."

Rachel wondered how she'd become the third wheel when she was the one who'd originally been talking to him!

"I can't get it wet or in the sun, so probably not the best timing," Marin said. "But whatever. All right, I'm going back to sleep."

With that, she marched into the house, the screen door slamming behind her.

Luke's eyes followed her, his tongue practically hanging out. Rachel sat back in the rocking chair and resumed reading. Or, rather, she pretended to resume reading.

"Your sister's a character," he said finally.

"Half."

"She's half a character?"

"She's my *half* sister."

"Yes. I remember." He ran his hand through his hair, a gesture she found riveting, like everything else about him. "I'm going to get something to eat. Want to come?"

She looked at him in surprise, and then, with great effort to sound casual, replied, "Sure."

Luke led the way down Commercial. They stopped at a souvenir shop, where Rachel was delighted to find a postcard with the Beach Rose Inn on the front. She bought it and decided she would send it to her mother. One block later, Luke stopped in front of a small restaurant with a windowed storefront and a prominent rainbow flag: Café Heaven.

"When you try the food, you'll see it's aptly named." He smiled.

Food or no food, she was already in heaven.

Inside, the blue ceiling was painted with puffy, cartoonish clouds. Every table was full. The host told them it would be just a few minutes and pointed out the specials written on a wall chalkboard.

"Everything is great here, but my favorite are the homemade English muffins. You'll never buy one from the store again."

She nodded. A table was cleared and they were seated.

"So is Amelia taking you sightseeing? Whale watching? There's a lot for you guys to get in while you're here."

"I'm not sure," she said. Even if Amelia had committed them to a jam-packed daily schedule, she would not have admitted it. Was he volunteering to show her around? "What are you doing all summer?"

"Well, I want to help my dad out. And I'm writing a book."

"Like, a novel?" She imagined a sexy spy series—something like James Bond, but American. Or maybe something more literary. *The Corrections,* set in Cape Cod.

"Nonfiction. About the decline of American cities. Sort of an update on Jane Jacobs's classic *The Death and Life of Great American Cities*. Did they make you read that in school?"

"Um, no." Maybe if she'd finished college, she would have gotten around to that one.

"Well, we'll see how productive I can be out here. This is my first summer since high school I'm in Provincetown for two months straight. It's a little bit of an adjustment for me."

"Did you just need some time away from Rhode Island?"

"No. It was actually difficult and complicated to pack up and move here for two months. But when I visited at

Christmas, my dad didn't seem to be doing very well. I have this weird feeling it might be my last summer with him."

"I'm sorry," she said. "But he must be so happy you're here. I'm sure it means a lot to him."

"Yeah, but I felt bad imposing on Bart. I don't want to, like, crowd him or take away from his time with my dad. I talked to him about it beforehand, and he agreed I should come. He said it was a good idea."

Of course Luke would think of Bart. Luke was considerate. Luke was, as far as she could tell, perfect.

"I wish I could stay," Rachel said. "I thought a week would seem like a long time to be in a strange place with people I don't know. Now it feels like I've been here my whole life."

"P-Town has that effect on some people. I couldn't live here year-round, but my dad came here for a three-day writing retreat and literally never left."

If Thomas Duncan could just pick up and move to Provincetown, leaving behind a wife and son, surely Rachel could extend her visit.

"Maybe I'll stay another week or two," she said carefully. She didn't want to scare him off. It's not like she was staying for *him*. Three days into her trip, she still had almost no idea what her dad had been like. The photos were a first step. But a small one. She barely felt any closer to answering the question: Who *was* he?

More important, she felt she needed to start answering questions about herself. Not the least of which was whether or not she was falling in love for the first time.

Marin slept straight through the afternoon and through dinner, and now, at nine at night, she was wide awake.

She stood on the balcony of her bedroom, looking out at the backyard. Hours earlier, Amelia, Kelly, and her mother had had dinner out there together. Their voices had woken her from her last nap of the day. They spotted her up there, gazing out, and they waved her down. They were happy; it was a done deal—everyone was staying until the Fourth of July weekend.

Marin ignored them, though she would have liked to spend some time with Kelly. Instead, she retreated back to bed.

Now the backyard was dark and empty, lit only by the moonlight reflected off the bay. Maybe she should go outside, sit by the water for some fresh air. Afterward, she might be able to return to her room and slip easily back into sleep.

Movement caught her eye. Two shadowy figures close together near the roped-off, outermost edge of the property, just beyond the farthest point of the long table. Her first thought was that people were trespassing, and then she wondered if maybe that's what people did around there. She wouldn't be surprised. Everyone's boundaries seemed a tad fluid, to say the least.

Laughter floated up to her. That's when Marin realized it was Rachel and Luke Duncan.

I could have closed that deal, Marin thought, and then she hated herself for it. That was heartache talking. Oh God. It hurt. She missed Julian so much, she felt in that moment she would do anything to make it stop. Even something stupid, like call him again.

She closed the balcony doors and sat on the edge of her bed. Heart pounding, she dialed.

"Hello?"

His voice brought pain and relief in the same instant.

"Hey," she said. "Sorry it's so late."

"It's not that late," he said. His voice was warmer than it had been on their last phone call—she could tell that already. Or maybe it was wishful thinking.

"How was Chicago?" she asked.

"Well, the job's a long shot. So it went as well as could be expected." Silence.

She was about to say, *I'll be back in New York this weekend,* but then remembered they were staying. It was probably for the best. He wanted time and distance, and he was getting it.

"How's your vacation going?" he asked.

"It's not really a vacation."

Julian didn't ask her to clarify. She felt she would have given anything in that moment to be with him in person, to see his face. To look into his eyes and tell him everything. She remembered their last morning together, the Sunday after her visit to Philadelphia. Telling him how odd it was that her mother practically shoved her out the door. There had been a warmth and wisdom in his eyes that had calmed her then, and she needed it now.

"Can we FaceTime?" she said. It felt like a juvenile request, like they were teenagers talking surreptitiously under the covers in their respective bedrooms on a school night.

"Marin..."

"What? You don't want to see me even on a screen with two states between us?"

He sighed. "It's not that I don't want to see you. It's not that I don't care about you—because I do. But our relationship was a distraction, one that cost us both. I don't know about you, but I need to regroup."

She felt a surge of anger. "Regroup? You have no idea

what I'm dealing with here. Genie turned my whole life upside down!"

"Genie? What does that have to do with anything?"

In that instant, her sorrow turned to fury. She had lost more than he had. She'd lost her identity, the man she'd thought was her father, her relationship with her mother. And, yes, her job. What had he lost? Nothing that couldn't be replaced.

"Yeah, so, I'm sorry our relationship was a distraction. I won't distract you further with more phone calls."

She hung up.

And, remarkably, she felt better than she had in weeks.

Chapter Twenty-Three

The morning was cloudy, not a beach day. Still, Amelia and Marin had already left for Herring Cove. Blythe had her own plans for passing a few hours; she curled up on the porch rocking chair with a copy of Diane Keaton's memoirs. The last time she'd cracked it open had been the night before she went to New York to check on Marin, completely unaware how dramatically things were about to change. And now, Nick Cabral was back in her life. Or, rather, she was in *his* life—in the house where he had spent his summers. At the beach that she had seen in his drawings.

While parts of Nick's life had come to the surface, others were still deeply hidden. What had happened between him and Amelia? How had he died? She wanted to know but didn't want to risk upsetting the woman who had been so generous to all of them. Still, how could she leave this place without asking?

Another question gnawed at her: Should she tell Amelia the truth about her relationship with her son?

That he hadn't been an anonymous sperm donor? That she had, in fact, known him and cared for him—if only for a brief time?

After that first afternoon of passion at his studio apartment, she had started seeing him once a week. Then it was a few times a week. Oh, how it pained Nick—someone who loved spontaneity and impulse above all else—to have to plan. But these were the days before cellular phones (how different their affair would have been today with all the modern technology seemingly built for subterfuge) and they had to pick meeting places and times, and stick with them. Usually it was his apartment during the workweek. They made frantic love, and if they were lucky and had a few hours, they would lie in bed and talk. They discussed artistic and worldly things—conversations that made Blythe feel sharp and engaged. But when she tried to get more personal, he shut her down. He would not talk about his family, alluding only to a big falling-out with his mother. Once, when looking through his older sketchbooks and remarking on the recurring images of the ocean and beaches with high dunes dotted with flowers, he spoke of his Portuguese grandmother's house by the sea.

"We spent every Christmas and summer at her house in Provincetown. In the winter it's a ghost town, and at my grandmother's house, it was easy to feel like we were the only people in the world. And then in the summer, it's a carnival." He smiled and told her he never felt entirely comfortable far from the sea.

When she asked questions, thirsty for more, aching to know this man who was bringing her back to life, he diverted the conversation to more impersonal ground. He would distract her, taking her breath away with motorcycle rides on the Schuylkill Expressway. Her arms wrapped around him, the wind knocking against her, she felt she was holding on for dear life. He circled around the river, whipping past the art museum and the boathouses, and she shrieked in futile protest that he was going too fast. And she was reminded of having once read that the brain experienced fear and falling in love in the same way, often confusing the two.

The only thing predictable about their stolen hours together was that they always took place during the daytime, when Kip was at the office. There was just one exception, and it was the beginning of the end.

It was late August. Kip was out of town, and Nick invited her to go out clubbing with him and his friends. She was excited to have a whole night with him instead of just a few stolen afternoon hours. She dressed playfully in a black miniskirt with a T-shirt covered in geometric shapes in bright colors. She could remember the shirt exactly. God, she felt beautiful that night.

She met Nick at his apartment. He and his friends were already drinking shots and getting high. He put his arm around her, introduced her as his girl.

"Oh yeah," said one of the friends. "The married chick." No one seemed in a hurry to leave the smoke-filled apartment. Eventually, she looked at her watch; it was almost two in the morning.

"We should go," she said impatiently. She offered to drive. They all piled into her BMW, and Nick directed her to a desolate neighborhood filled with warehouses. The club had no sign and no name and it opened just as the legal bars were closing. She hadn't known such places existed.

She nursed a cup of water. After years of treating her

body like an instrument, she couldn't abuse it even for one night. Nick warned her not to put her cup down out of her sight, even for a few seconds. And then he wandered off, and she was left alone in the cavernous space.

What the hell? Why had he bothered to invite her? The music was so loud, she felt it in her chest. She wandered around in circles. She needed to pee but the line for the bathroom was so long—for people who weren't even using it as a bathroom. She wished she were at home, tucked into her bed.

She finally spotted one of his friends. "Have you seen Nick?" She wanted to leave but was afraid to walk to her parked car alone. The friend pointed in a vague direction.

"Where?" she asked, squinting in the darkness.

"By the stairs. See that exit sign?"

"Okay, thanks." She threaded her way through the crowd, doubting that she would find him.

She found him.

He was inside the stairwell. It was barely lit and it reeked. (Now she knew where people were going to pee, since the bathrooms were otherwise occupied.) A bleached blonde wearing a red miniskirt leaned against the wall, her head thrown back, exposing her long white throat. She was pinching her nose. Nick, standing next to her, was busy snorting coke off of a compact mirror.

Blythe backed away.

What was she doing there? The madness of it all was suddenly so clear to her. Sweating, she pushed her way through the club, desperate to get away. Outside, the North Philadelphia streets were dangerously desolate, and she realized how crazy she was being—risking her marriage and now her very safety over some temporary, lust-induced insanity. By the time she reached her car, her hand was shaking so hard she could barely get the key in the door.

When she was finally home, safe in her bedroom, she took off her clothes and threw the outfit in the garbage. She never wanted to see it again, to be reminded of the wretched night. Of her wretched behavior. Guilt-ridden and confused, she pulled her new journal out of her night-stand drawer and poured out her heart: *I've been so lonely, I don't think my husband loves me. I'm in a marriage with no purpose, we will never be a family, and so I did something reckless and stupid and now I'm more angry at myself than I ever was at Kip...*

Kip returned from his business trip the following afternoon; she was resolved to reconnect with him. She pulled his favorite bottle of red from the cellar and cooked sirloin and baked stuffed potatoes. Afterward, she steered him to the bedroom, where she closed her eyes and tried not to imagine her sensual, reckless, maddening lover. She didn't think she'd be able to climax—not only because she often did not with Kip, but also because of the guilt and the mental burden of trying to resist making comparisons. But surprisingly, it was the most physically gratifying sex of their marriage.

She wasn't the only one who noticed.

"Maybe I should go away more often," Kip said, kissing the top of her head. That's when the guilt came in, sweeping through her like a wave of nausea. *It's over with Nick,* she reminded herself. It was a temporary detour, but she was back on track now.

Blythe closed the memoir on her lap. She couldn't focus. Should she tell Marin the truth? Correct her assumption that her biological father was an anonymous sperm donor? Was the truth better or worse?

A woman walked up to the house smoking a cigarette and wheeling a suitcase. Blythe watched her collapse the handle, pick up the bag, then climb up the stairs briskly, without hesitation.

"Can I help you?" Blythe asked, standing.

The woman had thick brown hair threaded heavily with gray and sharp dark eyes above an aquiline nose. Blythe guessed she was around her own age. "I doubt it," the woman said. "I'm here to see my mother."

With that, she brushed past Blythe and strode into the house.

Amelia considered the morning a success.

Marin came up short on her quest for sea glass but Amelia was pleased to find several white wentletraps and a handful of shells from Atlantic razor clams. Marin picked up a sea urchin skeleton, which fascinated her, but it was ugly and she ultimately tossed it back into the sea.

When it was clear the beach had yielded all that it would that day, Amelia ventured to ask Marin, "Are you at all curious about my son? It's okay to ask, you know."

"I really don't want to talk about him. I mean, no offense, but he was just a sperm donor. My father is my father."

Amelia nodded. She did not take offense. It was a difficult situation, and Marin was handling it as well as anyone could be expected to. While she accepted the turn of events on the surface, she clearly rejected it on a deeper level. It was a process, and Amelia knew that one week wasn't enough for her to work through it all. She just hoped she would keep in touch, and if the day came when Marin wanted to really talk, Amelia would be there for her.

They got back into the car and Marin busied herself looking at the shells.

"Isn't it amazing how the beach gives up her treasures? Every day, a gift," Amelia said.

Marin smiled.

They inched along in the car, the five-minute drive now hitting the ten-minute mark. Commercial Street was jammed with traffic.

"I just realized something. There's no traffic light on this street," Marin said.

"Nope. And it's just going to get progressively more crowded all summer until the end of August, when we're about to lose our minds, and then everyone leaves and we feel sad."

A block away from the house, Amelia spotted Blythe waving at them from the porch. "Your mother seems to be trying to get your attention."

Blythe hurried down the steps and met them in the street, barely letting Amelia park the car before leaning in the open passenger-side window.

"Why aren't you answering your phone?" Blythe asked Marin, clearly frustrated.

"I'm not *carrying* my phone."

"Is everything okay?" Amelia said, stepping out of the car. Blythe took her by the arm.

"I didn't want you to be taken by complete surprise."

Amelia's stomach tensed. "What's wrong?"

"Nothing is wrong. But your daughter is here."

Amelia looked at Marin, the words not computing. *Does she mean my* granddaughter? *Is Rachel looking for me?*

And then it hit her.

Nadine.

"Where is she?"

Blythe pointed to the house, and Amelia walked as briskly as her aching legs would allow. For the first time in years, she bemoaned her lost ability to run, her joints as creaky as old floorboards about to give. The entrance foyer was empty. She rushed to the rear of the house. Of course Nadine would be out there, looking at her beloved bay.

Sure enough, Nadine was seated at the farthest end of the table, her back to the house. Amelia approached gingerly, quietly, afraid she would startle her off, like a fawn in the woods.

And like a fawn, Nadine sensed her and turned around.

Amelia's eyes filled with tears. All thoughts of restraint dissolved and she rushed to her daughter, pulled her close.

"You're here," she said, gasping. "You're really here."

Nadine pulled away first, and Amelia got the first chance to take in her face. The last time she'd seen her, she had barely been old enough to drink. Now she was a middle-aged woman. She was changed, and yet Amelia felt that time had stood still.

"The house looks different," Nadine said. "You must have put a lot of money into it."

Amelia almost couldn't process what she was saying. A dozen questions flooded her mind at once, causing a short circuit. So she just nodded, letting the moment wash over her, a tremendous wave that she could not master, could only give in to.

"How long are you here for?" she said finally.

"I'm not sure." Nadine shrugged, a familiar gesture. "A few days."

"You came to see your nieces."

Nadine glanced at the house. "I came to see you."

"I'm so grateful that you did. Whatever the reason."
Silence.

"So Kelly is still here," Nadine said. It wasn't a question.
"I've been following the inn on Facebook. You've really got
quite a business going."

"Yes, well, it's been a labor of love."

She had found Nadine online too. Not on Facebook,
but on her website. She sold handcrafted pottery. All in
the Portuguese tradition. It was beautiful, and she had
longed for a few pieces but didn't dare buy any. Doing so
would have felt like an intrusion.

Unfortunately, there were no personal details on Nadine's website. And so Amelia asked, "Are you married?
Children?"

Nadine shook her head. "I was living with someone for
a while. But we broke up."

"I'm sorry."

Nadine looked away. Amelia let silence sit between
them, resisting the urge to fill it with more chatter.

"So is there space for me to stay here? The website
said you're not taking guests this summer, so I figured my
room would be free."

"Of course! Of course. Come upstairs."

Nadine wheeled her bag into the house and followed
Amelia up to the third floor. Passing the closed door to
Kelly's studio, Blythe had the anxious thought that she
had to warn her about Nadine's arrival so she wouldn't be
blindsided.

"Who is the woman on the porch?" Nadine asked.

"Blythe? She's the mother of one of the girls."

"Interesting," Nadine said. "And where are these…
girls?"

"One of them should be here—she was with me when I returned to the house. Marin. She looks just like your brother."

"Does she now." Her voice was so flat, it was clearly a statement, not a question.

"And Rachel is probably here somewhere. Marin is somewhat guarded, a little tightly wound. Rachel is sunnier—very California. She's from LA." Amelia could hear the awkward nervousness in her voice. She opened the door to Nadine's old bedroom.

"I'd never recognize it," Nadine said.

"Thirty years is a long time."

Nadine pulled her suitcase onto the bed and unzipped it. "I'm going to sleep for a few hours, if you don't mind. I'm exhausted." She told Amelia she had flown from Italy to Boston two days ago, stayed with a friend, and then taken the ferry over that morning.

"Of course." Amelia resisted the urge to hug her and started to walk down the hallway, but then she poked her head back in and said, "I can't tell you how happy I am that you're here."

Nadine offered a tight smile.

Amelia closed the door behind her and made her way quickly down the hall to the studio. She knocked but got no response. The door was locked. She hurried down to their bedroom and dialed Kelly's cell. It went straight to voice mail. Damn it! Of course she didn't have her phone with her. But where had she disappeared to?

Chapter Twenty-Four

Rachel did little but daydream about Luke Duncan.

She kept mentally replaying the time they spent together, analyzing every word of the conversation, every shared glance between the two of them. Still, she had no clue as to how he felt toward her. On the one hand, they had spent a platonically friendly afternoon-turned-evening out. On the other hand, when he had walked her back to the inn, they'd spent a few minutes looking at the water in the bay and it was undeniably romantic.

But that would have been the perfect time for him to try to kiss her. And he hadn't.

She hated to admit that she had never felt this way before. Shouldn't a woman have at least one major love affair under her belt by this time? She blamed it on her upbringing. With no admirable examples of steady, secure coupledom, she did not know what to aspire to. Of course she'd had attractions and hookups. But she had never felt this mental preoccupation, the kind that left her constantly sleepless and dreamy at the same time.

How could she leave on July fifth and never see him again? Impossible.

Deciding she should get out of the house and do something productive, she walked to the post office to mail the postcard she'd bought for Fran. By the time it reached her, Rachel would be home already, but she sent it because she thought it would be a nice gesture. That, and because on some level, she wanted to prompt her mother into showing some interest in what was going on in her life.

Dear Fran:

Provincetown is beautiful and eccentric. Sand, surf, yoga, seafood, and plenty of outdoor drinking. It's your type of place. I thought you'd be happy to see where donor dad is from.

Love, Rachel

A block from the house, she spotted Kelly, wearing sunglasses and a faded baseball hat with a fish on it. She looked at the ground as she walked.

Rachel called out to her. Startled, Kelly stopped short.

"Oh, hi, Rachel. What's going on?"

"Not much. But Amelia was just looking for you."

"Thanks," Kelly said. Then: "I'm sorry. I'm distracted. Did you say what Amelia needed?"

"I think she wanted you to know that her daughter just showed up."

Rachel could have sworn Kelly paled under her freckles.

Blythe couldn't believe it. Nadine, the sister Nick had spoken about with such affection. The sister he'd left Philadelphia to visit, never to return. *Here.*

It was the closest she'd felt to seeing Nick again. And this feeling helped answer one of the questions she'd been grappling with, the question of whether she should tell the truth to Amelia.

She would do it. And it was the first step toward telling Marin the truth, if she was ever going to be able to actually go through with *that.*

When would be the right time to talk to Amelia? She pondered this for a full five minutes, pacing the floor in her bedroom. Then she realized there was no right time—the time was now.

On her way down the stairs, she heard movement on the floor above. Amelia must be in the studio with Kelly. Fine; she would tell them both at the same time. She backtracked and headed to the third floor but stopped midway down the hall when she heard their raised voices.

"Can't she stay in one of the first-floor bedrooms? It's awkward having her right next door to the studio. It's just..."

"It was her old bedroom. Kel, I really need you with me on this. Try to be happy for me."

"I *am* happy for you. I just don't want any negative energy around here. Not now."

"The energy isn't negative. Why would she bother coming here to be negative? It's a turning point. The one I've been waiting for all these years. And I really need you to be less cynical."

"I'm not being cynical! She shows up after thirty years of demonizing us, of punishing you, and I don't get to say, *Hey, let's just make sure there are boundaries here?*"

"She wasn't punishing me. She was hurt. We hurt her."

"She didn't tell you Nick was gone until after the funeral. She buried him on another continent. That's not punitive? Frankly, I don't understand why you don't have a little more anger of your own."

"You don't understand because you're not a mother."

"Oh, I have nothing to contribute to this conversation because I'm not a *mother?*"

"That's not what I meant."

Blythe turned at the sound of movement behind her.

"Mom? What are you doing out here? Eavesdropping?" Marin said, hands on her hips.

"No, I was just...never mind. What are *you* doing up here?"

"I'm helping Kelly with a project."

"What kind of project?"

"Forget it. Don't say anything."

"Why would I say anything?"

"I don't know. Why would you be standing in the hall listening to their conversation? Clearly with nothing better to do, you're turning into a busybody."

"Marin, I've had about enough of your attitude. You're upset—I get that. I can't change the past, but I'll be damned if I'm going to be punished for it for the rest of my life!" She was surprised to find herself choking up, tears in her eyes.

The door to the studio opened. Kelly and Amelia looked at them.

"Everything okay out here?" said Amelia.

"Just fine!" Blythe said before turning to run down the stairs.

Was there a more awkward family dinner imaginable?

Marin wanted to drink, but ever since the afternoon

binge at the A-House, she couldn't even look at a glass of wine. Across the table, her mother was getting good and hammered, and for the first time that week, Marin couldn't blame her.

"So let me get this straight," Nadine said. "Rachel, you knew that your father was a sperm donor, but you"—looking at Marin—"thought your mother's husband was your father until last week."

"That's right," Rachel chirped.

"And you found each other through a *website?*" She said the word *website* as if it were *spaceship*.

"Yes."

Silence at the table.

Marin couldn't believe this woman was her aunt. When Marin met Amelia, despite her feelings of betrayal and her sense of loss with her dad, she'd felt at least a warmth and connectedness. She was able to accept and embrace the woman as her relative. But this black-eyed shrew was pissing her off with all her questions. Or, more specifically, with the tone of her questions—as if this were all some dubious tale.

Amelia had cooked fish stew, apparently Nadine's favorite.

"I'd love to learn how to make this," Rachel said. "It's just so good!"

"I'd be happy to share a few recipes," said Amelia. "We Portuguese have such wonderful food traditions. I would be thrilled to introduce you to that part of your culture."

"You know," Nadine said, addressing the entire table, "the last time I had this meal, Kelly and I were best friends."

Rachel and Blythe looked at her. Kelly stopped eating.

Marin, knowing where this story might go, looked at Amelia, who subtly squeezed Kelly's arm.

"Really? When's the last time you saw each other?" said Rachel.

Nadine seemed about to say something but then thought better of it. Finally, she said simply, "A very long time ago."

"Well, it's great you're here now."

"That's the thing about this town," said Nadine. "People come, people go. Sometimes forever."

"Thanks for that bit of philosophy," Kelly said.

Amelia shot her a look.

"I totally get that," Rachel said. "This is a really special place. So I was thinking, Amelia, if you didn't mind—I'd love to stay for the summer."

"What?" Marin and Blythe said in unison.

"Oh, Rachel, of course. That would be wonderful," Amelia said.

Nadine narrowed her eyes. "You know, that's not a bad idea. I think I'll stay awhile myself."

Crazy, all of them. Marin didn't care what Rachel did—she was leaving after the Fourth, with or without her.

Chapter Twenty-Five

A giant pink whale made of papier-mâché and wood took up most of Bart and Thomas's front lawn. Bart was administering to it with a tape dispenser while Paul spray-painted its tail.

"For heaven's sake, it looks like a giant sperm," Kelly called out her window as she pulled her truck into their driveway. "Gotta love Fourth of July," she said to Rachel. "It's Mardi Gras, New Year's Eve, and the Gay Pride Parade rolled into one. And that's *before* the fireworks."

Bart and Thomas were borrowing Kelly's truck so they could transport their Fourth of July float to the East End for the start of the parade at eleven.

Rachel opened her door and hopped out. On a morning when she should have been packing up to leave the next day, she was instead throwing herself headfirst into summer, Provincetown-style.

"A giant sperm is exactly the look we were going for," Paul said, spraying the lowermost point of the whale's belly.

Rachel couldn't help glancing around for any sign of Luke.

"Luke's out back," Bart said.

Damn! Was she that obvious?

"Oh? I was just...great whale."

"Thanks, kid. Go on back to the pool."

She looked at Kelly. "Do you need me to—"

"I'm all good. I just want to hear their justification for this pink monstrosity, then I'm walking home." She winked at her.

Okay.

Rachel walked around the side of the house, following a flat-stone path to the pool. The walkway was lined with purple flowers; they smelled like the blooms her mother had had outside of the first house they'd lived in, when Rachel was in elementary school. She felt a pang of nostalgia for a time she didn't particularly want to revisit; somehow everything was starting to feel precious and acute, and she wasn't sure what to do about the emotions that seemed to wash over her every five minutes.

Luke was perched on the edge of a lounge chair, just as he had been the day of the party. But today he wore swim trunks and a heather-blue T-shirt that tugged at his wide shoulders as he typed into his phone.

"Hey," she called out, trying to sound casual.

He turned around, surprised—understandably—to see her.

"Oh, hey, Rachel," he said. "What's going on?"

"Kelly just brought her truck over so Bart and your dad can get their float to the East End. Are you going to the parade?"

"Probably. But first I want to get a few laps in. Back home I go to the gym, but here I have to be disciplined and get what exercise I can from swimming."

"Totally, I get it. I should exercise more." Ugh. She felt like an idiot.

"You're welcome to stay and use the pool."

Her heart leaped. Sure, it might just be a pragmatic invitation from someone who believed in the importance of exercise. Or maybe it was more.

"Are you sure? I don't want to, like, get in the way."

He smiled, dimples and all. Oh, she wanted to get in his way.

"You're not in the way. I give myself an hour or so out here in the morning before I get to work."

She shrugged her beach bag off her shoulder and sat on the lounge chair next to him. He looked up at the sun.

"I was waiting for it to get warmer, but I guess I should stop being such a wimp," he said.

"You really should."

"Oh yeah? Okay, Esther Williams—you first."

"Who's Esther Williams?"

"You don't know who Esther Williams is? She was a major actress in the forties. She swam in most of her big roles."

"Never heard of her."

"How old are you?"

"Not old enough to have gone to the movies in the 1940s."

He laughed. "Okay, so maybe I'm a little extra into old movies because of my dad. Anyway, stop stalling. Into the pool."

Rachel pulled off her T-shirt and cutoff denim shorts. Underneath, she had her favorite tie-dyed bikini from Beach Bunny on Robertson. It had been a rare splurge; she'd seen it in the window driving by and couldn't resist.

She had a feeling it was about to pay for itself.

Luke was definitely noticing her body, but as soon as he saw her noticing him noticing her, he looked away. She loved that reticent quality he had—so unlike most guys! Maybe it was because he was older. Either way, it just stoked her slow burn.

She would have loved to do a big, splashy dive, but the pool wasn't deep enough, so she settled for wading into the shallow end and pushing into a quick breaststroke.

Damn, it was cold. She let out a little yelp despite herself.

"Hate to say I told you so," Luke called from the side of the pool. She kept moving, her heart pounding from the cold and from her acute awareness of him watching her. She stopped in the deep end, treading water. She felt her hair fanning out around her like a mermaid's. Luke had gotten into the shallow end and was moving into his own set of laps.

They swam in opposite directions, passing each other every half minute or so, their bodies far enough apart not to collide but close enough to thrill her. But too soon, she felt herself grow tired, and she cursed her lack of stamina. *More cardio, less yoga,* she told herself. Breathless, she was finally forced to paddle over to the side of the pool and hold on to the ledge.

Luke swam over to her.

"Quitting time already?"

"Just a little break." Their faces were inches apart. His eyes were the color of the pool and the sky. His skin, tanner than it had been just two days ago, glistened with water. The word *godlike* came to mind.

Get a grip!

She felt like she should say something along the lines of *Don't let me slow you down,* but she didn't want to break the moment. It was eye-lock, and she didn't dare breathe, let alone speak.

Was he going to kiss her?

And then a tapping sound, metal on glass. They both looked up; Thomas waved to them from a second-floor window.

"He must need something. I'm going to check."

He hoisted himself out of the pool, his arms all lean muscle. She had to force her eyes away, knowing that Thomas was watching them.

"Are you going to Paul's party tonight?" he asked, toweling off.

"Paul's party? No, I think we have some dinner thing on the East End." Damn. Why weren't they going to Paul's party?

"Well, maybe I'll see you guys at the pier for the fireworks after." He grinned.

She would definitely be at the pier if she had to go on her own. If she had to ride there on her own on the back of a pink whale float! Rachel climbed out of the pool by the metal ladder in the deep end, and Luke handed her a towel. "Thanks. And thanks for the swim. Clearly, I need the cardio!"

"Anytime. See you at the fireworks."

She dressed and walked back out front to her bike, more buoyant than she'd been in the water.

Marin woke up feeling as exhausted as if she hadn't slept at all, even though she'd gotten ten hours. She wanted to go back to sleep, but at ten in the morning, Commercial Street sounded like Times Square on New Year's Eve at midnight. Somewhere in the distance, an early firework exploded.

She groaned and burrowed under the covers.

By this time tomorrow, she would be driving back to New York City. She had to admit, there were a few things she would miss about Provincetown. At the top of the list, Kelly.

Marin looked at the flower inside her wrist. Kelly had pulled her right out of her funk, if only for a little while. She was thankful she'd run into her in the hallway the morning she'd meant to slink off and drive away. That ride to the East End, the wind blowing through the truck's open windows, the sun on her face—it had been a pure moment of summer, a deep exhale.

She decided she would get her alone so she could thank her—if it wasn't too late. She'd probably left to watch the parade. And then they were all going to Sandra Crowe's house that night, so she might not have time alone with her at all.

At that hour, breakfast was over. She looked out her window, and, sure enough, only her mother and Amelia were still at the table. They looked deep in conversation; Amelia was downright transfixed by whatever her mother was saying. Good. Hopefully they'd be at it for a few more minutes and she'd have time for some private words with Kelly.

She went down to find her.

The sound of blaring pop music and raucous cheering on Commercial Street reached them even in the back of the house. There had been a time when Amelia wouldn't have missed a second of the parade. But she felt oddly removed this year. Perhaps it was because she didn't have the pressure to show Beach Rose Inn guests the way the Fourth of July was done in Provincetown. Or maybe because she was so consumed with meeting her new granddaughters, figuring out what it all meant. The usual P-Town revelry was no match for the happiness Rachel and Marin had brought her.

"I really appreciate you having us here," Blythe said.

Amelia poured them both more coffee. "Oh, my dear. You can't imagine how much it's meant to me. I'm sorry to see you go! Though if you have to leave, we will at least give you a spectacular send-off tonight. We do the Fourth of July like no one else."

Blythe nodded. "Yes. Well, before we leave, I feel like there's something I should tell you. That you deserve to know."

Amelia looked at her expectantly, but it took Blythe a moment to speak. It was clear she was struggling with whatever it was she had to say. Amelia had to hold herself back from prompting her, afraid she would shut her down completely. The sounds from the street seemed to grow more boisterous in the silence.

"Nick wasn't my sperm donor," Blythe said.

What? Amelia felt an immediate sense of loss. Marin wasn't Nick's daughter? How could that be? She looked just like him.

"I don't understand…"

"He was my lover. We had an affair."

It took a moment for her words to sink in. Nick had known this woman? Loved this woman?

"Oh my God."

Blythe nodded, openly sobbing now. "I've never told anyone—not in all these years. It was the summer, and he left to visit Nadine in Italy, and I never saw him again. By the time I realized I was pregnant with Marin, Nick was long gone and I was working on my marriage."

Amelia began crying herself and reached for Blythe's hand.

"Oh, dear. What secrets we all keep. It must have been difficult."

Blythe nodded, trying to pull it together.

"Thank you," Amelia said. "Thank you for telling me." She looked at Blythe as if seeing her through fresh eyes. Imagining her as her son might have seen her thirty years ago. It was the closest Amelia had felt to Nick in a long time.

Amelia leaned forward, embracing her, and they cried together for the man they had both lost.

Marin climbed the stairs to the third floor. The door to the studio was closed, but she heard Kelly's voice from inside.

"I appreciate the follow-up call. I just have to process—yes, I know. Look, if you need me to say that you've made my options clear so that you feel you've done your job as my oncologist, then consider it said."

Marin froze.

The door opened.

"Hey," Kelly said casually—so casually that if Marin hadn't just overheard the snippet of conversation, she wouldn't have known anything was wrong.

"What's going on?" Marin said.

"Nothing."

"Oh no, you don't," said Marin. "We got drunk that first week and I told you all my messy shit." She flashed her wrist tattoo.

"Marin, not now."

"Then when? I'm leaving in the morning. In case you've forgotten, I'm not a fixture here like everyone else in this town."

Kelly seemed to consider this. "Fine. If you're leaving tomorrow, you can take a secret with you."

Marin nodded.

"I don't want to talk here."

"Where, then?"

The A-House was decked out in Fourth of July splendor, complete with red, white, and blue pinwheels on the bar, mini–American flag toothpicks garnishing every drink, and a shirtless bartender wearing an Uncle Sam hat. The bar was packed, standing room only. Kelly elbowed her way to a spot in the corner closest to the video screen and waved the bartender over. He poured two kamikaze shots. Marin downed hers, even though it was not yet noon, even though she'd sworn off alcohol for the duration of her trip. Because on a gut level, she knew she was going to need it.

"So," Kelly said over the music—Whitney Houston's rendition of "The Star-Spangled Banner," complete with video accompaniment. "It appears that my cancer is back. It's in my lungs now."

The words stung like a slap in the face. *Think of something positive to say.*

"I'm really sorry, Kelly. I know this is not good news, not at all what anyone wants to hear. But—at the risk of sounding like a massive cliché—you can beat this."

Kelly shook her head. "Well, that's the thing, gorgeous. I can't beat it—the doctor was pretty clear on that. I can just maybe buy some time. Hence his follow-up call this morning to make sure I didn't pull a Virginia Woolf."

It took a beat for Marin to get the reference.

"Oh, Kelly! How does your doctor know for sure?"

Kelly smiled. "Marin, come on. We're both grown-ups here."

"You need a second opinion. Come to New York. My former boss knows the head at—"

"Marin, no. There isn't a fancy doctor in New York or in Boston or on the moon who can fix this. It's spread to my lungs, and my brain could be next. He said I'd be lucky to get six months. And who knows what state I'll be in by the end."

Kelly called out for another shot. "Can you imagine that? To me, there's nothing worse. Actual death isn't as bad as living death."

"Kelly, don't go there. You have to think positive. They say your mental outlook is really important—"

Kelly touched her hand. "Marin, you have to promise me—swear to me—that you won't tell Amelia."

"What? Kelly, you have to tell her. You can't just blind-side her one day, months from now. She needs to know what's going on." She couldn't imagine Amelia without Kelly. With their twenty-year age difference, Amelia surely had always assumed she would be the one leaving Kelly behind. She had no doubt planned for that.

Not for this.

"I'm not going to blindside her. But I do want to enjoy this Fourth of July—and I want her to as well. Because it will be our last together."

Chapter Twenty-Six

"Happy Fourth of July!" A waiter uncorked a bottle of champagne in Sandra Crowe's foyer.

"Fancy, fancy," Nadine said.

There was no kitschy Fourth of July décor in sight. The house was all white and beige and cream.

"It's a good house," said Amelia. "Strong bones. Not my taste, but these high ceilings do make for a dramatic space. So where's your piece, hon? I can't wait to see it."

Kelly glanced around. "The dining room, I think? Sandra will show us, I'm sure."

"Unbelievable what rich people will waste their money on. Never fails to amaze me," said Nadine.

Kelly threw Amelia a look and said, "Okay. Well, then—I'm off to find the bar. Anyone else need a vodka shot?"

Amelia wanted everyone to get along. It was Kelly's favorite summer holiday. And now Nadine was being sour and threatening to spoil it. Her daughter obviously had mixed feelings about being back, and that was understandable. Kelly just had no patience for it, which was unlike her.

Something was up with Kelly. Amelia had been eager to talk to her all day about Blythe's revelation. She'd been involved with Nick! But Kelly had made herself scarce, skipping the parade and instead taking a long solo bike ride to the beach. When she finally got back, she had barely enough time to shower and change for the dinner party, never mind have a long conversation. And now they were at the party and she was already drifting away.

Maybe she was just trying to give Amelia space to reconnect with Nadine. But it was impossible to entirely focus on Nadine when it was Blythe and Marin's last night. She hated to admit it to herself, but Blythe's confession that morning affected the way she felt toward Marin; she wasn't just the product of an anonymous sperm donation. She was a love child. Nick's love child!

"There you are!" Sandra breezed into the entrance hall, her outstretched, beckoning arms covered in chunky gold bracelets. "The guest of honor!"

She gave Kelly the European two-kiss greeting. Then she turned to Amelia and took one of her hands in both of hers. "It is so lovely of you to make it. Thank you for sharing your magnificent, talented wife with me. I am in love with the piece—*in love*."

"Amelia taught me everything I know," Kelly said.

Sandra clapped her hands together. "You two are *adorable*." She turned to Nadine and introduced herself.

"Oh, I'm sorry—where are my manners?" Amelia jumped in and made the round of introductions.

"Are you ready to see my mermaid?" Sandra said. "I've named her: Ariel. *The Little Mermaid*! One of my favorite movies," she said.

"The *cartoon?*" said Nadine incredulously.

Amelia bit her lip to keep from smiling.

"What do you think?" Sandra asked Kelly. Amelia knew what Kelly was undoubtedly thinking: that Sandra had turned her mythical Siren into a Disney character.

Before Kelly could respond, Sandra said, "We're still on for you to do the window in my master bathroom, right? If anyone here tonight tries to steal you away from me, you just let me know. They'll have to wait their turn."

Amelia squeezed Kelly's hand.

"Sure," said Kelly.

"How soon can you start?"

"I have one piece before it. But I can come measure the window soon and we can talk about color and design."

"Fabulous! This weekend?"

Kelly hesitated, then said, "Sure. Why not."

Sandra snapped her fingers at Tanya. "Gather everyone in the dining room."

Amelia, Kelly, Nadine, and the girls followed Sandra across the foyer into a cavernous room with a marble table that could seat twenty. On the farthest wall, behind the head seat of the table, was Kelly's mosaic. It looked absolutely magnificent, dramatic in the space. The room, painted oxblood, picked up all the deep tones of the piece.

Waiters handed them flutes of champagne. Behind them, voices of the other party guests filled the hall.

"Everyone, gather round," Sandra sang out, moving a chair out of the way so she could stand at the head of the table. "I'm so delighted to have you all here to celebrate the Fourth of July. Tonight, we have a special guest, the brilliant artist Kelly Hanauer. This fabulous piece behind me is her work, so, Kelly, why don't you come up here and tell us a little bit about it."

Kelly looked at Amelia, a deer in headlights.

"Might as well get it over with," Amelia murmured to her.

"If I'd known this was going to be a dog-and-pony show, I would never have come."

"It's the price of doing business, my dear," Amelia said. "I'll hold your drink."

Kelly reluctantly walked to the front of the table and stood next to Sandra.

"Thanks, Sandra. I'm so happy to see it in this space—you gave her a perfect home. As you can all see, the design is a mermaid, and she's formed from a combination of materials including stones, shells, mother-of-pearl, stained glass…"

Across the room, Amelia saw Nadine and Marin talking. Amelia's vision blurred, and for a fraction of a second, it was Nadine and Nick.

Her heart beat fast at the thought of the last time she'd seen her children together. They'd come at her like wolves, Nick shouting, Nadine crying and breaking things. Had she deserved it? Yes. When parents hurt their children, purposefully or not, they get what they get.

The first fear, her immediate thought when Nick discovered her with Kelly, was that he would tell Otto. Oh, how foolish she'd been. As if her marriage mattered at all in the big picture. By that time, it was already over. They were both drifting, going through the motions. Still, the horror she'd felt at the thought of him learning of her affair. It was funny how much time one wasted worrying about the wrong things.

In the end, Otto had forgiven her. And when he died,

she'd genuinely mourned him. Without her family, because Nick was gone by that time and Nadine did not come home to bury her father. Even for that unjustifiable, selfish act, Amelia blamed herself. She had set the family adrift, and so in the end it all came back to her.

Yes, Otto had forgiven her. But Nick...

"I *love* her," he'd spit.

"Love who?" Amelia had asked, genuinely bewildered. The conversation took place in the kitchen the day after Nick had walked in on her and Kelly.

"Kelly!"

"What? Since when?"

"Since freshman year! I'm the one who convinced her to spend the summer here!"

Amelia panicked. Had Kelly been with Nick and then turned to her?

"You've been dating her? Why didn't you say anything?"

"No, I wasn't with her! She's barely been around this entire month. And now I know why."

"What's all the screaming about?" Nadine appeared in the doorway.

"Oh, nothing much," said Nick. "Mom's just been fucking Kelly."

Nadine, her olive skin burnished even darker from a month in the sun, turned white.

"Stop it," Nadine said. "That's not true."

"Tell her," Nick said.

Amelia looked helplessly between the stricken faces of her two children. "I'm sorry."

"How could you do this to Dad?"

Ah, yes—there it was. Nadine had always been very much a daddy's girl, which had been adorable when she was a child. But it became less adorable as Nadine grew older and forgave Otto for every misstep while blaming Amelia for everything. It did not matter that for all the summers in recent memory, Otto had made it clear that he preferred twelve-hour days of fishing to any time spent as a husband or father. Otto, who drank from the moment he stepped foot in the house at six at night until he passed out. She had been sleeping on the foldout couch in her studio at the house in Boston for years and had moved into one of the extra bedrooms on the second floor at the beach house—not that her children thought anything of it. She didn't know what she had done wrong as a mother to make Nick and Nadine think of herself and Otto only as their caregivers, not as individuals with their own needs and frailties. Maybe that was how all children were until they became parents themselves. Amelia never got the chance to find out.

And so Nadine, in her furious defense of her father, came at Amelia.

"I hate you!" she screamed, lunging for her. Amelia jumped aside, and Nadine grabbed the serving bowl of seafood paella and threw it to the floor. Shrimp, mussels, lobster, risotto, and glass flew everywhere. Nadine was not finished; she started for a shelf filled with plates but Nick restrained her.

Amelia realized, as Nadine tried to tear apart the kitchen, that she had given her daughter the perfect excuse to turn her adolescent rejection of her mother into something far more damning. And something much more permanent.

Marin wondered if she could go home early without seeming rude. How could she spend the night making small talk, waving miniature American flags and watching fireworks, knowing that Amelia was oblivious to the fact that her life was about to be shattered?

She didn't agree with Kelly's decision not to tell her that the cancer was back, and she especially didn't agree with her choice not to tell her that her doctor had given her such a grim prognosis. If it were Marin's spouse, she would want to know, to have time to prepare. If Amelia knew how few nights she had left with her wife, Marin doubted she would waste one of them at this stuffy party.

A waitress passed around crab cakes with aioli sauce served on red, white, and blue herringbone-patterned china. She bit into one and spotted Nadine heading toward her. Oh God, just who she didn't want to talk to.

"So this is it. Your last night," Nadine said. She held an hors d'oeuvres plate in one hand and a glass of champagne in the other.

"That's right."

"Too bad we didn't really get to talk very much. Hopefully the trip wasn't a total wash for you."

Marin frowned. "Not at all. Why would it be?"

"I don't know. You tell me."

"I have no idea. I came to meet my grandmother. And I did, obviously."

"You came here with a woman you'd never met before so you could both meet your *grandmother?* I would imagine you have a pretty full life back in New York City, complete with grandparents from the people who actually raised you."

"It's complicated," Marin said.

Nadine nodded, raising her glass of champagne to Marin's glass of ice water. "To complications," she said.

"Yeah. Sure." Marin glanced at Rachel across the room, hoping she'd catch her eye and come rescue her.

"Although you know what I bet you don't have in New York City?"

Losing patience, Marin simply shrugged.

"An enormous beach house," said Nadine.

"Excuse me?"

Amelia joined them, smiling at the sight of her daughter and granddaughter together, oblivious to the fact that her daughter was basically accusing Marin of being a sleazy opportunist.

"Hi, girls. Come out back. There are tables by the pool."

Nadine smiled at her mother. "Lead the way."

"Oh, Marin—since you have a handbag, can you take this home for me?" She slipped her one of the china plates.

"What's this for?"

"Mosaics," Amelia whispered with a wink.

"Oh, Mother," said Nadine impatiently. "Is that any way to behave at your age? Stealing from a dinner party?"

"Do you think Sandra Crowe is going to miss one plate? Look at this place. Besides, she appreciates Kelly's art. She'd be flattered."

Nadine shook her head.

Amelia touched Marin's arm to bring her along.

"You know what?" Marin said. "You two go on ahead. I'm going to find the bathroom." Actually, she was going to find Kelly.

An idea was forming, one she wasn't entirely comfortable with. But she realized she wasn't choosing the thought—the thought was choosing her.

* * *

Sandra Crowe's guests, several dozen of them, gathered by the pool. Red, white, and blue paper lanterns were strung all around the veranda, and glowing paper lanterns floated in the pool. Rachel sat with Nadine and two couples visiting for the weekend from New York and Connecticut. The man to Rachel's left spent a full twenty minutes telling her all the ways Provincetown differed from the Hamptons. He went through it in such meticulous detail, it was as if his assessment were the result of a long scientific study.

She half listened, all the while thinking of the way Luke had looked into her eyes. Had he been about to kiss her? What would have happened if Thomas hadn't knocked on the window?

Rachel's talkative new friend mercifully wandered off to visit another table. She wasn't alone for long. Sandra Crowe slipped into the seat next to her.

"I have been so looking forward to meeting Amelia's granddaughters and I've barely had time to *look* in your direction," she said. "Are you enjoying yourself?"

"Yes! This is such a great place you have here. I love your house."

"I love *your* house," Sandra said, touching her arm. She wore a pile of gold bracelets that made a clinking noise when she moved her hand. Rachel wasn't sure what Sandra meant but then realized she was talking about the inn.

"Oh, it's not really my house," she said.

"Damn right it's not," chimed in Nadine from the other side of the table.

Rachel was momentarily startled, but the sweet smile on Nadine's face contradicted her sharp tone.

Sandra turned to her. "Nadine, do you know how

many times I've offered to buy that house? And now they're not even running the inn—probably because it's too much work. And really, at your mother's age, who needs that much work? Don't you agree?"

"As a matter of fact, I do."

"You tell your mother that when she's ready to unload it, I will write her a check for the asking price."

"We'll talk," said Nadine.

Rachel, having nothing to add to the real estate conversation, glanced at her phone to check the time. She was itching to leave and looked around for any signs that dessert was on its way out.

Was it too late to head over to Paul's party? She was ready for some fireworks. And she wasn't thinking of the ones in the sky.

Marin watched Kelly from across the table. The way Kelly talked and laughed and toasted the holiday, Marin almost wondered if she'd imagined their conversation at the A-House. She *wanted* to believe she'd imagined the conversation.

Finally, Kelly excused herself, and it was the opening Marin had been waiting for. She trailed her into the house, calling out to her in one of the beige living rooms.

Kelly turned around, startled.

"Jeez, Marin. You scared me. What are you doing?"

"Following you."

"Obviously." She tugged her long hair out of its ponytail and shook it loose. Her cheeks were flushed under the smattering of freckles.

"Are you okay?"

"I'm fine," she said irritably. "Go back to the party."

"Kelly, I'm really afraid you're not dealing with this

news at all. How can you be here talking and laughing like nothing is wrong?" Her eyes filled with tears.

Kelly put her hands on Marin's shoulders. "Marin, keep it together. It's the Fourth of July. The official start of the summer season. And it's your last night here, so please—if I can have a good time, so can you."

"What if it's not my last night?" she said.

"Meaning?"

"I'm thinking of staying. I know you don't want to tell Amelia what's going on right now. But I want to be here when you finally do."

Kelly gave her a quizzical look, wrinkling her pert nose and narrowing her eyes.

"Stay for how long?"

"A month. Or maybe until the end of the summer. I don't know exactly. I'm just not ready to leave. Would that be okay with you?"

"Don't do this because of what's going on with me."

"It's not just that," Marin said, and she realized it was true. She wasn't ready to get back to the mess of her own life yet. "I like it here."

"Well, in that case, I'm all for it. I told Amelia we should have kept the inn open this summer. She is happiest with a full house, and to have it filled with family? It's a dream come true." Kelly stepped forward and hugged her. "Having you here for the summer will be good for all of us."

Marin exhaled in her embrace, feeling good about her decision.

"Marin—hey. Are you heading out?" Rachel had somehow snuck up behind them.

Marin did want to leave. She was exhausted.

"Yeah. Soon."

"You girls should go to the pier and get a good spot for the fireworks. We'll meet you there soon."

"No fireworks for me. I'm going home," Marin said.

"I was thinking of stopping by Paul's party," Rachel said.

Kelly looked at her phone. "It's probably winding down. It's almost fireworks time. Come on, Marin. It's the best part of the day. I'm going to round up Amelia and your mother now."

When she was gone, Marin turned to Rachel.

"What's the deal with Paul's party? Everyone we know is here." Oh—not everyone, she realized. Marin sighed. "For God's sake, Rachel. Stop chasing that guy."

Rachel looked stricken. "What do you mean?"

"Paul's party? Luke? I *mean,* it's obvious every time I see that guy he's ready to jump into my pants."

"Oh my God, you're disgusting!"

"I'm disgusting? Okay, fine. Disgusting, but accurate."

"You're just jealous!" said Rachel.

"Of what?"

"Your boyfriend dumped you so you don't want anyone else to be happy!"

Rachel turned on her heel and stormed off. Marin felt a small flicker of regret—had she been too harsh? But she was too worn out to care.

"Oh, good—you're still here," Amelia said, rounding the corner and entering the room with Kelly close behind. "Kelly said you're going home without seeing the fireworks? I won't hear of it. Come along. You don't mess with tradition."

Kelly touched Marin's shoulder. "Come on, kiddo. *Carpe diem* and all that."

Marin was about to protest but... where had she just

heard that expression recently? It was Paul—that first day at the A-House. When he told Marin that Kelly was a cancer survivor.

She followed them out the door.

* * *

Marin hadn't spent much time at MacMillan Pier, though she passed it every single day. Right in the center of Commercial Street, it was where the ferry came in from Boston and where you could catch a whale-watching tour. There were quirky little art studios and a pirate museum. But tonight, the pier had one purpose and one purpose only: serving as one of the penultimate stops for the daylong Fourth of July extravaganza. Nine hours since the parade started, and the revelers were still going strong.

Personally, Marin was over it.

Amelia and Kelly set up folding beach chairs they'd picked up at the house on the way over. They wore red, white, and blue foil Uncle Sam high hats that were being handed out, and an artist painted a small American flag on Kelly's cheek.

Rachel perched on a narrow plank that bordered the walkway and the beach, facing the water, still pouting about what Marin had said to her, yet clearly craning her neck and looking around for Luke Duncan. Well, at least she couldn't say Marin didn't warn her.

"I'm going to walk to the water," Marin said to Amelia.

"Okay, hon. If you see Paul or Bart, send them over."

Marin threaded her way through the crowd. Someone was blasting the Sia song "Chandelier" and something about the song and the pier and the water gave her a flash of déjà vu. It was a memory of a late-winter evening in New York, sometime well past midnight, walking along the East River promenade with Julian. He held her hand, something they had sworn never to do in public. But in that moment, he clearly had not cared; he had reached for her hand, and her heart soared.

She shook the thought away, trying not to wonder what he was doing for the Fourth. She'd thought about it earlier and Googled where the Manhattan fireworks would be this year. Where she would have been, had life not laughed in her face.

"Hey, Marin!"

She turned at the sound of her name and saw Luke Duncan making his way toward her with long strides. It was no wonder Rachel had such a crush on him. His eyes were the brightest blue, the stubble on his jaw gold even in the fading light of the setting sun.

"I thought that was you," he said, grinning.

A perfect, dimpled smile.

"It's me," she said.

"How was the dinner party?"

"What, do you have our whole itinerary memorized?"

He laughed. "No. I saw Rachel earlier. She told me you were all heading over to the East End."

"Yeah. It was fine."

"Not exactly a glowing review. Rumor has it Sandra Crowe is usually quite the hostess."

"What's your deal?" she said.

He cocked his head. "I didn't realize I had a deal."

"Well, you're wasting your time flirting with me when Rachel is clearly interested."

"Rachel? We're friends. She's—I mean, she's a kid."

"She's twenty-two."

"Exactly."

Marin sighed. "Okay, well, then maybe you should stop leading her on."

Luke ran his hand through his hair, wrinkling his brow in a way that was so adorable it almost cracked through Marin's annoyance. Almost. "I've never been anything but friendly toward her."

"Whatever, Luke. But FYI, *this*"—she waved her finger between the two of them—"is never going to happen."

He laughed.

"Is this amusing to you?" she said.

"No. It's just—I'm not hitting on you, Marin. Obviously, you've got a lot going for you. But I'm not looking for anything. I left enough complications behind in Rhode Island. Sometimes it's just nice to talk to someone who's close to my age and isn't a gay man."

Marin turned red.

"I'm sorry. I feel like an ass."

"Don't. I'm sure ninety-nine point nine percent of the men who talk to you are hitting on you. I just want to put your mind at rest that I'm not one of them. That probably goes for any of the other guys out here."

She laughed. "Okay, then. But—you still shouldn't lead my sister on."

"Point taken. Friends?" he asked, holding out his hand.

"Friends," she said, placing her hand in his. He pulled her into a quick hug. When she stepped back, still feeling more than a little silly about her assumption, she spotted Rachel a few yards or so behind Luke—too far away to hear their conversation, but close enough to see them embrace. Rachel looked stricken, and before Marin could wave her over, she turned and disappeared into the crowd.

Oh, for heaven's sake. Marin couldn't take any more drama.

She said a hasty good-bye to Luke and headed back to the house to go to sleep just as the sound of fireworks erupted behind her.

Chapter Twenty-Seven

Marin woke up in a panic.

Last night, just before going to bed, she looked through her calendar to decide what weekend she'd leave in August. The calendar must have played on her subconscious overnight, setting off the alarm bell she'd somehow failed to notice in all of the drama of the past two months.

She'd missed her period. Two periods.

Her exhaustion took on new meaning. What if it wasn't just the emotional strain after all? She dressed quickly, planning to go to Adams Pharmacy, the only drugstore in town as far as she could tell. She hoped it was open early.

"Marin!" Her mother poked her head into her room. "Amelia just told me at breakfast that you're *staying?* I'm literally packing to go. When were you going to tell me?"

"Not now, Mom. I have to run out for a few minutes. Just—hang tight for a half an hour. I'll be right back."

She hurried down the stairs.

Outside, the day was bright and cloudless, warmer at

early morning than it had been on most of the other days. She was sure Amelia was already beachcombing.

She turned right, toward the pharmacy. It wasn't until she spotted the white clapboard building that she began to feel nervous. The place looked so old-fashioned, it felt unseemly to be searching for a pregnancy test. A blue plaque outside read ADAMS PHARMACY, ESTABLISHED 1869 BY DR. JOHN M. CROCKER. PURCHASED IN 1875 BY JOHN D. ADAMS. OLDEST BUSINESS IN CONTINUOUS OPERATION IN ONE LOCATION IN PROVINCETOWN.

She wondered, if in that long history, anyone had ever been more distraught than she felt in that moment walking through the door. She was going to bet not.

Marin, panicked, felt a wave of nausea. Or maybe that was the pregnancy. *Stop it,* she told herself. *Think positive. Or, rather—not positive. Think negative! Negative test results.*

The old-timey pharmacy limited her buying options. Instead of the dozen pregnancy-test varieties she would have had to choose from at CVS or Duane Reade, Adams had only one—First Response. One line, she wasn't pregnant; two lines, she was pregnant. Simple enough.

She was so out of sorts she nearly shoved it into her handbag and just walked out, but she remembered to pay at the last minute. That's when she literally bumped into Kelly.

"What are you doing here so early?" Kelly said, before noticing what Marin was holding. Kelly's mouth formed a silent O.

"I don't know yet, okay? Just please don't say a word!"

Kelly raised a small white prescription bag. "One big secret deserves another."

* * *

Blythe was beyond frustrated with her daughter.

One minute Marin couldn't wait to leave Province-town; the next she was suddenly staying for the entire summer. And she didn't even have the courtesy to tell Blythe herself! She'd had to hear it from Amelia, who, when she realized Blythe didn't know, could only look at her with pity. After weeks of punishing rudeness, this was adding insult to injury.

And where had she run off to this morning like the proverbial bat out of hell? Just wait, she'd said. As if Blythe had any choice. She *would* wait, if only to tell Marin that she could do what she wished with the rest of the summer, Blythe was leaving. She'd already checked the ferry schedule and booked a flight from Boston.

She paced impatiently in Marin's bedroom.

"What are you doing in here?" Marin asked when she walked in, clutching her handbag to her chest as if expecting Blythe to snatch it away.

"Waiting—like you asked me to. But I'm leaving in an hour."

"Just—sit, okay? Sit on the bed, and just... I'll be right out."

Marin ducked into the bathroom and closed the door. Blythe sighed, crossed her arms, and perched on the edge of Marin's bed.

Marin emerged a few minutes later and sat next to her mother wordlessly.

"As I was saying, Marin. I'm leaving in an hour. You'll be officially unburdened by my presence and can enjoy your summer." She stood to leave.

Marin looked up at her, her big dark eyes wide with emotion.

"I'm pregnant."

* * *

Marin walked along the water's edge, just close enough to the ocean so it licked her feet when the tide rolled in.

It was the hottest morning so far, but still she wrapped herself in a lightweight cardigan. She felt raw and vulnerable and would have hidden beneath a full-length ski coat if she could justify wearing one. The sweater had a hood and she pulled it over her head, though the breeze kept blowing it off. As she strolled, she hugged her midsection, newly aware that it wasn't perhaps as flat as it had been two months ago. And no, she wasn't imagining it; her jeans had gotten tighter.

As angry as she had been at her mother all this time, she had to admit her mother had taken the news well and had jumped into action. She made Marin an appointment to see an obstetrician in Hyannis on Tuesday.

She didn't know how she would wait. The drugstore test told her she was pregnant, but it couldn't tell her how many weeks pregnant. And the answer to that question was everything; timing was the only clue for Marin to guess who the father was.

She hated to admit it, but there had been a brief window when she was still sleeping with her fiancé and also hooking up with Julian. It had been such a confusing time, she had mentally edited it out of her own history. But now there was no denying it. The baby might have been fathered by either Greg Harper or Julian.

Tears welled in her eyes, and she brushed them away. She wasn't going to feel sorry for herself. She didn't deserve it.

"Hey—Marin!"

Rachel plodded toward her as quickly as the soft sand

terrain would allow. Her long hair waved out behind her, and she held her ubiquitous flip-flops in one hand.

Marin wanted to tell her she needed time alone, but from Rachel's determined pace and her less-than-pleasant facial expression, she doubted she'd get off that easily.

Rachel stopped in front of her, out of breath. Perspiration beaded at her hairline. It was hot already. Marin had barely noticed before now.

"You have some nerve," Rachel said.

"I'm really not in the mood for this, so could you be a little more specific?"

"You tell me that I'm chasing Luke just so I back off and you can go after him!"

"Oh my God, that is ridiculous."

"Really? Like you didn't make a beeline for him the second we got to the pier last night? How long did it take for you to throw yourself in his arms?"

"Rachel, you have this *all wrong*. I have zero interest in Luke, and he has zero interest in me. Unfortunately, he doesn't seem to have much interest in you either. But that's not my bad. So if you want to keep wasting your time and making yourself miserable, be my guest. But if you don't mind, I have bigger things to worry about right now. And I came out here to be alone."

Rachel crossed her arms, shaking her head slowly. Marin turned her back to her and walked off.

Chapter Twenty-Eight

Blythe crouched over a shady patch of the backyard. After dampening it with water, she dug up a small sample with a kitchen spoon. She rubbed a bit between her thumb and index finger. Gritty. She tried molding a handful into a ball, and it fell apart. Amelia's soil was too sandy, as she'd been warned. But the soil could be enriched, the problem fixed. She'd had the opposite issue in her backyard in Philadelphia—too much clay. And therein was the reason Blythe loved gardening; in gardening, unlike life, there was a solution to almost every problem.

She was going to be a grandmother! Oh, how she was dying to tell Kip. But Marin insisted that she not tell anyone.

"Not until I know more," she'd said. Blythe would try to contain herself.

In the meantime, her thoughts kept turning to the day Marin was born. Kip drove her to Lankenau Hospital at four in the morning, and she remembered wondering if he would leave her in a few hours to go to the office. She asked him if he would, and he shook his head. "Is that what you think of me?"

Sadly, it was.

Her parents drove in from Michigan, and the Bishops of course were there. Kip was not in the delivery room with her, and in the clutches of labor pain, she preferred it that way. She couldn't imagine him acting like a typical father-to-be did in movies, holding his wife's hand and mopping her brow and saying, "Push! You can do it!" The very thought was worse than the contractions bending her insides.

After four hours of labor, Marin was born. Eight pounds, eight ounces, with a headful of dark hair and big gray-brown eyes. Blythe clutched her to her chest, and the tiny thing claimed her breast with an energy and confidence that flooded Blythe with a love she'd never felt before.

Kip rushed into the room. He had tears in his eyes. She was shocked, genuinely floored, by the raw emotion in his face. He kissed her, then gingerly kissed the baby.

"I love you," he told Blythe.

Blythe cried, completely overwhelmed. Kip sat on the edge of the bed. He took her free hand, closing it in his own.

"We're a family now," he said. Blythe nodded through her tears.

Kip's mother proclaimed she'd never seen a newborn with dark eyes. Blythe's parents happily decided she looked just like the Welsh Madigans. Blythe, of course, knew otherwise. And in the first, and last, acknowledgment of the man who gave her baby life, she named her new daughter Marin, "of the sea."

Blythe looked up; Amelia waved at her through the

kitchen window. She was busy cooking away with Rachel, and Blythe was thankful they were too preoccupied to pay her much mind. She pulled out her phone and dialed.

Kip answered his cell on the second ring. Then she realized: it was a Saturday and he was not at the office.

"You back home?" he asked.

"No," she said. "In fact, we've decided to stay the summer."

Kip made a familiar, disapproving tsking sound. "This your idea, Blythe? I can't see Marin making this decision."

"And why not?"

"Because she is happiest when she is productive and working. She needs to get back to real life. Enough of this licking her wounds."

She sighed. "You are so infuriating sometimes." The truth was, even this aggravating conversation was of strange comfort to her. As irrational as it was, hearing his voice made her feel like everything would be all right. It always had. "If you're so sure what's best for her and disapprove of what's going on, then come out here for a day. I need to talk to you, and, more important, your daughter needs you."

"Don't be melodramatic."

She couldn't hold back. Marin might not want her father to know, but he should know. And if that's what it would take to get him out there, Blythe would tell him.

"Marin's pregnant."

A brief silence. "I'll see what I can do."

Rachel would not, as Marin had put it, waste her time and make herself miserable. No more hours spent pining after Luke Duncan. She'd come out there to get to know Amelia, and that was exactly what she was going to do.

Especially now that Amelia had invited her into her ultimate domain: the kitchen.

It was a foreign environment. Fran had told her one thing and one thing only about cooking: Don't start. "Once you're cooking for everyone, they expect it of you." *Her* mother, Rachel's grandmother Esther from Philadelphia, had been on call in the kitchen her entire life. "And what kind of life is that?" Fran said.

She repeated her mother's only culinary wisdom to Amelia.

"I feel sorry for your mother that she would feel that way."

"Oh, it's fine. I'm just saying I really don't have any cooking experience. My grandmother did cook a lot, but she lives on the East Coast and we see her only once a year for the Jewish holidays."

"Where was her family from?"

"Russia. Poland. Eastern Europe. So her cooking was pretty meat-heavy—lots of brisket. And potatoes. And this stuff called kasha varnishkes."

"Did you enjoy it?"

Rachel nodded. "I did."

"I bet if you had it right now, you would feel like you were at that house. And you would feel like a child again."

She smiled. "Probably."

"Food is so powerful. It connects us to the past. It sustains us. It's personal but also communal. So I am happy, deeply happy, to teach you a few Portuguese dishes. We have such a rich culinary tradition."

"I love Mediterranean food," Rachel said.

"Our dishes use the flavors of Mediterranean

cooking—the olive oil, the bay leaves, coriander, onions, paprika. But it's the way these flavors are combined that make Portuguese dishes unique. Our food is influenced by many cultures going back centuries: the Phoenicians, the Turks, the Moors."

"Sounds amazing. I'm just warning you that I have zero technique."

Amelia laughed. "It's not a matter of technique. We cook *com gusto*—'to your liking.' The way I do it might not be the way a neighbor does it. Forget about right or wrong. I'll show you the way my mother taught me and the way her mother taught her and so on. And someday, you might show your daughter." Amelia pulled out a white tin box from one of the cupboards. She lifted the lid and showed Rachel what had to be a hundred index cards separated by divider tabs.

"You should look through here. Familiarize yourself. Let me know what interests you the most. It's organized alphabetically but the recipe names are in Portuguese, so write things down as you go or you might lose track."

"Nadine's lucky she grew up with this," Rachel said.

Amelia's face clouded. "Nadine did not have much interest in the kitchen. Maybe she does now, living in Italy. I don't know. But I did not get to share most of this with her—not the way I learned with my *mãe*."

"Oh." She didn't know what else to say. She looked out the window and saw Blythe digging around in the ground.

"What's Blythe doing?"

Amelia glanced outside. "She's trying to figure out a way to grow a vegetable garden back there." She turned back to the task at hand. "So. The first meal. As you have seen, we cook once a week for Thomas. Bart has two jobs—running the art gallery and directing the theater company. And Thomas has bad days where he can't get out of bed."

Rachel nodded. "Luke told me he's really worried about him."

"We all are. This town has been so afflicted by the AIDS crisis. But we have learned as a community how to make this a place where people can *live* with the disease. Painters can paint and writers can write and not worry about where their next meal will come from."

"I want to help."

"And you will. We'll make a roast chicken for tomorrow night. And Thomas likes my homemade cheese. It needs to sit for twenty-four hours, so we'll get that going and then move on to the main course."

Rachel had never considered the notion of actually making cheese. Cheese was something that simply existed. She shared this thought with Amelia, who told her, "When I was growing up, making cheese was a weekly Sunday-afternoon activity with my mother. She took her cheese very seriously. When I first met my husband, Otto—your grandfather, by the way—and he came for lunch to meet her, he declined the cheese and I don't think she ever forgave him."

Rachel laughed.

"I'm quite serious," said Amelia. "I'll admit, it doesn't look that pretty if you're not used to it. But a good Portuguese man should have known better. It was a sign."

Cheese is important. Noted.

"We only use three ingredients: whole milk, rennet tablets, and coarse salt."

"What's rennet?"

"Rennet causes milk to become cheese by separating it into solids and liquids—the curds and the whey."

"But I mean, what is it? Is it a chemical?"

"No—it's all natural. It's an enzyme, usually extracted from the stomach lining of young calves."

What? Oh no. This was a problem. No, she wasn't vegan—she would eat dairy and eggs. But this was pushing it. Really pushing it. She would have to refuse the cheese, repeating the bad juju started by her grandfather decades ago. "Um, Amelia—I'm a vegetarian. I can't...I just..."

Amelia shook her head. "What's with all this vegetarianism? I don't get it. If you ask me, women need red meat." And then, maybe seeing Rachel's look of agony, she relented. "You don't have to eat the cheese. You just have to watch and learn. Deal?"

"Deal," Rachel said, smiling.

Chapter Twenty-Nine

I can't believe you're still collecting all this crap, Mother," said Nadine, watching Amelia carefully organize her latest beach finds into their appropriate bins.

"And why not? As an artist yourself, you of all people should understand."

"It's hardly the same thing."

Amelia rolled her eyes. Thirty years might have passed, but Nadine was the same recalcitrant daughter, always finding a way to needle her.

"I would like to say I am extremely pleased to see that you've made a life of creative work. It feeds the soul even through tough times."

"Yeah, well, it feeds the soul but doesn't always pay the rent," she said. "And what can I say? It's in my blood."

"That it is." Amelia had the urge to reach for her, to pull her into her arms as she hadn't in decades. But she didn't want to push. "I was surprised to find that Marin and Rachel don't do anything creative."

Nadine snorted. "Why? I mean, how do you know they're really even related to us? Where's the proof?

These people just show up out of nowhere. You have to wonder about their motives."

Amelia felt her first flash of genuine irritation. "Oh, for heaven's sake, Nadine. What *motives* would they have?"

Nadine sighed. "Mother, please. I think you're being a little naive here." Nadine focused her eyes on her, eyes that were so much harder than Amelia remembered. Her skin was weathered, more so even than Amelia's had been in her fifties. They loved the sun, all the Cabrals. But it was more than that. She'd caught Nadine smoking in high school and come down hard on her. She had probably never quit. Or perhaps she drank a lot. Whatever the case, she looked years older than Blythe, who was her peer. But her hair was still thick and cut in stylish layers, barely threaded with gray. And she was a handsome woman, moving with a confidence—almost aggressiveness—that gave her presence.

Amelia didn't want to take the bait in this conversation. She'd forgotten how dramatic Nadine could be, the way she could triangulate between her and Otto to get what she wanted. It had caused a lot of arguments with Otto because Amelia had recognized it and Otto had not.

And yet, Amelia found herself asking, "How on earth do you figure?"

Nadine drummed her fingers on the corner of the easel. "Do you have any idea how much this place is worth?"

Amelia laughed. "Oh, please. I don't want to hear this nonsense."

"I'm sure you don't. But I'll tell you, it's a good thing I'm here to be the voice of reason. Wake up, Mother. This isn't the tiny fishing village it was when our ancestors bought this house. And you've made it into something extremely valuable. As your daughter, I would be remiss if I didn't ask you what you plan to do with this house after you're gone."

Amelia shook her head. "Oh, Nadine."

"What?"

"Well, the house will go to Kelly when I'm gone. She's my wife."

Nadine nodded. "Of course. I understand. But you two don't have children together. So what will she do with the house?"

"Nadine, you've been here all of forty-eight hours. After decades of silence. And I'm thrilled about it—I am. But frankly, this conversation is out of line."

"Is it? I think mothers and daughters have this conversation. I'm sorry if it makes you uncomfortable. But before the end of the summer, we should finish it."

Amelia walked to her studio door and closed it. "There's a conversation we need to have that's going to make *you* uncomfortable. What happened with Nick that summer in Italy?"

Nadine stiffened. "You know what happened."

"I don't. I heard nothing from you—nothing—until the day after you buried your brother. How could you do that?" Amelia found herself shaking. "I didn't deserve that. For many years, I believed I did. But I don't think that way anymore. And I'm sorry if you do. But now you're here, in my house, under my roof, and the least you can do is tell me how my son killed himself."

"He crashed his motorcycle late at night. I told you this at the time. You want more details? Why don't you ask your lovely guest Blythe? Mother of his child. Ask her why he came to me; no doubt he ran to Italy to get away from *her*. He was not in a good emotional state."

Amelia sucked in her breath. "I thought you said he killed himself because of me. Now you're saying it was because of Blythe?"

"Apparently, there is plenty of blame to go around." Nadine brushed passed her and opened the door. "I'm going to take a walk over to the pottery shop."

Amelia, shaking, watched her leave without a word.

Blythe insisted on doing the driving to Hyannis even though she wasn't comfortable behind the wheel for long distances if she didn't know the roads by heart. She didn't like relying on her phone for directions, was unnerved by the turns and exits relayed in a systematic monotone. But she was there to take care of Marin.

"Mom, I'm fine. I can drive! I'm just going for an exam, not to deliver the baby."

"You just relax."

Marin fell silent, and it felt to Blythe like her own secret rested between them with all the weight of the world. She couldn't stop thinking about Nick—the way it had started, the way it had ended, all the passion and fear and guilt and worry playing in an endless loop in her mind. And Blythe understood that on some level, she was mentally preparing herself to tell Marin the story.

Nick had called her a few days following the club disaster, during the afternoon when he knew Kip would be at work.

"Can you come into the city? I really need to see you." When Blythe heard his voice, her resolve to just cut it off cold disappeared, and she agreed. For the entire drive downtown, especially when the stately profile of the art museum came into view, she justified her actions by thinking the least she could do was say good-bye in person.

When he opened the door, greeting her with his dark-eyed gaze and his mouth slightly open, as if he had just kissed her, the anger from the night at the club was gone. She wanted him instantly, and yet she'd had satisfying sex with her husband just two nights ago. It seemed like no matter what she did, she would be betraying them both.

"Sorry I called you at home," he said, pressing his mouth to hers. She felt herself opening up to him, her insides unfolding like a bird spreading its wings. "But I needed to reach you because I'm leaving tomorrow."

For a second, she forgot that she was there to end it. All she could think was *Leaving? To go where? For how long?*

"I don't understand," she said.

"My sister, Nadine, invited me to Italy. She has a house with a bunch of friends. It's a great setup."

"What about your classes?"

He shrugged. "I'll pick them up in the fall. You gotta live life, you know?"

Yes, she did know. And that's what she'd felt she was doing when she was with him. But she had to focus on her real life—her life with Kip. She had to try to make her marriage work. Despite all the times she had felt like Kip did not care for her, surely he cared more than this stranger. The night at the club had shown that.

"So, this is good-bye," she said.

"It's not good-bye. I'll be back in the fall."

"Nick, we really should make this good-bye."

He seemed to consider this. He moved closer to her, cupping her face with his hands. "You think too much. Maybe it's not up to us. Maybe the universe has its own plans." He pressed his lips to the hollow of her throat, and her body swayed against his, his hand already underneath her dress, moving between her legs. It was difficult—so achingly difficult—but she pulled away.

"Good-bye," she whispered.

She never heard from him again except for a single letter one month later.

When she saw the Italian postmark, she dropped the rest of the mail on the dining-room table, took the letter up to her bedroom, and closed her door even though she was alone in the house.

She cried because, damn it, she missed him, and also because she was thankful she'd gotten out when she did—relatively unscathed, her marriage intact.

She knew she should throw away the letter, but she hesitated. On the back, Nick had rendered a beautiful pencil sketch of the Italian coastline, remarkable in its stark detail. She could throw away his words, but she couldn't quite bring herself to throw away his art. Instead, she took the letter and her barely used Degas journal, stuck them both in a shoe box, and shoved it into the back of her closet. It was done.

Until she'd discovered she was pregnant.

Blythe squeezed the steering wheel now, fighting back tears. "Marin, we need to talk." Blythe turned off the radio.

"Okay," Marin said, glancing sideways at her.

"I've been waiting for the right moment and, really, there isn't one."

"You're freaking me out. What now?"

Blythe took a deep breath. "You know your biological father is Nick Cabral."

"Yeah, I get that part. What I don't get is how or why. Did you have trouble conceiving or something? And then go behind Dad's back to use a sperm donor? That's what

I figured. You wanted to do fertility treatments and Dad didn't."

"No. It was nothing like that."

"What, then?"

"I knew Nick."

Marin leaned forward, her hand on the dashboard, scrutinizing Blythe's face. "How?"

Blythe shook her head. "It was crazy. It was..."

"Mom, just spill it."

"It was early in my marriage. Your father was working all the time. Things were not great between us. I was young—ten years younger than you are now."

"Mom, please. I don't need a long setup here."

"I met him at the art museum one afternoon and it turned into a summer affair. It was over by the time I realized I was pregnant."

Marin slumped back in her seat. "I can't believe it."

"I'm sorry."

"I don't get it. What about Rachel's mother? Was he a sperm donor for her?"

"I don't know. He might have been. Maybe he needed money—he was an art student. Estranged from his parents. That might be what happened with Rachel's mother. Regardless, when Rachel told you her story and you assumed mine was the same, I wasn't ready to correct you with the truth."

Marin nodded slowly. "So when you found out you were pregnant, you didn't know who the father was?"

"Oh, I knew. Six weeks pregnant...I knew absolutely."

Marin gave an odd laugh. "Well, then you're a better person than I am."

It took a few seconds for her to process what Marin

was saying, and then she gasped. "You don't know who the father is?"

"That's right."

Blythe, overcome with sadness for her daughter, reached for her hand. Marin turned to look out the window.

Chapter Thirty

Kelly, do you have a sec?" Rachel jumped up from the porch rocking chair when she spotted Kelly coming from the back of the house. Kelly seemed deep in thought. Rachel thought twice about interrupting her, but she just *had* to talk to someone.

Kelly looked up, startled. "Hey. I'm making a quick run to Sandra's house to measure something. You can ride along if you want."

Rachel climbed into the passenger seat of the truck and Kelly started driving.

"So what's up?" Kelly asked.

"You've known Thomas so long, I figure you've known Luke a long time too, right?"

Kelly started to say something, then coughed. "Can you find me a tissue in my bag?" she asked, coughing again. Rachel opened the knapsack between them on the seat. "Front pocket," Kelly said.

Rachel found a packet of Kleenex and handed her

one. Kelly pressed it to her mouth, then balled it up and shoved it into the bag.

"Are you okay?"

"Sinus infection," she said. "So what do you want to know about Luke?"

"What's his deal? I just can't figure him out. Sometimes it seems like he's into me. We've hung out a lot, and on the Fourth, when we dropped off the truck? He was like, hey, you can stay and swim. And in the pool, I swear he was going to kiss me. I mean, it felt like he was going to. But that night at the pier, I saw him talking to Marin and it looked intense. What do you think?"

"What do I think? I think you should talk to Luke. If he's giving you mixed signals, call him on it. And by the way, there's nothing going on with him and Marin."

"How do you know?"

"I know."

Rachel felt a wave of relief.

"Okay, I'll talk to him."

"People play games—especially in the beginning of relationships. You know that."

"I haven't had many relationships. Just hooking up, you know? And that's pretty straightforward. But I'm thinking about Luke nonstop and it's making me crazy."

"How old are you?"

"Twenty-two."

"And you've never had a serious relationship?"

Rachel shook her head.

"I was with Amelia by the time I was your age."

That gave Rachel pause. "How long did it take before you knew you were in love with her?"

"About two minutes," Kelly said with a smile.

So it wasn't so absurd that she had such strong feelings

for a guy she'd known for two weeks. "Okay. I'll talk to him," she said.

"Glad that's settled." Kelly pulled the truck into the driveway. A familiar white Honda was parked at the top.

"Isn't that Amelia's car?" Rachel said.

"That's weird. I swear when we left, she was home." Kelly slammed her door shut.

Tanya answered the doorbell.

"Hi, Kelly. Is she expecting you?"

"I think so."

Tanya came out, closed the door most of the way, and stood out on the porch with them. "Between you and me, if you hear of any other jobs opening up in town, let me know. She's driving me crazy."

"You got it," Kelly said with a wink.

"This way—she's in the breakfast room." Tanya showed them into space off the kitchen that was blindingly white—white furniture, walls, and tiled floor with sun streaming through a massive skylight. Sandra sat at the Lucite table drinking coffee. Next to her, Nadine.

"What a lovely surprise," Sandra said.

"What are you two doing here?" Apparently, not so lovely for Nadine.

"I'm working. What are *you* doing here?" Kelly said.

"Kelly. Rachel—come sit," Sandra said with a smile. "I wasn't expecting you today. For the measurements?"

"Yes. For the measurements." Kelly put her hands on her hips.

"Sit down. Have some coffee. This is actually good timing."

"Sandra…" Nadine began in protest.

"Coffee? Scones?" Sandra said, pointing to a plate.

"What's going on?" Kelly sat at the foot of the table,

facing them both. Rachel awkwardly pulled out a chair next to her and helped herself to a blueberry scone.

"You know, life is all about timing. I've really come to believe that." Sandra poured herself more coffee.

"You don't say?" Kelly narrowed her eyes.

"It's amazing that Nadine should arrive this summer just as you've closed the inn for business and just as I've been thinking so much about how I'd love to take that large property off your hands. Nadine agrees it makes perfect sense. I'm prepared to make quite a generous offer."

"Um, Sandra—can you excuse Nadine and me for a minute?" Kelly stood, her chair making a loud noise against the tiled floor.

Sandra smiled graciously. "Of course."

When Sandra was out of the room—though probably not out of earshot—Kelly turned to Nadine and slammed her hand down on the table.

"Who the fuck do you think you are to start negotiating the sale of the house? It's our *home*."

"It's my family home—has been for generations. And in case you haven't noticed, I'm the last of the generations. The buck stops with me, Kelly. Not with you—me. Amelia's daughter. Not her lover."

"We're married. Your legal claim to the house does not supersede mine."

"This isn't about legality, Kelly. It's a practical issue. Sandra Crowe will pay enough for the house that my mother won't have to worry about money for the rest of her life."

"She's not worried about money. We're doing fine."

"It's also about doing what's right. The house is part of my family legacy. The conversation about what happens to it is one that involves me. Now, I know you've had it pretty easy since you waltzed into town that summer, torpedoed my family, and never left, which meant I had to leave. But I'm back, and I'm not going anywhere until this business with the house is settled."

"There's no business to settle. Your mother loves that house. If she moves somewhere to live alone, it will be the death of her."

"Well, she won't be alone. She has you, doesn't she?" Nadine picked up her handbag and pulled it over her shoulder. She looked at Rachel. "And don't *you* get any ideas. I don't care how many test tubes my brother jerked off into. You have no part of this—understand?"

She walked out the door, calling back to Sandra that they would talk soon.

Blythe was at the beach when the call came.

The day was hotter than usual. She sat in a folding plastic chair, wearing a new turquoise-blue bathing suit purchased at a small shop on Commercial Street and a big striped hat she'd borrowed from Marin.

Today, she'd managed to find the "straight people" beach. She had not understood the various strata of beach geography and a few days ago had accidentally planted herself in the lesbian section, where she soon realized she was one of the few women wearing a top. Farther down, the gay men congregated, and she was even more out of place there. When she returned to the house, frazzled, Amelia graciously drew her a map on a paper towel.

The buzz of her cell phone startled her. She hadn't even meant to pack it in her beach bag. She didn't think she had reception at the beach and had biked the short distance thinking she was giving herself an hour or so of being completely out of touch. Frankly, she needed it.

"Hello?" She fumbled with the phone as a strong breeze swept over her and she had to hold on to her hat.

"Blythe, it's me. I'm in town."

Kip!

"You're here? In Provincetown?"

"Yes."

"I can't believe it," she said, more to herself than to him.

"Well, I want to see Marin. And you said you needed to talk to me, so we can take care of that while I'm here. What's your availability this morning?" Kip, always to the point. Always goal-oriented. He no doubt had his entire Provincetown visit scheduled to the last minute, the agenda filed with his secretary back in Philadelphia.

Blythe tried to stand and instead sank further into the sand, the chair folding in on itself.

"Shit!" she said.

"What?"

"Nothing. Hold on."

How could she be so unprepared for this moment? Had she really thought he would refuse to come? They were going to be grandparents.

"Where are you staying?" she asked, stalling.

"The Sutter Hotel. Where are you staying?"

"The Beach Rose Inn."

"I saw that online but it's supposed to be closed this season."

"Long story," she said. Where should they meet? Should she have him just come down to the beach? She wanted to see him immediately. But she looked a mess—windblown, no makeup, dressed in just a bathing suit.

No, for this conversation she needed to be pulled together. She was delivering extremely difficult news. And faced with the task, she wished she had told him the truth about Marin's paternity before this—any time before this. It would be hard enough for him to deal with the fact that Marin was not his flesh and blood, but now that unfortunate reality also extended to the new baby.

Blythe took a deep breath. "Are you still there?"

"Yes, Blythe," he said, and she could imagine the taut, impatient line of his jaw. "Can you meet in an hour? Pick a place on that main street in town. We can have coffee."

Where? At Joe, so every coffee klatch in town would overhear their messy personal business? No, thanks.

"Actually, there's a better place. Less crowded." She told him how to get to Pilgrims' First Landing Park, at the westernmost end of Commercial Street. The park—a monument, technically—had stone benches and grass and it overlooked the jetty. The fact that she could pick a place like the park—not just the obvious coffee shop—made her feel pleased, like she was a local.

"I'll see you in an hour," he said.

She pressed the phone to her chest.

Rachel, with her marching orders from Kelly, did not want to waste any time. She found Luke at the pool.

He didn't notice her at first. She sat on a chaise longue while he did laps, feeling, yes, like a stalker. She hadn't even bothered to ring the doorbell—she just walked right around to the back of the house. Questionable behavior? Maybe. But she couldn't wait another minute to follow Kelly's advice. Kelly was the boss. She'd been with the love of her life for three decades; surely, she had some relationship wisdom.

When he finally noticed her sitting there, he climbed out of the pool.

"Hey—sorry to intrude."

"What's up?" he asked, toweling off. Maybe she was paranoid, but he did not seem happy to see her. *Bad idea. Bad, bad idea! Rachel, what were you thinking?*

She had to work really hard not to look at his body.

"I just wanted to talk to you for a sec."

He sat down on the edge of the chair next to her. After an excruciating minute of silence, she knew she had two choices: say something, or slink off and never come back. In that moment, it was actually a tough decision.

"So, I just wanted to, um, say something," she managed.

"Actually, if you don't mind, I'd like to say something first."

Okay, this was a curveball she hadn't expected.

"Sure."

"Rachel, I've enjoyed spending time with you and talking. I have. But I'm afraid I've given you the wrong impression about our...friendship."

Her stomach dropped. "In what way?"

"You understand that we're just friends, right? Nothing more?"

Oh.

"It felt like something more," she said. "I don't think I was imagining it."

He sighed. "Don't get me wrong. You're extremely attractive. It's not about that."

"What, then?"

He smiled kindly at her. "Come on. We can be friends, right?" He held out his hand to shake. Rachel placed her hand in his. What else could she do? She wasn't going to win this one. She felt sick with defeat. And as soon as her hand touched his, she felt something else—the searing, electric chemistry she'd felt that first day at the beach.

It propelled her, with a centrifugal force, right onto his lap.

Startled, his arms instinctively closed around her to keep her from toppling onto the ground. In his embrace, she seized the moment, kissing him full on the mouth. She figured what the hell—might as well go out in a blaze of glory. Surely he would push her away, let her fall to the ground after all.

But no.

He pulled her closer, kissing her back with as much fervor as she had fantasized about. Her heart beat wildly in her chest, and she was barely breathing but would not stop for air—would keep going forever, if he would let her.

"Rachel," he said, almost inaudibly. He pulled back, and she noticed his chest was heaving. His bare chest that had moments ago been pressed against her breasts, which were covered only with a flimsy tank top…

"Rachel," he said again, louder this time.

"Yes," she breathed.

"You should go."

Chapter Thirty-One

The sight of her husband affected Blythe in a way she hadn't anticipated. She finally understood the expression *to have one's heart in one's throat.* That's what it felt like, and when he hugged her hello, she started crying.

She had underestimated just how very much she missed him.

"What's wrong?" he asked, alarmed.

"Nothing," she said, dabbing at the tears in her eyes with a paper napkin pulled from her handbag. "Here. Let's sit." She headed toward a stone bench on the outer circumference of the small park, but Kip was busy reading the monument.

"So the Pilgrims first landed here, not Plymouth?" he said.

"Apparently."

"Hmm. Learn something new every day."

They sat side by side on a bench with a view of the ocean and a three-mile-long stone jetty.

"Okay, what the hell is going on with Marin?" Kip finally said.

"Oh, Kip." This was more difficult than she'd anticipated.

"I assume the father is that fellow from the law firm?" Kip said. Blythe hesitated, then nodded. She felt it would be crossing a line to confide the entire truth, the messy ambiguity of it all. Especially in light of what else she had to tell him—her own messy truth. She started to speak but he interrupted her.

"I know you're concerned about Marin—I am too. But we can't let that become a distraction from what's going on between the two of us."

Blythe couldn't help but feel a plunging disappointment. He wanted to talk about the divorce? Now? She thought he was there for Marin, but apparently he just wanted to take care of business. Well, it hurt. But it also made it easier to admit the truth to him. She would not lose him over it. He was already lost.

"Kip. There's something I need to tell you—"

"Please. Let me finish," he said. "I want to apologize about Candace. It was wrong. I should have dealt with what was going on with us, with myself, in a more honest way. An affair was lazy and ultimately just made things worse."

Wait, *what?*

"Are you saying you're not with her anymore?"

"That's what I'm saying. It was a distraction. Not from you, but from what's been going on at work. That firm has been my whole life, you know."

"Believe me, I know."

He nodded, looking out at the water. "To the detriment of our family, yes. I admit it. It didn't mean I didn't love you and Marin. I never meant to make you feel that way. It's just who I am. Who I was." He turned to her.

"They want to buy me out. They want me gone. The young bucks don't need an old-timer like me anymore."

"Oh, Kip. Can they do that?"

He shrugged, looking uncharacteristically forlorn. "They can't force me to leave. But if I stay, I'm a lame duck. Frankly, I don't want to be where I'm not wanted. Not valued. For a while now, I've tried to deny it. I think Candace was a way to say, *See, I'm still vital. I'm still young and wanted.*" He took her hand. "It had nothing to do with you. Not that it's any excuse."

"What are you saying? Do you still want the divorce?"

"I don't know what the answer is, Blythe. Do you? I think we need to focus on getting Marin back on her feet before we make any big decisions about our marriage."

Blythe's mind raced. Her prayers had been answered; there was a reprieve. The marriage might be savable.

"Yes. Okay," she breathed.

"So what did you want to tell me?" he said.

Oh my God. No, not now. This was the last thing she wanted to talk about *now.*

"Just…Marin," she said. "Let's go find her."

Marin used both hands to squeeze the wheel cutter and slice through a piece of dark blue tile. A tiny sharp corner shot up and then fell to the floor. She had yet to master precision.

"This makes me realize how long it's been since I actually used my hands for anything except typing on the computer and my phone. It's kind of crazy."

"It is," Kelly said. She glanced up from the piece she was gluing onto the mosaic. "So, as much as I love the meditative silence in here—are you going to tell me what's going on with you or what?"

Marin had known the question was coming. Since the morning at the pharmacy, Kelly obviously knew. It was okay; she wouldn't judge her too harshly. The only person she truly dreaded telling was her father. All her life, she'd wanted to make him proud. Now look at her: unemployed, single, and pregnant, sitting around doing arts and crafts in the middle of a workday.

"I'm pregnant," she said to Kelly. "As you clearly figured out."

"Well, the test could have been negative."

"Yeah. It wasn't."

"How far along are you?"

"About eight weeks." She couldn't believe it.

"So...is this good news? Bad news? Mixed?"

Marin shrugged. "I can barely process it, to tell you the truth."

"What are you going to do?"

"I'm going to have the baby. Aside from that, I don't know." She hadn't considered not keeping the baby. This surprised her, actually. Finding a job at a law firm while pregnant would be challenging. No one would admit it, but of course firms didn't want to hire someone who was going on leave in a few months. And raising a child as a single mom? What would that do to her billable hours? She understood these complications, but they did nothing to change the strange certainty that she should keep the baby. She was afraid hormones had already overtaken the logic side of her brain. Or maybe it was her new understanding of her own all-too-complicated origin story.

"What's the deal with the father?" Kelly asked.

Marin groaned. "I don't want to get into it."

"Why not? Talking helps. And I trusted you with something major. Something really big and really bad."

Marin looked at her. "Yeah, about that. I'm not the only one you should be talking to. I really think you need to tell Amelia. She'd want to know."

Kelly shook her head. "I want to spare her for as long as possible."

"I don't think you're doing her a favor."

"Don't get off topic. We're talking about you. You and your baby. Hell, Amelia's going to be a great-grand-mother." She coughed. "This will be good for her. Just what she needs after…" Kelly teared up. Marin moved from behind the table and put her arms around her.

Kelly pulled back after a minute, wiping her eyes. "Nadine is trying to get her to sell the house."

"This house? Well, that's ridiculous."

"It's not as ridiculous as you would think. Amelia has a lot of guilt about our relationship, estranging the kids. Now I'm sick. I'm worried the two things are enough to tip the scales and make her do something really mis-guided."

Someone knocked on the door. "Marin, there's a call for you on the house phone," Rachel said.

Marin put down the cutter. "Really? Are you sure? Who is it?"

"Julian Rowe?"

Julian? Why hadn't he called her cell phone? Then she realized it had been days since she'd looked at her phone. It just wasn't a natural part of life's rhythm out there. How strange that she hadn't looked at it, hadn't even thought about it.

Marin brushed past Rachel and ran down the two flights of stairs. The receiver was set on the top of the front desk.

* * *

Marin took the phone into the office and closed the door. She sat at a desk, surrounded by calendars and vendor-order forms and a dozen framed photos of Amelia and Kelly and groups of smiling people at the inn, guests from summers past. Three framed wedding photos were on the walls, different couples posing with their bridesmaids and groomsmen on the steps of the front porch.

"Hello?" she said, heart racing.

"Marin—finally. I've been trying to reach you for two days. Your phone goes straight to voice mail."

"How did you get this number?"

"You mentioned where you were staying, and I looked it up." Had she mentioned it? She couldn't remember. She was amazed that he had. "I thought you would be back in New York by now."

"Um, yeah. Change of plans," she said.

"I was hoping to talk to you in person. When are you coming back?"

"I'm not sure exactly."

"Marin, I feel bad about our last conversation. I'm sorry for cutting things off so quickly. It was a difficult situation. I was stressed out, and I couldn't think about our future until I figured out my future."

"It's okay."

"No. It's not. I'm sorry."

Her stomach was in knots. *Don't be so sweet. It makes this harder.*

"Babe, listen," he said. "I have some good news. Genie offered me a job as in-house counsel. I can stay in New York."

"Julian, congratulations. I'm happy for you." And she was. She also felt wistful. Their lives were taking opposite turns.

"I want to see you. We need to get back on track."

"What?" Her hand instinctively went to her belly.

This could not be happening. The conversation she'd dreamed about—at the worst possible time. "Well, I'm not going to be in New York for a while."

"Okay," he said slowly. "I'll come out there for a few days."

"No! Don't." The only thing worse than losing him the first time would be losing him a second time, face to face, when he learned she might be pregnant with another man's child. No—the worst would be if she found out it was his and he still rejected her. Julian might be willing to see her now, maybe talk about how things would work out in the future. But if the messiness of what happened at the firm was too much for him, how would he handle *this?*

"Marin, I reacted badly last month. There's no excuse, no denying it. And I'm sorry. Please give me a chance to make it up to you. I've missed you very much. Let me come out there so we can talk in person."

"There's nothing to talk about," she said.

"Marin..."

"No," she said, her voice catching. "Please don't call me again." Marin disconnected the call, set the receiver down on the desk, and cried, her arm bracing her midsection. *Stop it,* she told herself. *You have to be strong. For two people now.*

She walked out of the office, determined to keep it together.

"Marin, there you are!" said Blythe. "I've been looking all over for you."

Her mother. Standing with her father. Marin lost it all over again.

Chapter Thirty-Two

Amelia didn't like to lie, had sworn never to lie again after her disastrous falling-out with her children. But now Blythe was asking her to do just that.

She turned away from the kitchen window, where she had been peeking out at the handsome man talking to Marin, the two of them sitting side by side on one of the benches, gazing out at the water. Their heads occasionally bent together.

"I'll tell him the truth eventually. I will," said Blythe. "But our relationship is in a very fragile state right now."

"So why does he think you are both out here? Who does he think I am?"

"Marin lost her job in New York. Her boyfriend broke up with her. She needed to get away, and Kip knows that. I told him you and Kelly are friends of Marin's."

Amelia shook her head.

There was another reason, a deeper and more disturbing reason, why Amelia wasn't in the mood to do Blythe's bidding. The conversation with Nadine was bothering her more than she cared to admit. Whatever had happened between Blythe and Nick was none of her business, but the thought of their affair being the last straw, the event that drove him to end his life…it was tough. She had long blamed herself for his unhappiness. But to learn that he had had his heart broken all over again by someone else?

"I don't appreciate being a party to this. Especially since my son was the one hurt the most."

"What?" Blythe looked stricken.

"Nadine told me he came to Italy heartbroken after your affair. Why? Did he ask you to leave your husband and you refused? Did he know you were taking his baby away from him?"

Blythe's eyes widened. "Amelia," she said slowly. "I don't know what Nadine told you—but none of that is true."

"Well, it might be unpleasant. But that doesn't mean it isn't true."

"No. Nick did not leave Philadelphia heartbroken. He was excited to leave Philadelphia, to see his sister. He told me he never felt comfortable far from the sea. He wasn't in love with me. It was a passing thing. By the time I found out I was pregnant, we were out of touch. He told me he was never coming back—that he was happy in Italy."

Amelia shook her head. "If he was happy in Italy, why did he kill himself?" she shouted, her voice shrill despite her best efforts to stay calm. Blythe flinched.

"I don't know anything about how he died. That's something I'd hoped to learn on this trip and I just never found the nerve to ask you."

"He drove his motorcycle off a dirt road one night."

Blythe shook her head. "It was an accident. It had to

be. The Nick I knew loved life. He was reckless, maybe a little lost. But that's it."

"I wish I could believe you."

"Amelia, I want you to know, for your own peace of mind, that Nick never wanted anything more from me than the brief affair we had. And he wrote to me about how happy he was in Italy."

Blythe seemed so earnest. Either she was in denial or she had rewritten the script of her own history. "You don't have to tell me these things just to appease me. I won't give away your secret."

Amelia couldn't look at that woman another minute. She tossed her apron on the counter and walked out of the kitchen.

"Dad, I can't believe you came all the way out here," Marin said, wishing for a more private place to talk with him. But the season was peaking and the town was jam-packed. Amelia's house was a refuge—albeit an emotionally complex one.

It was a comfort to look into his sharp, confident blue eyes, to feel his steady arm around her shoulder. His calm, his confidence, had been her emotional benchmark for her entire life, and she had been foolish not to reach out to him sooner.

But her happiness at seeing him was tempered by her certainty that he was disappointed in her for the pregnancy, and also by her mother's terrible secret. A secret Marin was now complicit in keeping.

"I considered coming up to New York to talk to you after the whole situation at Cole, Harding," he said. "I didn't know you would be leaving."

"It was a spur-of-the-moment decision."

"It's not like you to run away from problems."

She sighed. "It's complicated." *Understatement of the year.*

"Marin, I think the best thing you could do for yourself is get your career back on track."

"Dad, come on. You know better than anyone that would be challenging enough after the way things went down at Cole, Harding, and Worth, the gossip item in the *Post*. Now I'm pregnant. I'm not exactly a desirable candidate."

"It's a temporary setback."

"You really believe that?"

"I can pull some strings."

She shook her head. "Dad, no. That's the last thing I want."

"We'll discuss that more another time. The most important thing is your health. You're okay?" He turned to her, his eyes crinkled in concern.

"I'm fine, Dad. The doctor said everything looks good so far. Strong heartbeat."

Kip nodded and squeezed her hand. "And the father?"

"I haven't told him yet. I'm sorry," she whispered. "You must be so disappointed in me."

He tightened his arm around her. "Never. We all make mistakes. I think you're handling yours with great strength. I've never loved you more."

It suddenly felt difficult to breathe. The weight of it all was just too much. In that moment of unconditional love, she couldn't keep her mother's secret. Her parents' marriage was over, but he would always be her father. In the end, her paternity was her truth to tell.

She turned to him.

"Dad," she said. "I didn't come out here for a vacation."

Chapter Thirty-Three

Amelia insisted on cooking dinner at Thomas's house instead of doing the usual prep at her house and then walking it over.

"Marin's father is visiting," she said. "I want to give them some privacy."

Rachel felt a pang of envy. Her mother hadn't so much as texted her, and Marin had both parents with her. She shook the thought away. She hadn't done yoga all month; no wonder she was slipping into negative energy.

She turned her focus to the *pão de milho,* mixing corn-meal, salt, and boiling water, stirring vigorously. She'd been practicing the recipe and could make it completely on her own, freeing Amelia up to focus on the main course: hake stew. Hake was apparently in the cod family. Which was in the fish family, which meant of course Rachel would not eat it.

"This was your great-grandmother's signature dish," she said, tossing onions, scallions, and two cups of water into a large heavy pot to boil. "Her mother was born in the Azores—a cluster of islands off the coast of Lisbon.

She was from the largest island, São Miguel. I didn't learn this dish properly until I went back to visit after she died." She glanced at Rachel. "Will you never eat fish?"

"Probably not," Rachel said.

"How can you cook what you don't eat?"

"I probably won't be cooking meat and fish."

"What about for your children?"

Children? Rachel would settle for a boyfriend.

Bart poked his head into the kitchen. "I'm going to the gallery. Everything under control here?"

"Everything's fine," Amelia said. "Good luck with the show. Don't worry about us."

Bart kissed her on the cheek. "You're the best." He peeked over Rachel's shoulder. "Whatcha making there?"

"Corn bread," she said.

"Rachel is becoming quite the cook," said Amelia. "Bart, I'm going to refrigerate leftovers for you to reheat when you get home. Is Luke here for dinner or will it just be Thomas?"

Rachel's heart soared with hope. She had not seen him in a few days—not since the kiss. He obviously could have found some excuse to stop by the house if he'd wanted to. Clearly, he didn't. It hurt and it was confusing. The way he'd responded to her by the pool—that had been real. So why was he rejecting her?

"Luke's helping out at the gallery but he said he'd be home by six."

Rachel glanced up from the baking pan she was greasing, and Bart caught her eye. He winked. Oh, great—so Luke had told him that Rachel had thrown herself at him and that he was avoiding her. That wasn't at all humiliating. Well, she'd made her bed and now she had to lie in it.

Bart left, and the two of them settled into busy silence.

Rachel glanced at the clock, now unable to resist counting the minutes until Luke showed up.

* * *

The hostess at the Red Inn, one of the town's oldest and most upscale restaurants, smiled at Blythe. "Bishop, party of three?"

"Actually, it's just two of us." Blythe glanced at Marin. She'd thought Kip would stay at least one night in town, that they could have dinner together as a family. But he left immediately after his visit with Marin without so much as a good-bye to her.

The hostess led them through the spacious waterfront rooms to a table with a view of the lighthouses of Long Point.

"Enjoy your dinner," the hostess said, handing them menus.

Blythe looked out at the water. "I thought we could at least have a meal together with your father."

"I don't know why you would expect that, Mom. You two are divorcing."

Blythe didn't bother responding.

How could she resist getting her hopes up after their conversation that morning in the park? She knew most women would be too badly hurt by the affair to be thinking about a reconciliation, but she couldn't hold it against him, considering her own history.

Early in their marriage, after she almost ruined it with that reckless affair, she'd resolved to accept Kip's workaholism. She knew she had to either accept it or leave. She couldn't spend her entire life seething with resentment or, worse, acting out. And once she'd made that choice, to stay even though she understood that Kip was always going to put work first, it got easier. Still, she'd never expected him to admit his shortcomings. Certainly, she'd never dreamed of hearing the apology he'd given her that morning. For it to come as their marriage was ending just seemed like a terrible, ironic waste.

"Look on the positive side—we get some time together," Marin said, opening her menu and smiling at her across the table. Blythe smiled back. It was such a relief to see Marin let go of her anger toward her. Blythe wasn't happy that Marin's pregnancy was a complicated situation, but the one bright spot was that it clearly gave Marin some empathy where Blythe was concerned.

She reached across the table and squeezed Marin's hand.

It seemed their trip to Provincetown had served its purpose. With Marin expecting a baby, and with the small window she sensed for a reconciliation with Kip closing, it was time to leave.

A waiter took their drink orders: pinot noir for Blythe and a club soda with lime for Marin. "I really want the Wellfleet oysters but I'm not supposed to eat them now," Marin said.

"Why not? Because of the baby?"

Marin nodded.

"So many more rules now than when I had you. Marin, you really need to get established with your doctor in Manhattan. And I need to get back to the house." She paused, then said gently, "We should plan to leave this week."

Marin shook her head. "I can't."

"Why on earth not? Your father said you were avoiding dealing with everything and I told him he was wrong. Now I'm starting to wonder."

"I told Kelly I would stay."

What was she talking about? "I think Kelly will understand."

Marin reached across the table and took a sip of Blythe's wine.

"Marin, don't."

"One sip won't hurt." Her eyes filled with tears. Blythe felt a pang of alarm.

"What's going on?"

"Kelly has lung cancer."

What? "Good Lord. Was she a smoker?"

"Mom, I have no idea."

Blythe, her hand shaking, reached for her wineglass.

"Don't say anything. I shouldn't even have told you. But I want you to understand why I'm not leaving right now. I want to be here for her—and for Amelia."

Blythe nodded. There were no words. How could Amelia bear it?

"Amelia seems so strong! I'd never guess."

"She doesn't know," said Marin. "So seriously, Mother—not a word."

Blythe assured her she wouldn't say anything. She thought again of their uncomfortable conversation in the kitchen earlier.

"Amelia got upset with me today. Now I feel even worse about it."

"Upset with you? Why?"

"I asked her not to say anything to your father about how we knew her—that I wasn't ready to tell him the truth. She got defensive and said her son was the one hurt by all of this, getting involved with a married woman. But Marin, it isn't true. Nick Cabral was not upset by whatever happened between us. I'm sure of it. He liked his freedom. And the worst part is Nadine said he killed himself because he was upset by the end of our affair. Why would she lie?"

"He killed himself?" Marin said, blinking hard.

"I don't know. None of it makes sense."

Marin shook her head. "Nadine's got an agenda. She's trying to get Amelia to sell the house, and now Kelly's worrying about that on top of everything else."

Blythe sighed. "Well, Amelia doesn't see it that way. She believes her. I felt bad about the conversation all day, and now hearing what's going on with Kelly...I wish I could put Amelia's mind to rest over the past."

"So tell her."

"I did! She doesn't believe me. She thought I was just trying to make nice so she wouldn't spill the beans to your father."

Marin sat back in her seat. She twisted her cloth napkin in her hands. "Mom..."

"Marin, before you start, please let me just say something to you. I know we're just getting back on track here, and at the risk of irritating you, I'm going to put my two cents in where maybe it doesn't belong. I assume you will at some point determine who is the father of your baby. And when you do, I hope you will let him know. It might be uncomfortable and messy but if we've learned anything, I think it's that the truth has a way of demanding its day. There's no use fighting it."

Marin nodded. "Yeah. About that: I told Dad the real reason we're here. I told him the truth about my paternity."

Blythe, mid-sip of her wine, dropped her glass. The white tablecloth turned deep burgundy as the glass rolled onto the floor and shattered. A waitress and two busboys scurried around to clean up the mess. Blythe could barely breathe. Marin was saying something to her, then to the waitress, but Blythe heard none of it.

Well, that was it. Any chance of reconciliation was no doubt ruined. No wonder Kip left so quickly. He never wanted to see her again. He hated her. She was lucky she hadn't had to face him.

"It's okay," Blythe finally said, a new plate before her, her wineglass replaced and refilled. She touched the stem, her eyes filling with tears. "Here I am, lecturing you about the truth. Of course you don't want to live a lie. I don't know how I have for so long."

"Well, that's the thing. You haven't been."

Blythe looked up. "What?"

"Dad knows. He's known all along."

Chapter Thirty-Four

By the time Rachel served the coconut lemon cake she'd baked using Amelia's dog-eared recipe for *bolo de coco e limão,* Thomas, Kelly, and Amelia were deep into the wine and on an extensive trip down memory lane.

Rachel and Luke, excluded from the conversation, ate silently, pretending not to steal glances at each other. At least, that's what she thought was going on. Maybe she was stealing glances at him, and he was looking at her wondering why she was staring at him. It was so hard to know!

Things got more confusing when he helped her clear the table; while she was loading the dishwasher, he said, "It's really great of you to help Amelia and Kelly. Spending hours in the kitchen probably isn't what you expected when you came to the beach."

"It's better than what I expected," she said.

He looked at her as if seeing her for the first time.

"Is that true?"

She nodded.

"It's funny," he said. "When I told colleagues at the university I was spending the summer in Provincetown, they basically rolled their eyes like I was going on a two-month party bender. But the truth is, life is more real here than anywhere in the real world. Do you know what I mean?"

"Yes," she breathed. He was so close. She tried not to think about touching him. She knew it was important that she understand what he was saying—that whatever was being communicated to her was more important than any poolside kiss. She just wasn't completely sure what that thing was yet.

"Trust me, you'll feel it even more when you leave."

She didn't want to think about leaving Provincetown. She didn't even want to think about leaving that kitchen.

Amelia walked in. "Kelly's not feeling well. Are you okay finishing up here? I want to get her home."

"Yes, sure. Is she okay?" Rachel said.

"Nothing a little rest won't cure." She put one of the half-finished bottles of wine on the kitchen island. "And maybe a little less of this." She smiled and kissed Rachel on the cheek. "You're a huge help. Thank you, dear."

Rachel and Luke finished up the dishes, Rachel slowing and stalling when it came to the last few pots and pans. Just when there was absolutely no excuse to linger at the house, Luke said, "I could use some air. Want to go for a quick walk?"

She looked into his beautiful blue eyes. She felt no confusion, no nervousness. Deep down, she knew something was happening between them. She was not imagining it, and she was not going to let it slip away this time.

"Sure."

Amelia sat on the edge of the bed, rubbing her hands with an organic lavender moisturizer. One of the small daily annoyances of aging was that her skin was always dry, even in the middle of summer. And in the winter? Forget about it. One year, she had mentioned this in passing to one of their summer regulars, a retired flight attendant who had battled dry skin during long flights, and the woman had given her a tube of her favorite moisturizer as a thank-you at the end of the week. Amelia had been a devotee of the product ever since. It had even inspired an ill-fated attempt at a lavender garden.

"Remember that summer when we tried to grow lavender?" she called out to Kelly, who was in the bathroom. "Maybe we should give it another try? I think Blythe has quite the green thumb. Maybe she can help."

Kelly, behind the closed bathroom door, began coughing with alarming ferocity.

"What's going on with you?" Amelia asked when she finally emerged, pressing a tissue to her mouth.

"Sinus infection," Kelly said, crawling into her side of the bed and closing her eyes. Amelia moved closer to her and rested her head on her pillow.

"We should take a vacation. Travel somewhere this winter."

"Oh? Why's that?" Kelly rolled toward her and propped herself up on one elbow, prompting more coughing.

Amelia hesitated. "I'm thinking we should free ourselves of the responsibility of this big house. We won't be bogged down by the upkeep, by the decision of whether or not to run the inn. We can travel. Who knows what we'll fall in love with? We'll feather a new nest—one for this chapter in our lives. I'm seventy-five years old. If not now, when?"

"Nadine got to you," Kelly said.

Amelia sighed. "I know you don't understand, but I do feel a responsibility to her. If I couldn't be the mother she wanted or needed, I can at least help give her some financial security. And ourselves too. Sandra Crowe is offering above and beyond what I would have asked—"

"I can't tell you what to do with this house. But I think you should know the big picture before you make such a major decision. I won't be traveling with you this winter. I won't be feathering a new nest."

"Well, you don't have to say it like that. We don't have to go anywhere. But this house issue is complicated for me—"

"I might not be around this winter," Kelly said.

Amelia felt her entire body go cold.

"Don't," she said, turning away from Kelly, her heart pounding. On some primal, deep level, she knew what was about to be said. And if she could just refuse to hear the words…

"The cancer is back."

It was dark, and up above, it seemed every star in the universe was visible.

"Just take it slow. Follow my lead," Luke said.

The rocks formed a mile-long jetty into Cape Cod Bay. Luke walked one step ahead of her, holding out his hand, leading her along the rocks that afforded the most stable footing.

"I would not want to do this drunk," she said.

"No, you wouldn't. I have, and it wasn't pretty."

The signs warning of sharks and dangerous currents were not comforting. Yes, it was definitely a walk to be made sober, and probably best in daylight. But there she was, following Luke Duncan into shark-infested waters on some questionable rocks.

Luke set a slow but deliberate pace. They made their way in silence, not speaking until he stopped a quarter of the way out.

The wind picked up. Surrounded by lapping waves, under the stars, she felt like they were standing at the edge of the world, exhilarating and terrifying at the same time. She'd grown up at the beach; water was as familiar to her as land. But this felt somehow different. She shivered, and Luke put his arm around her.

What was going on? Should she play it cool? How could she? She had no game—she wouldn't even try.

He looked up at the sky and sighed. "I wish you were a little older."

What? *That* was the stumbling block?

"Older? Why? Kelly met Amelia when she was younger than I am. They have a twenty-year age difference. And look at them!"

"I'm not saying our age difference is empirically wrong. But it does make things more difficult—as I learned the hard way in my last relationship. I'm not a big fan of making the same mistake twice."

"You dated someone younger, it didn't work out, and now you'll never date someone younger again? Sorry, but that sounds a little crazy to me. And as someone *older*—you should know better." She shook off his arm.

He laughed. "Touché. You sure Marin's the only lawyer in the family?"

She didn't smile back at him. This was not a joke to her. It *hurt*. She was putting herself out on a limb—or, to be accurate, a jetty.

"I don't think I can be *friends* with you," she said.

"Oh, Rachel." He put his arm around her again, and despite her feelings of indignation, she couldn't bring herself to shrug it off. "A month before I moved out here, I was living with my girlfriend, Vanessa. She's a first-year grad student in ancient history. We were planning to spend July in Greece. I went shopping for a ring. But then Bart confirmed what I'd suspected at Christmas: my father was deteriorating, and I decided I needed to be out here for the summer. Vanessa was upset—she doesn't like it here very much."

Rachel felt a stab of irrational jealousy. He'd brought a woman to Provincetown? Had they stood on that very spot, his arm around her? Probably. He had no doubt kissed her, the water rolling gently all around them in the romantic way it was at that very minute.

"So she broke up with you?" The woman must be crazy.

"No, not exactly. But she put me in a position of choosing between her and my dad. I realized I couldn't marry her."

Her loss.

"Okay, that sucks—I get it. But I don't know what that has to do with age."

"Vanessa isn't a bad person. She's just young. She doesn't understand taking care of someone other than herself."

"So you're lumping me in with her? I *am* helping take care of other people—including your father. In case you hadn't noticed dinner tonight."

Who was he to judge her limitations? It felt good to be angry, to push back a little. She wasn't just begging for whatever crumbs he tossed her way.

"Of course I noticed. It makes it hard for me to stick

to my feelings on this. But Rachel, you don't know who you are yet—what you're going to do with your life. I've answered more questions than you've probably begun to ask."

"I've answered questions you've never *had* to ask! That's why I'm here this summer. Learning about my father is the biggest thing that's ever happened to me. If that's not life-changing, I don't know what is."

They balanced on the same rock, glaring at each other in the moonlight.

"You're right," he said. "I'm sorry. It's not all on you. I'm still getting over Vanessa. But even under better circumstances, you live in LA. I don't want a summer fling. That's not what I need, and I'm guessing it's not what you need either."

Actually, a summer fling sounded good to her! But whatever—she wasn't going to beg. She was too young, he was still hung up on what's her name in Rhode Island, they lived far away from each other. How many excuses did he need to reject her?

"I get it," she said. She eyed the distance back to dry land. If she had any dignity, she would turn around and march herself home. But she was a quarter mile out on the jetty.

"Shall we?" he asked, turning around, holding out his arm for the trek back. He looked at her with such friendly affection, she couldn't offer anything less than a tentative smile. How could she help herself?

She was completely in love with him.

Chapter Thirty-Five

In the morning, there was no breakfast.

"Amelia always has food and coffee out. *Always,*" Blythe said.

Marin nodded, concerned. When Amelia wasn't waiting for her in the front hall for their morning walk on the beach, she went around back to find her. Instead, she found Blythe sitting alone sipping coffee from a Joe takeout cup.

The day was bright and particularly warm, nearing eighty degrees even early in the morning. Marin pulled off the long-sleeved cotton T-shirt she wore over her tank top and tied it around her waist. She sat opposite her mother at the table.

"Marin, you look so beautiful," her mother said. "You have the glow."

"I don't feel it. I'm exhausted." Even though she had slept better last night than she had in a while.

Thanks to the conversation with her father yesterday, she finally had some relief from the shadow of dread she'd felt ever since that first e-mail from Rachel.

Sitting with Kip, just inches from where she now sat with her mother, she'd felt as if she were watching someone else tell him. She couldn't now, for the life of her, remember exactly what she'd said. But she would never forget how her father responded.

"You're my daughter. You've been my daughter since the moment I set eyes on you."

"Dad, I don't think you understand." She started in again about the genetics and he stopped her midsentence.

"Marin, hon, *you* don't understand: I've always known. It makes no difference to me. You're my daughter, always have been and always will be." She found it difficult to believe that he could mean it. And yet, the knowledge of Nick Cabral didn't change the fact that Kipton Bishop was her dad. What were genetics compared to love?

Her mother had an equally hard time wrapping her mind around his reaction. She made Marin repeat it twice, word for word.

"Are you upset with me for telling him?" Marin had asked.

"No," Blythe said quickly. And then she reiterated what she'd said, that Marin had to deal with her own pregnancy paternity issue as honestly and as forthrightly as she could. This irritated Marin.

"Mom, please. Don't turn this around on me."

Still, she'd thought about her mother's words as she fell asleep. It wasn't the same situation, she assured herself. She wasn't *lying* to Greg or Julian. She just wasn't telling them.

Rachel walked out of the house, and seeing that the table was empty, she turned right around to make coffee and breakfast.

Marin stood up from the table. "I'm going to pick up a croissant at Joe and take a walk." No more coffee for her. No caffeine, no alcohol. Oddly, she didn't miss either one. All she wanted was sleep. It was tempting to just go back to bed, but she refused to let the first-trimester fatigue hobble her. At least some shred of her type A personality was left.

"Do you have your phone with you?" Blythe asked.

"No. Why?"

"Maybe bring it? Just in case." Blythe nodded her head toward the house, widening her eyes. Marin got it; Amelia might be a no-show at breakfast because she was upset. Maybe Kelly had finally told her the truth, or maybe Amelia figured it out for herself. Either way, she might need their support.

"I'll get my phone. Call me if anything's going on."

Crossing the street, Marin was distracted; a bicyclist had to ring her hand bell so she didn't collide with her. Car traffic was already at a standstill. She could see from two buildings away that Joe had a line out the door. In the late weeks of July, the town had swelled into something unrecognizable from the intimate community she had met just a month earlier.

Marin pulled her hair off her neck and into a ponytail. She wiped her forehead with the back of her hand and took a place in line. It moved quickly. The server behind the counter was the blond-dreadlocked girl from the first day they arrived in town. Today her T-shirt read VAGITARIAN.

She ordered her croissant just as her phone vibrated in her pocket. Marin so fully expected it to be her mother that she barely registered the incoming number before hearing his voice.

"Hey, I'm glad you finally answered," Julian said.

"Hold on a sec." She paid quickly, cradling the phone between her cheek and her shoulder, and rushed back outside. Bart was seated at one of the tables with a bunch of friends, and he waved at her. She waved back, then turned left on Commercial, falling into the tide of pedestrians.

"Julian, I told you not to call me."

"I know. And I probably deserved that. But Marin, we need to talk. I don't care how many times you make me beg."

In the middle of the street, a drag queen dressed as a mermaid had halted traffic. Cars honked—tourists, no doubt. She knew by now the locals had infinite patience for traffic stoppage on Commercial. The mermaid handed out paper flyers. A sequined lobster appeared beside her, hoisting a 1980s-style boom box in the air and blasting "The Edge of Glory" by Lady Gaga.

"Come one, come all—it's the sixth annual Lobsterfest to Benefit Outer Cape Health Services!"

"Hold on a second. I need to find a quieter place—" Marin ducked into Marine Specialties, a quirky cavelike place that was part thrift store, part gift shop, part she didn't quite know what. She walked toward the back, weaving through racks of cargo pants, a display of thermal underwear, a box piled with straw hats, and a low-hanging smattering of piñatas. She found a quiet spot next to a box of movie posters.

She took a breath and put the phone to her ear. "Okay," she said. "I'm back." Julian began talking, something about time and thinking about everything and realizing how much she meant to him...

Marin could still hear the Lady Gaga music and the shouting mermaid. *From Julian's end of the phone.*

"Julian," she said, barely daring to breathe. "Where exactly are you?"

Kelly was wrong. Amelia did not need a house that was full of people. She didn't need the house itself. Amelia needed *her*.

She pulled her suitcase from the top of her closet and began throwing clothes into it. She didn't know yet where they were going; all she knew was that they had to get away.

The universe was punishing her. It was very clear. Loving Kelly, leaving her marriage—it was a transgression for which she had been paying ever since. Loss after loss. When Nick died, she had the same thought, and in her heart and mind she told God that she accepted her penance. She would have to live with it. But now this.

Last year, when the cancer first appeared, she felt it was the universe wagging a finger at her, saying, *Don't get too comfortable*. Kelly told her she had to stop with the magical thinking.

"It doesn't work that way," she'd said.

Amelia closed the bag, knelt on the floor, and dissolved into tears. She indulged herself, because while she was determined that after last night she would not cry again in front of Kelly, at the moment, Kelly was not in the bedroom. She had gone to her studio to work, as she did every morning.

"I don't want anything to change," she'd told Amelia, kissing her before she rolled out of bed, that cough trailing after her like a blaring alarm.

Her bag packed, Amelia sat immobile on the floor until she heard a knock on the door. She wiped her eyes.

"Who is it?"

"Blythe. I have coffee for you."

Amelia took a deep breath and forced herself to do the right thing and open the door.

"We missed you at breakfast," Blythe said. She held a tray with Amelia's yellow coffeepot and set it on the wooden bureau. Amelia did a quick calculation on the odds that Blythe knew about Kelly's illness; Kelly had admitted to Amelia that she'd told Marin, "Only because she busted me on the phone." The question was, had Marin told her mother?

"I overslept," Amelia said. "Thanks for the coffee. That was so thoughtful of you."

"It's the least I could do," Blythe said. There was something about the expression on her face, a look that was both sorrowful and searching, that gave Amelia her answer. But she would not acknowledge it. She refused.

Blythe eyed the suitcase. "Are you going somewhere?"

Amelia nodded. "The Cape is so overrun this time of the summer. We need to get away for a few days."

"Oh, dear," Blythe said. "Are we crowding you? I can round up the girls. We don't want to outstay our welcome. You two have been so generous, but of course you must want some time to yourselves—"

"No, no—please. Don't be silly. We're thrilled to have you here, and in fact I'm more comfortable leaving when I know the place is being looked after. Rachel has been such a help and I know she'll step in if Thomas needs anything."

"Yes. Absolutely." Blythe stood awkwardly, wringing her hands.

Amelia smiled patiently, waiting for her to leave. Blythe walked to the door, reached for the knob, then paused. She turned back to her.

"I wanted to give you some good news," she said. Amelia looked at her, wondering if she was hearing correctly.

"Good news?"

"Yes," Blythe said, smiling tentatively and moving closer to her. "Marin is pregnant. You're going to be a great-grandmother."

"What?"

"She just found out last week."

Blythe went on and on, but to Amelia it was white noise. She searched deep inside herself for some feeling, some hint of joy. All she felt was a sense of betrayal, that the universe was playing a cruel joke on her, taunting her with its ability to deal its cards of life and death. She began to sob, and Blythe's hopeful smile quickly faded. She embraced her, telling her it was going to be okay—that they would be there for her. Amelia searched for words, a way to express her feeling that everything she loved was eventually taken from her and so how could she feel joy even about this good news?

"What's going on?" Rachel appeared in the doorway.

Amelia and Blythe looked at each other. Amelia mouthed, *No*.

Blythe invited Rachel in and closed the door behind her. When she turned around, she had a smile planted on her face. "We have some good news," she said, her eyes shining with tears that only Amelia knew were sorrowful. "Marin is pregnant."

* * *

Julian looked so good! She had almost forgotten the intensity of her attraction, but when he pulled her into his arms and she breathed in his scent, she felt she could faint from it. He held her wordlessly, and it felt like they were alone in the world there in the musty air and dim light of Marine Specialties.

She'd fantasized about their reunion endlessly, but in her daydreams (a) she had not been pregnant, and (b) it hadn't taken place under a movie poster from the 1987 vampire film *The Lost Boys*.

"My God, I didn't even realize how much I missed you until this second," he said, pulling back and looking at her.

"I can't believe you're here," she said, uncomfortable under his gaze. Would he be able to tell? Did she look different? It was vitally important to her to get through whatever time they had together without mentioning the pregnancy. There wasn't even a question; she would not tell him. Seeing him again was a gift—a fleeting, impossible offering from the universe that was knocking her about just to show her who was boss. She had capitulated: *Universe, you win!* But here was one last thing, at least, she could control.

She would not ruin their reunion with the messy truth.

He kissed her and murmured something about getting out of there.

"Where are you staying?" she asked him.

"A place called Captain Jack's. You have to see my room. It's like being on a boat."

They walked down Commercial, his arm around her waist, keeping her close. Every guy they passed shot him an appreciative glance, and it gave Marin an odd sense of possessive pride. For just a few minutes, she let herself feel like she was part of a normal couple, reveling in the mundane happiness of being in love.

Captain Jack's was a quirky hotel out on a wharf, a long string of cabins right on the water. It was the type of establishment you'd be hard-pressed to find outside of Provincetown. Julian led her to a shingled cabin painted bright green and facing the bay. The building was framed by dock pilings decorated with old buoys flaking with paint, threaded with long ropes of Christmas lights. A sign outside the cabin read NO SMOKING. NO CATS.

Inside, the room had vaulted wood ceilings, white wood floors, French doors opening onto the deck, and plenty of wide windows. It was decorated with nautical bric-a-brac. He had a view of the Long Point lighthouse in the distance.

"This is beautiful," she said, feeling nervous.

Julian reached for her wordlessly and led her to the bed. His touch felt so good she could barely breathe, but she worried that he would notice the distinct new curve to her belly, the fullness of her breasts.

"God, I've missed you," he murmured.

"I missed you too," she said, her body arching toward him. And when he was inside of her, her thoughts were no longer coherent enough for worry.

Afterward, she curled against him, willing herself to just enjoy the moment and not think about the reality that, when confessed, would destroy this very temporary happiness.

"Is that a tattoo?" he asked.

"What?" She'd forgotten about the beach rose. It was already a part of her—the new her, the woman who woke up to take long walks on the beach instead of a walk to the subway, who spent her morning cutting tile instead of filing briefs, and who had a baby growing inside of her.

"Yes. It's a beach rose. I got it the first week I was here."

"Interesting."

"Interesting good or interesting bad?"

"You tell me," he said, stroking her hair. "Marin, what's going on? You're not just out here to get away from everything that happened in New York, are you? Why did you get so mad on the phone and bring up Genie?"

She rubbed the inside of her wrist, and it all came pouring out: her Genie results, Rachel's e-mail and phone calls and the road trip and all that had happened since the last time she saw him.

"You were trying to tell me that morning after you got back from visiting your mom in Philadelphia," he said. "When you asked me about the statistical likelihood of error?"

"I wasn't trying to tell you. I wanted plausible deniability. I didn't want to admit it to *myself,* let alone you."

He started saying all the right things, about how she could have talked to him about it—should have talked to him about it. It should have been a comfort to her, but it just made her feel that much worse about the one thing she still was not telling him.

"Can we go to the inn?" he said. "I want to see where you've been staying all summer."

"This wasn't how I envisioned you meeting my family," she said.

"I never knew that you had envisioned me meeting your family," he said, smiling and squeezing her hand. She pulled her hand away, not wanting to encourage him. This could not go anywhere. They would have a good day or two, and then he would go back to New York. And by the time she returned to New York, visibly pregnant, it would be over.

Just because Julian had missed her, just because he had shown up to visit, didn't mean he wanted a baby. And it certainly didn't mean he wanted a baby that might belong to her former fiancé.

But for now, he was there with her. *Stay in the moment,* she told herself. *You can have one day of happiness.*

"We'll see who's home. It might be just Kelly in her studio." She felt a flicker of excitement to introduce him to Kelly. Then, afterward, she could talk to Kelly about all of her complicated feelings. Kelly would understand.

"Marin, I want to make this work. Let's turn all of the craziness of the past few months—the work stuff, all this upheaval with your family—into something positive. Let's build, okay? We can do this."

She closed her eyes. *We can do this.* Oh, how she wanted to believe he was right.

Chapter Thirty-Six

Blythe knelt on the grass and hammered the last of four wooden stakes into the ground to wall off the patch of fresh soil she'd tilled. Next, she would cover the garden bed with compost. Working in the heat, panting with exertion, she still couldn't quiet her mind.

How could Kip have known the truth about Marin all along and never said a word? It should be cause for relief, but instead it made her feel that not only was her marriage over, it had never been what she'd believed it to be in the first place. She always felt that Kip loved her more after Marin was born; he tried harder to connect with Blythe, and even though he fell short in many ways, the new effort, combined with motherhood, cemented Blythe's conviction that she needed to make her marriage work. And for so many years, it had worked. There had been genuine love, happiness, and, yes, even passion between them. Sure, it had fallen off in recent years. But she thought that was the normal course of things. Now she wondered if there had ever been a "normal" moment between them after her pregnancy.

The answer was probably no. And there never would be. The marriage wasn't ending because of his affair with Candace, and it wasn't going to be saved because the affair was over. It was fatally flawed.

Nadine stepped out of the house, wheeling a suitcase. "Have you seen my mother?"

"She's in her room," Blythe said, squinting against the sun.

Nadine consulted her phone. "Can you tell her I'm going to visit friends for a few days? But I'll be back."

"Yes, I'll let her know. She and Kelly are going away too."

Nadine raised an eyebrow. "Really? Well, looks like you'll have the house all to yourself. How convenient. What are you doing, anyway?"

"Gardening."

"Does my mother know you're digging up her property?"

Blythe, summoning all the patience she could muster, said, "She knows, and she's all for it. There's nothing like garden-to-table food, Nadine. You might like it too."

"You three have gotten really comfortable here," Nadine said. "Just don't get too comfortable."

Where was all the hostility from? Did she really believe that Blythe had somehow hurt Nick? That he had run to Italy to get away from her? If she did, that was her problem.

But it sure as hell didn't have to be Amelia's. Blythe had an idea. Maybe a crazy idea, but an idea nonetheless. She walked into the house and poured herself a glass of water.

Think carefully about this, she told herself. *Once you do it, it can't be undone.*

She went upstairs, pulled her barely used cell phone from her bedside-table drawer, and dialed Kip's number.

"I was wondering if you'd call," he said.

"Why did you rush off without saying good-bye?"

"I said good-bye when you left me to talk to Marin."

"Yes, but I thought I'd see you later." Silence. "Marin told me about your, um, conversation with her. Kip, why didn't you ever say anything to me?"

"Blythe. It's water under the bridge. Let's not."

How? How could they not talk about it? She supposed, in his mind, the marriage was over. Kip was very much like that; either things were being debated or the case was closed.

She'd thought, that moment at Pilgrims' Park when he told her it was over with Candace, that he'd been making his way back to her. Clearly, she had been mistaken.

They had now been separated for four months. He'd come all the way out there to see Marin and didn't say so much as a good-bye to Blythe. And then there was the deeply confusing news that he had known about her infidelity all along and never confronted her. Now it was all out in the open, and he couldn't even be bothered to talk about it. It wasn't worth his time. His mind was made up.

Understanding all of this should have made what she needed to ask easier. But it didn't, and she found herself stalling. "What's going on at work?"

"I've decided to take the package they're offering. I'm leaving at the end of the year."

"Oh, Kip. I'm sorry. I know it's not what you wanted."

"I'm making the best of it. Marin's feeling well?"

"Yes. She's fine. But we all got some bad news. One of the women we're staying with found out she had terminal cancer. It's quite upsetting."

"Marin's grandmother?"

"No. Her partner."

"I hope Marin isn't taking it too hard. She needs to keep her spirits up."

"She's fine. I'm actually concerned about her grandmother—Amelia. That's why I'm calling." Deep breath. "There's something I want to show her. It's at the house and I was wondering if you could find it for me and mail it here."

"I can do that."

"It's a shoe box. I know this is a lot to ask, but please don't open it. Just put it in a FedEx pack and send the whole thing. It's . . . personal."

Blythe told him where to find the last words she'd ever heard from Nick Cabral.

Rachel rolled her yoga mat out on the front porch and stretched. Her original plan had been to take it to the beach, but she couldn't wait to get there. She needed to meditate and quiet her mind. She was going to be an aunt! It was hard to keep a secret, but who would she tell, anyway?

She was excited, but at the same time, the news made her a little sad. Marin had her parents and now she would have a baby. Amelia and Kelly had each other. But at the end of the summer, Rachel would have to go back to LA and she would feel more alone than ever.

Rachel rolled onto her back.

"Rachel—you're here," Marin said, appearing on the top step. Rachel, surprised, looked up at her.

"Oh my God, Marin, hi! Congratulations! A baby! I can't believe it."

Marin's eyes widened, and she shook her head. And then a gorgeous man with dark hair and big brown eyes appeared behind her.

"What did she just say?" he asked Marin.

Oops.

"Julian, this is my half sister, Rachel," Marin said quickly, as if a conversational bomb had not detonated. "Rachel, this is my friend Julian. I'm just going to give him a fast tour of the house."

Really, there was nothing she could do but nod as Marin took him by the hand and tugged him toward the kitchen. The "friend" glanced back at her, as if Rachel were going to offer up one last parting gem. She looked away.

Disaster! But how was she supposed to know someone was right behind Marin? She'd seen only Marin, and she was just so excited about the idea of becoming an aunt. Well, if that was the baby daddy, he had to find out sooner or later. Right?

Amelia made her way down the stairs, dragging luggage.

"Are you *going* somewhere?" Rachel asked. The idea of Amelia leaving was almost unthinkable, like the backyard table just getting up and walking away.

"Yes. Kelly and I are going on a little vacation. I'm hoping you can keep an eye on things while I'm gone? Please just check on Thomas for me on Thursday? It's Paul's turn for dinner, but I'd just feel better if you confirm with him."

The front door opened and in walked a bunch of people Rachel had never seen before, a man and woman who looked to be in their forties and two young teenagers, a boy and girl. The boy carried a guitar case and the girl held a skateboard.

"Amelia!" The woman, stout and dark-haired, smiled and ran over to hug Amelia while the man waved from the doorway, a pile of bags at his feet.

"Joan...Frank. What are you doing here?" Amelia dropped her own bag.

"I know, right?" the woman said, looking around the room and beaming. "August already! Every time we walk in the door, it feels like we never left."

Kelly walked down the stairs, and Amelia turned to her and whispered, "The Millers are here. I thought you said you were going to call them?"

"I forgot!"

An odd welcome ritual ensued, lots of catching-up talk that excluded Rachel. She looked at the two kids shuffling their feet and checking their phones while their parents exulted in their reunion with Amelia and Kelly. Finally, the woman turned to Rachel.

"Joan Miller," she said, her hand outstretched. "Are you staying here too?"

"Oh! I'm sorry. Where is my head? Joan, this is my granddaughter Rachel."

More exclamations. Joan didn't know Amelia had a granddaughter! (Of course she didn't. Amelia hadn't known she had a granddaughter until three months ago.)

Kelly pulled Rachel aside.

"Listen, we have a somewhat awkward situation on our hands," she said, breathing heavily. "The Millers have been coming here every summer for the past two decades. I canceled their reservation this year because we closed the inn, but clearly they didn't get the memo. Now that they're here, I can't see making them leave, but Amelia really wants to get away for a few days—" A coughing fit interrupted her, and Amelia rushed over.

"Hon, go to the car. I'll handle this," she said, her face creased with concern.

"Amelia, I can take care of things here. Just tell me what to do," Rachel said. Amelia glanced back at the Millers, who had congregated on the front porch while waiting for their room.

"Are you sure?" Amelia's face was pinched with doubt.

"Yes. Absolutely. Just tell me what room to put them in and I'll take care of it."

"It's a lot of work. The linens, breakfast…"

"I can handle it! It's the least I can do. I mean, we all showed up here and never left. I feel bad that you and Kelly have to leave in order to get some peace and quiet—"

"Oh, my dear. That's not it at all."

"Just let me do this. Let someone do something for you for a change."

"It *would* be a huge help," Amelia admitted. "But only if you're sure…"

"I'm sure," Rachel said.

What could go wrong?

Chapter Thirty-Seven

Marin sat on her bed, in the same spot she'd occupied all summer yearning for Julian. Now he was there, and things couldn't be worse.

He paced in front of her. "I just don't understand why you would keep this from me."

"Really? Maybe it's because you handle complications and setbacks so well!"

"You're comparing this pregnancy to us losing our jobs?"

She shrugged. He sat next to her and gripped her shoulders, forcing her to look him in the eyes. "I know what it's like to grow up without a father and I would never do that to my own child."

She broke his gaze. "That's noble of you, Julian. But what if it's not *your* child?"

His hands fell from her shoulders and he sat back, a stricken expression on his face.

"It's not?" he whispered.

"I don't know, okay? I mean, you do the math."

His eyes narrowed and he got the faraway expression

she'd seen when he was poring over a case, trying to solve a problem or answer a complex question. After what felt like forever he said:

"How could this happen?"

"I assume that's rhetorical," Marin said.

Julian stood and pressed his hands to his forehead. "Goddamn it, Marin."

"You should leave," she said, fighting back tears.

She didn't have to tell him twice. When he was gone, she closed the door and leaned against it with a sob. That's when she noticed a piece of Beach Rose Inn stationery had been slipped under it.

"Hello over there? I'm looking for Nadine."

Blythe glanced up from the patch of soil she was raking. It was marked off from the rest of the yard with wooden stakes, and the next step would be to buttress the garden with wood planks, which she would hopefully find at the garden shop.

Blythe wiped the soil from her hands and adjusted her sun hat so she could see the person calling out to her from the side of the house. It was Sandra Crowe.

Sandra was dressed in a salmon-colored sundress and strappy gold sandals. Her dark hair was sleek, cut sharp at her jawline, and despite the relative humidity of the afternoon, her face was fully made up. She looked like she was going to an audition for *Real Housewives of Provincetown*.

Blythe stood. "Nadine's not here. She went away for a few days. Can I help you?"

Sandra looked at Blythe's hands and dirt-smudged shorts.

"What are you doing?" she asked.

"I'm gardening," Blythe said.

"Can you please not dig up this property?"

Good Lord, not this again.

"Excuse me?" Blythe said. "I don't see how that's your business."

Sandra cocked her head, smiling with amusement. "It is literally my business. I'm buying this house. Now, if you don't mind, Nadine told me I could take some measurements inside."

"It's not a good time," Blythe said. Did she have a right to interfere like this? Hell yes. More than a right; she had a duty!

Sandra started to protest, but Blythe plastered a smile on her face and said, "The exterminator is here. It's being fumigated."

"Exterminator? For what?"

"Well, now—that's not *my* business. You'll have to come back when Nadine is here." Blythe steered her back to the front of the house and left her at the sidewalk with a wave.

Blythe walked up the steps and took a seat on the porch. She felt she should have a shotgun, like a settler defending her home on the range. After a few moments of reveling in her role of domestic protector, she decided she'd check out the gardening shop she'd seen on Race Point Road.

The front door swung open, startling her. She turned, hoping to see Marin, who had disappeared after breakfast, but instead she found a tall, dark-haired, extremely handsome young man.

"Excuse me. Can I help you?" she said, standing quickly.

"I was just leaving," he said. He was dressed in khaki pants and a white button-down shirt with rolled-up sleeves. The clothes were casual but not quite as casual as the norm around here. He was a visitor, but who was he visiting? Or was he looking for a room?

"I don't mean to be rude, but this is a private residence. The inn is closed this season."

"Like I said, ma'am, I was just leaving."

His eyes were dark, long-lashed. His voice held a hint of a British accent.

Oh, happy day!

"Are you Julian?"

Now it was his turn to be startled. "Yes, I'm Julian."

"I'm Blythe Bishop, Marin's mother. Oh, I'm so glad she called you about the baby and that you came!" Blythe wanted to hug him. He had proven her right: Marin had to embrace the situation, be honest, not try to hide the complicated truth. It was all going to work out for her.

He didn't say anything, just looked at her. Then: "It's nice to meet you, Mrs. Bishop."

Oh, dear. Something was wrong.

"Are you leaving?"

"Yes. I'm leaving."

Blythe's maternal alarm sounded.

"So soon? Please don't go. I know it's complicated. But you came here to see Marin so you must want to be with her."

He looked at her like she was crazy.

"With all due respect, Mrs. Bishop, I need some time."

Time? That's what he'd said when they lost their jobs. But now he was here, so he must have realized he didn't need time, he needed Marin. Why go through that same useless exercise? "You two can work this out. I know she cares about you. More than she's cared about anyone. I saw that the first day she told me about you."

He shook his head. "I know you're trying to help."

Blythe glanced back at the house. There was so much she needed to say, things he had to know before he made a decision that would hurt him and Marin and, yes, maybe even the baby. Things she'd learned only in the past month, like the way the truth always comes out. That maybe the truth isn't as scary as you think; it's the running away that's the problem. The fact that family has to do with so much more than biology. That investing in loving someone is worth it.

The front door swung open and a strange woman and teenage girl walked out carrying beach chairs. The woman smiled at Blythe.

Who on earth were they? She was in the midst of a crisis, and that damn porch was becoming Grand Central Station. Before she could salvage the moment, Julian walked away.

Chapter Thirty-Eight

Rachel's first morning running the inn, and breakfast was late.

She completely misjudged how long it would take to prepare Amelia's usual spread. She thought since the only food that took real time was the *broa* and the orange muffins, that was all she had to account for. But it was the little things, like hard-boiling the eggs and squeezing the orange juice and cutting up the fruit salad, that threw her off. Even simply putting the organic granola into the bowl, setting out the yogurt—it all added up. The Millers patiently drank coffee while they waited. Well, the parents were patient. The two teenagers protested loudly, wanting to skip breakfast and head to the beach.

When she finally set the food out, they all made such a big deal about how good it was, she stopped beating herself up on the timing.

"This is all so delicious, Rachel—just like your grandmother makes!" Mrs. Miller said. Her husband nodded his agreement, his mouth full. Mrs. Miller told her daughter not to drink too much coffee, which got an eye-roll.

Rachel was heading back to the kitchen when Mrs. Miller called out to her.

"You don't, by any chance, have that incredible cheese?"

Cheese? Did she mean the homemade cheese? She'd forgotten all about that. She hadn't seen it after she and Amelia had spooned the curds into cheese molds and put it in the refrigerator. Things had gotten so crazy around there.

"I don't, but..." Was this something Amelia always put out for her guests? Did she have a responsibility to make it? There was no way. She'd mess it up. "Maybe tomorrow?"

Mrs. Miller clapped her hands like a little kid. "I just love it here. We've missed it so much."

Rachel nodded, hoping the panic didn't show on her face. She headed back into the kitchen, where Marin was making herself decaf.

Oh God. She hadn't seen Marin since the horrendous faux pas yesterday afternoon. Marin hadn't shown up for dinner, and neither had Blythe. Rachel ate a lobster roll alone at the Canteen.

"Marin, I'm so sorry about yesterday. I was just so excited about the baby. I hope it didn't upset you. Or him. Was that your boyfriend?"

"He used to be my boyfriend. It's okay. It's not your fault. He had to find out sooner or later."

Rachel covered her face with her hands. "I'm such an idiot."

"No, really. You did me a favor. It was like pulling off a Band-Aid, you know?" She looked out the window. "So I don't get it. These people just showed up thinking they had a reservation and Amelia said let them stay?"

Rachel nodded, weak with relief that Marin forgave her.

Marin groaned. "I'm just not in the mood for randoms."

"Well, think of it this way: Two months ago *we* were the randoms. Imagine how Kelly felt. We invaded."

"We're not *randoms*. We're family."

"Yeah, well, I think that's sort of how Amelia and Kelly feel about the people who have been coming here for decades, so try to roll with it."

"I guess. Oh—Luke's out front. He wants to talk to you."

"Here? Now?"

Marin nodded, poured her coffee and snagged a hard-boiled egg, and headed back up the stairs.

Rachel looked down at her flour-covered T-shirt, then brushed it off. She pulled her hair out of its rubber band and shook it loose. Oh, what difference did it make what she looked like? Friends.

She found Luke standing on the top step, facing the house. He wore navy cotton shorts and a baby-blue University of Rhode Island sweatshirt, his jaw notably covered in gold stubble. Oh, Lord help her.

"Hey," she said as casually as she could manage. "Marin said you wanted to see me?"

Luke smiled. "Any interest in going whale watching with Bart and me? The boat leaves at eleven."

Luke, a boat, four hours at sea in hopes of catching a glimpse of a majestic creature. It was her mermaid TV movie come to life.

"I'm busy. Thanks anyway."

He looked genuinely disappointed. "Rachel, I meant what I said. I really do want us to be friends."

Who cares what you want? she thought, suddenly irritable. It hurt to want someone so much. Still, it was tempting. But the laundry. The cheese!

"It's not that. I'm actually busy. Amelia and Kelly are away, and a family showed up because they never got the cancellation of their reservation, so I'm running the inn all week."

"Really," he said. "That's... great."

"Yeah. Hey, why don't you ask Marin to go?" There. That's what a friend would say.

"I don't think a whole afternoon on a boat would be her first choice for passing the time, considering..."

"Oh, you know about that?"

"Word gets around in this place."

They stood awkwardly. "Well, thanks anyway." With great effort, she turned and walked back into the house.

Thank you, cheese. Thank you for helping me do the right thing.

Marin couldn't stand being alone with her thoughts. It was agony. The baby, Julian... her life was completely out of her control. There was nothing to do to occupy her mind except work on the mosaic.

It felt strange to be in the studio without Kelly, almost as if she were trespassing. Before she started working, she reread the note that had been slipped under her door:

Marin: You'll be happy to know I told Amelia. It was rough. She wants to get away for a few days and how could I refuse? But this is throwing off my timeline for the mosaic. I really need you to start applying some of the pieces. Do the sapphire, bluebell, and arctic Venetian tile—follow my drawing.

I started that area so just keep going with the pattern. When in doubt, check the sketch. Remember what I showed you about buttering the tile with the adhesive. Thanks so much and have fun with it! XO K

Marin would not let Kelly down. She worked methodically, and her panic subsided after about a half hour. Once she fell into a rhythm, she realized she'd learned more from her afternoons alongside Kelly than she'd thought. Somehow, she'd absorbed some of Kelly's technique. And Kelly had known this.

The thing she loved about working with her hands was how it stilled her mind. No agonizing thoughts of Julian, no worry about the pregnancy and her future. There was just the work, a beautiful pattern taking shape under her fingertips.

Three different shades of blue tile joined together to great effect. If she ever made her own mosaics, she would probably have to plan out the patterns a few different ways before deciding. Okay, to be honest, a dozen different ways. She would obsess about making it perfect before giving in to the idea that it was good enough. Maybe that was okay.

She was startled by a knock on the door. She'd locked it out of habit; she and Kelly were always careful to do it so that Amelia wouldn't walk in unannounced and accidentally ruin her own surprise.

"Just a sec." Marin wiped her hands on a cloth. Whoever it was would have to be sent away quickly. She was on a mission and in a groove.

She unlocked the door and her breath caught in her throat.

"Your mother said I could find you up here," Julian said.

Marin put her brush and glue down on the table. "I don't know why you came back. There's nothing left to talk about."

"There's a hell of a lot to talk about."

"Julian, I know you probably prepaid for a few days at Captain Jack's. That doesn't mean we have to drag out this conversation."

He shook his head. "So cynical."

"Don't I have reason to be? You freaked out over the job thing, were barely able to talk to me for a month. I can't imagine you handling this baby situation even under the best of circumstances, never mind with this ambiguity. And it's fine—really. I don't blame you. *I* don't even know how to handle it. So let's just call it a day and save ourselves the drama."

"Marin," he said. "Look at me."

She couldn't. Why did he have to show up again? She'd spent all night telling herself it was for the best that he left—it took the pressure off. Some people weren't meant for lasting relationships, and she was probably one of them. Maybe she would raise the baby in Provincetown, get a job in one of the small law offices nearby. Or she would live in a small place on the beach, become an artist. Not much money in that, but she could make it work...

Julian was saying something. She tried to focus.

"I'm sorry," she said. "Say that again?"

"I came out here because I missed you. We started something amazing and, well, I did a lot of soul-searching in New York and I really want to see where this thing can go."

"What are you saying?"

"I overreacted when we lost our jobs. I don't want to make the same mistake now. I think we need to just...take things slow and get all the facts."

"The facts."

"Come on, Marin. You worked with me on Genie. You understand all the advances of DNA testing. We can find out the paternity in, what—a few weeks?"

Yes, she'd thought of that. And she'd dismissed it. She didn't want to know who the father was because she loved the baby no matter what. The messy reality could come later.

"And then what happens? You find out the baby isn't yours and you just walk away? No, thanks. Let's just end it right here and now."

"Marin, we've been together only a few months. We haven't even gotten to the point where we know for sure about each other, never mind raising a child together. But either way, I want to know. And, frankly, Greg has a right to know."

It was true. She hated that he was right.

She didn't say anything. He looked down at the mosaic.

"Did you make this?"

"No. It's Kelly's—my grandmother's wife. I'm just helping."

Julian looked around the studio, walked over to the bins filled with shells and colored glass and tile. He examined a few of Kelly's pieces on the walls. "She sells these?"

"Yes. My grandmother taught her when she first moved out here because she needed something to do. Now houses and restaurants all over town have her mosaics."

"Impressive."

"People out here make a living without showing up at a big corporation every day. It's just a whole way of life I never thought about."

"Is that what you want? To give up law and live out here doing something like this?"

She shook her head. "No. It just gives me a different perspective, that's all. Why? What do you want?"

"The same thing I've always wanted. I'm the same ambitious lawyer you met two years ago when you came to the firm. And so are you. So let's do what we do best: get the facts. Then make decisions." He took her hand. "What do you say?"

Slowly, she nodded.

"It will be all right," he said, leaning forward and kissing her on the cheek.

She hoped he was right.

"Let's find a computer," he said. *What's the big rush?* she wanted to say. But didn't.

"My laptop's in my room," she admitted.

She hadn't once taken it out of her suitcase and felt self-conscious retrieving it from the closet, feeling Julian's eyes on her every movement. It was strangely intimate to be together in that space, somehow much more so than any of their moments at his apartment in the city, including that first night. She had no idea why this was so, but it made her feel skittish.

Julian sat on the edge of her bed while she plugged in the computer and logged on to Genie. It took her a few seconds to find the prenatal genetics section. Her mind clouded with anxiety; she thought about the previous time she'd logged on to the site, prompted by Rachel's e-mail. This was even more terrifying.

She clicked on the order form for the testing kit and began typing in her info. He moved closer to her, rubbing her shoulders.

"Do they have a next-day-delivery option for the kit?" he said.

She nodded. It was done.

"Now what?" she said.

"Now? Now we go on a date. Why don't you show me what this town of yours has to offer."

Blythe found Amelia and Kelly's matching blue bikes propped at the side of the house. Amelia told them all they could use the bikes whenever they wanted, but as Blythe admitted to Rachel early in the trip, it really had been about thirty years since she rode. And as Rachel told *her,* getting back on would be like she'd never stopped.

Blythe, wobbling her way onto Commercial, hoped Rachel was right. The congestion on the street made her nervous. It would be embarrassing enough to topple over, but running into a pedestrian or car was her worst-case scenario. She reached for the hand bell more times than was necessary, and a few people looked at her funny. Or was she imagining it?

Still, it felt incredibly liberating to be on two wheels. A giddiness overtook her, and she picked up speed when she turned toward Race Point Road. Why, oh why, had she not been on a bike in so long?

She pulled into the gravel path entrance of Garden Renovations Nursery. From much past experience, she knew she could get a little crazy in garden shops, so she stuck to her list: a forty-pound bag of compost, wood planks, trays for transplanting, and loose-leaf lettuce, mesclun, Brussels sprouts, and carrot seeds.

Oh, but that wooden birdhouse would look so adorable in Amelia's front yard...

"I see you have your hands full there. Can I help you take some of that up to the counter?"

He sure could. The man was handsome as could be, with a thick head of silver hair and smiling brown eyes. He was tall and tan, and for the first time since falling into her casual beach routine, Blythe felt self-conscious about her unkempt appearance. Her hair was loose and slightly wavy, her face completely bare of makeup. In Philadelphia, she wouldn't drive to the WaWa convenience store looking like that, never mind walk around town.

With a smile, she handed him the heavy bag and trays. "Thank you. I should have gotten a cart, but then I have a bad habit of filling it with more than I need."

"You're not the first to strategize how to get out of here with minimal damage to the bank account. I know more than a few people in town whose significant others don't let them set foot in here by themselves."

"Well," she said, following him to the front counter, stopping to admire a potted orchid, "that makes me feel a little better."

"Do you want this packed up for delivery?" he asked. She found herself looking at his hands, one of the first things she noticed about men, even back in the days when she was assigned a dancing partner. This man had wide, shapely hands with neat nails. She wondered if he gardened or just happened to work here. Or did he own the place? And she noticed he did not wear a wedding ring. Then she pretended to herself she hadn't noticed.

She realized he was looking at her expectantly. "Oh— my address. Right." She gave him the street number of the house.

"And your name?"

"Blythe Bishop."

"Nice to meet you, Blythe Bishop. I'm Warren Ames. You're staying with Amelia and Kelly?"

"Yes. You know them?" Stupid question. Everyone knew everyone in this town.

"I certainly do. But you are definitely a new face around here. What brings you to Provincetown?"

"Just...visiting."

"Last I knew, Amelia didn't have a garden." He printed the sales slip and slid it across the counter for her signature. "You must be very ambitious to tackle that soil."

"I guess you could say I need a project."

He smiled. "How long are you in town for?"

"Until Labor Day weekend," she said. "I originally just came for a week with my daughter but we ended up staying."

"This place has that effect on people."

A short line had formed behind her. If Warren Ames noticed, he certainly didn't seem to care. He slid a few packets of Buttercrunch and Red Sails lettuce seeds across the counter, telling Blythe why he preferred them to the varieties she'd selected. "I'm throwing these in the bag for you. Give them a try."

Surprised by the gesture, marveling at how lovely it was to be in a town where people were so warm and welcoming, she thanked him profusely. She turned to leave, but then he said, "Blythe? One more thing. Can you put your phone number on the delivery slip?"

"Oh! Of course. The house number or—"

"Your cell number would certainly make me happy," he said.

Biting her lip to contain her smile, she scrawled it on the paper.

She started heading back to the house, but instead turned to go to the beach.

When the dunes came into view, she slowed to a complete stop. The sun was bright and hot. She straddled the bike with both feet on the ground and looked through the small handbag she'd placed in the wicker basket in front of the handlebars; it held her wallet, her phone, Nivea lip sunblock, and a bottle of water. She took a sip of the water, then kicked the bike back into motion, cycling through a path to the beach. It was already crowded.

She parked the bike and walked a few feet into the dunes. They were high, threaded with grass and vibrant green plants and dotted with bright pink beach roses. She turned her face to the sun, willing to risk a few seconds of UV exposure to bask in the glorious feeling that there just might be life after being Mrs. Kipton Bishop after all.

Marin walked Julian to the Pilgrims' monument, then up and down Commercial. They hit all the highlights: Cabot's Candy. Shell Design. Atlantic Accents. She saved her favorite store, Provincia, for last. An adorable white clapboard shop toward the western end of Commercial, Provincia was filled with Portuguese fine pottery and art, a heavenly little gift shop that tempted her every time she walked past on the way to Thomas and Bart's.

But she'd never enjoyed it more than she did in that moment, looking through the shelves with Julian, pointing out hand-painted olive dishes, floral-patterned earthenware dinner sets, glazed tiles, Luxo Banho soaps, and mugs and pitchers decorated with images of fish or olive branches.

"What's with all the roosters?" he asked. Ah, yes, the roosters; lots and lots of clay roosters, tiny three-inch roosters, giant bookend roosters, roosters half a foot tall. All painted with black bodies and adorned with colorful flowers and hearts. A quirk of the shop she'd never questioned. "I don't know," she said.

"They're good luck," said the man behind the front counter.

"Is that so?" Julian picked up one of the larger birds.

"According to Portuguese folklore, that is so."

"Well. We could use some luck." Julian carried the bird to the counter.

"Is it a gift?" the man asked, removing the price tag.

Julian winked at Marin. "As a matter of fact, it is."

Chapter Thirty-Nine

Rachel woke up, slipped on her orange flip-flops, and headed down to the kitchen, as excited as a kid on Christmas morning. It was the moment of truth for her cheese, which had been resting in the molds, refrigerating, for a full twenty-four hours. She'd drained the last of the whey yesterday afternoon. If she'd done everything right, it should be ready to serve.

As she pulled it out of the top shelf of the fridge and set it on the kitchen counter, she noted the cheese was white. A tad lumpy. Not, to be honest, very appetizing. Was it okay? She clearly should try a piece before serving it to the guests. But the thought of the rennet...

Still, she knew it was her job as hostess. What if it was horrible? She would disgrace the family! She had to take a bite.

She sliced into it with her knife and scooped a piece into her mouth.

"Oh my God." It was heaven—perfection. What to compare it to? Maybe the best cottage cheese imaginable but more firm. She had done it!

It was, unbelievably, the most accomplished she'd ever felt in her life. She wanted to feel this way every day. Could she possibly be a cook? Was that the calling she had been searching for?

Rachel walked outside, smiling at the early-morning sun, setting out the corn bread and coffee and fresh fruit, consumed by the fantasy of running her own little Provincetown restaurant.

Molly, the chocolate Lab, bounded in from the street, wagging her tail and sniffing around the table.

Rachel peeked around the corner of the house, wondering if Bart was nearby. But apparently Molly had just made her way to the house, as Rachel had learned that first day Molly had a tendency to do.

The Miller daughter appeared wearing very short shorts and a Marina and the Diamonds concert T-shirt.

"Good morning!" Rachel sang.

"Hey." The girl patted Molly. "I remember this dog from last summer," she said, pouring herself coffee. "Can I ask you something?" she said, shaking long bangs out of her eyes.

"Sure," said Rachel.

"Is there anything to do in this town? It's so fucking boring. Like, am I missing something?"

"Boring?" Rachel said, as if the word were utterly foreign. "I don't know. I think it's pretty great."

"Well, clearly you've never been anyplace cool. No offense."

"I live in LA, and I'm having the best summer of my life here."

"Okay, then—can I have some of whatever you're smoking?"

Before Rachel could begin to think of a response,

Marin rolled out, hand in hand with the Boyfriend. Crisis averted? Maybe ripping the Band-Aid off really was the best thing. Life lesson noted!

"Wow. You really have Amelia's whole thing down," Marin said, taking a hard-boiled egg and pouring orange juice.

Rachel beamed.

"Good morning," Blythe called out, walking to the table in her bathing suit and terry-cloth cover-up. It had taken some time, but she'd finally let go of the cardigans and linen pants. She sat across from Marin and the boyfriend. "Julian, glad to see you decided to give Provincetown another day or two."

Blythe introduced herself to the Miller daughter just as Mrs. Miller strolled out wearing her pajama pants and a P-Town sweatshirt.

"The Millers have been coming to the inn for twenty years," Rachel told Blythe.

Joan Miller looked around the table. "So you're all relatives of Amelia? I'll be darned. We never knew she had so much family. I feel like we're here for reunion week!"

Rachel and Marin looked at each other.

"Yeah, well, it's been that kind of summer," said Marin.

And then Rachel was struck with inspiration: Why stop at making breakfast? Why not have a family dinner tomorrow night? Or more than family; she would invite Luke, Thomas, and Bart. A *friendly* dinner.

She walked back into the kitchen to look through Amelia's recipe box and make a shopping list.

Marin and Julian rented bikes and rode to Herring Cove. They walked along the ocean, the same path she'd been taking on her mornings with Amelia.

Marin picked up shells as they went, pointing out the different varieties to Julian.

"Quite an education you're getting out here," he said.

"I take walks with Amelia almost every morning. She's been collecting shells all these years for Kelly's mosaics. And stones and sea glass."

She handed him a pristine wentletrap.

"What's it like? Being with this woman who's suddenly your grandmother?" he asked, putting the shell in the pocket of his bathing shorts.

"It's strange, but not as strange as you'd think," she said, stopping and looking out at the horizon. "I like her. It's easy to like her." The waves rolled in and she bent down to rinse off her sandy hands. Standing up, the sun kissed her face, and she closed her eyes. "And I love it out here."

"I can see why," he said.

"Obviously, I wish I were here under less complicated circumstances. But the thing I worried about the most— telling my dad the truth—turned out to be the most painless part."

"He took it well?"

She turned to face him. "He said he knew all along. It never made a difference in how he felt about me."

Julian looked away, distracted. Two children, a boy and a girl with sun-bleached hair and tans the color of caramel, ran past them to the water's edge. The boy, taller by a head, splashed the girl, and her shrieks of laughing protest made Marin and Julian share a smile.

"It's interesting we're both only children," he said.

"I never thought of that before, but yeah, you're right."

He put his arm around her and they watched the brother and sister until their mother called them farther down the beach.

Someday our child will play on this very spot, she thought.

"It's a great place for kids," he said, clearly having similar thoughts. She felt a swell of happiness. Until he asked, "What time does FedEx show up around here?"

"I'm not sure." He was thinking about the test kits?

"Maybe we should head back to the house and wait for it," he said.

She looked at him, a chill running up her spine as the water licked her feet.

"Okay. Sure." And in that instant, she knew.

If this baby wasn't his, they were over.

* * *

Rachel jotted down her shopping list on the Beach Rose Inn notepad Amelia kept on the counter next to the toaster.

4 lbs. of fresh cod
4 lbs. of ripe tomatoes
4 large sweet onions
8 cloves of garlic
1 small bunch of parsley
Lentils
Quinoa
Kale
Eggs

What else? She glanced at the index cards—stained from years of consultation mid-cooking—then looked through the pantry to make sure she had enough flour and sugar to make dessert. In the front of the house, Molly barked relentlessly.

"Molly!" she called out, penciling in a few more vegetables. "Quiet!"

The barking grew more excited. Was someone out there? She put down her pen and headed to the front door.

She was halfway through the entrance hall when, disbelieving, she spotted the woman on the couch, leafing through a copy of *Provincetown* magazine.

It couldn't be. It was her mind playing tricks on her.

"Hello?" she said quietly, as if she were talking to an apparition and if anyone heard her, she might be committed. At the moment, the notion that she was losing her mind was a best-case scenario, the one that made the most sense. The alternative was too crazy.

"Hey there." Her mother closed the magazine and looked at her calmly, as if Rachel had just happened upon her in her own living room.

"Fran? What are you *doing* here?"

"Didn't you get my texts?"

Texts? When was the last time Rachel had even seen her cell phone? She honestly couldn't remember. It was a vestigial organ from her distant life in LA. It served no purpose here. People didn't text; they walked over and said hi. Or you met at Joe as part of a routine. Or you ran into them at the Canteen or at the beach. And she hadn't thought of anyone from the outside world. Provincetown had become her world—she just hadn't realized how completely until that moment.

"No. I didn't," she said.

"Sean and I are doing the Love Yoga Fest in Cape Cod. I took a detour to see you."

"You came all the way east for a yoga festival?"

"It's a big one."

Was her mother just looking for an excuse to check on her? Was she being motherly after all?

"Did you stop in Philly to see Nana?"

"On the way back. Maybe." She stood up and held out her arms. "Give me a hug, kiddo."

Rachel walked into her mother's embrace, willing herself to be happy for the visit but feeling mostly uncomfortable.

"So are you staying in town? Is your boyfriend here too?" Rachel asked.

"He's seeing friends on the Cape. I thought I'd just drop by for the afternoon and drive back after dinner, but it took me a pretty long time to get here. I'm reconsidering. Is there room for me to crash here?"

"Not really," Rachel said quickly. "But you're welcome to have dinner here. I'm having a few other people over."

"Very cool. Do I get to meet the grandmother you told me about? How's that going?"

"She's actually away."

"But you're still here?"

"Yes. I'm helping out around the place. It's a long story."

Fran walked to the front door, looking out at the porch. "It's a gorgeous day. Why don't you show me the beach?"

Rachel tried to imagine herself and her mother biking over to Herring Cove, finding a spot on the beach, and just sitting quietly in the sun. When was the last time they'd spent an afternoon together? What would they talk about? Rachel could try to tell her about all that had happened in the past month, but did Fran really care? Or would she just wait for a conversational opening to jump in about her latest boy toy, as was her typical MO? Rachel didn't have the time or patience to find out.

"I can't right now. I have to shop for dinner."

"We can pick that up on the way back."

"I'm cooking, Fran. It's going to take most of the afternoon."

"Since when do you cook?"

"Since my grandmother showed me how."

Fran gave her an odd smile. "Well, that's great. Glad your little vacation has been worth it."

It's not a vacation, Rachel thought. Vacations come to an end. And that's when she admitted to herself that she had no intention of leaving.

The paternity testing was painless. At least, physically.

Marin and Julian showed up at the lab with the testing kits, had their blood drawn, and signed all the paperwork. Now there was nothing left for them to do but wait.

"I'll be back in nine days," Julian said, kissing Marin good-bye next to his parked car.

Nine days. That's when the results would show up in the mail. Nine days, and then Julian had the excuse he needed to walk away for good. She felt like saying, *Why bother coming back?* Did she really want to open the envelope in front of him, like the Academy Awards of genetics? But when she suggested she just call him, he wouldn't hear of it. "We need to get the news together."

Okay. Whatever.

By the time his car pulled away, swallowed up in the pre-weekend traffic of Commercial Street, her mood plummeted. Forget about it, she told herself. *Put him out of your mind for now.*

Back at the house, Marin planned to head straight to her room and close the door for a few hours, if not the entire rest of the day. But she couldn't make a break for it because Rachel was in the living room talking to an aging hippie with long hair and a deep tan wearing a tie-dyed romper.

Had Rachel lost her mind and opened the inn to more guests?

"Marin—hey. Come here for a sec."

Rachel introduced the woman as her *mother*.

Looking at the two of them next to each other, she could see it. Their jawlines, the shape of their noses. The mother's hair was threaded with gray but cascaded down her back just like Rachel's. Their style was similar, though where Rachel was boho chic, the mother was mostly boho.

"Nice to meet you," Marin said.

Fran squinted her eyes and looked back and forth between them. "So is there a resemblance? I don't see it. Are you sure you're related?"

"Yes," Rachel and Marin said in unison. Rachel shook her head, clearly irritated.

"How long are you in town for?" Marin asked politely.

"Just until after dinner. Rachel invited me to her little fiesta."

Marin looked at Rachel, who explained she was cooking dinner at the house and had invited Luke, Thomas, and Bart. "I figured you and Julian would be here so...it will be a fun night."

"Julian went back to New York," Marin said.

Fran yawned. "Well, I'll leave you girls to figure out dinner. I'm going to get some sun." She consulted her phone for directions to the beach, then left with a jaunty wave.

"Fuck," Rachel said.

"You had no idea she was coming?"

"None."

"Well, it's nice. She must miss you."

Rachel shook her head. "I don't know. It's weird. She always goes away for weeks and weeks at a time. Now she suddenly misses me? Maybe she just doesn't like the role reversal."

The screen door flapped open and closed, and they turned to see Amelia dragging her bag into the house.

"You're back!" Rachel said, a smile taking over her face.

"We're back," Amelia said. Marin could see the hollows under her eyes. Kelly, a few steps behind her, looked thinner than she had just three days ago. Her stomach churned with worry.

"How's everything going here?" Kelly asked, notably breathless.

"Great! The Millers have been so cool, and everything is running smoothly. They're leaving in the morning, so perfect timing."

Rachel prattled on about what she'd been cooking, about some cheese she'd made, and about the Millers' comings and goings, all the while oblivious to Amelia's distracted expression and Kelly's evident exhaustion.

Marin realized that her sister had not been clued in to what was going on with Kelly.

"I'm sure they want to unpack," Marin interrupted. Amelia cast her a grateful smile. Marin helped them get their bags upstairs, and when Amelia used the bathroom, she was shocked to find Kelly leaning on the dresser.

"Are you in pain? What's going on?"

"I feel like shit."

"Can I do anything for you?"

Kelly shook her head. Marin looked down at the inside of her wrist, at their shared tattoo. She was so grateful Kelly had convinced her to stay on the morning she'd wanted to run away—a state of mind that was difficult to imagine now. Now it was her turn to help Kelly at a time when she couldn't possibly be thinking clearly. "Kelly, if you're in pain, you need to ask for help—"

The bathroom door clicked open. Marin gave Kelly a quick hug, feeling her shoulder sharp against the arms she wrapped gingerly around her.

"Marin, thank you, dear. We're just going to rest for now," Amelia said.

"Do you need me to do anything?"

Amelia shook her head, and Marin understood: just leave them.

Fighting back tears, she walked slowly down the stairs. She found Rachel in the kitchen, bending over the counter scribbling on a piece of notepaper. Peering over her shoulder, she saw that it was an elaborate grocery list.

"Listen, you can't have a dinner party here tonight," Marin said. Rachel glanced back at her.

"Why not?"

"Trust me, they need peace and quiet."

Rachel turned around and leaned against the counter, holding her list. "Says who?"

"Says me, okay? Tonight's not a good night."

"I already invited everyone. I'm going right now to do the shopping," Rachel said.

"Stop being such a baby!" Marin said, frustrated. "You're like a child looking for Amelia's approval with all this cooking and cleaning and trying to run the place."

Rachel's cheeks flushed, and Marin instantly wanted to take it back. "I'm sorry."

"Oh, I should be like you? Moping around half the summer so they have to spend all their time kissing your ass hoping you stick around? Screw you!"

Rachel grabbed her straw handbag off the counter, shoved the list inside it, pulled it onto her shoulder, and headed out the back door.

"No dinner party!" Marin called after her.

Chapter Forty

It had taken Warren Ames exactly three hours to call Blythe and invite her to dinner. She dressed for it carefully, almost giddily. For the first time in weeks, she wore linen pants and a turquoise blouse with her pearls. She set her hair and did her makeup and then slipped out as quickly and quietly as possible lest she, God forbid, run into someone and have to explain where she was going.

She had such mixed feelings about meeting Warren Ames for dinner (she could not in her mind call it a date) that she absolutely could not tell anyone else about it—least of all Marin. On the one hand, she was having a difficult time dealing with the idea that her marriage was over. But after four months of lying to herself, of denying what was happening, she was starting to feel foolish. And she had, after all, asked Kip to unearth the shoe box.

He was going to move on, and she would have to eventually too.

Warren made reservations at the Red Inn. It was an unfortunate selection on his part; she couldn't help but think how she had wanted to have dinner there with Kip back when she thought there was still hope for her marriage.

She found Warren waiting for her at the bar. It was a warm room, buttery yellow, with wood-beamed ceilings and a red-brick fireplace.

He stood when he saw her and kissed her on the cheek. "You look beautiful," he said. She felt herself flush. He was more attractive than she'd remembered, and she wondered why he was single. Divorced?

"I'm a widower," he told her once they'd moved to a table overlooking the water. He had two grown sons, one just finishing up at the University of Wisconsin, the other a marine biologist working in Santa Barbara. The garden nursery had belonged to his wife, Catherine. In the five years since she'd died from complications of multiple sclerosis, he'd been running it by himself. They'd moved to Provincetown early in their marriage, and he admitted to Blythe it was not an ideal place to be a widower. "It's lonely, especially in the winter. But at the same time, all of my memories of Catherine are here so it's difficult to just pick up and leave."

She did not want to talk about her own situation, though she did explain that she was still married, at the very beginning of the divorce process.

"It's still very new. And complicated." A part of her hoped that would give him pause, that he would pull back and then she wouldn't have to deal with her own highly uncomfortable, ambivalent feelings about the evening. But he was understanding and sympathetic, and he deftly turned the conversation to more neutral territory: their former careers. In another life, he had been a CPA. She told him about her barely there ballet career.

"A ballerina. I'm not surprised. You still carry yourself so gracefully."

Oh Lord, it was too much. He was so lovely, so utterly focused on her in a way that was flattering without being too obsequious. She tried to imagine an evening out with Kip without him looking at his phone every few minutes. It was unthinkable. So why was this dinner making her miss Kip even more?

"It was a long time ago," Blythe said.

"You never went back to dancing, even as a hobby?"

"No," she said. "Once I had my daughter, I didn't have time or interest."

And yet, that wasn't exactly true.

After two years of being home with Marin every day, of baby music classes, of teaching her her letters and cooking three toddler-approved meals a day, Blythe hired a part-time babysitter, a Nepalese woman named Pema. She was sweet and had a teenage daughter of her own, and Blythe was comfortable leaving Marin for a few hours while she drove to Center City to take ballet classes three mornings a week. Oh, how good it felt to get back in front of the barre, to have her muscle memory kick in and feel a reclaiming of her own body. For a few weeks, it was the happiest she'd been in a long time. Her life felt whole. She had her beautiful daughter, she was in a decent place with Kip, and after a few years of safe distance, she could return to ballet with all of the love and none of the pressure and sense of failure.

But one Tuesday, she pulled into the driveway of the house and heard Marin's bloodcurdling cries before her key was even in the back door.

Blood rushing to her head so hard and fast it was deafening, she ran into the living room where Marin was standing next to the couch, howling. With Pema standing uselessly nearby.

"What's wrong with her?" Blythe asked, just as she noticed the welts on Marin's neck and collarbone. Her first thought was that she was having an allergic reaction. But Pema started saying something about hot tea, and Blythe finally comprehended that her daughter was seriously burned. "Why the fuck didn't you call me?" She'd left the number for the ballet academy. She always did.

With shaking hands, she pulled Marin into her arms and dialed Kip. She should have called an ambulance first, but all she could think was that she needed Kip.

His secretary pulled him out of a meeting. He told her to call an ambulance, that he would meet her at the hospital.

In the ambulance, riding to Lankenau Hospital where Marin had been born, she felt calmer and more in control. Hearing Kip's voice had snapped her out of her hysteria. And in Blythe's arms, listening to her soothing words of comfort, Marin calmed down just a little bit too.

For ten days, Blythe and Kip had to change the dressings on Marin's bandaged burns. It was imperative that they keep it sterile and prevent an infection. Every time they touched her bandaging, Marin cried like she was experiencing the burns all over again. Blythe could barely endure it, but Kip was there with a sure and steady hand.

The burn specialist told them if they kept the areas out of the sun, chances were it would heal so well, they'd never even know it had happened. Sure enough, the marks disappeared. But Blythe's guilt over the whole incident didn't fade one bit.

She stopped going to the ballet classes. If she hadn't been so selfish in the first place, if she'd just been home with her baby as she should have been, there wouldn't have been an accident. Oh, how she blamed herself. Kip, to his credit, never did.

It was so easy, in retrospect, to cast herself as the victim in her marriage, the selfless mother who did all the heavy lifting while her husband put his career first. Yes, in many ways, he did. But if Blythe had wanted to find her way back to a career, he would have been supportive. The simple fact was, after Marin was born, she wanted to be a full-time mother. Maybe it was her own insecurity about that choice that made her resent Kip's ability to have it all—the family and the blockbuster career. And that was certainly why she had been so appalled by Marin's broken engagement. It seemed she was making the opposite choice that Blythe had, that in a sense, she was rebuking Blythe. Of course, that hadn't been it at all. Marin had simply been in the midst of making her own messy decisions.

Warren lifted his glass of wine. "To past lives," he said.

She touched her glass to his, trying to offer the man the genuine smile he deserved.

When Rachel called Luke to cancel the dinner—blaming it on Marin's making her feel bad about crowding Amelia and Kelly—he said, "If you still want to do it, bring everything over here. My dad and Bart will be into it. Just count Paul in because he's here swimming and will probably stay for dinner."

Rachel, already emotionally invested in the dinner plan, agreed.

The only wrinkle in the whole thing was Fran. What would Luke think of her mother? Oh, who cared? It was never going to happen between them. His opinion didn't matter. She had to change the way she thought. She had to let it go.

In the kitchen at Thomas and Bart's house, Rachel squeezed one last burst of lemon juice onto the kale salad, then tossed it. She sprinkled pine nuts on top of that, then handed the bowl to her mother to carry to the table.

"I love this kitchen!" Fran said, toying with Thomas and Bart's mint-green vintage toaster.

"Can you stop fondling the appliances and help me get food out to the table?" Rachel said.

"But this toaster," cooed Fran. "So smooth…so shiny."

Rachel looked at her. "Are you high?"

Of course she was. She had disappeared for a while with Paul. Rachel sighed and carried the salad into the dining room herself. By the time she returned to the kitchen, Fran had drifted off to another room.

Rachel twisted the cap off a bottle of Kim Crawford sauvignon blanc and poured herself a glass just as Paul walked in and deposited a bottle of Tito's vodka and half a dozen limes on the counter.

"I thought we'd do kamikazes tonight," he said. He pulled one more bottle out of a brown paper bag. "The secret ingredient: Combier."

"Go for it. I'm sticking to wine."

He found a handheld juicer in one of the utensil drawers, then cut a lime in half and squeezed it into a shallow glass. "Let me ask you something. What the hell is going on with Kelly?"

Rachel looked at him blankly. "I have no idea. What do you mean?"

"Oh, cut the shit. I've known her a lot longer than you. I'm family too, you know."

"Paul, honestly, I don't know what you're talking about. She and Amelia have been away for a few days. They got back earlier but I haven't really seen them. Why? What do you *think* is going on?"

"Maybe her cancer is back. This is how she acted last year when she was diagnosed, going MIA."

This was all news to Rachel. She didn't know anything about Kelly having cancer in the past and had no reason to think she was sick now. She decided that Paul was just paranoid from the pot.

"I have to get dinner on the table."

The mood was festive. Everyone seemed genuinely thrilled to have Fran in the mix. Thomas was clearly having a good night, Bart was celebrating a big sale at the gallery, and Paul was happily infatuated with a guy he'd met at Lobsterfest. The wine flowed, Rachel's cod was apparently superb—she had to take their word for it, since she wouldn't eat it—and Fran was trotting out her most debaucherous LA stories, including her classic one-night stand with Anthony Kiedis.

"Was that during the One Hot Minute tour?" asked Bart.

"Their worst album," muttered Rachel. It was true, but she wasn't sure why she felt the need to say it. Except she was suddenly angry at Fran. Furious.

Fran was oh so fun, oh so amusing—unless she was your only parent.

"Rachel, this cod is truly fantastic," said Thomas. "I think it's the paprika that really makes it pop."

"I can't believe you can cook," said Fran.

"Yeah. Amelia's a great teacher," said Rachel.

"Unlike me," Fran said, laughing like it was a joke.

"That's right," said Rachel. "Unlike you."

Fran, realizing this was not just banter, put down her fork. "What's that supposed to mean?"

"Well, I mean—that's a fact. You never taught me much of anything."

"*I knew* that's what this whole trip was about! I wasn't a good enough mother, so you have to run off looking for something better."

"That's not what this is about. Although, yeah, if you were more of a mother, I might not have felt like something was missing my whole life. But you know what? I guess in the end you did me a favor, because it pushed me to find the rest of my family."

"You have no idea what it's like being a single mother!" Fran yelled.

"That was your choice!"

"Okay, Rachel?" Luke said. "Why don't you and I take a walk, get some fresh air. Bart and Paul can clear the table? Right?"

"Yes," Bart said. "Absolutely."

Rachel threw down her napkin and followed Luke to the door.

After dinner, Warren insisted on walking her home. Blythe couldn't refuse without being exceptionally rude, but the truth was she was terrified that they'd run into someone. She practically held her breath passing Bart and Thomas's house, and by the time they reached Amelia's front porch, she knew she was acting like a skittish house cat.

"Everything okay?" Warren asked.

"Yes—of course. It's just that I didn't tell my daughter I was going out tonight and...I know it's silly."

"No, not at all. I might feel the same way if my boys were here."

"I had a lovely evening. Thank you so much. A night out like this—it was the last thing I expected."

He smiled warmly and she smiled back, trying not to worry about whether or not he was going to kiss her. When he did lean toward her, it was clear he was only going in for the cheek.

"I had a great time with you, Blythe. I think at this stage of life, it serves us well to be open to the unexpected."

Rachel took Luke's outstretched hand and walked from rock to rock. They made their way slowly across the length of the jetty.

"This is far enough," she said when they were about a quarter mile from land. She was feeling the wine and assumed Luke was in a similar state. It was dark, the water choppy. She was nervous.

"A little farther? We should make it to the end at least once this summer."

"No." She wrapped her arms around herself. There had been a time when she would have followed Luke anywhere. Not now.

He didn't push.

"So," he said. "That's your mom."

"Yep."

"Interesting woman."

"That's one way of putting it," Rachel said.

"I'm sorry you're upset."

"You know, the crazy thing is I didn't realize how angry I was until she showed up here. I see Marin and her mother, their closeness, and I'm jealous. I feel how nurturing Amelia is, and I realize how much I've been missing that all my life. I really don't know why my mother even had me."

"Well, the important thing is that she did have you. And considering the circumstances, it wasn't an accident. She really wanted a kid. And she loves you even though maybe she's not what you would have picked for a mother. But we don't get to pick. Look, I love my dad. But there were times when I was really angry. He abandoned us. Eventually, I realized he did the best he could. It's the same with your mom. And hey, she came out here to see you. She didn't have to do that, right?"

Rachel nodded. He had a point. "Thanks for stepping in before that got even uglier tonight."

"No problem."

She sighed. "You know, I'm glad I said those things. I said it, I got it out."

"Do you feel better?"

"I do."

"The thing with parents is it's a relationship, just like any other we have. It takes work. But it's worth having. You don't want to write her off."

"No. I don't. I think I was starting to, on some level. And then she showed up here and I felt like she was intruding. It was easier to push her aside than to admit how angry I've been." She turned around. Dry land seemed very far away. "We should get back."

He touched her arm, and she thought he was helping her keep her footing as she pivoted on the rocks. But when she looked up at him, he looped his arm around her waist, pulled her to him, and kissed her.

What was happening? Her first instinct was to respond, her mouth opening to his. But then her mind kicked in and was like, *Danger...danger!* She'd finally accepted that he would never think of her that way and there he was...thinking of her that way. She pulled back and said—with a Marilyn Monroe breathlessness that sounded contrived but wasn't—"I'm too young for you, remember?"

"Yeah. About that: I've been an idiot," he said. And he kissed her again.

Chapter Forty-One

Marin woke up to pouring rain. She felt almost as depressed as she had the first morning at the house. She stared at the Portuguese good-luck rooster on her nightstand for a long while before forcing herself out of bed.

The Miller family showed up in the kitchen just a little after eight for their last breakfast at the inn, and Marin made coffee since Rachel was MIA. She pulled corn bread, hard-boiled eggs, raspberries, and orange juice out of the fridge and set it out on the round kitchen table, whose white paint was chipped just enough to be charming.

While Mr. Miller loaded up the car, and the kids looked around for outlets to give their devices a last-minute charge, Mrs. Miller told Marin how sorry she was that she'd barely gotten to see Amelia and Kelly.

"Please tell them we look forward to seeing them next summer. I'll be e-mailing as soon as I get home to make my reservation."

Molly jumped up, tail wagging with a thump against the table at the sound of someone coming down the back stairs. "Maybe that's Amelia and you can tell her your-self," she said.

But it wasn't Amelia. It was Nadine, dressed in a black sundress and carrying a laptop. Molly barked and Nadine shushed her.

"You're back," Marin said.

"I am. And…who are you? Another long-lost rela-tive?" she said to Mrs. Miller.

"What? No…we're guests. We stay here every August."

"I thought the inn was closed this summer," Nadine said to Marin. Mrs. Miller looked at her in confusion.

"No. Obviously not," Marin said quickly. "We're up and running."

"Closed? Don't even say such a thing!" Mrs. Miller said with a small laugh. "I was just telling Marin, I'm al-ready reserving our rooms for next summer."

"Well, that might be a bit premature," Nadine said.

Mr. Miller appeared in the doorway and announced that the car was packed and the kids were just doing one last bathroom run.

"I'll see you out," Marin said, glancing over her shoul-der and shooting Nadine a look that she hoped read, loud and clear, *Just keep your mouth shut.*

After a quick good-bye on the porch, waving as the Millers drove away, she hurried back to the kitchen. Na-dine was busy eating the last of the orange muffins.

"What was that about?" Marin said. Nadine poured herself coffee and shrugged.

"You tell me. My mother said she closed this place to guests this summer."

"It's a long story. You didn't have to be so rude."

"That wasn't rude. That was honesty. This place won't

be taking guests next summer so that woman might as well hear it here first."

"How do you know what Amelia will or won't be doing next summer?"

Nadine glared at her. "You should just go back to New York. Pack it up like those other guests. I don't know how long you think you can sponge off my mother, but I'll tell you one thing, it's going to be coming to an end fast. She's selling this house."

Rachel awoke to the sound of rain pattering against the window. It took her a few seconds to remember she was in Luke's bed. She smiled contentedly, turning to look at his sleeping face. She couldn't believe it; after all that time fantasizing about having sex with Luke Duncan, it had actually happened. Just thinking about the way he'd touched her made her stomach do a little flip.

And then she realized that her alarm had never gone off.

"Shit!" She sat up and searched the nightstand for her phone. It was almost eleven.

"What's wrong?" Luke said groggily, reaching for her.

"I overslept," she said. "I meant to get back to the house for breakfast. It's the Millers' last morning."

"Don't worry. Amelia's back. I'm sure she has it covered."

She sank back into her pillow, pressing against him. He kissed the top of her head.

"This is crazy," she whispered.

His arms tightened around her. She wondered if she should get dressed. He probably wanted to get some work done on the book.

"I should go," she said.

He sat up, looking across the room at the rain-splattered window. "Not a beach day," he commented.

"No," she said.

"We could see a movie."

"Luke, it's okay. You don't have to, you know, entertain me."

He shook his head. "Silly. I know that. I wasted this whole summer pushing you away. Now I want to make up for lost time."

She smiled. "Really?"

"I'm starving," he said. "Let's see what my dad has in the kitchen. Breakfast is the one meal of the day I can manage to pull together. Do you like eggs?"

"I like eggs," she said, slipping on the jeans she'd worn the night before; they had been hastily discarded next to Luke's bed. He pulled a blue University of Rhode Island sweatshirt from his closet and passed it to her. "When it's cool outside, the kitchen has a draft."

She felt mildly self-conscious walking down the stairs holding Luke's hand as they made their way to Thomas and Bart's kitchen. In weather like that, there was no doubt they were both hunkered down inside the house, and this made Rachel feel she was doing the beach-house version of the walk of shame. Except there was nothing to be ashamed of. And, really, Thomas and Bart would not exactly be scandalized. There had been more than a few wink-winks along the way that summer. If she was surprised about last night's turn of events, she was probably the only one.

"There you are!" Fran jumped up from the kitchen table. "I went back to the other house looking for you."

"Well, you found me," Rachel said, sitting in one of the Arts and Crafts chairs across from her.

"I'm taking off after lunch," Fran said.

Rachel wondered if Fran was at all upset about their conversation last night, but she seemed to be in her usual chill mood.

"Coffee, Fran?" Luke said, pouring a mug for Rachel.

Fran said no, she was starting a cleanse. Luke made small talk with her about the Cape Cod yoga retreat, and Rachel was content to just revel in the luxury of looking at him. At one point, he caught her eye and winked, and she felt she could die of happiness.

The doorbell rang, and he excused himself to go answer it.

"Well, well," said Fran. "Good for you. No wonder you stayed here all summer. You should have mailed me a postcard of *him*. No further explanation needed!"

Rachel shook her head. She wasn't about to get into it. Fran wouldn't understand. She would have somehow managed to sleep with him the first day they met.

"I should get going," Rachel said.

"Why?"

Why? Because this was making her uncomfortable. She didn't need a post-hookup brunch with her mother. "Come by the house to see me before you leave."

Rachel glanced at the kitchen door, wondering what was taking Luke so long. She climbed the stairs back to his room and found her handbag. Looking out the window, she decided to keep his hooded sweatshirt for the walk to the house. He wouldn't mind. She looked at the disheveled bed and smiled. *This is really happening.*

Back downstairs, heading to the front hall to find him, she heard his voice before she saw him. He wasn't alone.

She followed the sound of conversation into the living room. Luke's back was to her, and so she was greeted by a surprised expression from a very lovely Asian woman. She was around Rachel's age, with prominent cheekbones, a heart-shaped mouth, and shoulder-length hair styled with neat bangs.

Luke, following the woman's gaze, turned around.

"Hey," he said, clearly trying to sound casual. But the set of his jaw and the way he squared his shoulders undermined that completely.

"Hey," she managed in a way that hopefully conveyed *Who the hell is that?* Even though she knew. Of course she knew: Vanessa.

Luke stumbled through the awkward introductions, and Rachel's body went cold at the same time her face turned hot. In all their intense talking the past fifteen hours—not to mention intense fucking—how had he failed to mention that his girlfriend was coming to visit? Okay, maybe the timing was a surprise. But surely he knew it was on the table, so to speak. No wonder he'd been pushing her away all summer. He was still involved with Vanessa!

Rachel almost knocked over an end table on her way to the front door. She ignored Luke's pleas to wait, stop, hold on a sec. Outside, the rain pelted her hard and she welcomed the punishing needles. She deserved to be soaked, drenched, washed out to sea. She was an idiot! When the Beach Rose Inn finally appeared in the distance, she ran the rest of the way.

Chapter Forty-Two

The days passed quickly, melting into one another. Marin felt herself growing lazy. She didn't know if it was the pace of life in a beach town or her hormones, but the only thing getting her out of bed some mornings was Kelly's knock on the door to get her ass up to the studio.

Marin was beginning to realize something. Or, rather, Kelly had realized it and pointed it out to her: Marin actually had some artistic ability. While Kelly worked on some of the more intricate parts of the Beach Rose Inn mosaic—the rose design was complicated because the pieces had to be cut in very deliberate angles to form the blossoms and the leaves and stem—Marin started her own small piece. It was a starfish, inspired by the stained-glass mosaic hanging in the living room. But instead of stained glass, Marin was creating hers entirely from smalti and tiles. And she loved it. It felt natural; she had an absolute vision for how she wanted it to look, and cutting and gluing the pieces to match that mental image was incredibly satisfying.

"I'm not surprised you've got a knack for this," Kelly

said. "I told you Amelia's the one who taught me how to do it, and her son, Nick, was an incredible sketch artist. It's in your blood."

Funny, she had always believed being a shrewd attorney was in her blood. And she had worked hard to fulfill that destiny. Not anymore. *Nature versus nurture.*

"I want to show you how to grout," Kelly said. Grout was the mortar that filled the space between the pieces, creating an additional bond to the glue.

"Sure. Let's do it."

Kelly walked her over to a small hutch and pulled out a few pieces, showing her the difference between a finished grouted mosaic and ones that were not grouted.

"It serves a technical purpose but also a visual one."

Marin nodded.

"Choosing the right color grout matters. When in doubt, go with your lightest option. You can always make it darker. Once you use black or dark blue, you're stuck with it."

Kelly dragged a big bucket to the side of the table, breathing so hard Marin jumped in to help her. "I already mixed this. It's pretty simple. Just add water until you get the consistency of mayonnaise. Then let it sit for fifteen minutes. But this batch is ready to go. So watch. I'm going to grout one of these small pieces that I have sitting around because I'm not at this stage yet for Amelia's."

She pulled on a pair of rubber gloves and told Marin if she ever got grout on her bare hands, she should rinse them in apple cider vinegar.

"My go-to tools. This is a float," she said, showing her a flat metal base with a handle. "And this is a trowel." She picked up a metal tool that looked like a cake knife without the serrations.

Kelly dropped a glob of the grout right on top of the mosaic.

"You just smear it all over? Don't you just go in between the cracks?"

"No—you have to cover the piece and then wipe away the excess. I know it looks strange to do it this way, but trust me." She smeared the thick gray mixture with the float, working right to left and then top to bottom. "Don't leave any gaps."

She started coughing and had to put down the piece to retrieve tissues out of the pocket of her apron. Marin gasped when she saw them spotted with red.

"Kelly! Jesus. You take it easy. We don't have to do this now."

Kelly shook her head. "I'm fine. This has to sit for ten minutes anyway."

They moved to a couch by the window. Marin, shaken, couldn't think of a thing to say.

"How are things going with your baby daddy? Have you heard from him since he was here?" Kelly said finally.

Marin shook her head. "Well, he might not technically be the father of the baby. And no, I haven't heard from him."

"I'm bummed I was away and didn't get to meet him. Bad timing."

"Yeah. Timing is everything." Especially when you get pregnant by accident. "I have a sonogram later today."

"Marin, have you considered it might be time for you to go back to New York? It seems like you have some pretty important things to take care of. You better not be waiting for me to kick."

"Kelly! I am not waiting for you to…kick. That's not it," Marin said.

Kelly cocked her head and narrowed her eyes. "You were all set to leave after the Fourth of July—actually, correction: you weren't even going to stay the full first week. Then you found out I was sick and suddenly you decided to stay the whole summer."

Marin shook her head. "It's partly because I wanted to be supportive of you and Amelia. But it's not entirely unselfish. I like being here. It's helping me regroup."

Kelly nodded. "Regrouping is good. Can't argue with that. But at some point, you have to get your shit figured out. You have someone else to think about now," she said, glancing at Marin's belly.

"I know. I'll go back to New York when the summer is over."

"So that's the mark for you? End of summer?"

"Yes. Labor Day."

Kelly's breathing was so strained Marin felt afraid.

"Are you in pain?"

"I don't feel great, I can tell you that."

"Is it...like, your chest hurts?"

"Yes, that's part of it. But it's more than that. While we were away, Amelia insisted I get checked in Boston. They found bone metastases, which the doctor here didn't see or didn't mention. The pain from that is hard to treat."

"Isn't there anything they can do?"

"I'm taking the meds. It barely helps and when I take too much it makes me loopy. I hate not thinking clearly. The doctor wants me to go in for radiotherapy next week. So we'll see."

Someone knocked at the door.

"Who is it?" Marin called out.

"Paul. Open up. I come bearing gifts."

Marin unlocked the door for him and he walked in with a plate of brownies.

"What do you know—we were just discussing pain management," Kelly said.

"What's *my* excuse for eating them?" he said, sitting at the table and moving Marin's mosaic to make room for the plate.

"You have none," Kelly deadpanned.

Paul took a bite of one and passed it to Marin.

"She can't eat pot brownies, Paul. She's pregnant," Kelly said.

"Pregnant! Mazel tov. Who's the lucky guy?"

"It's a long story," Marin said. She checked the time on her phone. Only two hours until her sonogram appointment. She had to find her mother and get going.

"Good luck!" Kelly called out as she left. Closing the door, Marin heard Paul say, "It's a little late for luck. She's already knocked up."

Marin heard Kelly's throaty laugh, and she smiled.

Blythe sat outside at the table planting lettuce seeds in trays. She decided to try the varieties Warren had given her. She had considered texting this to him, but she held back. While they'd spoken on the phone a few times since dinner, he must have sensed her reticence because he did not ask her out again. Or maybe he just didn't feel a connection. Either way, it didn't bother her and she had to read that as evidence that she simply wasn't ready to meet anyone new.

As always in times of stress, she turned away from her heart and toward her green thumb. In two weeks, the seeds she was pressing into little beds of soil would sprout up an inch or two, and she would transplant the leaflings to the garden.

Her phone rang, startling her. She jumped up to find it in her bag and saw the incoming number was Kip's.

"Hello?" she said. She squeezed her fist, her nails digging into her palm. By now, he had to have located the shoe box. The question was whether he'd looked inside before he packed it up and mailed it to her. No matter what Marin said about him knowing all along, seeing proof of an affair in black and white would be difficult for anyone to take. Ever since asking him to mail it to her, she'd second-guessed herself.

"How's Marin?" he asked.

"She's hanging in there. Julian came to visit and he's handling the news of her pregnancy fairly well. I just don't want her to feel alone in dealing with all this."

"She's not alone. She has us." *Us?* Of course—parents. Always they would be parents together. "Blythe, I found the shoe box you asked me to unearth from the back of your closet."

She looked down at her nails, edged with soil. Her heart beat fast.

"Did you send it?"

"No."

"*No?*" *No as in "not yet"? Or no as in "I looked inside and I'm not facilitating your walk down memory lane with your former lover"?*

"I brought it to you in person. I felt we have some loose ends to wrap up. I have some paperwork. We can kill two birds with one stone here."

In person? Loose ends to wrap up? Kill two birds...what on earth was Kip talking about?

"I'm confused," she said. "Where are you?"

"I'm here—in Provincetown."

He'd rented a basement studio apartment; it was the

only thing he could find that week at the last minute. The entire town was booked up. It was a few blocks away, just off Franklin. "Can you come meet me now?"

By the time she reached the address, she was sweating. He opened the door and they greeted each other awkwardly, without touching.

She looked around. It was a cute place, with a dark wooden sleigh bed, crisp white walls decorated with framed autographed photos of Broadway stars, and an anachronistic stereo and a rack of CDs. The room wrapped around a small kitchen, where they sat at a wooden table.

"This is cute," she said, looking at the place. It was difficult to face him, knowing that he knew the truth about Marin. In some ways, this was the first fully honest moment between them in the past thirty years.

It was excruciating.

"How long are you in town for?" she asked.

"I had to book it for a few days—their minimum. But I'm leaving in the morning. I figured I could see Marin for dinner tonight."

"Right," she said. She looked him in the eyes, those intelligent, commanding blue eyes that she'd fallen for so many years ago, so many years filled with secrets and lies. "I don't understand," she said, her voice almost a whisper. "You knew about Marin, so why didn't you say anything? In all this time…"

"Maybe I should have," he said. "But I was hurt. Angry. Talking to you about it would have, in some ways, been letting you off the hook. I'm not saying I thought this consciously, but in some sense, not admitting that I knew the truth gave me a secret of my own. It leveled the playing field. That's petty, I know. That's the lowest point of my reasoning. I also didn't say anything because I wanted to protect Marin. I didn't want her to know. I never wanted to have to confront the issue of whether or not to tell her the truth. As far as I was concerned, she was my daughter."

Blythe fought back tears. "I'm so sorry."

"Don't be. I never was. If it had been up to me, we probably never would have had a child. I was too selfish. And it would have been the biggest mistake of my life. You saved me from that."

"Do you mean that?" she said.

"Yes."

He stood up, the chair startling her with a scraping sound against the floor. Kip walked to the bedroom area and when he returned, he had the shoe box in hand.

She closed her eyes. She had asked for it, but now that it was in front of her, she didn't want to confront the evidence of her betrayal.

"I know I shouldn't have looked inside, but I couldn't help myself."

"Kip..."

"I read how lonely you were. How miserable you were. And it was my fault."

The journal. She had been so focused on Nick's letter, she had forgotten about the journal!

Blythe felt hopeful. Not that she wanted him to blame himself—the affair had been her mistake, her transgression against the marriage. But if he was willing to take some of the blame for his own shortcomings, if he could see the big picture, then there was room for reconciliation. Maybe that was why he had come in person. Yes, that had to be it!

She took his hand. "There is no excuse for what I did.

And I wish you'd told me you knew all this time. But please know that as wrong as it was for me to have the affair, it really did force me to either accept you as you were or end the marriage. And I knew I wanted to be with you. I made the decision to end it before I found out I was pregnant."

"I know," he said, smiling wistfully. "I read your journal, remember."

She looked at him, trying to read his expression. Decades of litigating had made him inscrutable. And she had learned from him not to always speak—that there was truth at the end of silence.

Kip spoke slowly, with deliberation. "Blythe, I thought I had put it behind me. Years ago. I figured you had a one-night stand or something equally as insignificant. That's what I told myself. I made it a nonissue because I didn't want it to affect my love for Marin. And it never did. But seeing the drawing…that letter. It made it real. Makes *him* real."

She closed her eyes. "Kip, I'm so sorry."

Finally, he said, "We both made mistakes. I hope we can move on from them."

Her heart soared. It was going to be all right. All of this happened for a reason, leading to that very moment. The marriage was not finished. It was at a point of renewal.

"Yes—yes. Of course we can."

"I'm happy to hear that," Kip said, smiling at her. "We need to be on good terms. For our own sake, but especially for Marin."

Chapter Forty-Three

Rachel never thought she'd miss the days of her unrequited, lusting-from-afar feelings for Luke Duncan. Now, compared to her current hell, they seemed quaint and relatively joyful.

He'd called the house twice, but she refused to talk to him. Here was a guy who spent all summer blowing her off because she was too young for him and therefore couldn't possibly have her shit together, and then he decides he wants her, *sleeps* with her, and his ex-girlfriend shows up *the next morning?* If she even was an ex. Would someone really just show up randomly like that? Did he expect Rachel to believe that? Clearly, *he* was the one who didn't have his shit together.

"Have you seen my mother?" Marin walked into the kitchen wearing a decidedly unbeachy, distinctly non-Provincetown outfit of jeans, shoes rather than flip-flops or sneakers, and a button-down shirt.

"No, haven't seen her."

"So annoying. She was supposed to go with me to my

doctor's appointment this morning. If I wait any longer, I'm going to be late."

"I'll go with you," Rachel said. She could use the distraction. Besides, they hadn't talked much since Marin freaked out about the proposed dinner party at the house. It would be good for them to maybe reconnect.

"No, that's okay. Thanks. I just..."

"I want to. Really. I could use the company. I honestly had the most epic fail with Luke. The night I cooked dinner at his place—"

And then the pieces clicked. Marin overreacting to the idea of her inviting people to the house when Amelia and Kelly got back. Paul asking her at dinner if Kelly was sick. "Marin," Rachel said slowly. "Is Kelly sick?"

Marin hesitated. And then said, "We'll talk during the drive."

Blythe found a quiet spot on the beach, near the dunes. She rested the shoe box on her lap. She'd gambled in asking Kip to send it to her. Gambled, and lost.

We need to be on good terms...for Marin's sake.

Now she couldn't bring herself to open the damn box. It had cost her too much.

But no. Kip had been pulling away for a long time. Kip had had an affair. The marriage had ended months ago, and she'd just refused to see it. He had come back to Provincetown to talk to her in person, to make sure she did see it, once and for all. And he might have done that with or without the excuse of bringing her the shoe box.

So why didn't he just do it the last time he was in town? Maybe he'd tried that day at Pilgrims' Park but lost his nerve. Maybe he was on the fence, and then after talking to Marin about her paternity, he'd decided. But again—

he could have talked to Blythe that night. Instead, he left town.

She ran her thumb over the white-gold wedding band she'd worn for thirty-two years. And she slipped it off her finger and into her bag. The spot was still marked by a thin tan line. A few weeks in the sun, and that would be gone too.

The sun could cure a lot of woes.

Blythe brushed sand off the top of the box, wondering if Nick had sat near that very spot, sketching the ocean, back in the days when he had been happy in this town, when inspiration had come as naturally as breathing.

It all fit together now—why he had left, why he had cut himself off so abruptly from the place he had loved. And when she met him, he was still struggling with losing his muse. Maybe he had been looking for a new muse in Blythe, or in the party scene in Philly, only to leave and find it on a beach halfway around the world. But she did know one thing; there was no way Nadine's depiction of his mental state in Italy was true. He had not run away distraught from his affair with Blythe. And he had not been unhappy in Italy—and certainly not unhappy enough to kill himself. Because for the first time in years, he had been successfully drawing again.

A part of her wanted to open the box, to hold Nick's letter, see his drawing and close her eyes and maybe, for a brief moment, see him again. But a stronger part of her did not. She didn't want to revisit the past. She'd had an impulse to save the letter all those years ago, and now she understood the universe worked in strange ways, as Nick had predicted.

The letter was not for her. It was for Amelia.

But there *was* something she wanted to see again.

Slowly, almost holding her breath, she lifted the lid and pulled out her old Degas journal. How amazing that she'd bought the book maybe an hour before meeting Nick, before her life changed forever. She traced the cover painting with her finger, then opened to the first page and closed it again. The words were written by a lonely and confused young woman she would never recognize today. She didn't want to revisit that either.

Her phone rang. She reached for her handbag, happy to be called back to the present.

"Blythe? Warren Ames here."

She smiled. "Hi, Warren. I'm at the beach, so reception might not be great."

"Gotcha. Just wanted to see if you're free for dinner tonight?"

Blythe stood up, looking out at the ocean. "Yes. Yes, Warren—I'm free."

It was a day of dramatic news—good and bad. On the bad side, Marin had to break it to Rachel that Kelly had cancer. This resulted in Rachel crying the entire ride to Hyannis. But then, in the exam room, the teeny-tiny 6.7-centimeter baby waved at them. Well, moved a tiny hand in their general direction. Marin couldn't quite believe her eyes. She stared and stared, thinking, *That's my baby. My baby.* Rachel smiled and squeezed Marin's arm and squealed that she was going to be an aunt.

The doctor—a Cate Blanchett lookalike wearing on her lab coat a uterus pin that read POLITICS-FREE ZONE—asked Marin if she wanted to know the gender.

Rachel had immediately said, "Yes!" Marin had to shoot her a look to temper her enthusiasm. She needed a minute to think. *Did* she want to know? It was a moment she would want, ideally, to share with Julian. But Julian was not there, had in fact not called her in days. As far as paternity went, as far as their relationship went, it was wait-and-see. But there was no reason to wait to fall more in love with her baby.

"Yes," she said. "I want to know."

"Congratulations. It's a boy!"

Oh my God, Marin thought. *I'm a mother.*

"We have to tell Kelly and Amelia," Rachel said. "It's such good news and, well, they need good news." Of course, she was right.

And so, back at the house, armed with a thin paper printout of the sonogram and the news that Amelia had a great-grandson on the way, Marin set off to try to bring her grandmother some measure of happiness. (Honestly, she would have liked to share the news with her mother first, but oddly, she was still nowhere to be found.)

Marin didn't have to look far to find Kelly and Amelia. They were reading out back, side by side in lounge chairs, a pitcher of iced tea on the small table between them.

"Hey, you guys. Sorry to interrupt," Marin said. "I wanted to show you something."

Amelia moved over, giving Marin space to sit on the edge of her lounge chair. She offered her tea. "I'm good, thanks," Marin said, handing her the thin strip of paper with three images. Amelia straightened out the paper that was already beginning to curl and squinted.

"I need my glasses," she said.

"It's the baby," said Marin. "A boy."

Amelia looked up. "It's a boy?"

"Holy shit, Amelia, you've got a great-grandson!" Kelly said, lifting up her sunglasses. Her green eyes were bright with happiness.

"*We* have a great-grandson," Amelia said, leaning over and reaching for Kelly's hand. "Exciting, right?"

Marin passed the sonogram pictures to Kelly.

"It's so fucking amazing," Kelly said. "Look at that little nose! See, babe—life goes on."

"Yes. Something for *us* to look forward to," she said pointedly.

The two of them locked in a gaze that excluded Marin so completely, all she could do was back silently into the house. She left the sonogram photos behind.

Chapter Forty-Four

Amelia gave up on trying to read. She'd been reading all day, and now she was reading in bed, and not a word was sinking in. She set the book on her nightstand, moving carefully so as not to disturb Kelly, who seemed to have drifted to sleep. Amelia checked the time: 8:00.

"Where you going, babe?" Kelly asked groggily.

"Oh! I didn't mean to wake you."

"I'm awake," Kelly said, sitting up and pulling her hair away from her face.

"I thought I'd get some fresh air. Want to come out back for a little bit?"

Kelly shook her head. "You go. I'm going to work for a few hours."

Amelia nodded reluctantly, kissed her on the cheek. She had never felt so alone. Kelly, relatively communicative during the initial cancer diagnosis last year, was now shutting her out completely. She didn't understand why.

Frantic, Amelia had confided in Bart. He had listened empathetically, but in the end told her, "Terminal illness is very personal. We want to be with them every step of the way, partners as we are in everything else. But ultimately, it's impossible. The journey is theirs alone."

Amelia's stomach rumbled. When was the last time she'd eaten? She'd cooked dinner for Kelly but had barely eaten a bite. Amelia knew she had to take care of herself. It wouldn't do Kelly any good if she got run-down and sick.

She headed down to the kitchen. The fridge was full. That dear Rachel had clearly gone above and beyond in the cooking department. She pulled out a dish covered in aluminum foil. Was that cheese? She cut off a piece and couldn't help but smile at the fruits of her labor. All those years lamenting the lost opportunity to pass her recipes on to Nadine. If only she had known what life had in store for her!

A breeze blew off the bay through the open window. Amelia breathed deeply. She had to keep it together. She wouldn't give up hope, despite Kelly doing her damnedest to convince her to.

Amelia stepped out into the backyard. In the distance, the foghorn sounded. Above, the clear night sky framed the glittering stars. Loneliness washed over her, but she refused to give in to it. She took a deep breath, reminding herself that Kelly was upstairs. She was there. And all around Amelia, even in that solitary moment, was so much that she held dear: the water, the salt air, the house where she had labored and loved for so many decades. And later that night, the rest of the family would make their way back into the house, filling the rooms.

She looked up and saw the light go on in Kelly's studio.

Amelia sat at the picnic table, her back against it, staring at the stunningly visible stars. Next month would be September already. Where had the summer gone? She closed her eyes, thinking of that first September with Kelly. Oh, to be able to reset the clock, to live the past thirty years all over again. Of course, that was impossible. That was greedy, that was asking too much.

Okay, then, she bargained with the stars. *How about just one more summer?*

It was no use. Blythe had no business dating. With everything that was going on, she was barely able to keep her own head straight, let alone offer anything to a dear, sweet man like Warren Ames.

Oh, she tried. Their dinner conversation stayed light, both of them consciously avoiding talking about their marriages. It was as if, in the days since their last dinner, they had both consulted a midlife-dating handbook. Unfortunately, her present was so complicated, it made her past look like a cakewalk.

How could she enjoy dinner with Warren when she knew Kip was still in town?

Probably at dinner with Marin that very moment.

Still, she and Warren had managed to laugh a few times. But she was certain he knew, when he walked her back to the house, that the laughter had been between friends, not potential lovers.

The house was dark and quiet. Before she met Warren at the restaurant, she'd tried to find Marin, but she wasn't at the house. Now Marin's door was closed, without a crack of light underneath it.

Blythe, feeling ghostlike wandering the halls, headed down to the kitchen. She filled the teapot with water and set it on the stove. Only when rifling through Amelia's tin filled with herbal teas did she finally remember: Marin's sonogram appointment. She'd missed it!

She was just failing all around.

And then she noticed the light on out back. Through the kitchen window she could see someone sitting at the farthest end of the table, facing the water. Amelia.

It was not too late to redeem herself, to save the day from being a total loss. She turned off the stove and hurried up to her room, where she pulled the shoe box out from under her bed.

*   *   *

Amelia was startled by the back door creaking open. She turned around, hoping Kelly had changed her mind, abandoned her art in favor of a talk. When she realized it was only Blythe, the disappointment was so swift and heavy, it almost made her gasp.

"I hope I'm not intruding," Blythe said.

She was, of course. But Amelia pushed away the ungenerous thought.

"Not at all," she said. "I was just getting some fresh air. Did you have a nice night?"

Blythe sat across from her, nodding. "I did. Well, I tried to. I had dinner with Warren Ames."

Amelia smiled with genuine joy. "Oh, Blythe. That's wonderful. He's such a nice man. A terrible shame about Catherine. We all liked her very much."

"Well, I'm afraid I disappointed him. I'm not ready to date. I feel ridiculous even saying the word."

"I think it's our need to label everything. Puts too much pressure on ourselves. It's the summer. You're entitled to some fun."

Blythe looked very serious, and Amelia sensed that whatever was weighing on her had little to do with Warren Ames. Well, if she wanted to talk, Amelia would listen. She glanced back at the house. She had the impulse to go inside, but then she would only be tempted to disturb Kelly. The truth was, Blythe's intrusion was just what she needed.

"Shall I get a bottle of wine?" Amelia offered.

"Oh, no, thanks. At least, not for me. I'm going to bed. I really just came out here because there's something I want to show you." It was only then that Amelia noticed the envelope in her hand. Blythe, fumbling for a minute, pulled out a folded piece of paper. "This is a letter Nick sent to me from Italy."

Amelia shook her head. "What?"

"This is the last I heard from Nick. I saved it all these years. I think I was hesitant to throw it away because of the drawing. I could never throw away his art. And now I'm so thankful I didn't, because this letter tells a different story than the one you're hearing from Nadine."

She held out the paper and Amelia took it gingerly, as if it would dissolve at her touch. Blythe reached out and squeezed Amelia's hand. "But you read it for yourself."

Amelia couldn't say anything. She waited until Blythe was gone, until she was probably already in bed, before looking down at the paper in her hand.

On one side, a drawing: high cliffs framing a stretch of beach and the wide, expansive sea. It was black-and-white, but so finely etched it hinted at color. The water, blue stillness. The pristine, ivory beach. She traced his lines with her finger, imagining him bent over this very sheet of paper, his brow furrowed in concentration, his hair—always too long—falling into his eyes.

She blinked back tears. Was Blythe right?

His words could speak for themselves. Finally. She read them eagerly, her breath in her throat, her pulse racing.

Dear Blythe:

Sorry to leave in a way that I guess seemed out of nowhere. But now that I'm back near the sea, re-united with my sister, there's no question it was just what I needed. I'm drawing again, finally. This is where I belong. So I guess you were right: it was good-bye. But I do think of you. I imagine what this relentless sun would do to your pale beauty, burnishing it into something new and exotic. If we see each other again I hope it will be here. Though I suspect you are back in the arms of your husband, happily now, I hope.

He signed it *Always, Nick.* When she was finished, she read his words again. And again. How many times until she was satisfied? She didn't know. How many times more would she drink in his words? Endlessly. But for now, she closed her eyes, pressing the letter to her chest.

He had been happy.

Amelia, overcome with a sense of urgency, rushed back inside the house. She had to tell Kelly. Kelly, who had been right all along about Nadine, the extent of how unfairly punishing she had always been toward them both. That Amelia did not have to bear the weight of Nick's death so completely.

She made her way up the stairs, feeling light and energetic. She paused on the second-floor landing, catching her breath before ascending to the studio. Outside the door, she hesitated; she hated to disturb Kelly when she was working, but this was worth it.

"Kel?" she said, knocking. She looked down at the letter in her hand. She still couldn't believe it! She knocked again. No response. "Kelly?" She tried turning the doorknob, but it was locked.

She knocked again, feeling the first prick of alarm. "Kelly, open up." She banged on the door, open-palmed, so hard it hurt. She again tried to turn the doorknob, then stepped back. Her whole body had broken out in a sweat.

There was a key to the studio behind the front desk. She ran down the stairs, taking them nearly two at a time, ignoring the pain in her legs. In the dark, she bumped into the living room couch but didn't miss a step. She reached the desk, breathless, and pulled open the drawers, rummaging through the messy contents, dumping rubber bands and pens and Beach Rose Inn notepads onto the floor. There were a few loose keys, and she grabbed them all.

When she looked up from the base of the stairs, the climb seemed like Everest. Cursing her age, cursing the body that was betraying her as she wanted to leap up to the third floor, she huffed and dragged herself as fast as she could. Hands shaking, she tried the first key in the door.

"Kelly, open up!" She dropped the useless key and moved on to the next one. Mercifully, the knob turned. She burst into the room, rushing blindly and knocking over a chair and a container of tiles, sending it clattering to the floor. "Kelly!"

Kelly, wearing her green cargo pants and NO ONE LIKES A SHADY BEACH T-shirt, was curled up on the small couch near the window. Amelia, less panicked now that she was inside the room, rushed over to her.

"Kelly?" She knelt beside her, shaking her gently. Kelly didn't stir. It barely seemed like she was breathing. Amelia shook her harder. "Kelly, wake up."

Amelia shifted position, knocking over a glass of water Kelly had set by the sofa. That's when she noticed the prescription bottle. Feeling like she was moving in slow motion, she picked it up.

It was empty.

"What did you do?" Amelia shrieked. "Kelly, what did you do?"

Blythe and Marin rushed into the room. "What's going on?" Blythe asked.

"Call 911!" Amelia yelled, holding Kelly against herself, cradling her like a child and sobbing. She pressed her head down, burying her face in Kelly's hair, which had come loose from its ponytail. "I need you," Amelia cried. "I love you. Please, please don't go…"

Amelia didn't know what she was saying, she just knew she had to keep talking. She had to keep Kelly with her, even as a man tried to pull her away. "I'm sorry, ma'am. You've got to let us—"

Blythe was beside her, taking her by the arms, forcing her to let Kelly go.

Kelly, goddamn it. Don't leave me!

Chapter Forty-Five

The Church of Saint Mary of the Harbor was, like most everything in Provincetown, just a little bit different, with its rainbow flag and the carved words over the wooden doorway that read WHERE THE LAND, THE SEA, AND THE SACRED MEET.

The funeral was standing room only. Marin and Blythe made their way to the front. Paul, Bart, and Thomas sat behind them in the second row. Paul sobbed, and Marin reached over to hug him.

"I had no idea it would end like this," he said, his voice breaking.

"Paul, of course not. How could you?"

"The other day? When we were getting high in the studio? She seemed so peaceful. So calm. I should have known she was going to do something."

"How would you have known?" Marin said, though she too had struggled with what-ifs. She'd combed through every conversation they'd had since Kelly confided her diagnosis; her fear of losing control, her frustration with not being able to work. Her acceptance of the inevitability of death. That this was her last summer. "And even if you had suspected, you know how strong-willed Kelly was. There was nothing you could have done."

He cried harder. Marin hugged him harder. She wished she could let it all out like that. She could never cry in public.

"Hey, Marin—I'm so sorry." She turned to find Luke Duncan. She couldn't help noticing that he sure cleaned up nice. No wonder Rachel was losing her mind over the whole disastrous fling.

He asked her if she'd seen Rachel.

"We took the car over together but I'm not sure where she is right this second," Marin said. Luke went off to find her, and she felt a pang. She hadn't called Julian to tell him about Kelly. As much as she wanted him there, as comforting as it would have been to be in his arms, to feel his steadying hand on her shoulder, she didn't *want* to want him. She didn't need him. Besides, the phone worked both ways. If he'd called, she would have told him. But she wasn't going to beg him to be by her side.

A stately, handsome older man stopped to talk to her mother. He kissed her on the cheek before moving on to talk to Amelia, who was making her way toward the pew.

"Who's that?" Marin said.

"Just a friend."

A friend? From where?

There was no time to speculate because Amelia moved next to her, sitting between her and Rachel. In the three days since Kelly's death, Amelia had been largely absent, either out of the house making arrangements or closed off in her bedroom. Marin felt utterly useless. Rachel, at least, had found a way to be helpful, cooking for the past two days to host a gathering at the house after the service. Amelia liked the idea, said Kelly would have liked it too.

On the other side of Rachel, her mother. Fran had turned right back around from Cape Cod as soon as she heard the news and set up camp at Thomas and Bart's house. Rachel complained about her, but Marin knew she was secretly thankful she was there. Marin didn't know what she would do without her own mother at a time like this.

The minister took her place in the front of the church. Everyone settled into their seats. Marin turned around to see how many more people were trying to squeeze into the hot room and spotted her father standing in the back.

"Dad's here," she whispered. Blythe, surprised, turned around, following Marin's gaze.

"I'm sure he's concerned about you," Blythe said.

The quiet murmuring in the room turned to silence.

"Today, we gather to honor the life of our beloved Kelly Hanauer," the minister said. She had long gray hair, wore a flowing white robe, and spoke with a rich, warm voice. "While I am serving to lead you in prayer, please know that I grieve along with you. As we all know, Kelly was not a fan of organized religion. Of organized anything, frankly." Nervous laughter. "So some might wonder how I came to know her well—which I am honored to say I did. To answer that question, I ask that you look around. Each one of these magnificent stained-glass windows, a constant joy and comfort for members of our congregation, was created and donated by Kelly. And as I reflected on what to say today in remembrance of Kelly, such a valuable member of the artistic and spiritual community here in Provincetown, I found myself returning to the notion of her life's work: the mosaic. I know that Kelly's beloved wife, Amelia, taught her the craft, a family tradition. If we think about the mosaic, the beauty of the mosaic, it is perhaps the art form that most reflects family. All the different bits and pieces, some that clearly fit together, others not so obviously, joining to create one beautiful, colorful whole. Some mosaics are stained glass, others tiles or stones or shells. There is no one way, no right way. Kelly understood this about life; she assembled all the pieces to create a life that worked for her, even when that meant leaving some things behind or being left by people who did not approve of her choices."

Marin glanced at the end of the row, at Nadine, who stared straight ahead. She wondered what was going on in her mind. Sensing her gaze, Nadine turned to her and Marin quickly looked down at her hands. She traced her tattoo with her forefinger.

Now, and probably forever, the sight of the tattoo was achingly bittersweet.

Goddamn it, Kelly. It was taking a lot of effort for her not to be angry. How could Kelly do this to Amelia? To all of them? She could have had months left, maybe a year. Who knew? Any time at all would have been better than this. No one got a chance to say a proper good-bye.

"Kelly always did things her way. This was true in the end. It is why we are here today, sooner than we expected, sooner than any of us is prepared to deal with. But in honoring Kelly, we must make peace with the fact that her final choice was part of the big picture of who she was, of what made her so special to all of us. And so, in your grief, I ask that you remember the mosaic. A single piece of one, by itself, might not be a thing of beauty. By itself, it might not be anything we would choose. But when all of the pieces are seen as a whole, we find ourselves in awe. And we sit in gratitude for the gift."

Amelia sobbed, and Marin held her tightly. Her arm brushed Rachel's, who was also holding on to Amelia.

That's when Marin realized Kelly hadn't been selfish in taking her own life, in choosing the time and circumstance of her death. She'd done it to guarantee that when the end came, Amelia would be surrounded by family.

Her own tears came, a sob that started deep within her and shook her entire body. Huddled together with Amelia and Rachel, she looked up at the ceiling. *Okay, Kelly. I get it.*

* * *

There was a long moment outside of church where everyone emerged, slightly dazed, into the sunlight, and regrouped. Blythe saw Kip making his way toward her and felt a flash of irritation. How was she supposed to move on with her life and accept their divorce if he insisted on hanging around? It was especially irritating how good he looked in his suit. And leave it to Kip to travel with a suit at all times. You can take the lawyer out of the firm...

"How are you holding up?" he said.

"I'm fine." She crossed her arms. "I'm surprised to see you still in town."

"When all of this happened, I figured I'd see if there was anything I could do."

"We're fine, Kip. I know you're trying to be supportive of Marin, but we've made it through a lot of emotional ups and downs all summer without you. And frankly, it's making it difficult for me to move on when you're here."

"Just a few weeks ago you wanted me here."

"That was when I thought maybe there was still a chance we'd work things out." She paused. "But now, Kip, I'm sorry. It's time for you to go."

Chapter Forty-Six

It seemed the entire population of Provincetown and then some had shown up at the house to pay their respects to Kelly. The front yard was full of people. The first floor of the house was packed. The backyard was jammed from the door to the last inch of lawn, with the table and both benches covered with trays of food and bottles of wine. Marin recognized the man who owned Provincia. The maître d' from the Red Inn. The sales clerk from Marine Specialties. The owner of Café Heaven. And then there was the out-of-towner.

Her father looked so distinctly *not* of Provincetown in his dark suit and John Lobb shoes. It was oddly comforting.

They'd had dinner the evening Kelly died. He said he was just in town for the night, that he had some things for her mother. She assumed he meant papers to sign for the divorce, but when she pressed him on it, he deflected the questions. Now she was just thankful for whatever had brought him to be with them during a difficult time. It seemed meant to be, and she said as much to him as they sat in the crowded living room.

"I'm sure Mom really appreciates it too."

"I'm not so sure about that," he said.

"What do you mean?"

Rachel tapped her on the shoulder. "Sorry to interrupt, but Julian's looking for you."

What?

Marin turned, and sure enough, there he was, making his way through the crowd toward them. Her heart soared at the sight of him, but she squashed that with the thought that (a) she hadn't invited him, and (b) she didn't need him.

"What are you doing here?" she said.

He looked flustered. "Why didn't you call to tell me about Kelly?"

"You haven't called me."

"Marin, I said I'd be back in nine days. And I'm here. I would have come sooner…"

Nine days.

She'd forgotten all about the test results. Results that were probably sitting in the pile of three days' worth of unopened mail behind the front desk.

"Kipton Bishop," her dad said, offering his hand to Julian.

"I'm sorry," Marin said, flustered. "Julian, this is my father. Dad, this is Julian Rowe."

"It's an honor to meet you," Julian said. "I studied a few of your cases in school."

A lawyer love-fest ensued. It was surreal to be with the two of them in the same room. She had to admit it felt good—like the threads of her life knitting together. And she could tell they liked one another. Why wouldn't they?

Two ambitious lawyers, one at the start of his career, one at the end.

And they might have something else in common. They each might have loved a woman who carried another man's child.

She couldn't take it anymore, the not knowing. For weeks, she'd pushed the uncertainty out of her mind. But Julian was here, the results were probably here, and she couldn't exist in her little cloud of denial any longer.

"Excuse me for a minute." They barely heard her. She threaded her way toward the front of the house, to the small office behind the front desk. She closed the door, and against the buzzing backdrop conversation of all the friends and well-wishers, she rifled through the pile of mail. It wasn't hard to spot the envelope, the bright red-and-green Genie logo in the corner. She tucked it under her arm, made her way back through the crowded living room, and pulled Julian from his conversation with her father. When he hesitated to disengage from Kip, she waved the envelope at him.

"We're doing this now?" Julian said.

"We're doing this now."

She led him up the stairs to her room.

Blythe was happy to see Julian show up for Marin. She was happier still to see the two of them slipping upstairs together. Young love was so resilient.

Older love, apparently, not so much.

She pulled Kip aside. "Didn't you hear a word I said to you outside of the church?"

"I did."

"So why are you here?"

"You made an erroneous assumption."

"Don't lawyer me, Kip."

"You said I was here for Marin. And I thought about it and it's only partially true. I didn't fly back here with that box of stuff for *Marin*."

"I know. You came with that box so you could deliver your recriminations in person. Look, I get it. It was a lot to ask, and I'm sorry. But if you could have seen Amelia's face when I gave her the letter...I don't regret asking it of you."

"It was a gutsy move on your part."

"Maybe."

He took her hands and looked her in the eyes. "You're a good woman, Blythe."

"But not good enough," she whispered.

"No? So why can't I bring myself to leave?"

Blythe looked at him, incredulous. With some difficulty, she managed to say, "You tell me."

Kip's eyes, so steely, always so certain, the eyes that had guided her through a lifetime, locked on her. "Standing in that church, hearing the minister talk about pieces fitting together in unexpected ways—about there not being one right way. Talking about family. You're my family, Blythe. We're going to be grandparents."

Her heart skipped a beat. "Yes," she murmured. "But that's not necessarily a reason to stay together."

"It's a good place to start."

Amelia was touched by the turnout for Kelly, her heart warmed by the sight of old friends, new friends, and even some strangers. They were all a comfort—with one exception.

Sandra Crowe was dressed like a widow in a long black dress with cap sleeves and a pillbox hat. It was as if she had been waiting all summer for an excuse to get out of her beach casual wear. Amelia couldn't help but think she was also delighted for an excuse to be inside the house that she was negotiating to buy.

Blythe had told her about the drop-in when Amelia and Kelly were out of town. Thankfully, Kelly had been out of earshot for that little tidbit or she would have lost it.

Nadine spotted Sandra and made a beeline for her. Amelia's irritation turned to rage. She marched over to the two of them, but they didn't notice her. Their heads, bent together in conversation, left Amelia with no doubt about what they were discussing—and it sure as hell wasn't fond recollections of Kelly. Oh, it was partially Amelia's fault. She had entertained the idea of selling the house, even tossed a few numbers around with Sandra through Nadine. There had been a brief moment when the idea of a financial windfall for herself and Kelly was appealing. It would also be money she could share with her only surviving child. Guilt money.

But there was nothing left to feel guilty about. At least, not in the way Nadine had led her to believe. She knew that now, thanks to the letter Blythe had miraculously produced and shared with her. How lucky, how very lucky, that it had come before it was too late.

It took Sandra and Nadine a few seconds to even notice her standing there.

"Oh, Amelia. So sorry for your loss," Sandra said.

"I'm not selling this house!" Amelia yelled, loudly enough that people stopped midconversation to turn and look at her. She didn't care. The volume, as well as the sentiment she was expressing, was pure release. Maybe there was something left of her after all. She had not died along with Kelly, though the pain made her feel as if she might.

"Amelia, you're in mourning. Of course this isn't the time to discuss this," Sandra said.

"And we're not," Nadine jumped in quickly. "We're not talking about the house."

Well, maybe her daughter had a shred of decency. But, as they say, too little, too late. Trembling, Amelia looked at Nadine. "You've outstayed your welcome. I want you to leave in the morning."

In the kitchen, Rachel busied herself moving apples and pears from a fruit basket to a serving bowl. She glanced out the window and saw Thomas holding court at the table, reciting poetry.

The houseful of people gave her something to do—gave them all something to do. But what would happen tomorrow? And the day after that?

Fran walked into the room carrying a platter of whole steamed lobsters.

"Look what someone brought! This is the best shivah I've ever been to," she said. "Shellfish and all!"

"It's not a shivah, Fran," Rachel said, taking the food from her. "It's just a gathering to celebrate Kelly."

In her complete shock and freak-out the night Kelly died, Rachel texted her mother, who by that time was in Cape Cod for the yoga retreat. It had been an impulse; she hadn't expected her mother to get right back in the car and return to Provincetown. But that's what she did.

"Are you going to hide in the kitchen all day?" Fran asked.

"I'm not hiding. What are you talking about?"

"Luke is out there waiting to see you."

Yes, she'd seen Luke at the funeral. Devastatingly handsome in a dark suit.

"Please—don't. Just because you talked your way—or smoked your way—into crashing at Thomas and Bart's house doesn't give you the right to get involved."

"It's not about having the right or not having the right. I was there when the ex showed up, and I can tell you that he booted her out so fast it was like the house had a revolving door."

"You know what? I really don't care. There are more important things going on here." Rachel turned back to the fruit, and Fran grabbed her arm.

"You told me the other night at dinner, loud and clear, that I'd never been a good enough mother. I didn't teach you enough, I didn't give you any guidance. And maybe I didn't. But I'm trying to right now: That guy? Luke Duncan? He's gorgeous. He's smart. And from what I can tell from the way he talks about you and the way he's acting, he's really into you. So don't blow it."

Rachel, taken aback, could only stare at her.

"I'm not... hiding in the kitchen" was all she managed.

She wasn't hiding. She was busy—couldn't her mother see that? And fine, maybe Luke hadn't asked his ex-girlfriend to show up. And maybe he didn't ask her to stay either. But the whole incident made her feel a hurt she'd never experienced before, and frankly it scared her.

Carrying the fruit bowl, she headed to the living room with a glance back at Fran. *Happy now?*

And there he was, tan and golden, his suit jacket off and his shirtsleeves rolled up. She looked away, but it was too late; accidental eye contact. He crossed the crowded room toward her. She ran back to the kitchen. To hide.

Fine. Her mother was right.

There was a first time for everything.

Marin closed the door to her room. The space, her sanctuary all summer, had turned into the place where fate would deliver its verdict.

Julian sat on the edge of her bed.

"Marin, I feel really terrible that you felt you couldn't call me when Kelly died. I would have wanted to be with you at the funeral."

"I couldn't. Don't you understand that I can't get more emotionally invested in you? We might not get the answer we want. And then what? I know you must feel the same way because you haven't exactly been calling or texting."

He nodded. "I'm sorry. I wanted to. I thought about you nonstop, but you're right—a part of me was holding back. But I could barely wait for an excuse to come here. And if you had called me, I would have jumped at the chance to come sooner. It was wrong that you lost a friend and I wasn't here for you. It was wrong that I showed up at the house too late for the funeral. It felt really, really wrong."

She held out the envelope, her hand shaking. "You open it."

He waited a beat, then took it from her. Their eyes met, and she swallowed hard.

Julian glanced down at the envelope. And then he ripped it into pieces.

Chapter Forty-Seven

It was dark outside. All the visitors were gone, and the house was quiet, quiet in a way she hated—in a way only Kelly fully understood how very *much* she hated.

Amelia didn't know when the silence had become her enemy. Maybe it started in the days after Nick and Nadine first left. The silence came to mean loss. And now she would have nothing but silence.

But for tonight, her family was here. Marin, Rachel, and Blythe, under her roof. And, of course, Nadine. Who was probably packing to leave at that very moment.

Amelia didn't regret her outburst earlier in the day, but it didn't entirely sit well with her either. Did she really want her to leave? On some level, yes. It was frustrating to have her back and find how little had changed. On the other hand, Nadine was her only remaining child. It was Amelia's job, her maternal duty, to make things right. She knew that if she didn't, it would be a fresh emotional wound she would have to live with.

She picked up Nick's letter from her nightstand, handling it like glass. Then she took the stairs up to the third floor, flinching as she passed Kelly's studio. Lord only knew how long it would be before she could set foot in there. If ever.

Nadine's door was open, her room empty. Amelia headed back down the stairs, checking the first floor and the living room. No one. The kitchen—empty. Through the window, by the big table, she saw the glow of a cigarette.

The night had cooled considerably. Or maybe it was just her exhaustion that made Amelia shiver and hug herself. She turned on the porch light.

Startled, Nadine turned.

"I wish you wouldn't smoke," Amelia said.

"It's a bad habit. I've been living in Europe my entire adult life."

Her entire adult life. What an interesting choice of words. Because standing there, watching her sneak a cigarette just as she had thirty years earlier, Amelia had to wonder if her daughter had ever emotionally evolved past the resentful teenager she had been. Maybe, under normal circumstances, Nadine would have worked out her adolescent rage and become a better woman. But when Amelia fell in love with Kelly—well, Nadine had the perfect excuse not to grow. Not to learn about personal accountability. Looking at her middle-aged daughter, illuminated only by the yellow glow of a single lightbulb cutting through the dark, Amelia thought she might as well have been standing next to a fifteen-year-old.

"Nadine, I'm not selling this house. Not for money. Not for anything."

"I get it," she said, putting out her cigarette.

"No," she said. "You don't."

Amelia handed her the letter.

"What's this?" Nadine unfolded it.

"Your brother sent it to Blythe from Italy."

Nadine froze.

"Go on—read it," Amelia said. It took a moment, but Nadine finally bent her head over the paper. When she was finished, she looked up at her mother, tears in her eyes.

"Why did you tell me he was miserable?" Amelia said, her voice tight. "Were you lying to me to punish me, or did you truly believe that?"

Nadine cried softly. "We were never whole again after that last summer here."

"He was moving past it," Amelia said.

"Why be out on that dirt road in the middle of the night? It was reckless. It was asking for something bad to happen." Nadine reached for another cigarette and then stopped herself.

"Nadine, listen to me: You did a good thing inviting him out there. And that night, he was just a young man on vacation. He made a stupid mistake. It wasn't my fault. It wasn't your fault. You need to let go of all your anger."

Nadine leaned over the table, rested her head in the crook of her arm. Amelia touched her back. "Sweetheart, life doesn't have to be as hard as you make it. There have been tough times. I'm partially to blame for that. But you ran away, and pushed me away, and that made it impossible to fix. Nothing is perfect—no one, no family. But look, in the end, we're here together. This is what we have."

Amelia wiped away Nadine's tears, a gesture she had not been able to make since Nadine was a little girl.

"I'm sorry," Nadine said. And then: "It's good to be home."

* * *

Rachel sat on the front porch with the food and waited. It felt like the town should be quiet that night, everyone indoors mourning the loss of Kelly Cabral. But at nine o'clock, Commercial Street was loud with merriment, all the boys on their way to the clubs, couples strolling to and from dinner or headed for drinks on the waterfront. After midnight, the same tide would roll in drunken boisterousness to Spiritus Pizza. She hoped that by then she would be asleep, able to put the long day behind her. For the first time, she understood the expression *bone tired*.

But the food. There simply wasn't enough space in the refrigerator to store all of it. She called Bart, asked if she could bring the overflow to their house.

"I can't even carry it all. Do you have a sec to run over here and help me? It's, like, four trays."

"Reinforcements on the way," Bart said.

She waited until she saw someone turn off the street to the house. She stood and waved. But it wasn't Bart.

"Hey. I heard you were in need of some manpower."

Luke.

"I thought Bart was coming." She clutched a tray like he'd arrived to steal it.

"I offered to come instead."

She shook her head in annoyance. "You shouldn't have."

"I think you're being a little hard on me."

"Oh, you do, do you?"

He took the heavy tray from her hands and set it on the ground. "Yeah. I do."

"I might be young but I'm not stupid," she said, instantly regretting the comment. It had a playground quality to it and made her sound, in fact, both young *and* stupid.

"I never said you were stupid. Not even when I was busy finding the colossal strength to resist your charms."

She refused to let him be cute. "Stupid, naive—whatever I'd have to be to believe your so-called ex-girlfriend just showed up here after two months, uninvited. Without a word."

"Can we sit down for a second? Please?"

"I don't want to sit."

"Rachel, she and I had been together for a long time. Of course we were still in touch occasionally. And for the first month or so, I held out hope that she might change her mind about spending the summer here. But by the time you and I got together, I hadn't texted or spoken to her in a few weeks. I'd accepted it was over. I had no idea that in her mind, she was moving toward trying to work things out."

It made sense; of course it did. But an alarm had been switched on inside of her, and she didn't know how to turn it off. She'd spent so much energy figuring out how to get him, she hadn't given any thought to the emotional risk she'd be taking if it finally happened.

Hookups were easy; relationships were hard. That's why she never had them. She realized, in the depth of her exhaustion and sadness, that after a lifetime of being let down by her mother, she never wanted to give anyone else a chance to hurt her. And then she'd met Luke, and for some odd reason—maybe it was chemistry or that people dropped their defenses when they were on vacation—she wanted him in a way she'd never wanted anyone before.

"So what are you saying? Now it's *really* over?"

He nodded. "Yes. We talked, and it's over. She was at the house barely an hour. If you don't believe me, your mother can back me up."

"Yeah. My mother is a big fan." He didn't say anything, just focused those aqua-blue eyes on her. They had the same effect as that first day by the pool. She was defenseless. She bowed her head, and he tucked a lock of her hair behind one ear.

"Can this really work?" she whispered.

"I don't know," he said. "But I want to try. Do you?"

Rachel looked away, up at the sky. It seemed every star was visible. She wondered if Kelly was somewhere out there, watching over the house.

If she was, Rachel knew what she'd tell her to do.

Chapter Forty-Eight

The lettuce leaflings, a few inches tall, were ready for transplanting to the garden. And not a moment too soon; Marin was leaving that afternoon, and Kip was eager to get on the road as well.

Blythe had planned to start the process much earlier, teaching Amelia and Rachel all they needed to know to keep the garden going long enough to harvest in the fall. And the better they understood things now, the easier it would be for them to replant in the spring. But Kelly's death put all that on hold. Now, Labor Day weekend, it was gardening go-time.

With Amelia next to her, Blythe soaked the ground, then dug a two-inch-deep hole with her finger, looking up to make sure Amelia was watching. She added some extra compost to help the soil retain moisture and gestured for the tray packed with leaflings.

Amelia brought it and knelt beside her with the rows of lettuce in their square plastic beds. Blythe set the tray on the ground between them, and inched the first leafling free from its temporary nest.

"Want to do the honors?" she said, holding it out to Amelia.

"I don't want to set it wrong," she said, cradling the leafling as if it were a baby bird.

"It won't break—just place it in here and then bury it up to its leaves."

Amelia gingerly did as instructed. Blythe leaned close and followed her work with her own hands, pressing the soil down firmly, pinching it to make sure it was tight around the plant.

"I'm so excited about this, I can't even tell you," Amelia said, sitting back on her heels. Blythe felt a swell of satisfaction; she was returning to Philadelphia in the morning, but she was leaving something behind for Amelia, something green and alive and nourishing. After all, Amelia had given her so much that summer. By taking them all in and keeping them under one roof, Amelia had given Blythe the chance to heal her relationship with Marin. And in confronting Blythe with her long-held, albeit mistaken, beliefs about what had happened to Nick in Italy, Amelia had literally forced the issue out of the back of Blythe's closet, and now the decades-long chasm between Blythe and Kip was closed. Amelia had, in a sense, helped sow the seeds for the next season of Blythe's marriage.

"Hey, you guys should have called me out here for this," Rachel said, bounding into the yard.

"You really want to be in charge of the garden?" Amelia said. "It's a big responsibility."

"Are you doubting me?" Rachel said, hurt.

"No. I don't doubt you at all. I just don't think you realize how busy we'll be in the spring if we open the inn—"

"*When* we open the inn," Rachel corrected.

"The spring is a whole different issue," Blythe said. "I'll coach you through that over the phone. For now, the next few weeks are crucial. While it's still hot, you really have to water twice a day. Whenever the top two inches of soil are dry."

"How do we know when to pick the lettuce?" Rachel asked.

"You'll see when it's a full plant. You can either pick a few leaves at a time—you'd be surprised how little you need to make a salad—or cut the entire head at soil level with a sharp knife."

She glanced at her watch. There were still other seeds to plant and all the maintenance to teach them. Tips for harvesting.

"Will you come back in the spring?" Amelia said.

Blythe nodded. "Sure. I'll be back after the last frost or during the summer at some point—"

"No," Amelia said. "I want a promise that you and Marin will come back after the baby is born. Once the winter is past."

Blythe smiled. That's right; by the spring, the baby would be here. "Of course. I promise. We'll all be back. And when we are, I want to see this ground bursting with vegetables. Don't be intimidated! Trust me, the plants want to flourish. They will reach for the sun. All you have to do is nurture them."

Her last morning in Provincetown.

Marin woke up early and tiptoed around a sleeping Julian. Her bags were packed (how had she accumulated so much *stuff* in just two months?), the gas tank in her car was full, and she'd said her good-byes. Most of them.

She'd left the most difficult for last.

She hadn't gone back inside Kelly's studio. She thought maybe she wouldn't, that she would preserve the memory of the room as it had been with Kelly alive and creating, full of blunt conversation. But to leave without one last visit to the space felt like unfinished emotional business.

Still, every step up to the third floor was filled with trepidation. Marin opened the door to the studio very slowly. As quietly as possible. It felt like trespassing, like breaking in. She turned on the overhead light, and it flickered twice before it went on.

The scent of spicy vanilla still hung in the air; this— more than the sight of Kelly's art on the wall, the rows and rows of bins left filled with Amelia's decades' worth of beach collecting, the scattered blue tiles and smalti on the floor where Amelia had knocked them over the night of Kelly's death—hurt.

"Oh, Kelly," Marin said, her heart seizing in her chest. She stopped in the middle of the room and pressed her hands to her forehead. She should leave. And yet she felt compelled to be there. After standing still and agonizing over it, she finally realized why.

It took her a few seconds to find it.

Kelly had set up a scrim, shielding one drafting table from view. Marin peeked behind it, knowing she would find the Beach Rose Inn sign. What she didn't expect to find was a handwritten note on top.

Hey, Marin—

I knew you'd come back to finish this! You rock.
    Sorry for the hasty exit. But I think you under-

stand. You have to know when it's time to stay and when it's time to go. Right?

So: The mosaic. I know you can do it.

Congrats in advance on the baby. It gives me comfort to know Amelia has something awesome to look forward to this winter.

XO Kelly

Marin wiped away tears. She traced the shiny arc of tiles forming the base of the rose. *Okay,* she told herself. *It's going to be okay.* She put the note in her pocket, left the studio and closed the door behind her, then walked back to her room. Julian was just waking up, and he smiled at her.

"Where'd you run off to?" he said. "Did I oversleep?"

"No," she said, kissing him. "It's still early. But now that you're up, I need help getting one last thing into the car."

Amelia knew the box was in the attic somewhere, one among dozens.

The overhead light was out, so she went in search of a flashlight and then resumed her hunt through a forest of cardboard. Some were labeled *Mãe,* from back in the days she'd packed up the house after her mother's death. Some belonged to her former husband, Otto. (She made a mental note to go through those and clear them out. It was time.) There were other, more generic labels: *Books, Winter Clothes,* even simply *Hats.* She knew one day she would add more to the pile, boxes labeled *Kelly.* But she was far from ready to do that. The very thought of it made her feel claustrophobic, and it was difficult to breathe.

She had to force herself to push through; she was, after all, there for a reason.

The boxes she wanted were near the farthest wall, underneath a pile of albums (*Fleetwood Mac,* Joni Mitchell's *Blue,* Simon and Garfunkel's *Bridge over Troubled Water*) and an old hat stand. After brushing off the dust and more than one cobweb, she slid a few boxes away from the congested corner so she could get a good look at the contents. The one she wanted was marked *Nick/Baby.*

She sliced through the tape with an X-Acto knife. The first thing inside, at the top of the pile, was the blue-and-white blanket her mother had crocheted. Then a blue sweater with a red elephant on the front. Oh, she remembered that one. She couldn't recall who gave it to her, but Nick looked so adorable in it. A baby-blue knit cap, a navy sailor suit, a hand-knit onesie. Footed pajamas with a turtle pattern. Another blanket, baby-blue cotton edged with a navy satin trim. She shook them all out, then folded them in her lap.

There was something else she wanted, and she felt around at the bottom of the box until her hand reached cool metal. It rattled as she pulled it to the surface, a sound that took her back to another life.

She gathered it all in her arms and headed back down the stairs to the second floor. She found Marin in her room, sitting by the window with her packed bags at her feet, scrolling through messages on her phone. She looked up sheepishly when she saw Amelia.

"I'm already half back in the real world," she said.

"I know it's that time, my dear. But before you go, I wanted to give you a few things." She sat on the edge of the bed, and Marin set her phone down and joined her.

Amelia unfolded the blue-and-white crocheted blanket.

"My mother made this when Nick was born. I was afraid to use it in the crib when he was an infant because I loved it and didn't want him to spit up on it. So I ended up just keeping it folded on his dresser. When he was about one he began sleeping with it. And he had it on his bed until he was, oh, I'd say, twelve? I want you to have it for your son."

Marin's cheeks flushed pink. "Oh, Amelia! I don't know what to say. It's so...thank you." She reached out to touch it, then brought it to her lap.

Amelia reached into the center of the pile of clothes and blankets and pulled out a tarnished silver rattle.

"This was his too. It's been in our family for many generations. From Portugal."

Marin began to say something, then stopped. When she finally spoke, it was halting. "Amelia, I have to admit, thinking about Nick as my father has been really difficult for me because I have a dad. But now that I know you, I can think of him as your son, the person that links me to you. And that makes me so happy."

"Life is so strange," Amelia said, her eyes tearing. "It gives, it takes. I'll never understand it."

"Me neither," said Marin. "But I guess I'm realizing that's okay."

Amelia nodded, missing Kelly with an ache that took her breath away. Marin leaned across the bed and pulled Amelia into a hug, and it felt like a deep inhale after being underwater. Amelia let herself cry—for Kelly. For Nick. For the passage of years and for the turning generations. It seemed she cried for a very long time, and all the while, Marin held her close.

Provincetown

Spring

They had reserved the rooms ahead of time, way back in February when Rachel called to say the inn was being booked up solid and she was turning down reservations.

"I know it's hard to think of it now, but you have to pick a week and just commit."

Marin—with a three-day-old baby in her arms, attached to her like a new limb, and half a foot of snow outside the window of their Sixty-Eighth Street town house—could not imagine a trip to the neighborhood grocery store, never mind a drive to Provincetown. In full nesting mode, she hated leaving the house.

Marin had never dreamed, when Julian gave her the key that night that seemed so long ago, that the house would one day be her home. Their home, a family of three.

"You really want to take this show on the road?" she asked Julian later.

"It will be the first chance for everyone to see him at the same time," Julian said. "And besides, we promised we'd go back."

Yes, they had. And if Julian, with his demanding hours at the office, could commit to the week away, certainly she could. After all, Marin made her own work schedule. Marin had surprised no one more than herself by inching, piece by piece, into becoming a mosaic artist. She'd made her first sale, a tile-and-smalti Portuguese good-luck rooster, the week before Jake was born.

And so, in early May, they loaded up the car and set off for Provincetown, Julian at the wheel.

Had it been only a year ago that she'd packed in fifteen minutes for a spontaneous weeklong trip? Driving in a straight shot, stopping once for a couple of quick lobster rolls (only to have them snatched away by seagulls). Now, packing took as much forethought and precision as a military operation. How to fit a stroller, a Pack 'n Play, Jake's bouncy seat, and her breast pump all in the backseat? One entire suitcase was just diapers, bottles, bath toys, and burp cloths. She packed enough baby clothes so she wouldn't have to completely hijack Amelia's laundry machine.

Marin barely slept the night before the trip, and the drive itself, with all of their stops for feeding and changing, took close to nine hours.

And it was all instantly worth it the second Amelia set eyes on baby Jake.

"Oh my heavens. Pictures don't do him justice. Oh, he's just the most beautiful thing I've ever seen." She reached for him, and he hesitated for just a second before giving in to her embrace.

"Meet your great-grandma," Marin said. "How do you say that in Portuguese?"

"*Bisavó,*" Amelia murmured, kissing the baby. "He looks just like you, Marin."

Marin smiled, but she knew it wasn't exactly true. He looked more like his father, with his long-lashed brown eyes and his perfect, tiny, chiseled little Clint Eastwood nose.

"Come along—everyone's out back."

It was strange to step into the yard. The communal table, the stretch of beach, and the water all looked exactly the same, while so much in her life had changed. The only hint of the passage of time was the robust vegetable garden.

"It survived the winter," Marin said, hugging Rachel.

"I know—and so did I!" Her hair was shorter, her formerly bronzed skin a paler shade of honey. But her big brown eyes were just as bright and mischievous as they'd been the day Marin had first met her at the Starbucks in Times Square. She'd seen her only twice since last summer, one weekend in October on Rachel's way back from visiting Fran's parents in Philly, and the week Jake was born, when Rachel had weathered the freezing cold and an impending snowstorm to meet her new nephew. Amelia had planned to go with her but had come down with a bad cold and wasn't able to make it. Rachel said Amelia had made her nervous a few times during the winter months, taking to her bed for long stretches, seeming frail in body and spirit. But now, in the spring thaw, she seemed more like her old self.

Luke pulled Marin in for a hug, with Kip and her mother right behind for their turn.

"Where's the baby?" Blythe asked.

"Inside," Julian said. "Marin already has Amelia on diaper duty."

"In my defense, she volunteered!"

Julian and her father settled into a few minutes of

shoptalk. Now that her father was retired, he liked nothing more than to strategize vicariously through Julian's work. And he never stopped trying to talk him into going back to a big firm.

Marin put her hand on Julian's arm. "Maybe my dad and Luke can help you with that stuff out front?"

"Good idea."

Left alone with her mother, Marin sat at the table and wondered how long it would take her to notice the ring on her finger. Blythe was too busy eyeing the door.

"Mom, relax. I'm sure Amelia will be right out."

"There he is!" At the sight of her grandson, Blythe jumped up like the bench was on fire, arms outstretched.

"He is such a good boy," Amelia cooed.

He was a very good baby. But the trip had thrown him off his nap and feeding schedule, and Marin was afraid the clock was ticking on a major meltdown.

"I should feed him," Marin said, reaching for him.

"You're not still nursing, are you?"

"Yes, Mom. He's only three months old."

Her mother had given birth at the tail end of a time when formula was considered the right way to feed a baby, and she had made it clear that she didn't understand Marin's rejection of this modern convenience "that was good enough for you."

Marin unbuttoned her blouse. She was now a pro at getting Jake to latch on while she discreetly covered herself. The kid was probably going to grow up with a fetish for eating in tents.

Blythe did a double take and grabbed Marin's left hand.

"Marin, are you—"

"Engaged? Yes."

Blythe let out a holler of joy that startled the baby into tears.

"Mom, come on."

"Marin, congratulations," said Amelia. "He's a lovely young man."

"Did you set a date?" said Blythe. "Places in New York book up years and years ahead of time. But if you do it in Philly, I'm sure we can get the club."

"Actually"—Marin looked at Amelia—"since everyone's all together this week, we were thinking of doing it here."

"Here?" Blythe and Amelia said in unison.

Kip appeared, waving at them to come to the front of the house.

Blythe shook her head. "No, come *here!* Kip, Marin's engaged!"

Her father strode to the table and kissed her on the cheek. "Congratulations, sweetheart." He turned to Blythe. "See? And you were so worried."

Blythe, looking busted, insisted, "I wasn't *worried.*"

"What did I miss?" Rachel emerged from the kitchen carrying a fresh pitcher of iced tea and a big tomato salad. She set them on the table.

"Marin's getting married," gushed Blythe.

Rachel smiled, nodding. "Yeah. I noticed the ring. I just didn't say anything because no one else did." She hugged her.

Of course Rachel noticed the ring. She was a twenty-three-year-old woman deeply in love with her boyfriend. Marin was sure she would have a ring of her own very soon.

"Okay, switching gears for just a minute here, ladies," Kip said. "Marin, Julian's ready for you."

"Great! Amelia, come out front for a second?"

Marin detached Jake, touched his mouth with a cloth to clean up the dribble, then put him over her shoulder and rubbed his back to get a burp out of him as she walked. Blythe, Amelia, and Rachel followed her to the street in front of the house.

It took Amelia a few seconds to mentally register what was in front of her: Julian and Luke had removed the old wooden Beach Rose Inn sign and hung Kelly's mosaic by a strong metal chain. Marin had finished it in late fall, had considered shipping it to Amelia. Now she was thankful she'd waited. The whole family was there, in the fading afternoon sun of a perfect spring day. When Amelia finally realized what she was looking at, she clapped her hands together and made a childlike sound of pure glee.

"Marin, you made this?"

"No. Kelly did."

Amelia gasped. Her face clouded, and Marin reached for her hand.

"I don't understand," Amelia said.

"Kelly worked on this all last summer. She got the idea for it because you were debating whether or not to keep the inn going, and she was definitely in the yes camp. I helped out a little when she started teaching me how to mosaic. And then she got the diagnosis…I don't know. I think she realized I could do the last minor parts of it for her."

"I can't believe it," Amelia said, reaching out and tracing the shell lettering.

"She wanted to surprise you," Marin said. Amelia just stared and stared at the sign, as if reading something, finding the answer to something.

"I've never been more greatly surprised in my life," she said finally. "Except, of course, when you called me, Rachel."

Everyone laughed, breaking the intensity of the previous few moments. Jake began fussing, and Marin handed him off to her mother.

"I miss her so much," Amelia whispered.

"I know," Marin said, putting her arm around her. They all stood in silence, broken only when Amelia turned to Marin and Julian.

"So. A wedding by the bay?"

Marin and Julian shared a smile. "If that's okay with you," she said.

"*Okay?* It's more than okay. I can't think of a better way to start the season."

And then there was a loud warning bark before Molly bounded into the yard, pressed against Amelia, and nuzzled her waist.

"Are we late for dinner?" Bart called from the street, Thomas and Paul trailing close behind him.

"No, you're just in time," said Rachel. Luke put his arm around her shoulders.

"Nice sign," Paul said, winking at Marin.

Somewhere in the distance, a foghorn sounded. Gradually, they all made their way to the back of the house, settling around the table while Rachel prepped the food in the kitchen. Amelia was the last to return to the yard, reluctant to leave her gift from Kelly. Marin saved a place at the table between herself and Blythe.

Kip opened a bottle of wine.

"To the start of a new summer," he said, raising his glass.

"To the Beach Rose Inn," said Marin.

Amelia stood up, holding her glass against her heart. "To my family."

Acknowledgments

Hearing the news that *The Forever Summer* would be published by Little, Brown and edited by Judy Clain was an unforgettable moment. My deepest thanks to Reagan Arthur and Judy Clain. Judy, working with you is an honor and a dream come true. Thank you to the entire team at Little, Brown, especially Amanda Brower and Maggie Southard.

Thank you to my agent Adam Chromy, who believed in this book from day one and found the perfect home for it. There is no better agent in the business.

A special thanks to my lifelong friend Sherri Poall.

I want to thank all the bloggers, book-club leaders, and passionate readers out there, particularly Robin Kall Homonoff of *Reading with Robin* and Andrea Peskind Katz of *Great Thoughts' Great Readers*. To writers Brenda Janowitz, Fiona Davis, and DeLauné Michel: I'm grateful for your camaraderie and support. Special thanks to Provincetown's the Anchor Inn, my favorite place to stay in town and the inspiration for the Beach Rose Inn.

Thank you to my husband, who enthusiastically joined

me on an adventurous first trip to Provincetown in the summer of 2015. To my daughters, Bronwen and Georgia, and my stepchildren, Eleanor and Addison: my stories of siblings and complicated families are inspired by our life together.

Finally, to my family in Philadelphia: Dad, Josh and Rachel, Aunt Harriet and Uncle Paul, Alison and Stewart. It means the world to me to know I can always come home.

About the Author

Jamie Brenner grew up in suburban Philadelphia, where her Saturday routine of a diner breakfast followed by a visit to the local bookstore with her dad led to a lifelong love of reading. Her previous novels include *The Wedding Sisters*, *The Gin Lovers*, and *The Husband Hour*. She lives in New York City with her husband and two teenage daughters.

. . . and *Drawing Home*

An unexpected inheritance, a promise broken, and four lives changed forever: the newest page-turner from *USA Today*–bestselling author Jamie Brenner. Following is an excerpt from the novel's opening pages.

On summer weekends The American Hotel in Sag Harbor felt like the center of the universe. If you lived in town, you were stopping by for a drink, and if you were visiting, you wanted a spot in one of the eight guest rooms.

It was the Friday before Memorial Day, not officially summer but close enough. The Hampton Jitney stopped right in front of the hotel and unloaded a fresh batch of Manhattanites every hour.

Emma Mapson, a Sag Harbor native, had watched the summer crowds grow every year. She'd seen fancier restaurants open and higher-end boutiques decorate Main Street. But one thing that never changed was The American Hotel. The red-brick Colonial building looked and felt exactly as it had when Emma was a young girl, with the same antique wood furniture, nautical paintings, and Tiffany chandeliers. The lobby had the same well-worn couch and the same backgammon table where her father had taught her to play and where she, in turn, had taught her own daughter to play. It all seemed to say to her, *Go ahead, live a little*. At least, it used to feel that way.

"I have a problem with my room," a woman said, approaching the front desk.

"I'm sorry to hear that," Emma said, glancing down at the handwritten reservation log and trying to figure out which guest she was talking to. "What's the problem?"

"Everything!" the woman said. "I can't find a single outlet for charging my phone. There's no television, and there's no closet."

Emma arranged her face into a practiced, neutral expression. Too empathetic, and it was like she was admitting there was a problem; too quizzical, and the guest felt even more provoked. Best to look simply blank.

"What's your last name, ma'am?" Emma asked.

"Stoward." She spelled it slowly, as if Emma were barely familiar with the alphabet. Emma flipped through the reservation ledger and found the woman was booked in the Cooper Room. True, there was no television in that room—or in any of the rooms. And although technically there wasn't a closet, the room did feature a large antique armoire. She had no idea why the woman couldn't find the outlets.

"Mrs. Stoward, I'll—" Emma looked up and caught a glimpse of a familiar mop of curly dark hair across the lobby.

The American Hotel's front desk provided the best people-watching in town. Emma never knew who might be sitting on the sofa, which offered views of Main Street on one side and the hotel's always-full bar on the other; she might look up and see the town dockmaster, a tourist from the Midwest, a celebrity chef, or Billy Joel, a local.

But she was happiest when the person planted in that coveted spot was the one she saw now, her fourteen-year-old daughter, Penny.

Penny's thin frame was hunched over her drawing pad, as always. Emma couldn't see her face because it was hidden by hair. Oh, that hair. When Penny was a toddler, people had stopped Emma in the street to comment on her daughter's curls. Emma watched her now, willing her to glance up. She could always tell from Penny's eyes—big and dark and so unlike her own—whether or not she was in a decent mood. Emma didn't know if it was Penny's age or just Penny, but the mood roller coaster was something to be reckoned with.

Emma smiled at the hotel guest standing before her. "I'll be up to your room in a minute to see what I can do," she said, buying herself some time to find out why Penny had left school so early. When the woman was out of sight, Emma slipped out from behind the desk.

Penny, busy rummaging through her book bag, didn't notice her.

"Hi, hon," Emma said. "What are you doing out of school?"

Penny looked up, pushing her curls out of her face.

"It's a half day. You know, 'cause of the holiday weekend."

Of course. "Right! I forgot." She leaned down to wrap her arms around her but Penny wriggled away. Emma straightened up, trying not to feel rejected. "Okay. So what's your plan?"

"I'm going to hang out with Mr. Wyatt. But I need to buy a book first." She gave Emma her puppy-dog-eyed *I need money* look.

Emma sighed. "Can't you borrow it from the library?"

"They don't have it yet and I really want to show it to Mr. Wyatt today."

Emma turned to look at the corner of the bar where the old man, a world-renowned artist and her daughter's unlikely pal, could always be found in the late afternoon. "Don't bother Mr. Wyatt right now. He's talking to someone." She walked Penny to the front desk and handed her a twenty. Her daughter leaned over and gave her a quick kiss.

"I guess now I know the price of a little public affection," Emma said.

Penny rolled her eyes on her way out the door.

Emma answered the ringing house phone, booked a room reservation, and then walked up the stairs to the second floor to see what she could do to placate the complaining guest.

"Finally," Mrs. Stoward said when she opened the door. She was not alone in the room. Emma spotted a man—Mr. Stoward?—seated on the edge of one of the twin brass beds. He was busy tapping away at his phone and didn't bother looking up.

"See what I mean?" Mrs. Stoward waved her arm as if to say *Look at this disaster.*

Emma glanced around, taking in the antique full-length mirror, the red-and-gold-striped couch, and a set of Dominy chairs. The room also featured a beautiful armoire that could hold a full wardrobe.

It made her crazy when summer people didn't fully appreciate the charm of the hotel. The building dated back to 1843 and yet guests expected it to feel like the Four Seasons. And they never had any sense of the village's history. They didn't care that it had been a whaling port, a writers' colony, a historic African-American community, a stop on the Underground Railroad. Did they know that John Steinbeck had called Sag Harbor home? No; all they wanted was restaurant recommendations.

"Let me show you the outlets," Emma said. She bent down and pointed out one hidden by the legs of the wooden desk.

"Well, that solves one problem," the woman said, hands on her hips.

Emma walked to the armoire and opened it. "We have more hangers if you need them. I think you'll find this very spacious."

Mrs. Stoward peered suspiciously at the armoire. "Is this cedar?"

"Just use the damn cabinet, Susan," mumbled the man.

"And what about the television?" she said to Emma.

That got the man's attention. He directed his irritated gaze at Emma. "Yes, we need to get a television in here," he said. "There's a game at seven."

Before Emma could explain that they didn't have televisions at the hotel, she heard a scream from the ground floor.

"Excuse me," she said, and she rushed from the room to the top of the stairs. One of the housekeepers was running up.

"Someone just passed out at the bar!" the housekeeper yelled, almost breathless. Passed out? It was early afternoon. Had someone already overindulged? It had been known to happen.

"Did you call an ambulance?" Emma said, running down the stairs to reach the front desk. She pushed through the wooden door between the stairwell and the lobby, a door she knew was often blocked by a café cart or a table, but she would lose precious seconds if she used the patio door and went around to the front entrance.

Nothing was blocking the door to the lobby today. She grabbed the black landline phone on the front desk and dialed 911.

"It's Emma at The American Hotel. We need an ambulance for an unconscious customer." The dispatcher asked her for some specifics, but from her spot, she couldn't get a good look at the fallen customer, and the phone wasn't cordless. The old-fashioned quirks of the place sometimes posed a challenge. She should have used her cell phone, but service could be spotty.

Waiters and busboys gathered around the person on the floor; the bartender, Chris, was on his knees trying to help. Did Chris have EMT experience? She wouldn't be surprised. Most people working in town were, if not jacks-of-all-trades, skilled at a variety of jobs. The person taking your dinner order one night could very well be operating your water taxi the next.

She scanned the bar, looking for anyone she recognized, trying to get a sense of whether the guest on the floor was a tourist or a local. The bar had a few regulars who came for happy hour every day, year-round. They were the ones at the bar in the middle of a blizzard. The American Hotel was a club to these customers.

Emma realized one bar stool was empty, the one at the corner closest to the lobby.

Oh no. She hoped the person on the ground wasn't who she thought it was.

Penny crossed Main Street, heading for the bookstore. As far as she was concerned, the town had two major things going for it: the bookstore and the self-serve frozen-yogurt shop, BuddhaBerry. Somehow, between these two places, she would find a way to pass the three-day weekend.

Penny didn't do well with lots of free time. It made her anxious.

"Instead of worrying," her mom had said, "think of something you have to be happy about. Just one thing, even if it's small."

One thing she had to be happy about was that eighth grade was nearly finished. It had been a brutal year. She'd almost failed math. Her best friend, Robin, barely had time for her anymore now that she'd become part of the group of "basics"—the girls with the flat-ironed hair and the new iPhones and the right clothes. Then, in December, the town's only movie theater had burned down. Everyone freaked out—it had been a historic building, and that stretch of Main Street smelled charred for weeks afterward. The burned pit was nasty. Still, Penny was amazed how upset people got about it.

"It's symbolic," her mother told her. "It's a sudden loss. And too much about this town is changing as it is. We have to hold on to some things."

Without the theater, there was one less thing to do on the lonely weekends. And now, one less thing to do this summer.

But she still had this place, Harbor Books.

The bookstore smelled like fruit and spices from the Dobrá Tea bar in the back. The owner, a twenty-something woman named Alexis Pine, had told Penny about the tea thing months before it opened. Alexis was obsessed with it—oolong tea, pu'er tea, green tea. Alexis had long hair that had once been blond but was now the pinkish-red hue of hair that had been dyed with Kool-Aid. She had funky, boho clothes and was basically everything Penny wished she could be. Alexis also had two cats in the shop, a vintage-book collection in a glass case in the back, and an impressive working knowledge of graphic novels.

"Hey, Penny," Alexis called from the counter. "Your book came in."

Penny was moving on from her manga and superhero phase and getting into realism with the graphic novel *This One Summer* by Jillian Tamaki and Mariko Tamaki.

Penny slid her mother's twenty across the counter with her fingertips, trying to touch as little of the bill as possible.

"Whatcha doing this weekend?" Alexis asked, handing Penny her change.

Penny quickly shoved the change in her pocket, pulled her forbidden tube of Purell out of her handbag, and squeezed a fat blob of it on the backs of her hands and on her palms. It burned her skin, which was already dry and cracked from overwashing.

"I'm not sure what I'm doing yet," Penny said.

She was embarrassed to admit that she didn't have any plans. Why did she feel like such a loser lately? It wasn't just the usual things, like not having a dad around and living in a house that was small and in the wrong part of town. Her otherness felt deeper, more unshakable, with every passing week.

It was why she felt more comfortable around older people. They didn't seem to notice anything strange about her. Most were just nice. This was why she had gotten into the habit of hanging around the hotel where her mother worked.

That's why she was going back there now to show her new book to Mr. Wyatt.

Mr. Wyatt had white hair and always wore a tweed jacket and carried a nephrite walking stick from Fabergé. His usual seat was in the near corner of the bar, his back to the lobby, and he didn't talk to anyone because he was always bent over a cocktail napkin doodling. It had taken a while before she'd realized some of these napkin drawings were framed in the dining room. The night she'd noticed this, she wanted to ask her mom about it, but the bar had been packed, and if her mother had known she was still there, she would have sent her home. So she asked the old man, "How'd you get them to hang your drawings on the wall?"

"They fished them out of the garbage or retrieved them from a crumpled heap at the end of the evening. I had very little to do with it."

It took her a few seconds to process this, and then she told him, "I draw too." It was one of the few things she enjoyed.

"I'm surprised anyone of your generation lets go of the phone long enough to put pencil to paper," he said.

"I'm not allowed to have a smartphone," she said. Penny had OCD and anxiety, and the doctor said screens were the worst things for her. This didn't help her in the friend department.

"You're not allowed to have a phone but you're allowed to hang around in hotel bars?" he said.

"I'm just visiting my mother at work," she told him.

The old man looked across the room at her mother, then back at her. He smiled for the first time. "Emma's kid. I see the resemblance." He had to be lying. Her mother was beautiful and she was, well, not.

After that night, Mr. Wyatt asked to see her drawings. He met her in the lobby and they sat on the couch; she drank soda and he had martinis and he taught her about contour and proportion. A month or so later, she realized that Henry's drawings were hung in other places besides the hotel. His artwork was all around town. Henry was famous.

Now, as she was leaving the bookstore, her phone, her old, crappy, embarrassing flip phone, chirped with a text.

Don't be mad. You can totally come to the party. I'll send you the address.

Penny ignored it. She didn't need Robin's charity invitation. She had better things to do.

She headed back to the hotel. It took her a minute before she noticed the police cars. Two were parked at an awkward angle right in front of the building. Traffic was being redirected. A small crowd had gathered on the sidewalk.

She ducked her head and tried to slip across the front porch to the hotel entrance.

"Young lady, step aside. You can't go in there," an officer said.

Ushered to the sidewalk, Penny wondered if she could sneak around back. And then—

"Some old guy dropped dead at the bar," a man announced. "Right over his martini."

"That's how I want to go," someone said.

Penny stood very still. Sirens blared nearby, and she covered her ears, her anxiety officially triggered. In the midst of all this, the four o'clock jitney pulled up to the curb, and dozens of passengers disembarked, lugging bags and talking on their phones. Although Penny was desperate to get away, she was trapped by the swarm of summer people in a hurry to have fun.